MONSTER ON THE HILL

Rob Harrell

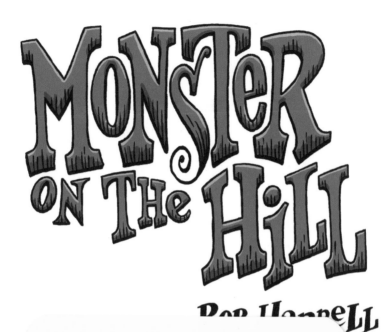

Editor-in-Chief: Chris Staros

Published by Top Shelf Productions, an imprint of IDW Publishing, a division of Idea and Design Works, LLC. Offices: Top Shelf Productions, c/o Idea & Design Works, LLC, 2765 Truxtun Road, San Diego, CA 92106. Top Shelf Productions®, the Top Shelf logo, Idea and Design Works®, and the IDW logo are registered trademarks of Idea and Design Works, LLC. All Rights Reserved. With the exception of small excerpts of artwork used for review purposes, none of the contents of this publication may be reprinted without the permission of IDW Publishing. IDW Publishing does not read or accept unsolicited submissions of ideas, stories, or artwork.

Visit our online catalog at www.topshelfcomix.com.

Printed in Korea.

ISBN 978-1-60309-491-7

23 22 21 20   1 2 3 4

For Bur

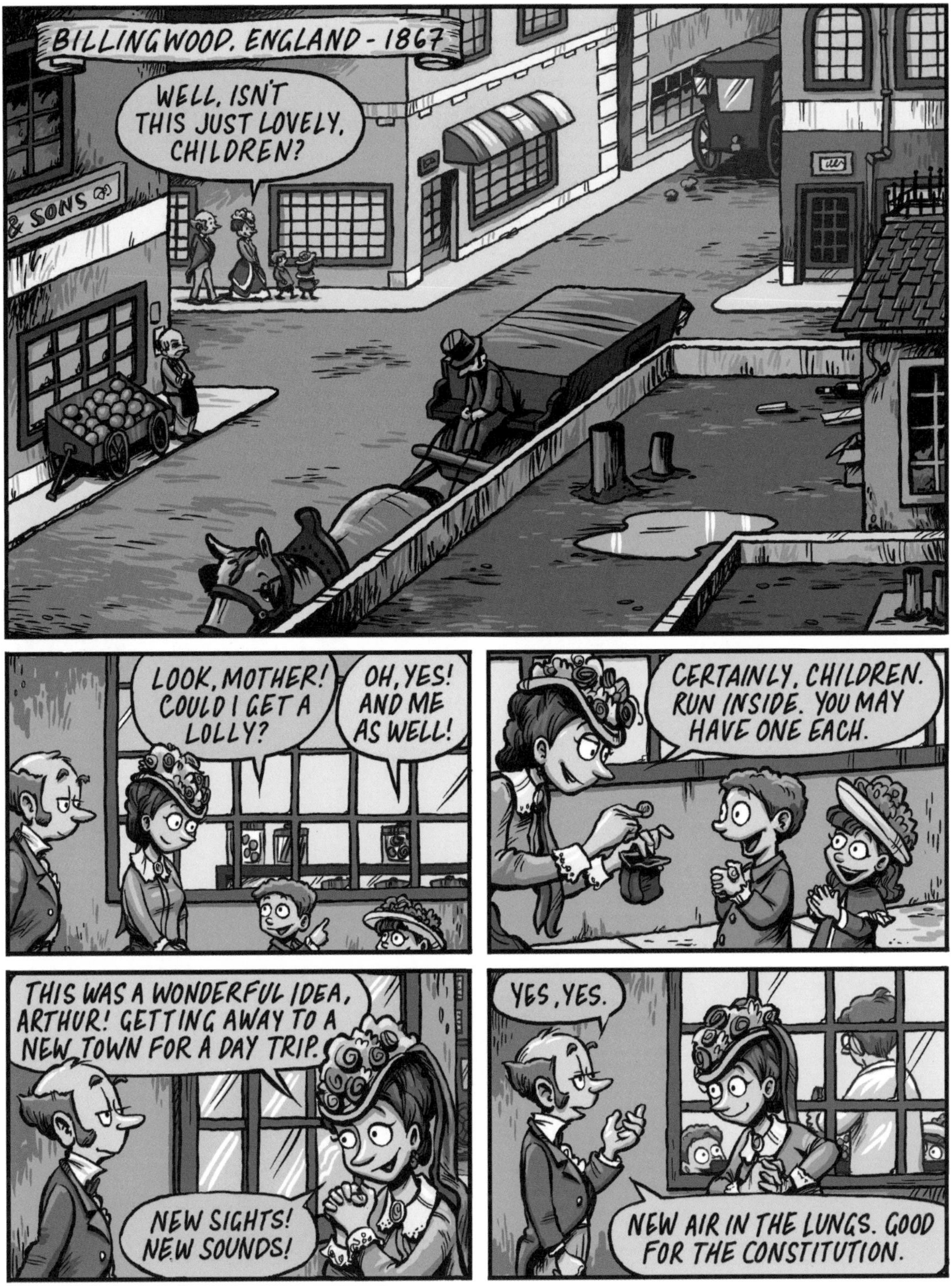
BILLINGWOOD, ENGLAND - 1867
& SONS
WELL, ISN'T THIS JUST LOVELY, CHILDREN?
LOOK, MOTHER! COULD I GET A LOLLY?
OH, YES! AND ME AS WELL!
CERTAINLY, CHILDREN. RUN INSIDE. YOU MAY HAVE ONE EACH.
THIS WAS A WONDERFUL IDEA, ARTHUR! GETTING AWAY TO A NEW TOWN FOR A DAY TRIP.
NEW SIGHTS! NEW SOUNDS!
YES, YES.
NEW AIR IN THE LUNGS. GOOD FOR THE CONSTITUTION.

IT'S EVER SO NICE FOR THE CHILDREN TO... OH!

RUMBLE

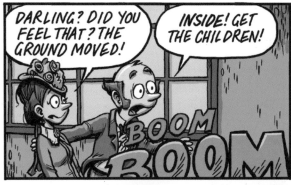

DARLING? DID YOU FEEL THAT? THE GROUND MOVED!

INSIDE! GET THE CHILDREN!

BOOM BOOM

IS SOMETHING COMING?

GATHER CLOSE, FAMILY!

RRUMMMBBLLE

IS IT THE MON...MON..?

I'M SCARED, FATHER!

GASP! IT IS! IT IS! IT'S THE MONSTER!

BOOM

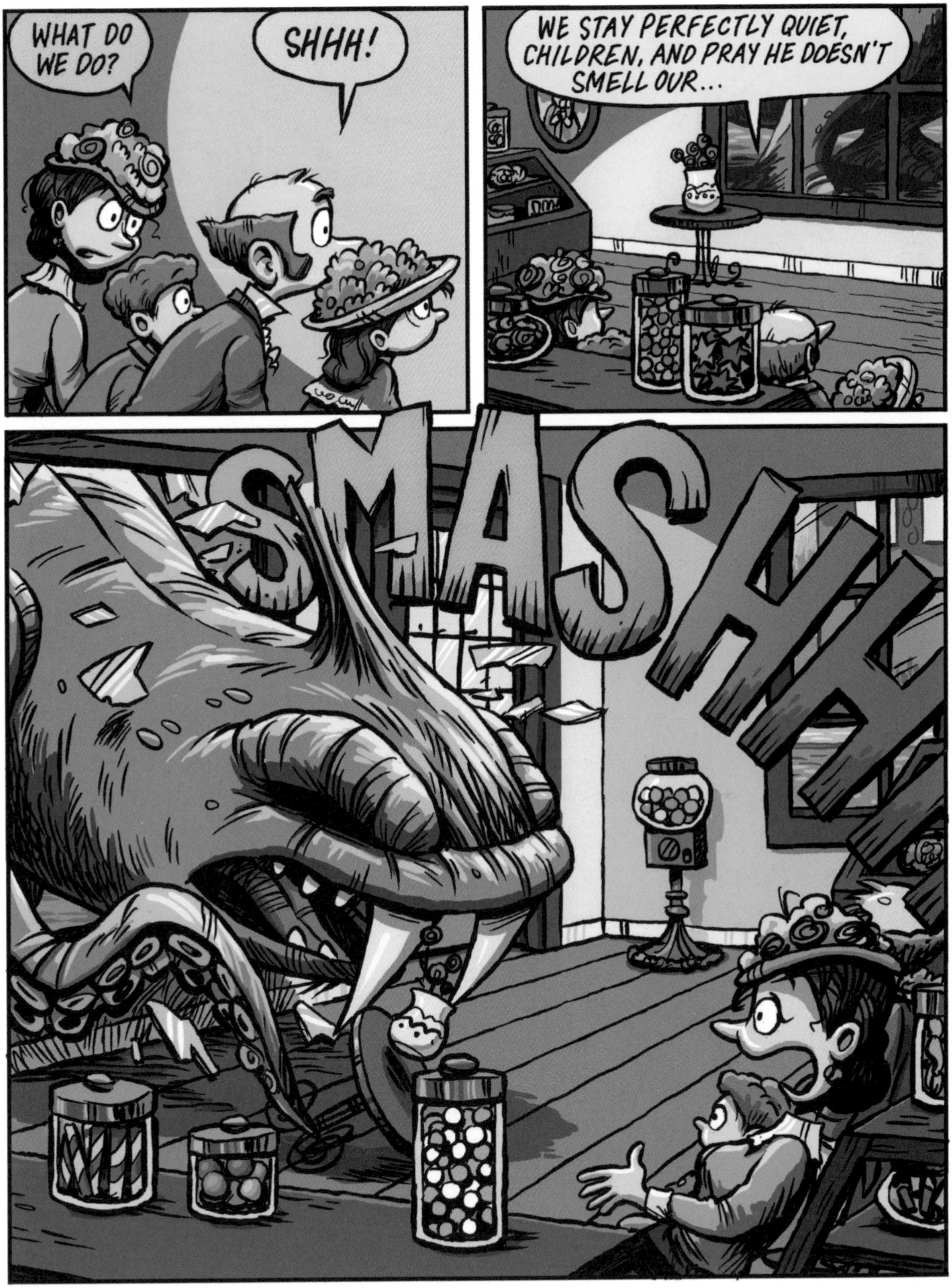
WHAT DO WE DO?
SHHH!
WE STAY PERFECTLY QUIET, CHILDREN, AND PRAY HE DOESN'T SMELL OUR...
SMASHH

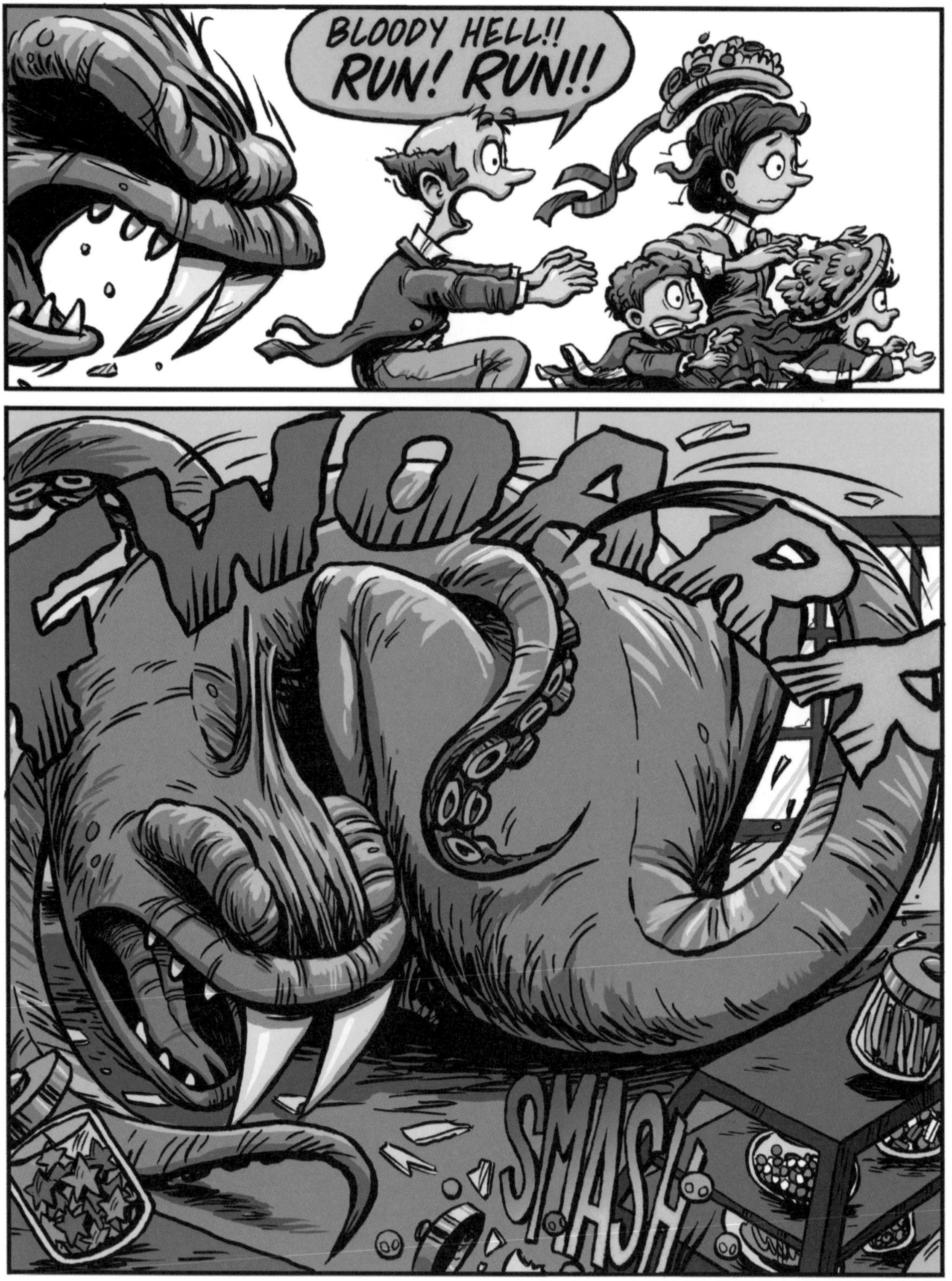
BLOODY HELL!!
RUN! RUN!!
WOA
SMASH

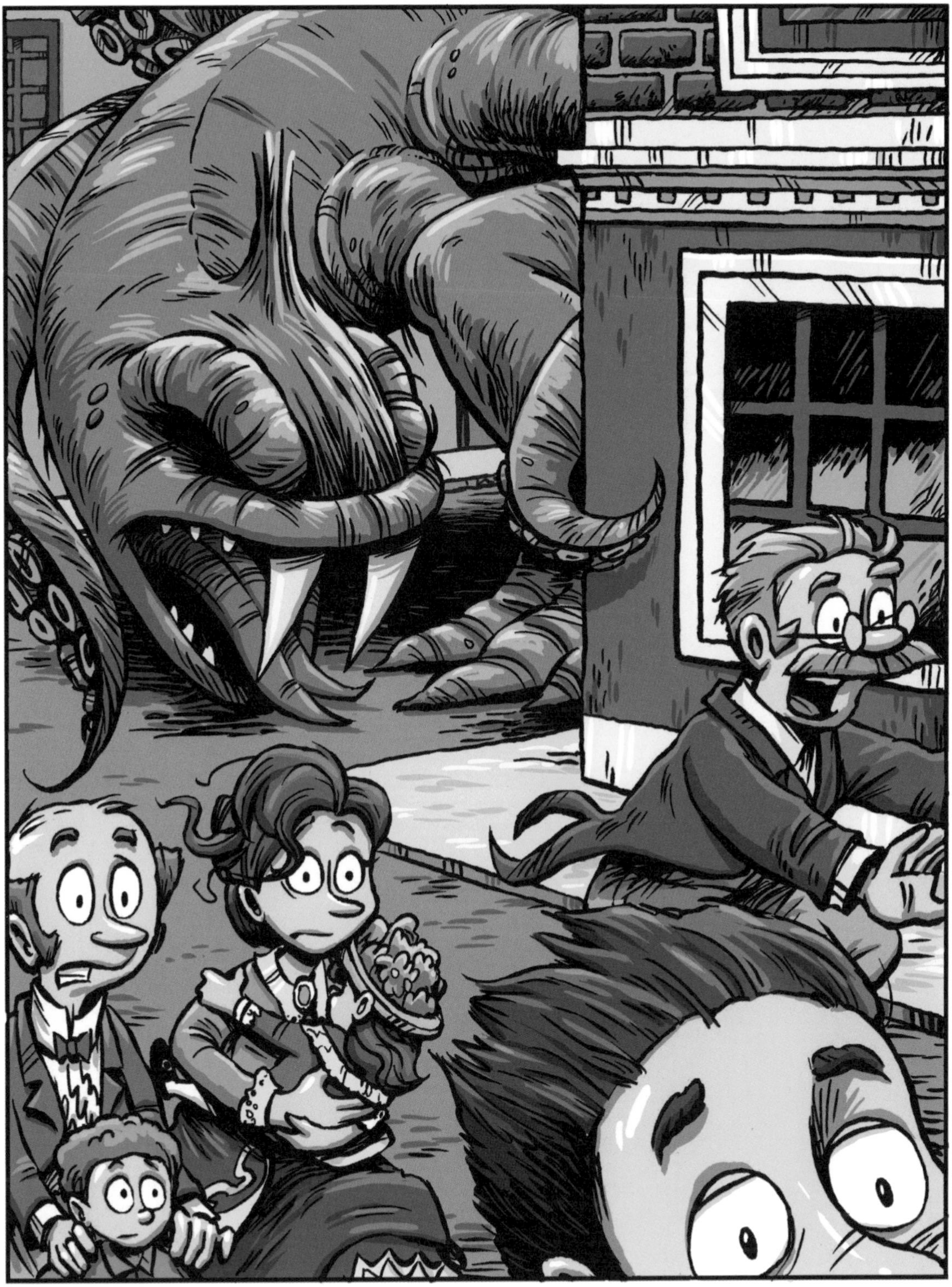

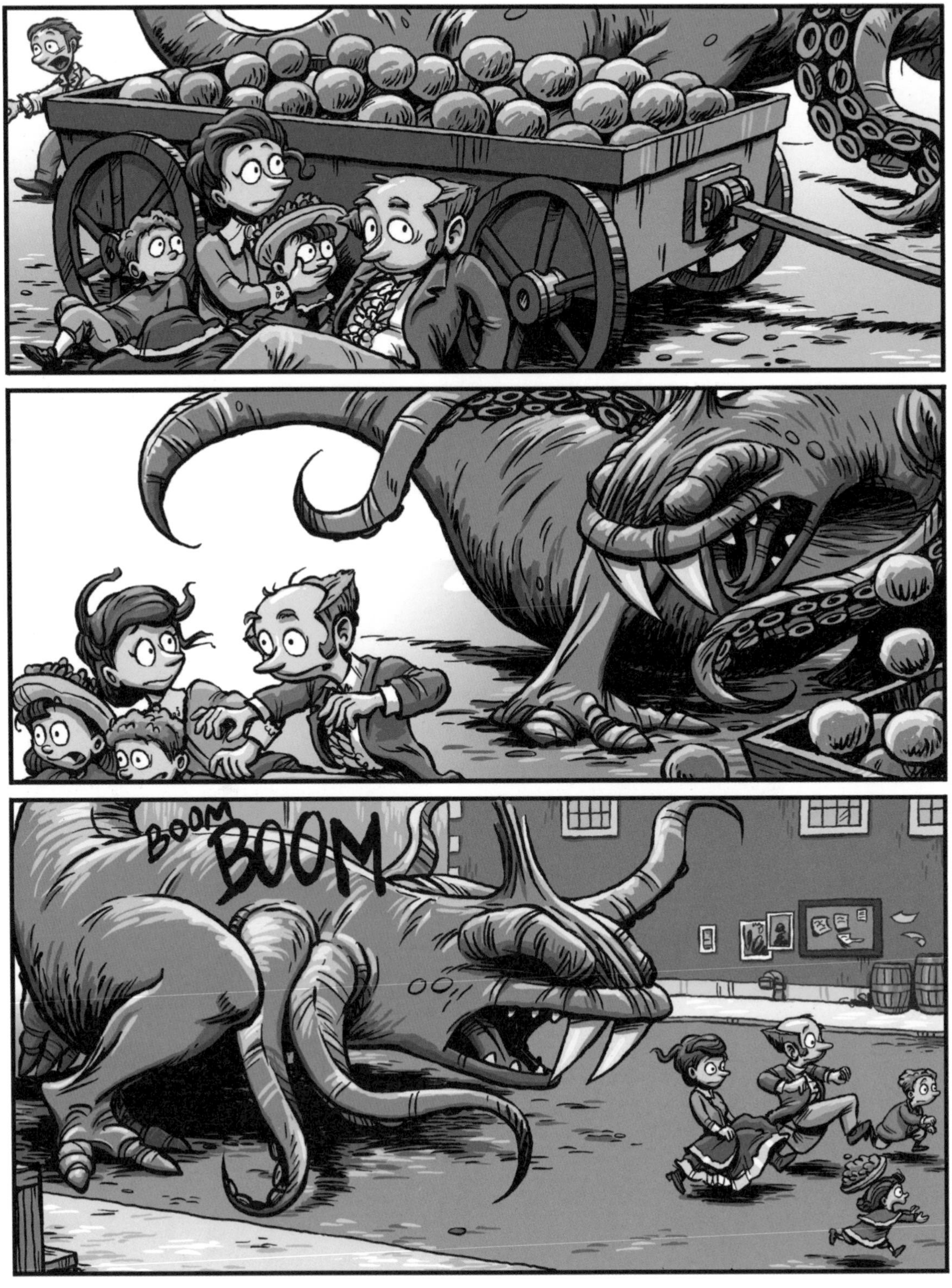
BOOM
BOOM

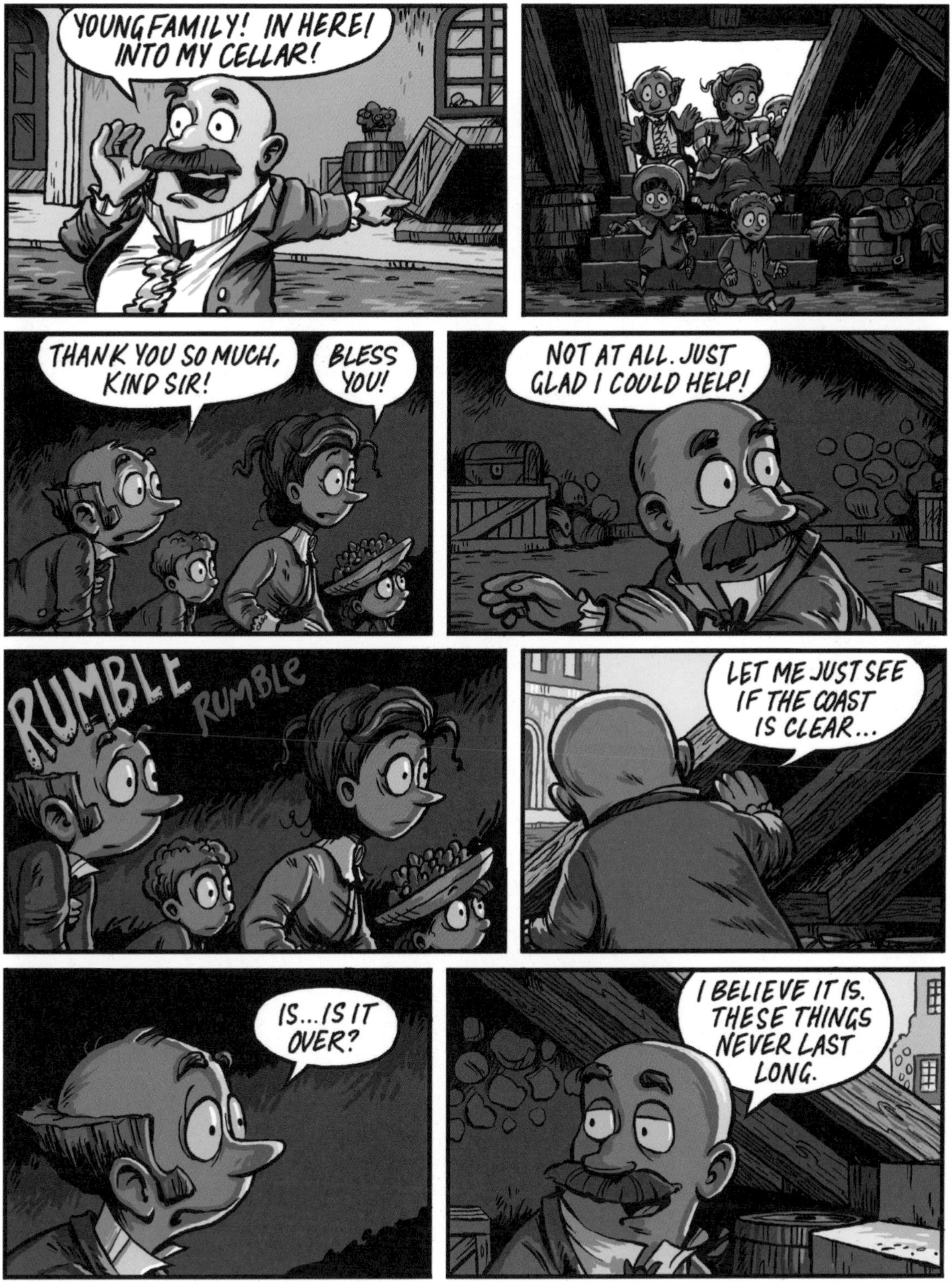
YOUNG FAMILY! IN HERE! INTO MY CELLAR!
THANK YOU SO MUCH, KIND SIR!
BLESS YOU!
NOT AT ALL. JUST GLAD I COULD HELP!
RUMBLE
RUMBLE
LET ME JUST SEE IF THE COAST IS CLEAR...
IS...IS IT OVER?
I BELIEVE IT IS. THESE THINGS NEVER LAST LONG.

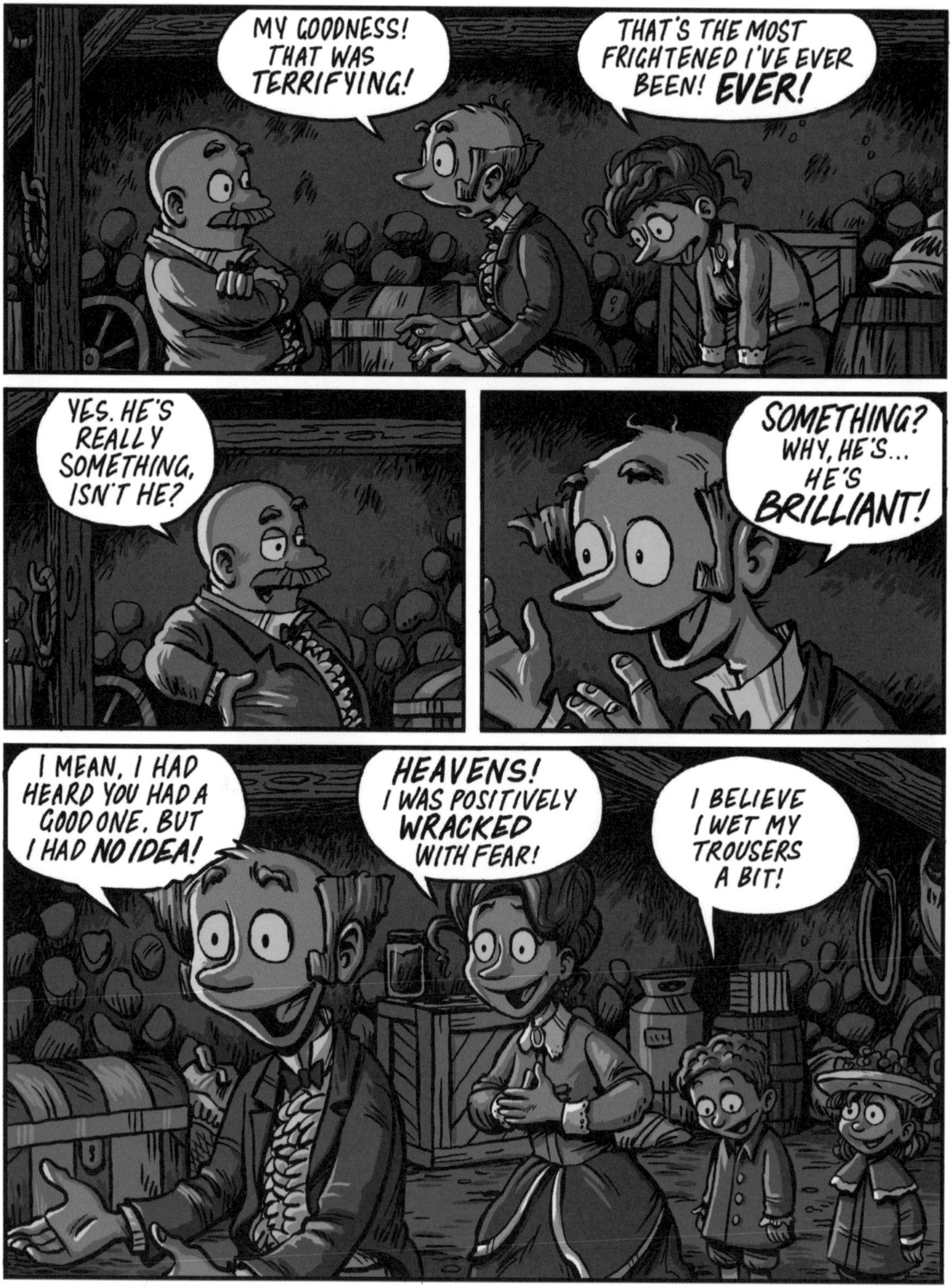
MY GOODNESS! THAT WAS TERRIFYING!
THAT'S THE MOST FRIGHTENED I'VE EVER BEEN! EVER!
YES. HE'S REALLY SOMETHING, ISN'T HE?
SOMETHING? WHY, HE'S... HE'S BRILLIANT!
I MEAN, I HAD HEARD YOU HAD A GOOD ONE. BUT I HAD NO IDEA!
HEAVENS! I WAS POSITIVELY WRACKED WITH FEAR!
I BELIEVE I WET MY TROUSERS A BIT!

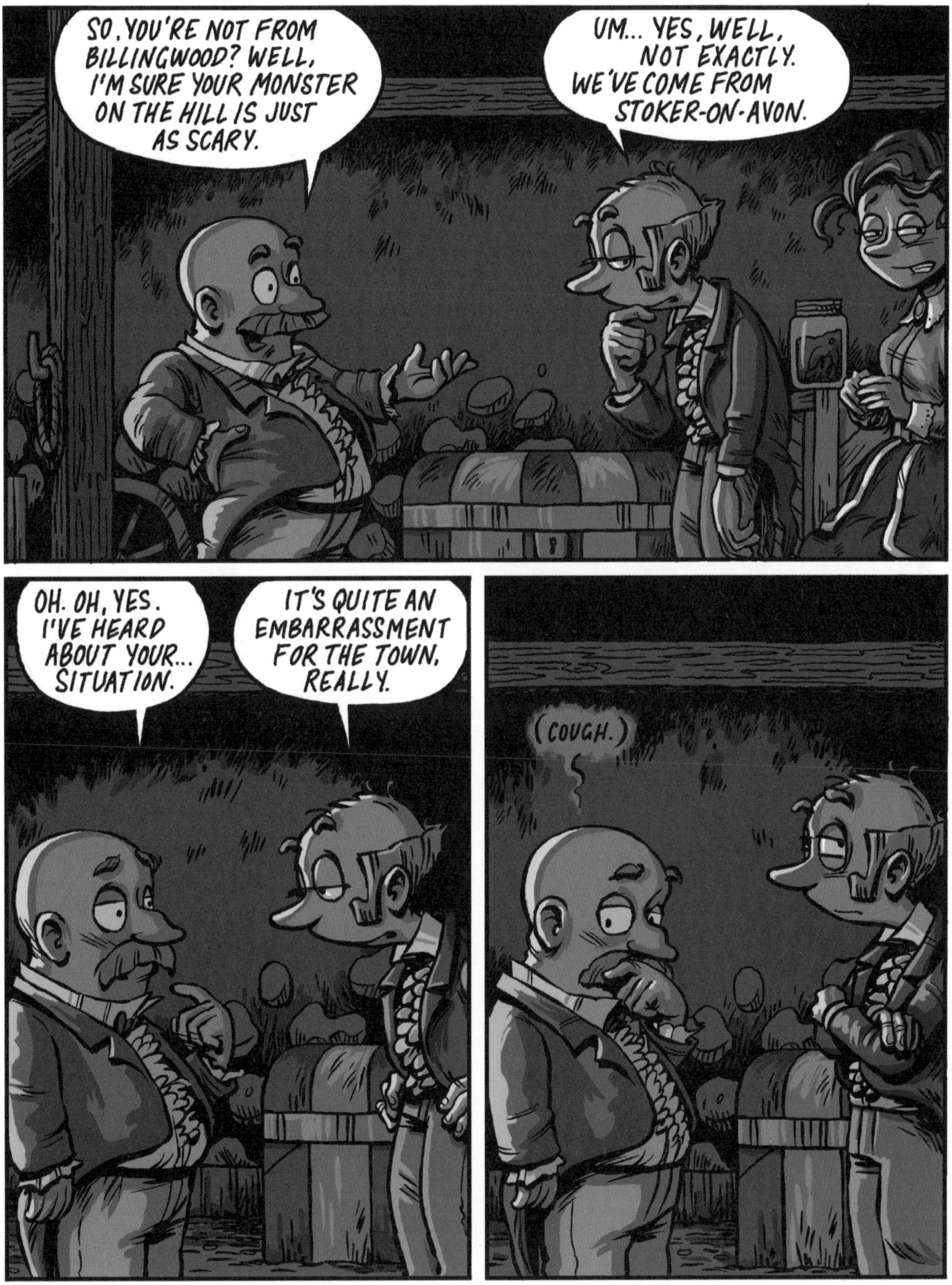
SO, YOU'RE NOT FROM BILLINGWOOD? WELL, I'M SURE YOUR MONSTER ON THE HILL IS JUST AS SCARY.
UM... YES, WELL, NOT EXACTLY. WE'VE COME FROM STOKER-ON-AVON.
OH. OH, YES. I'VE HEARD ABOUT YOUR... SITUATION.
IT'S QUITE AN EMBARRASSMENT FOR THE TOWN, REALLY.
(COUGH.)

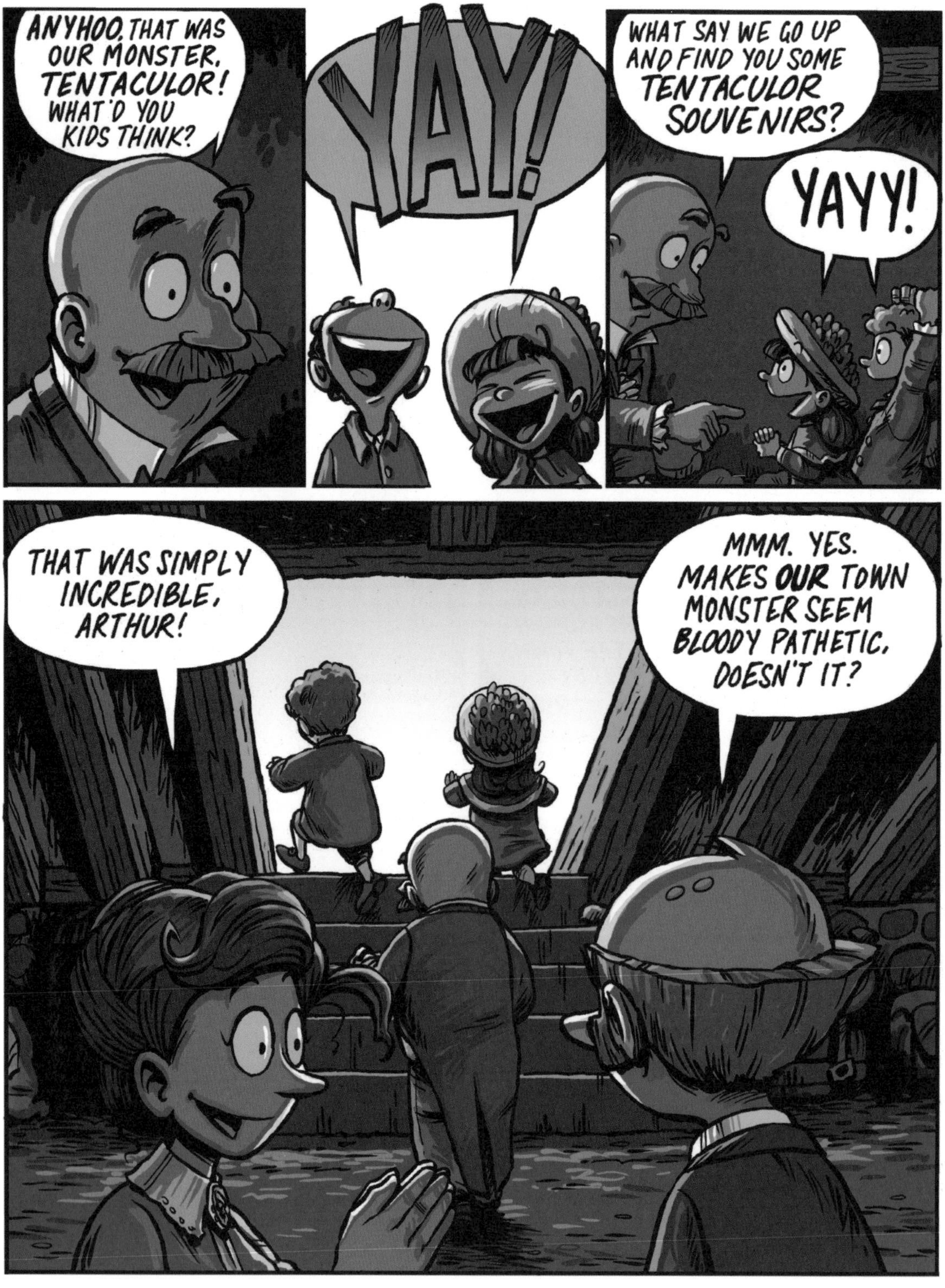
ANYHOO, THAT WAS OUR MONSTER, TENTACULOR! WHAT'D YOU KIDS THINK?
YAY!
WHAT SAY WE GO UP AND FIND YOU SOME TENTACULOR SOUVENIRS?
YAYY!
THAT WAS SIMPLY INCREDIBLE, ARTHUR!
MMM. YES. MAKES OUR TOWN MONSTER SEEM BLOODY PATHETIC, DOESN'T IT?

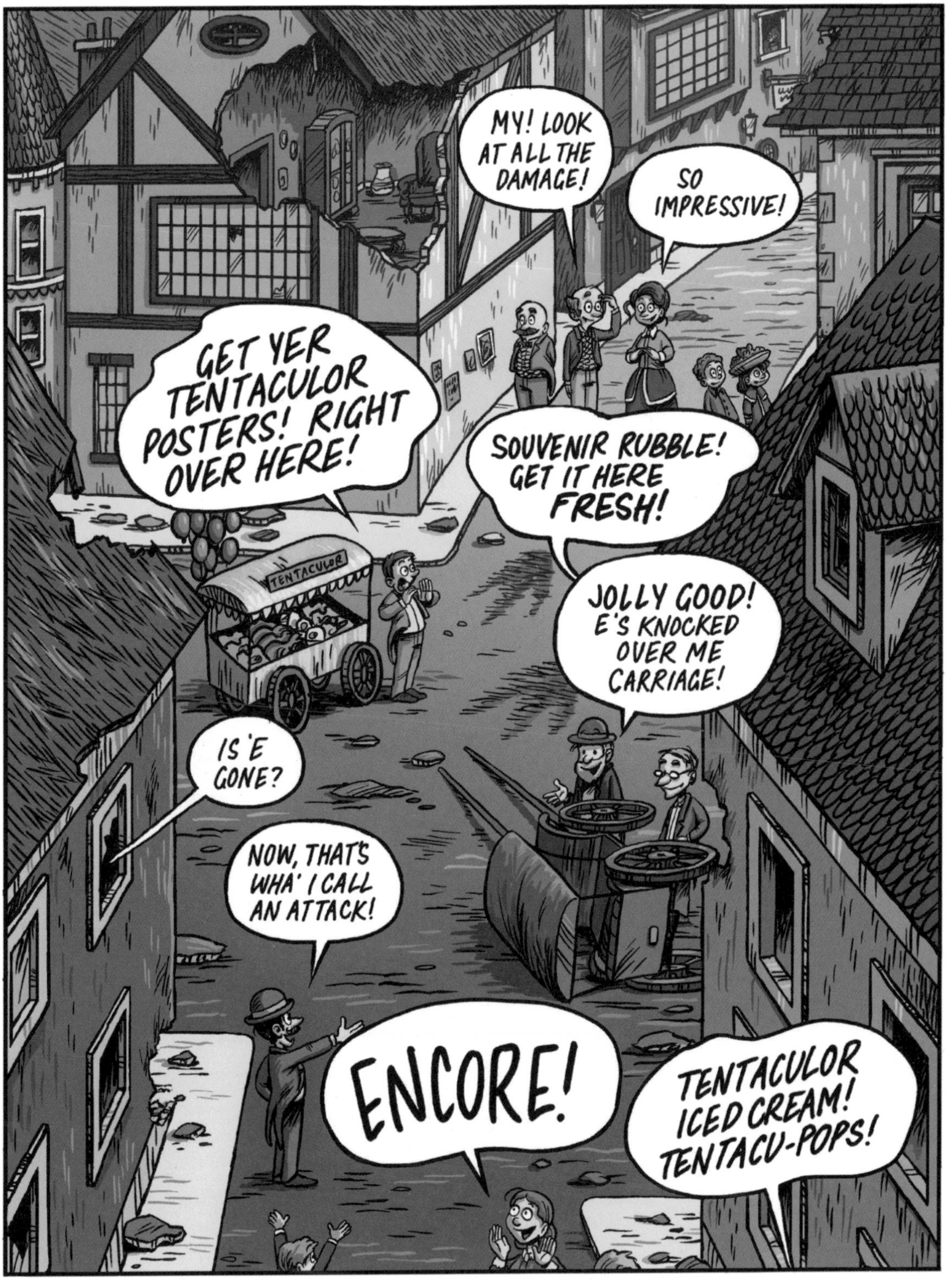

MY! LOOK AT ALL THE DAMAGE!
SO IMPRESSIVE!
GET YER TENTACULOR POSTERS! RIGHT OVER HERE!
TENTACULOR
SOUVENIR RUBBLE! GET IT HERE FRESH!
JOLLY GOOD! E'S KNOCKED OVER ME CARRIAGE!
IS 'E GONE?
NOW, THAT'S WHA' I CALL AN ATTACK!
ENCORE!
TENTACULOR ICED CREAM! TENTACU-POPS!

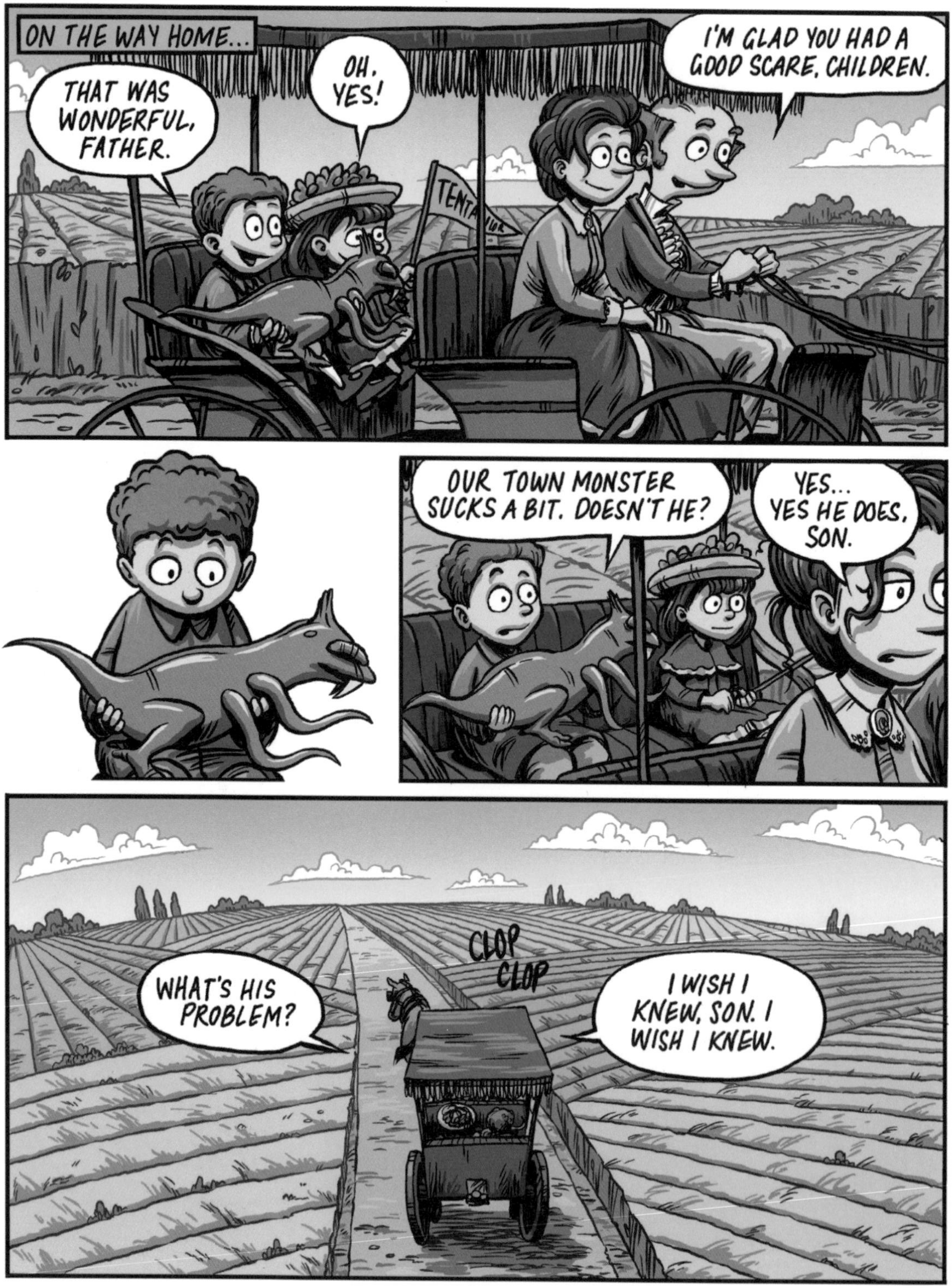
ON THE WAY HOME...
THAT WAS WONDERFUL, FATHER.
OH, YES!
I'M GLAD YOU HAD A GOOD SCARE, CHILDREN.
TENTA...
OUR TOWN MONSTER SUCKS A BIT, DOESN'T HE?
YES... YES HE DOES, SON.
CLOP CLOP
WHAT'S HIS PROBLEM?
I WISH I KNEW, SON. I WISH I KNEW.

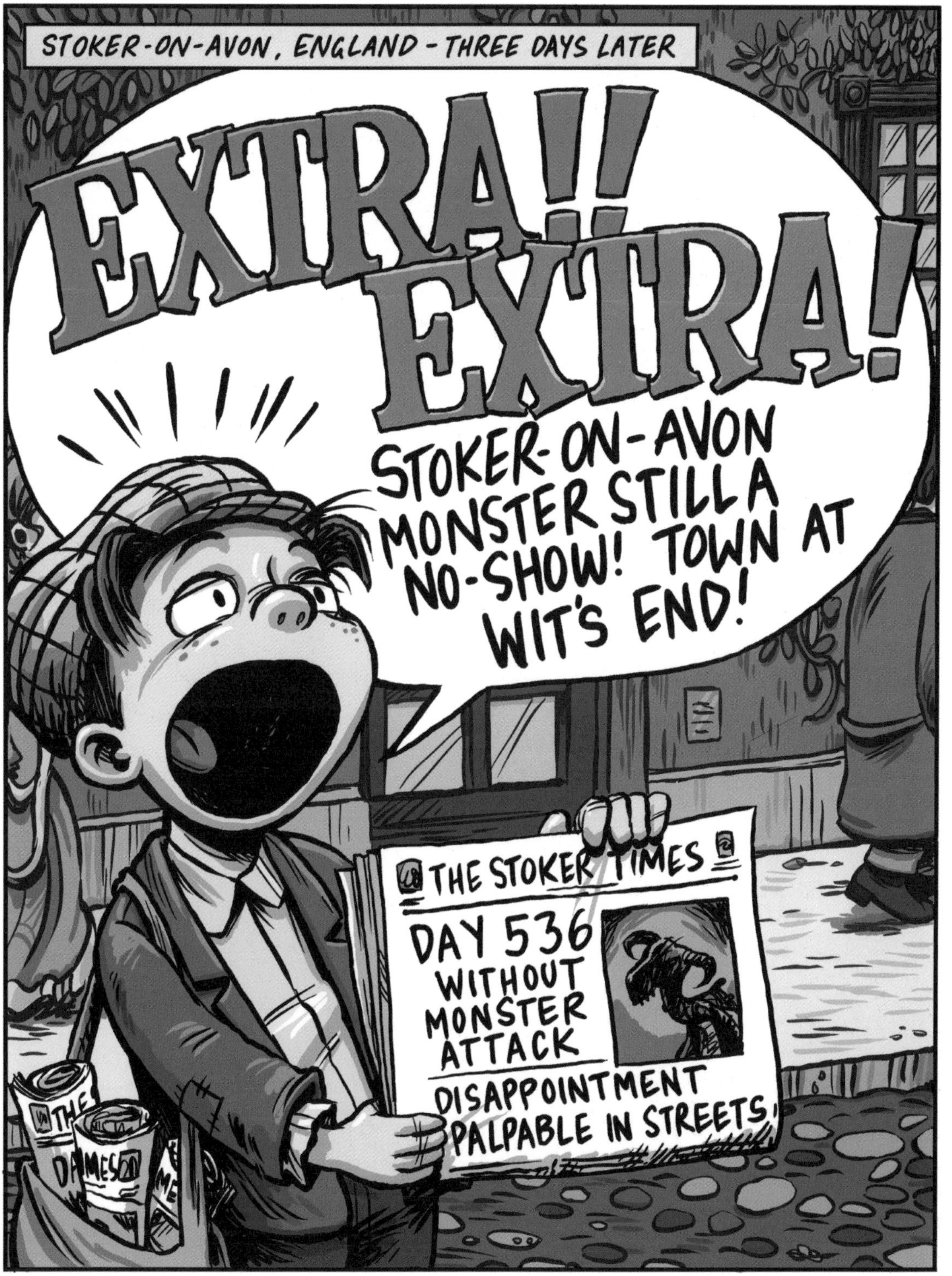
STOKER-ON-AVON, ENGLAND - THREE DAYS LATER
EXTRA!! EXTRA!
STOKER-ON-AVON MONSTER STILL A NO-SHOW! TOWN AT WIT'S END!
THE STOKER TIMES
DAY 536 WITHOUT MONSTER ATTACK
DISAPPOINTMENT PALPABLE IN STREETS

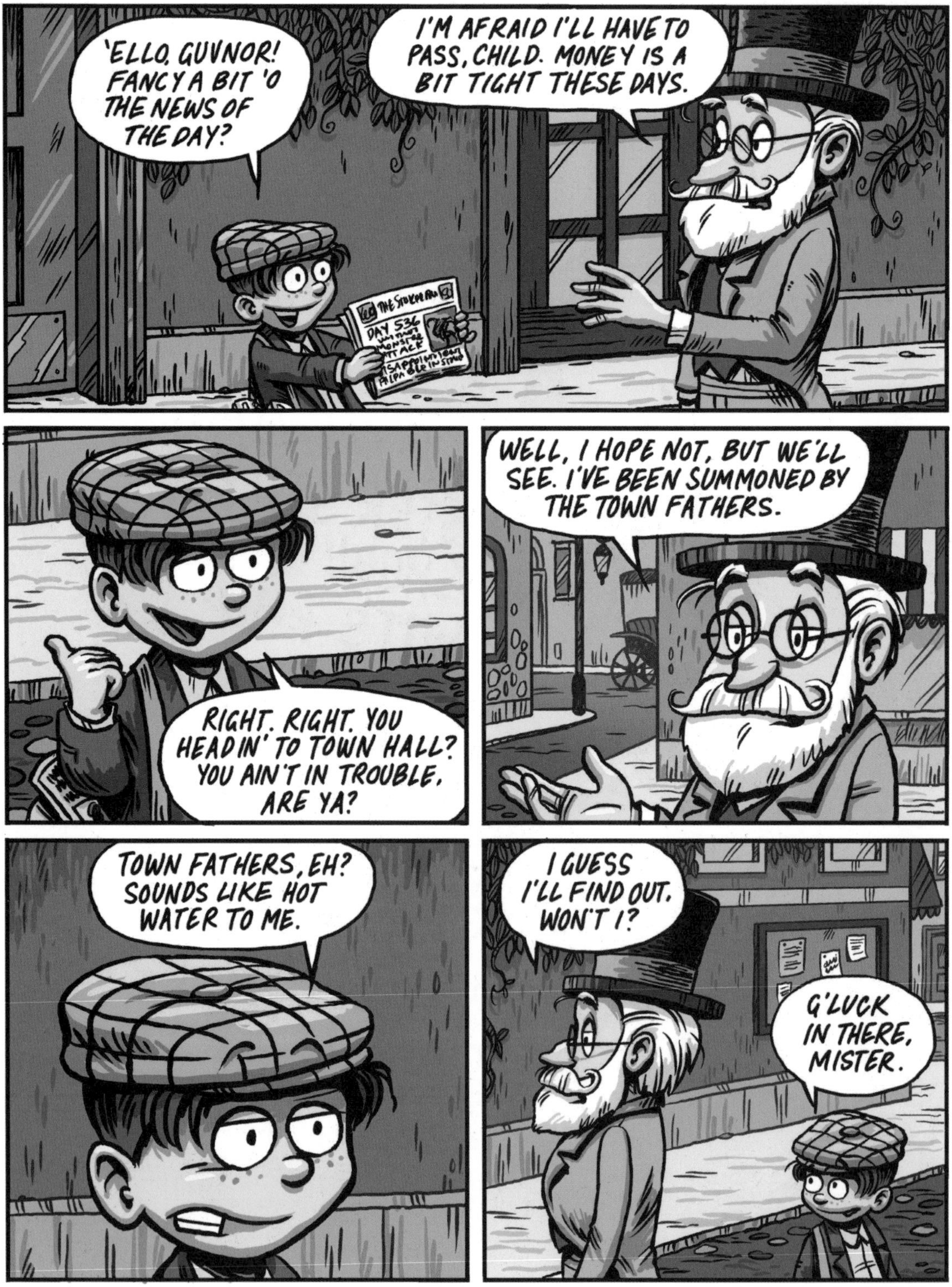
'ELLO, GUVNOR! FANCY A BIT 'O THE NEWS OF THE DAY?
I'M AFRAID I'LL HAVE TO PASS, CHILD. MONEY IS A BIT TIGHT THESE DAYS.
RIGHT. RIGHT. YOU HEADIN' TO TOWN HALL? YOU AIN'T IN TROUBLE, ARE YA?
WELL, I HOPE NOT, BUT WE'LL SEE. I'VE BEEN SUMMONED BY THE TOWN FATHERS.
TOWN FATHERS, EH? SOUNDS LIKE HOT WATER TO ME.
I GUESS I'LL FIND OUT, WON'T I?
G'LUCK IN THERE, MISTER.

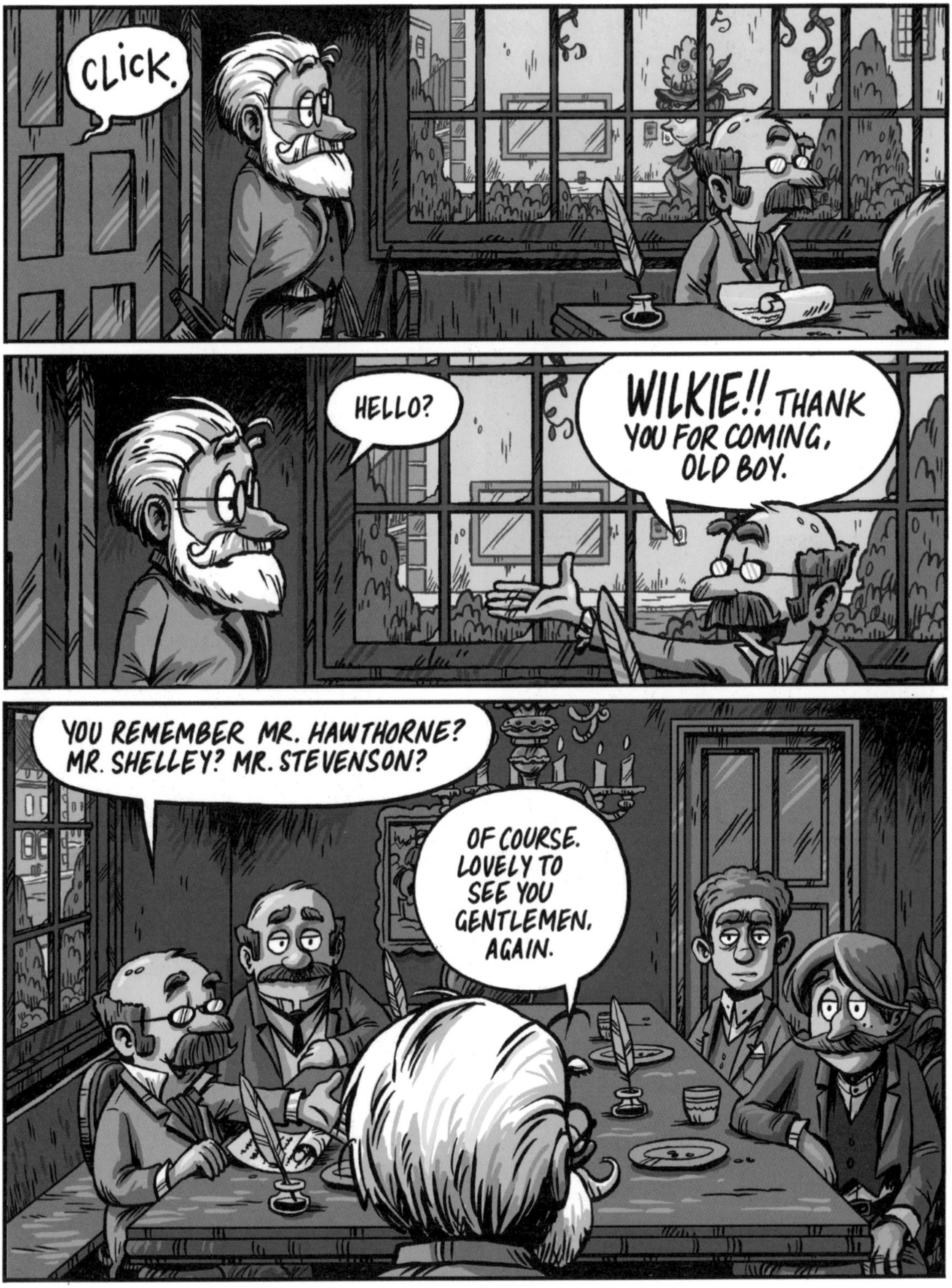
CLICK.
HELLO?
WILKIE!! THANK YOU FOR COMING, OLD BOY.
YOU REMEMBER MR. HAWTHORNE? MR. SHELLEY? MR. STEVENSON?
OF COURSE. LOVELY TO SEE YOU GENTLEMEN, AGAIN.

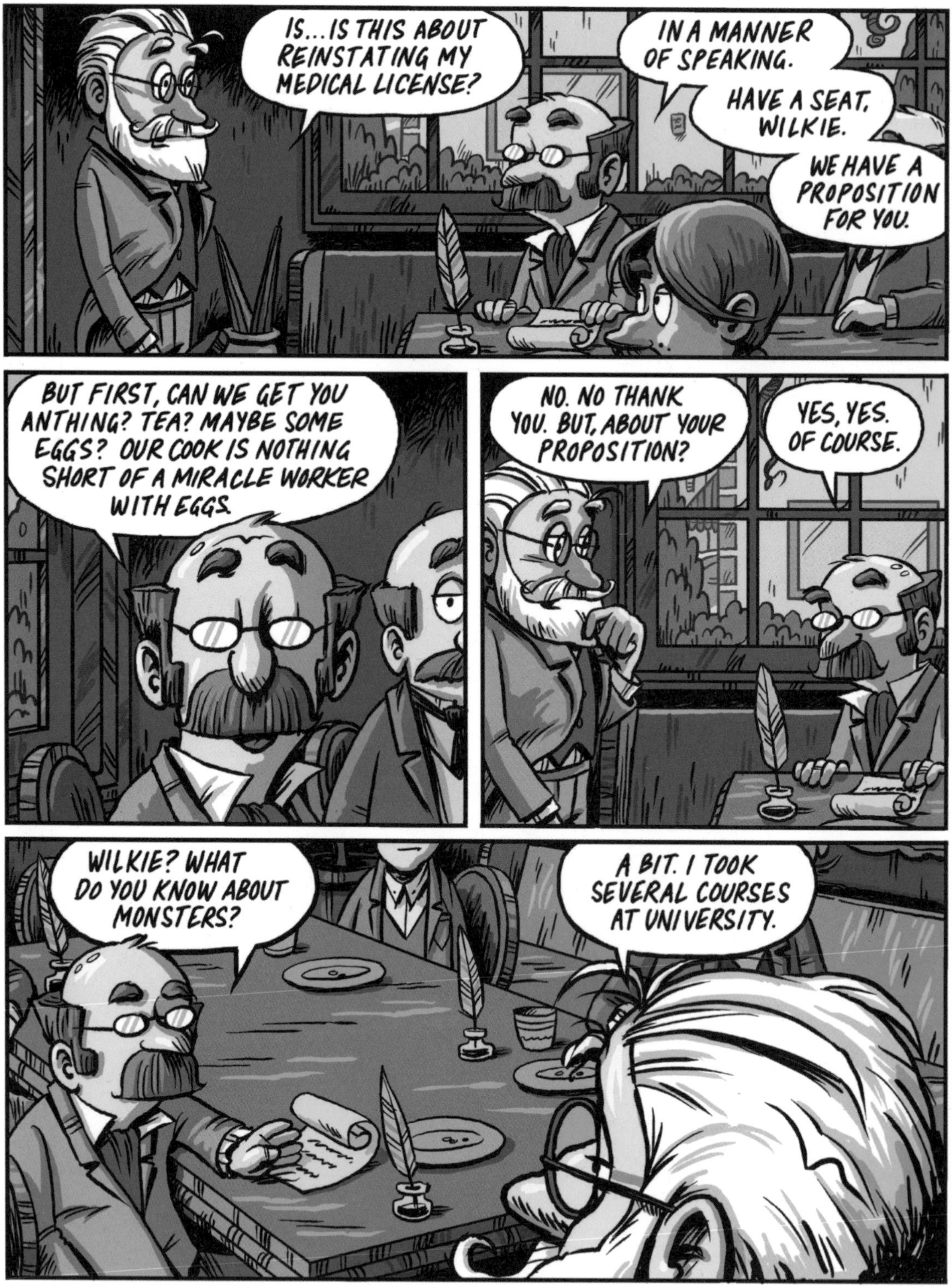
IS...IS THIS ABOUT REINSTATING MY MEDICAL LICENSE?
IN A MANNER OF SPEAKING.
HAVE A SEAT, WILKIE.
WE HAVE A PROPOSITION FOR YOU.
BUT FIRST, CAN WE GET YOU ANTHING? TEA? MAYBE SOME EGGS? OUR COOK IS NOTHING SHORT OF A MIRACLE WORKER WITH EGGS.
NO. NO THANK YOU. BUT, ABOUT YOUR PROPOSITION?
YES, YES. OF COURSE.
WILKIE? WHAT DO YOU KNOW ABOUT MONSTERS?
A BIT. I TOOK SEVERAL COURSES AT UNIVERSITY.

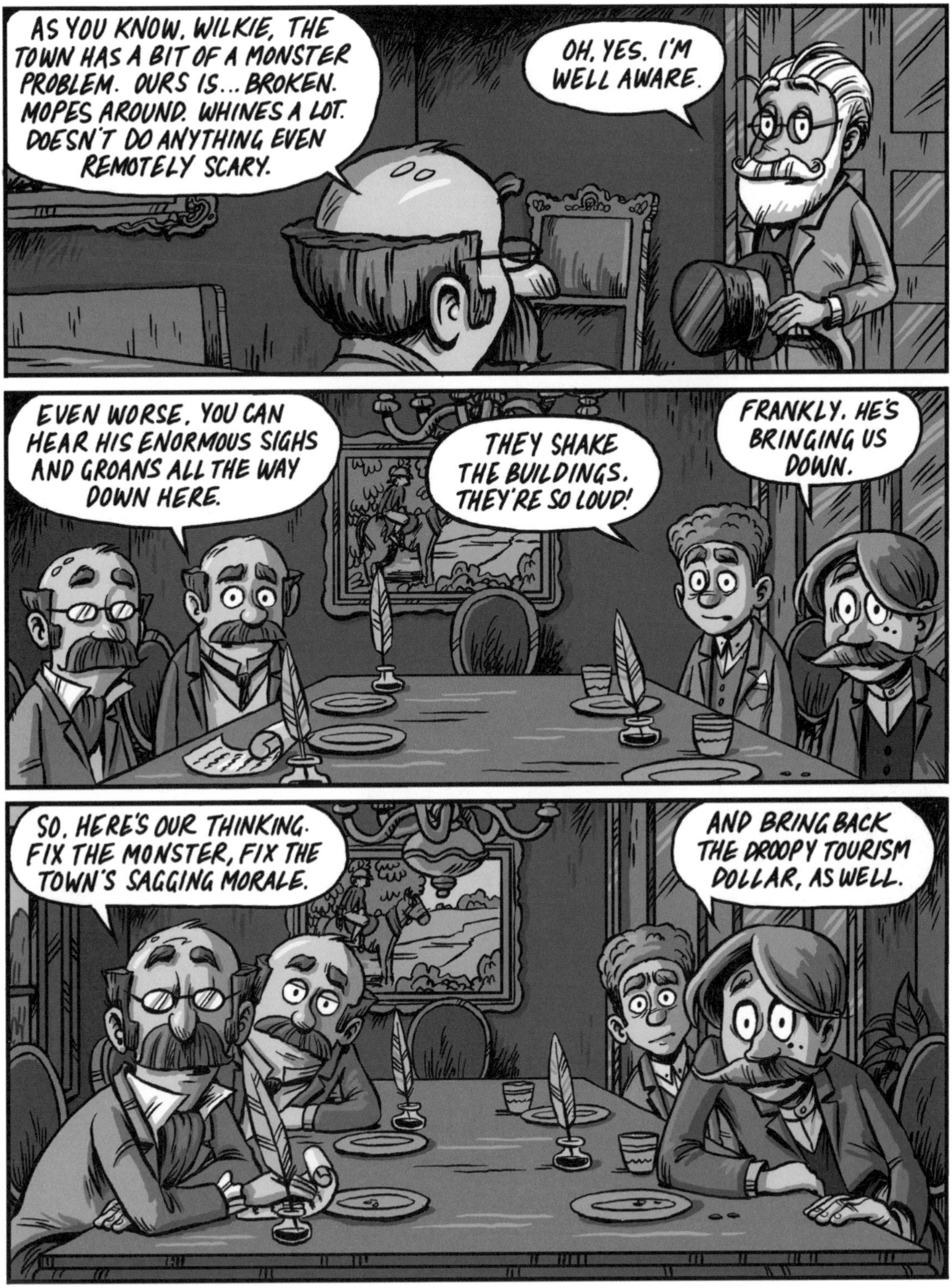
AS YOU KNOW, WILKIE, THE TOWN HAS A BIT OF A MONSTER PROBLEM. OURS IS... BROKEN. MOPES AROUND. WHINES A LOT. DOESN'T DO ANYTHING EVEN REMOTELY SCARY.
OH, YES. I'M WELL AWARE.
EVEN WORSE, YOU CAN HEAR HIS ENORMOUS SIGHS AND GROANS ALL THE WAY DOWN HERE.
THEY SHAKE THE BUILDINGS. THEY'RE SO LOUD!
FRANKLY, HE'S BRINGING US DOWN.
SO, HERE'S OUR THINKING. FIX THE MONSTER, FIX THE TOWN'S SAGGING MORALE.
AND BRING BACK THE DROOPY TOURISM DOLLAR, AS WELL.

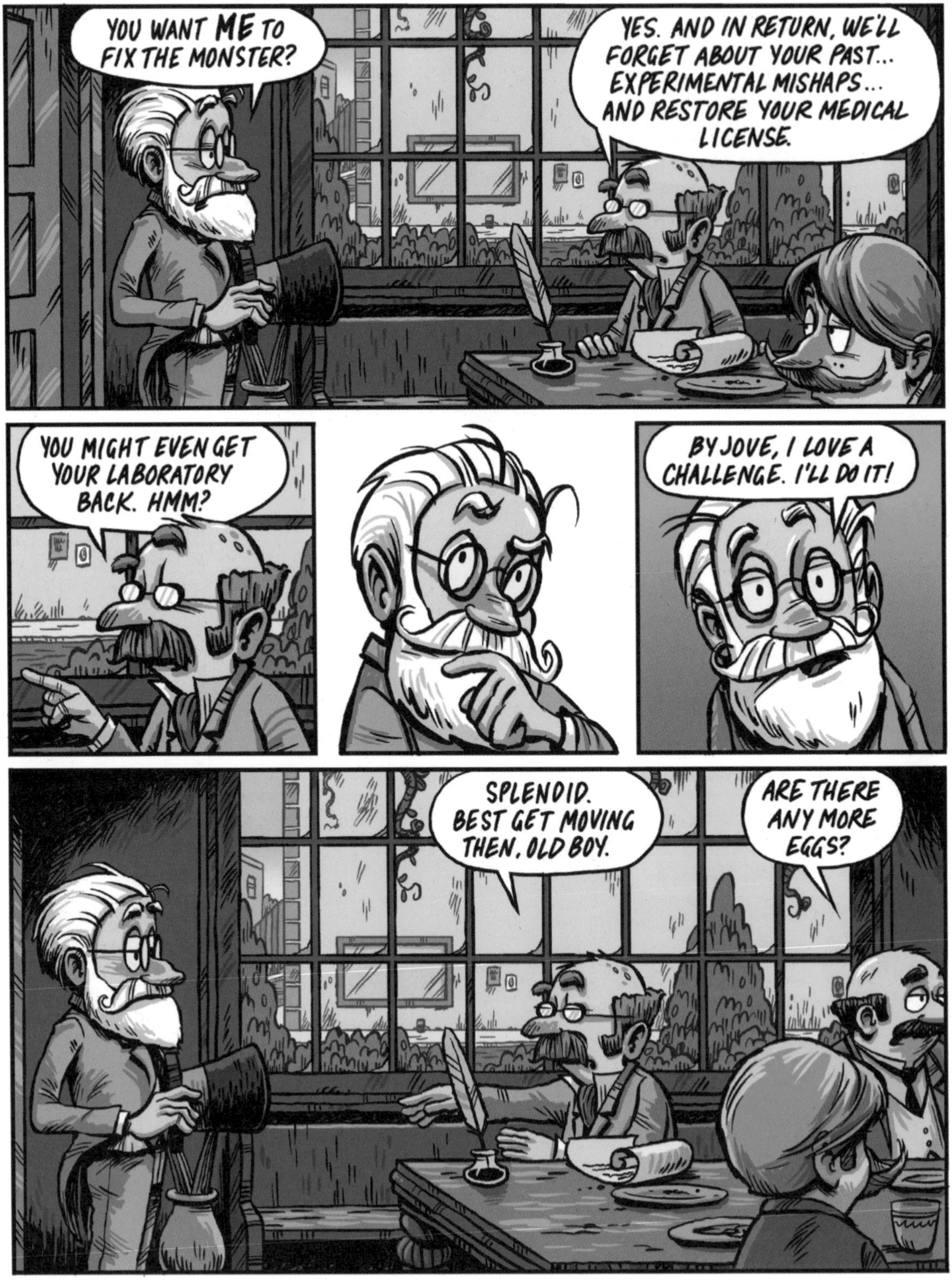
YOU WANT **ME** TO FIX THE MONSTER?
YES. AND IN RETURN, WE'LL FORGET ABOUT YOUR PAST... EXPERIMENTAL MISHAPS... AND RESTORE YOUR MEDICAL LICENSE.
YOU MIGHT EVEN GET YOUR LABORATORY BACK. HMM?
BY JOVE, I LOVE A CHALLENGE. I'LL DO IT!
SPLENDID. BEST GET MOVING THEN, OLD BOY.
ARE THERE ANY MORE EGGS?

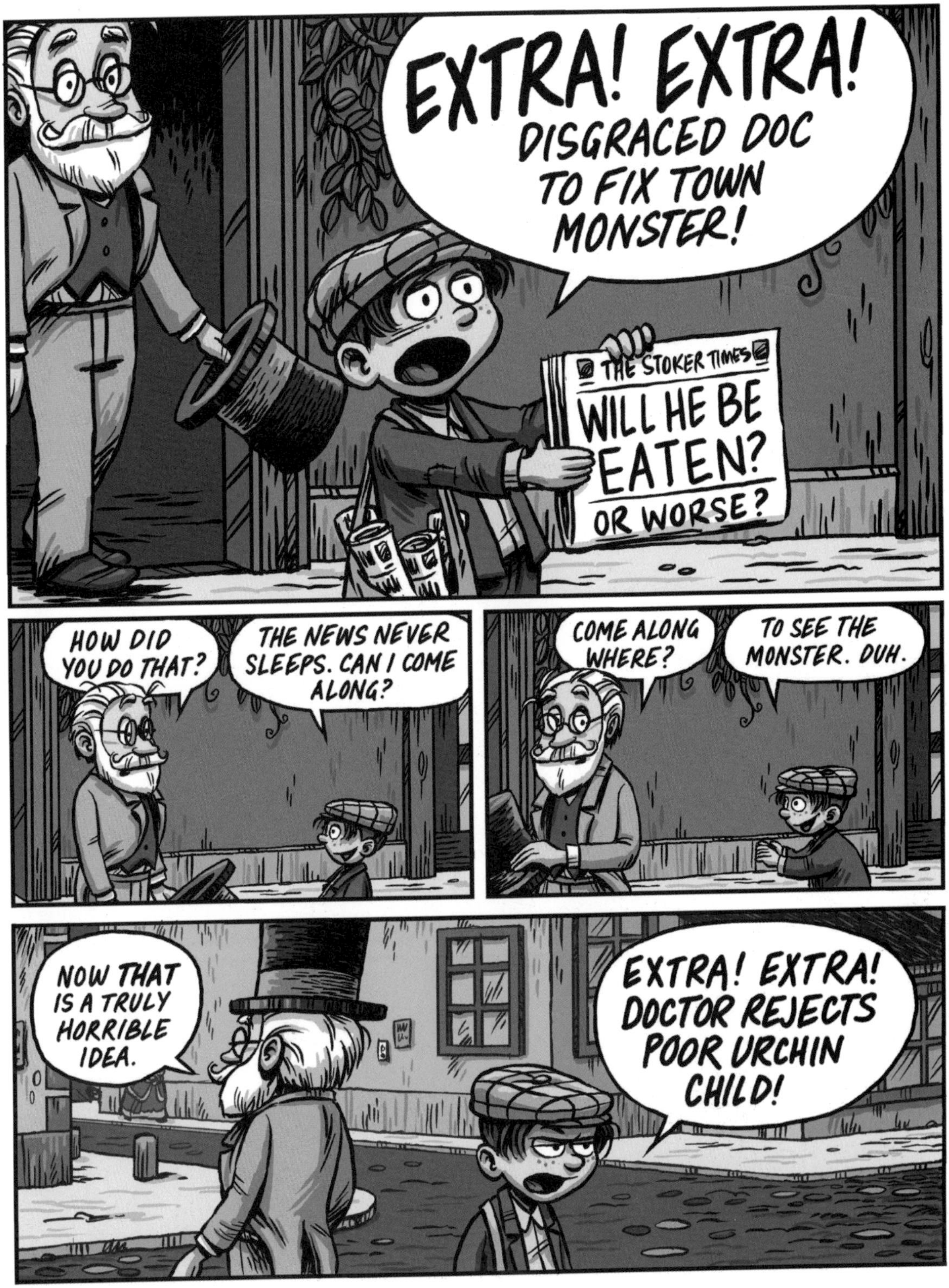
EXTRA! EXTRA! DISGRACED DOC TO FIX TOWN MONSTER!
THE STOKER TIMES
WILL HE BE EATEN? OR WORSE?
HOW DID YOU DO THAT?
THE NEWS NEVER SLEEPS. CAN I COME ALONG?
COME ALONG WHERE?
TO SEE THE MONSTER. DUH.
NOW THAT IS A TRULY HORRIBLE IDEA.
EXTRA! EXTRA! DOCTOR REJECTS POOR URCHIN CHILD!

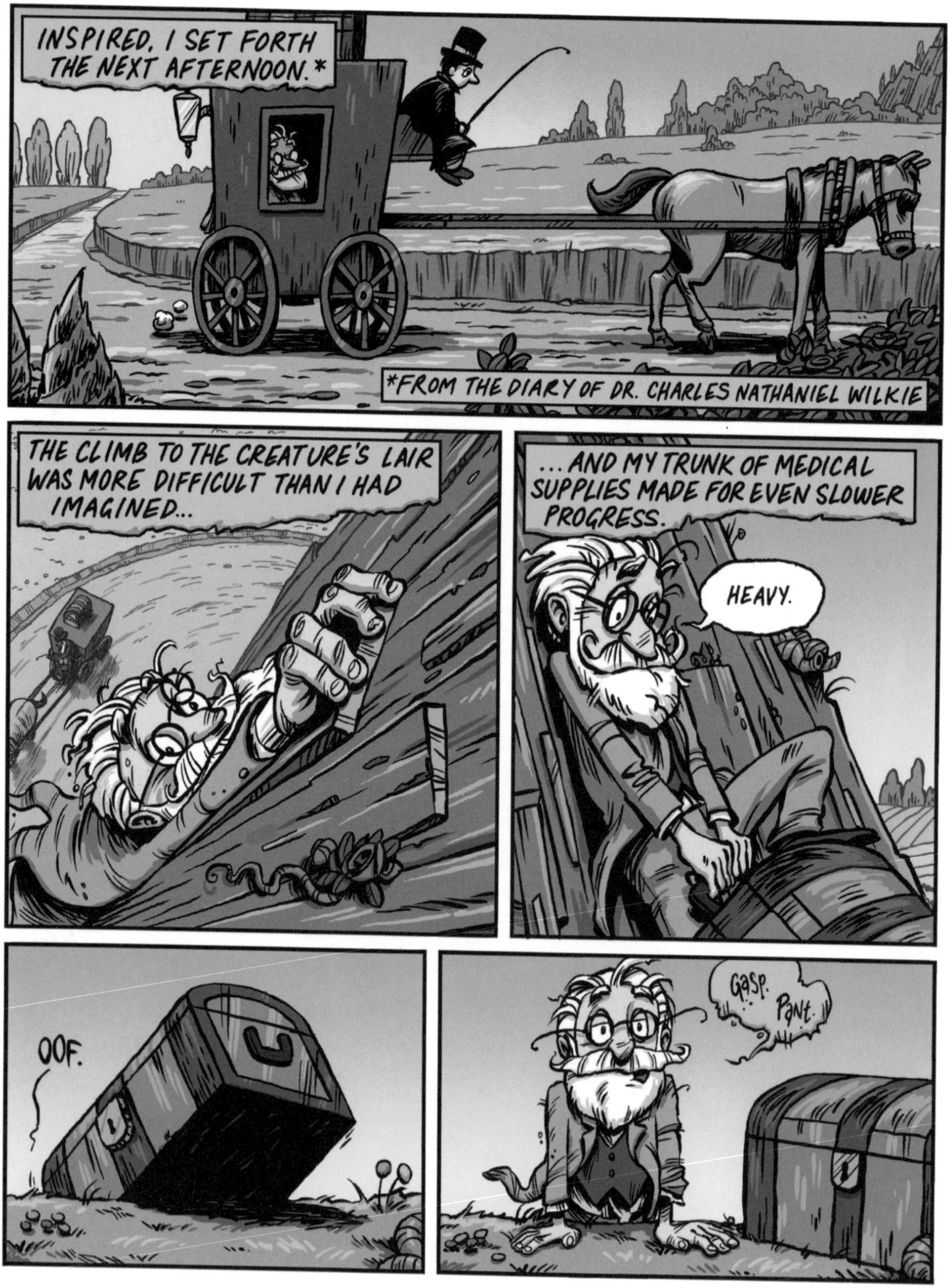
INSPIRED, I SET FORTH THE NEXT AFTERNOON.*
*FROM THE DIARY OF DR. CHARLES NATHANIEL WILKIE
THE CLIMB TO THE CREATURE'S LAIR WAS MORE DIFFICULT THAN I HAD IMAGINED...
...AND MY TRUNK OF MEDICAL SUPPLIES MADE FOR EVEN SLOWER PROGRESS.
HEAVY.
OOF.
GASP.
PANT.

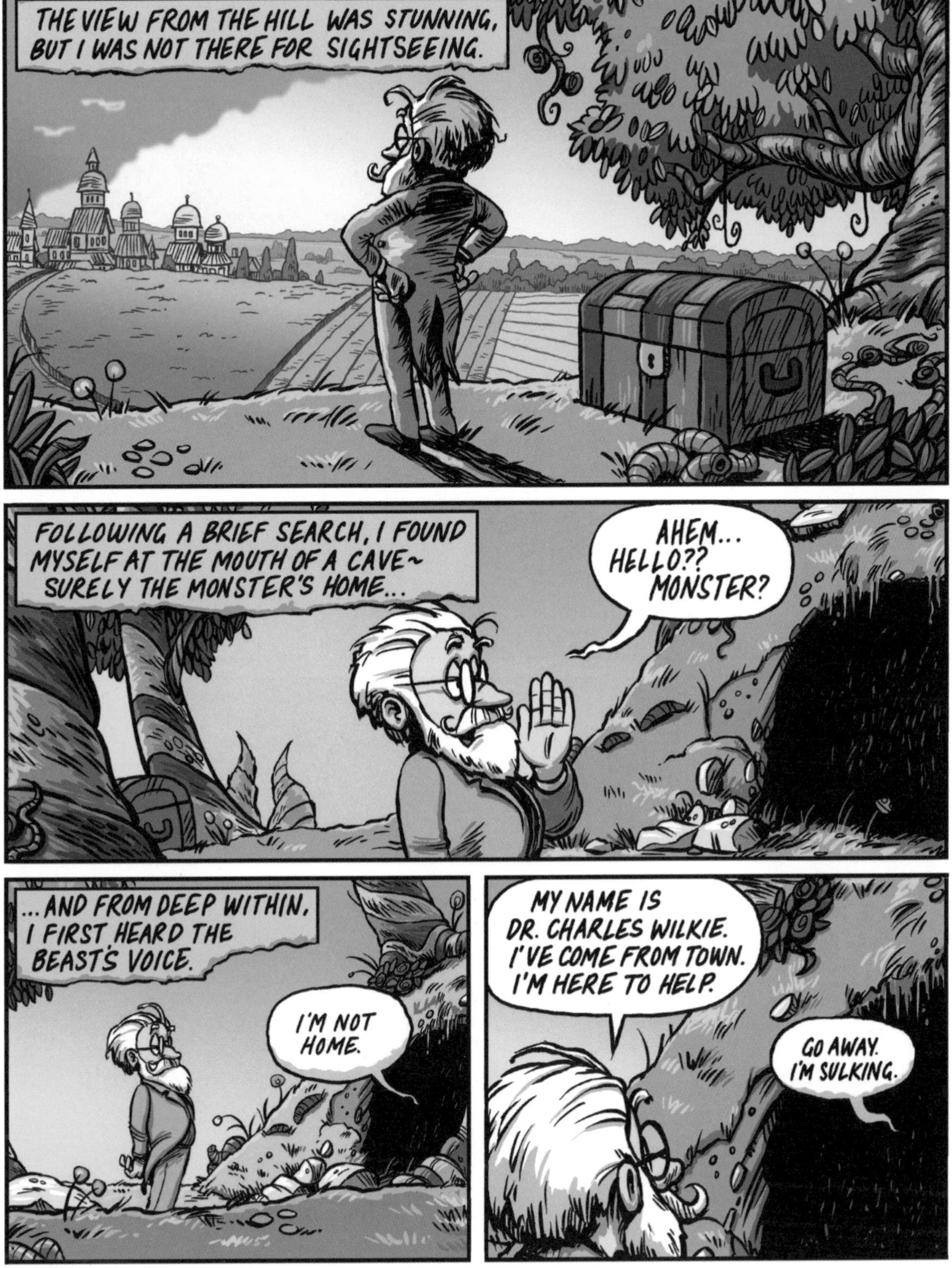
THE VIEW FROM THE HILL WAS STUNNING, BUT I WAS NOT THERE FOR SIGHTSEEING.
FOLLOWING A BRIEF SEARCH, I FOUND MYSELF AT THE MOUTH OF A CAVE~ SURELY THE MONSTER'S HOME...
AHEM... HELLO?? MONSTER?
...AND FROM DEEP WITHIN, I FIRST HEARD THE BEAST'S VOICE.
I'M NOT HOME.
MY NAME IS DR. CHARLES WILKIE. I'VE COME FROM TOWN. I'M HERE TO HELP.
GO AWAY. I'M SULKING.

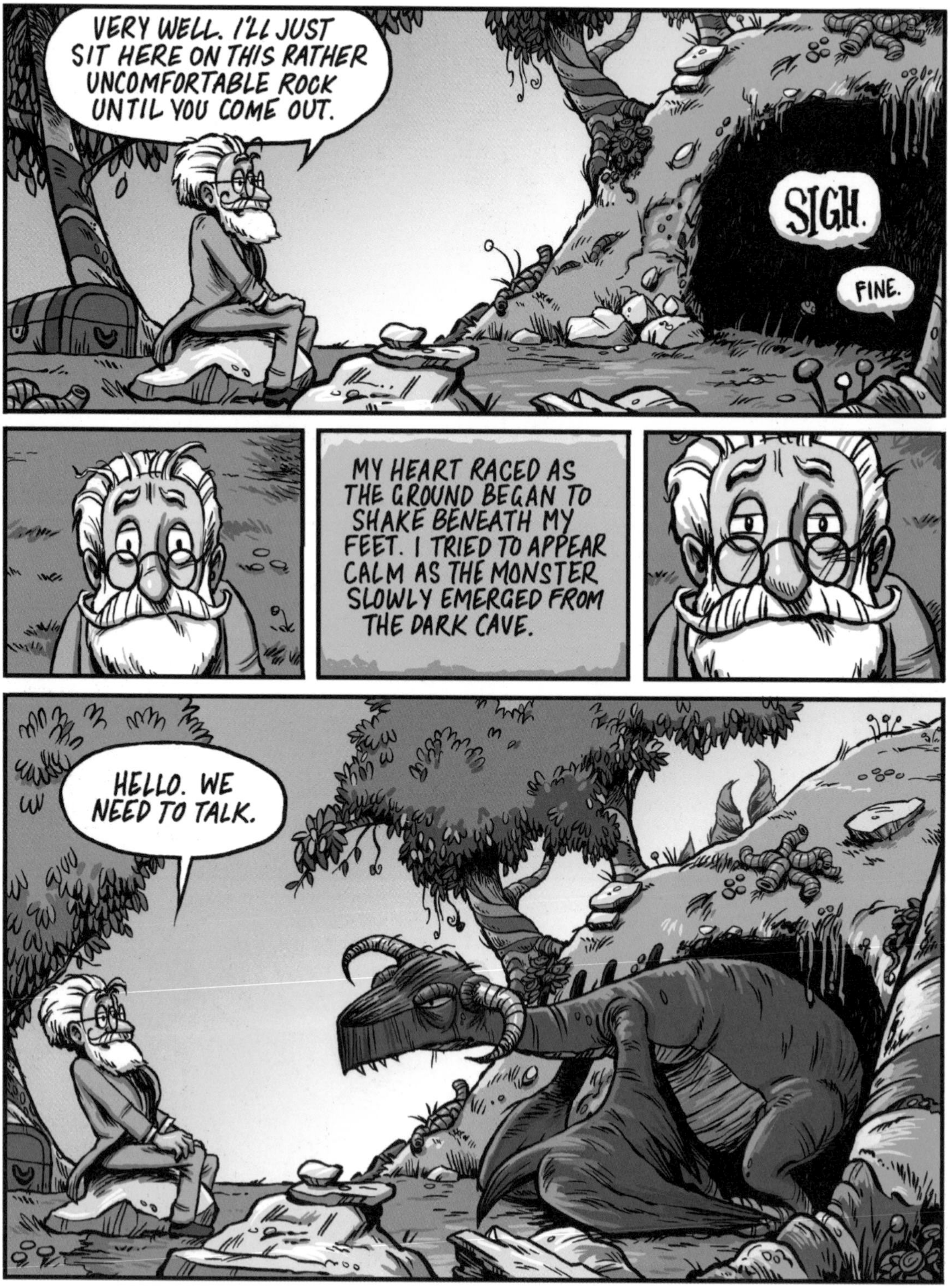
VERY WELL. I'LL JUST SIT HERE ON THIS RATHER UNCOMFORTABLE ROCK UNTIL YOU COME OUT.
SIGH.
FINE.
MY HEART RACED AS THE GROUND BEGAN TO SHAKE BENEATH MY FEET. I TRIED TO APPEAR CALM AS THE MONSTER SLOWLY EMERGED FROM THE DARK CAVE.
HELLO. WE NEED TO TALK.

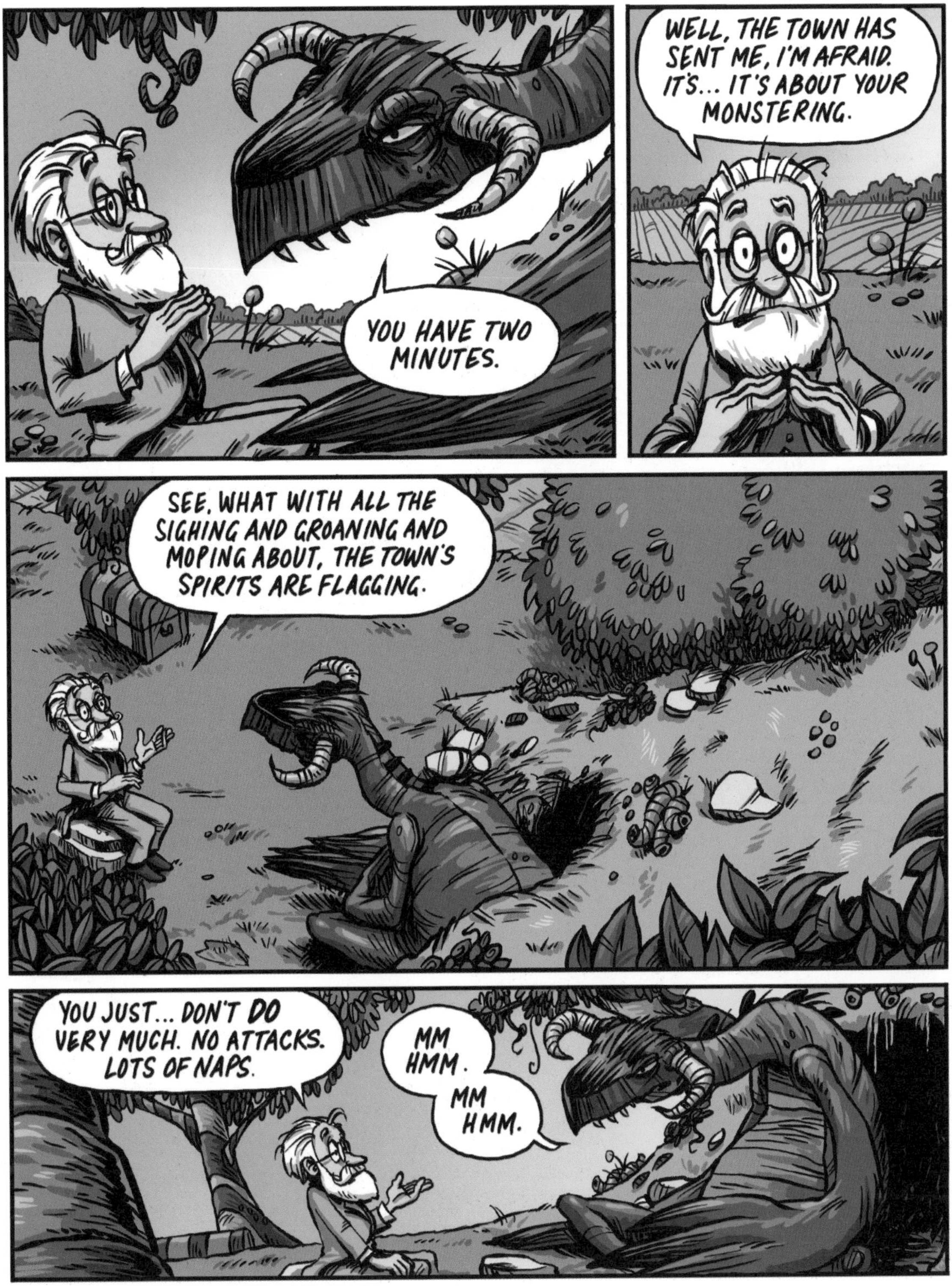
YOU HAVE TWO MINUTES.
WELL, THE TOWN HAS SENT ME, I'M AFRAID. IT'S... IT'S ABOUT YOUR MONSTERING.
SEE, WHAT WITH ALL THE SIGHING AND GROANING AND MOPING ABOUT, THE TOWN'S SPIRITS ARE FLAGGING.
YOU JUST... DON'T DO VERY MUCH. NO ATTACKS. LOTS OF NAPS.
MM HMM.
MM HMM.

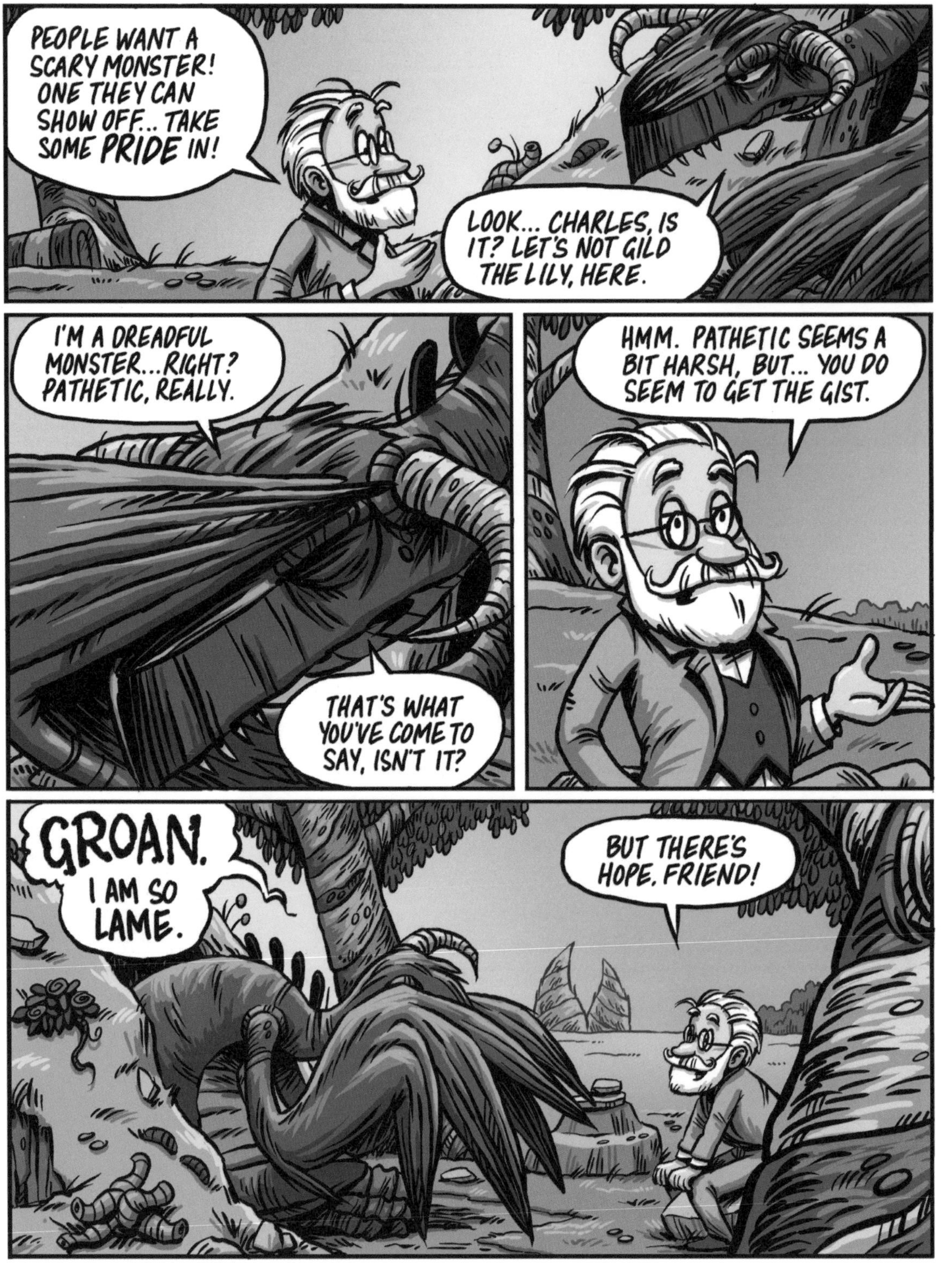
PEOPLE WANT A SCARY MONSTER! ONE THEY CAN SHOW OFF... TAKE SOME PRIDE IN!
LOOK... CHARLES, IS IT? LET'S NOT GILD THE LILY, HERE.
I'M A DREADFUL MONSTER...RIGHT? PATHETIC, REALLY.
THAT'S WHAT YOU'VE COME TO SAY, ISN'T IT?
HMM. PATHETIC SEEMS A BIT HARSH, BUT... YOU DO SEEM TO GET THE GIST.
GROAN. I AM SO LAME.
BUT THERE'S HOPE, FRIEND!

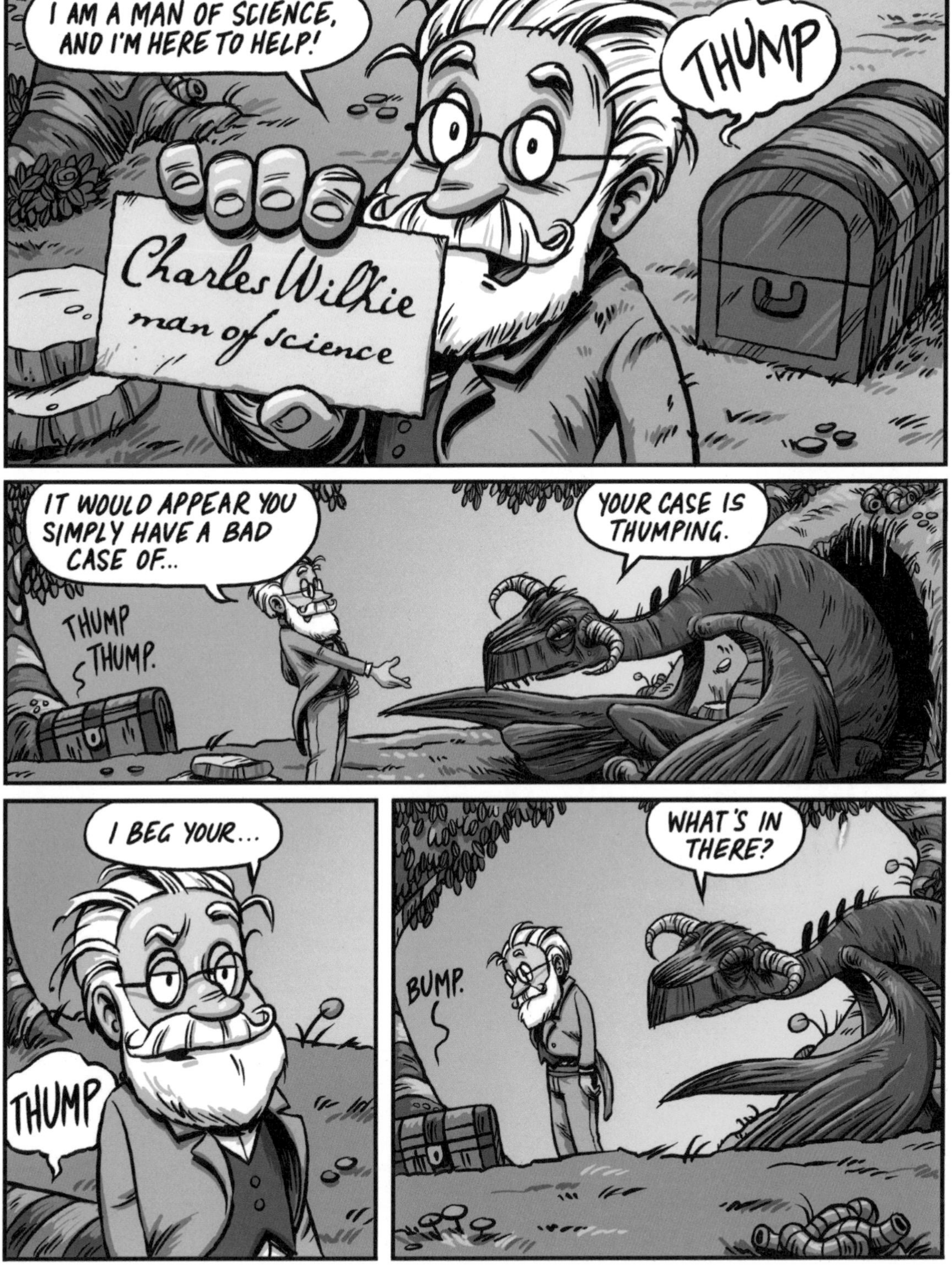
I AM A MAN OF SCIENCE, AND I'M HERE TO HELP!
THUMP
Charles Wilkie
man of science
IT WOULD APPEAR YOU SIMPLY HAVE A BAD CASE OF...
YOUR CASE IS THUMPING.
THUMP THUMP.
I BEG YOUR...
THUMP
WHAT'S IN THERE?
BUMP.

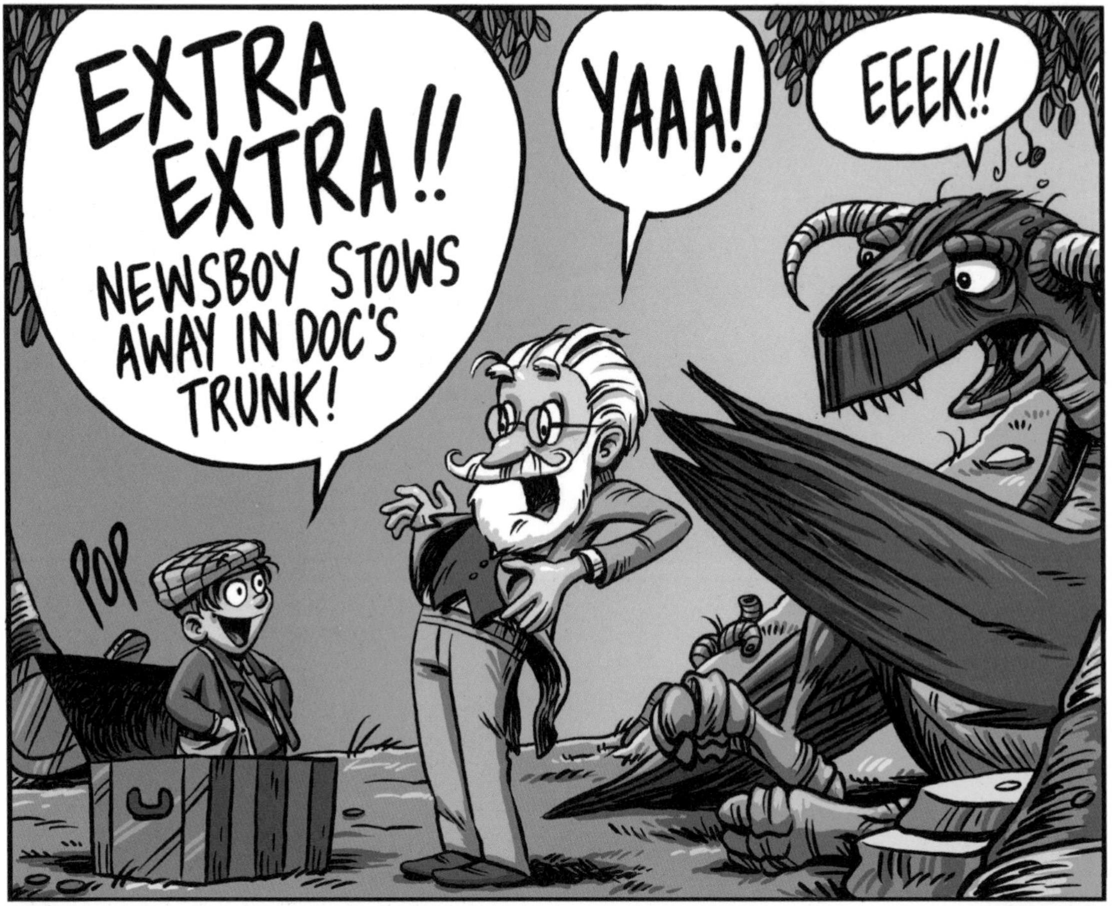
EXTRA EXTRA!! NEWSBOY STOWS AWAY IN DOC'S TRUNK!
POP
YAAA!
EEEK!!

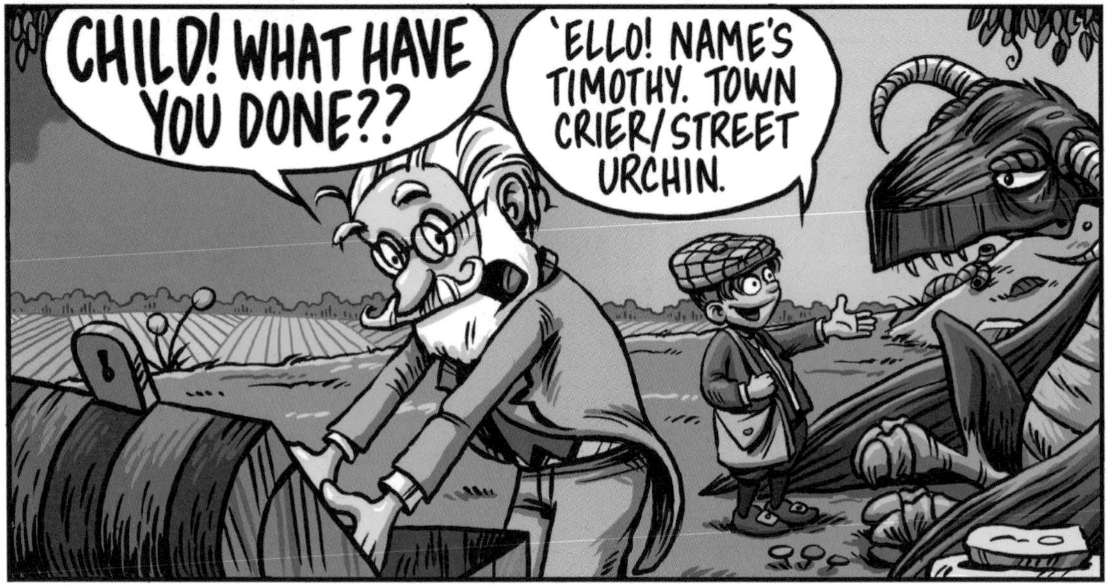
CHILD! WHAT HAVE YOU DONE??
`ELLO! NAME'S TIMOTHY. TOWN CRIER/STREET URCHIN.

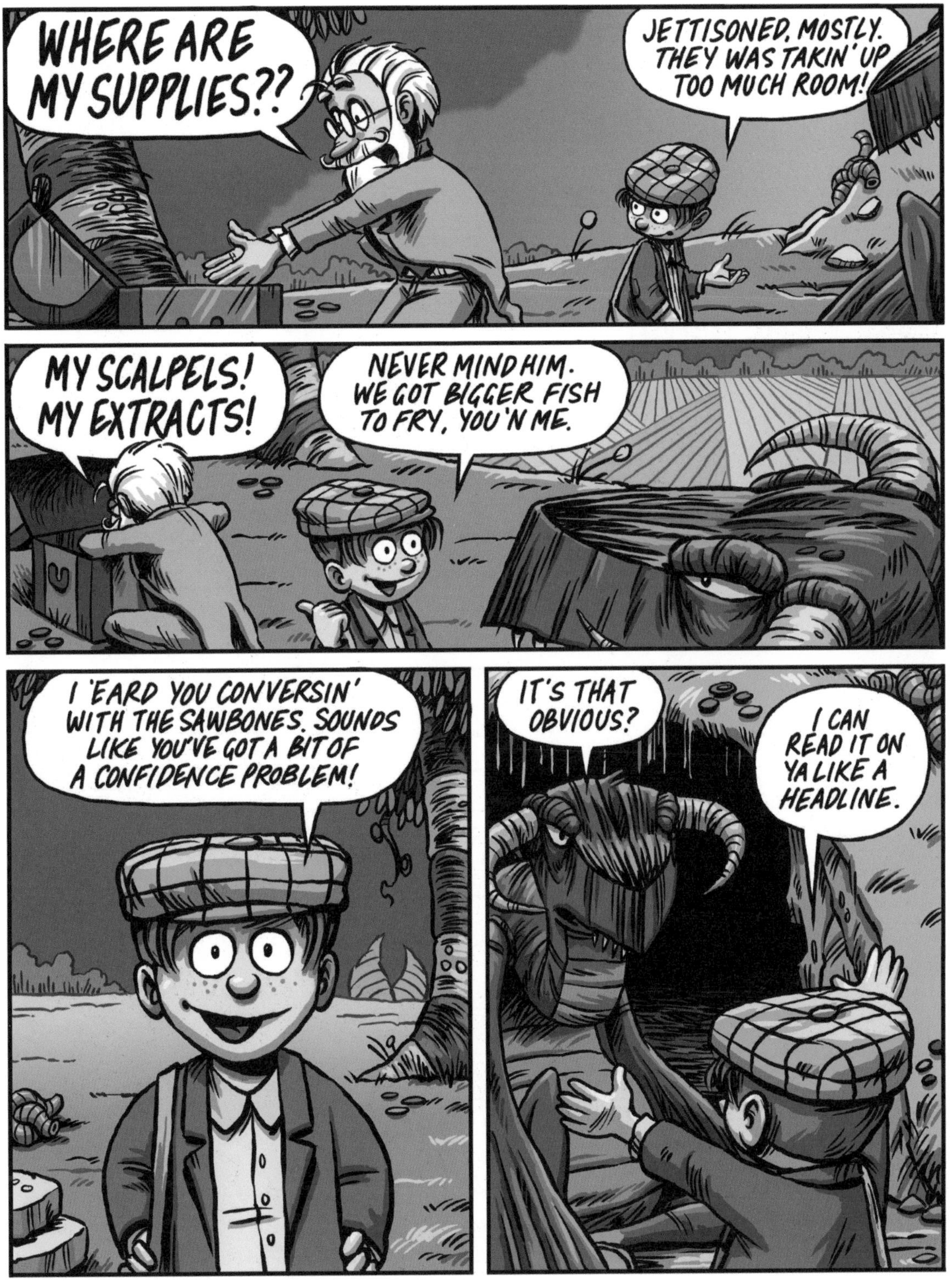
WHERE ARE MY SUPPLIES??
JETTISONED, MOSTLY. THEY WAS TAKIN' UP TOO MUCH ROOM!
MY SCALPELS! MY EXTRACTS!
NEVER MIND HIM. WE GOT BIGGER FISH TO FRY, YOU 'N ME.
I 'EARD YOU CONVERSIN' WITH THE SAWBONES. SOUNDS LIKE YOU'VE GOT A BIT OF A CONFIDENCE PROBLEM!
IT'S THAT OBVIOUS?
I CAN READ IT ON YA LIKE A HEADLINE.

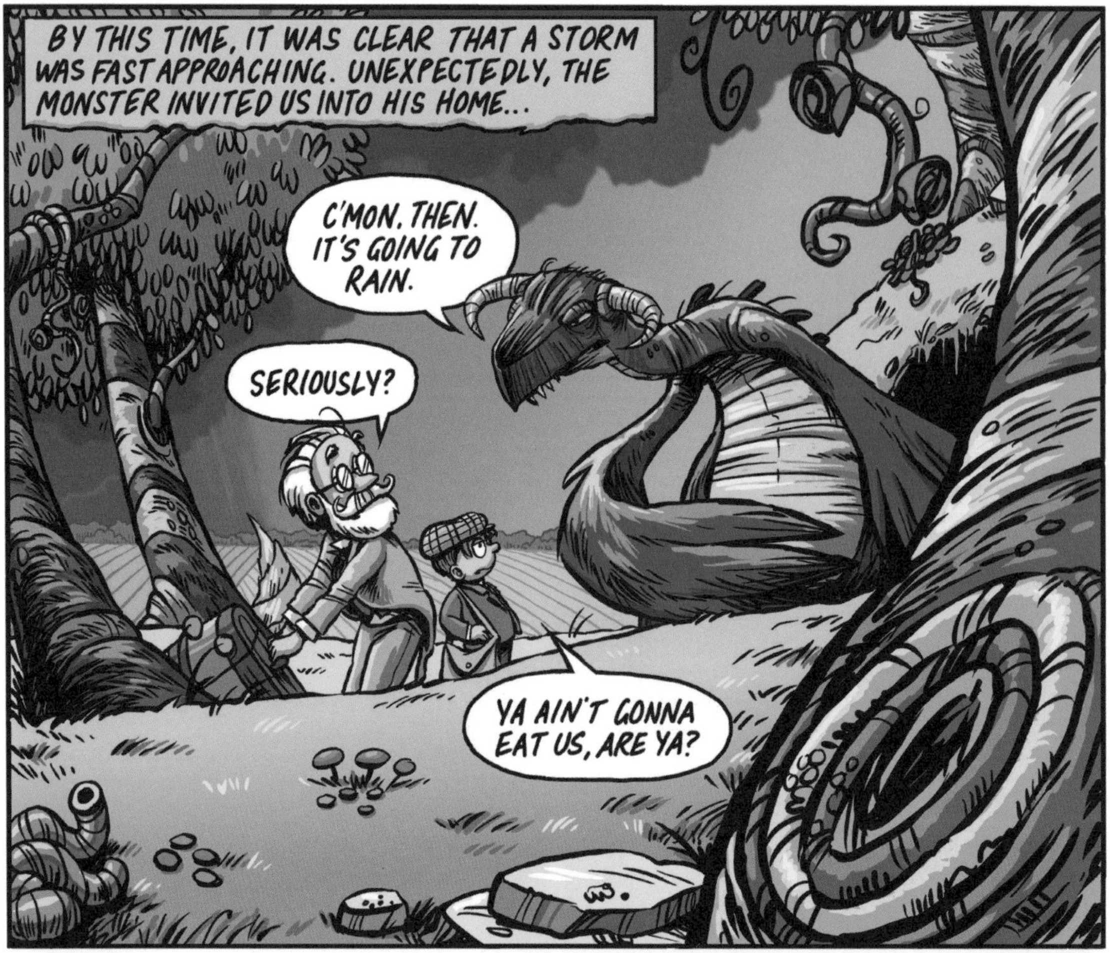
BY THIS TIME, IT WAS CLEAR THAT A STORM WAS FAST APPROACHING. UNEXPECTEDLY, THE MONSTER INVITED US INTO HIS HOME...
C'MON, THEN. IT'S GOING TO RAIN.
SERIOUSLY?
YA AIN'T GONNA EAT US, ARE YA?
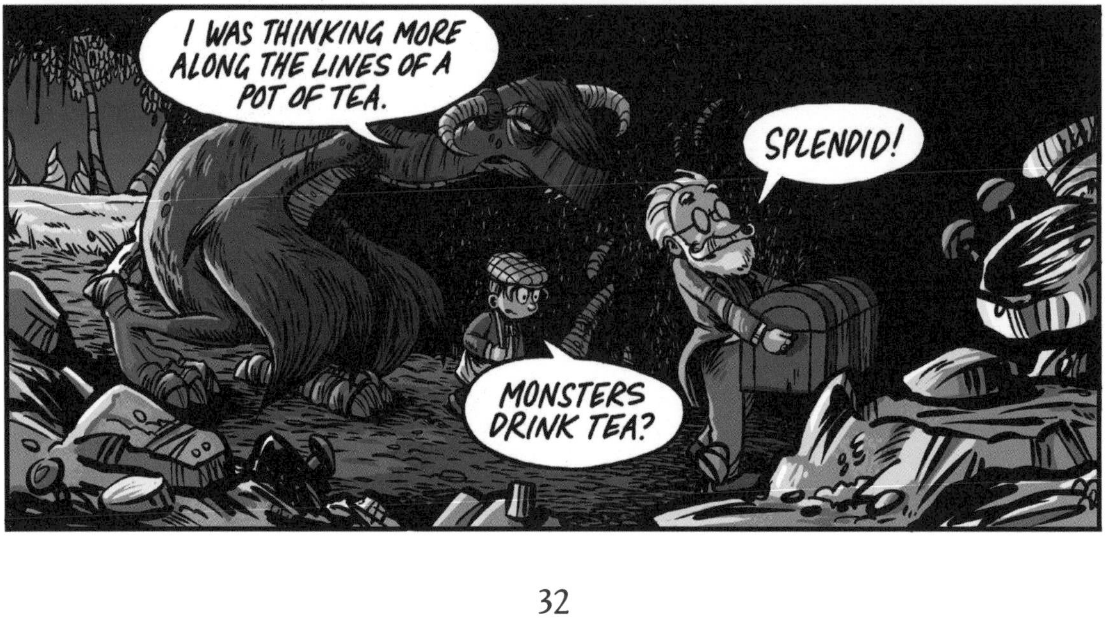
I WAS THINKING MORE ALONG THE LINES OF A POT OF TEA.
SPLENDID!
MONSTERS DRINK TEA?

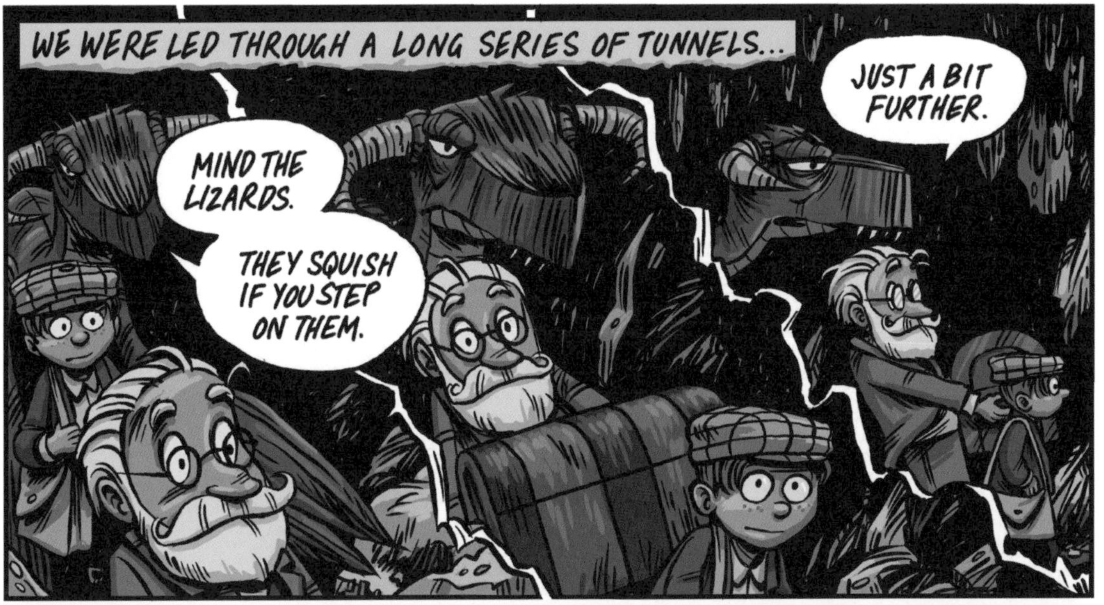
WE WERE LED THROUGH A LONG SERIES OF TUNNELS...
MIND THE LIZARDS.
THEY SQUISH IF YOU STEP ON THEM.
JUST A BIT FURTHER.

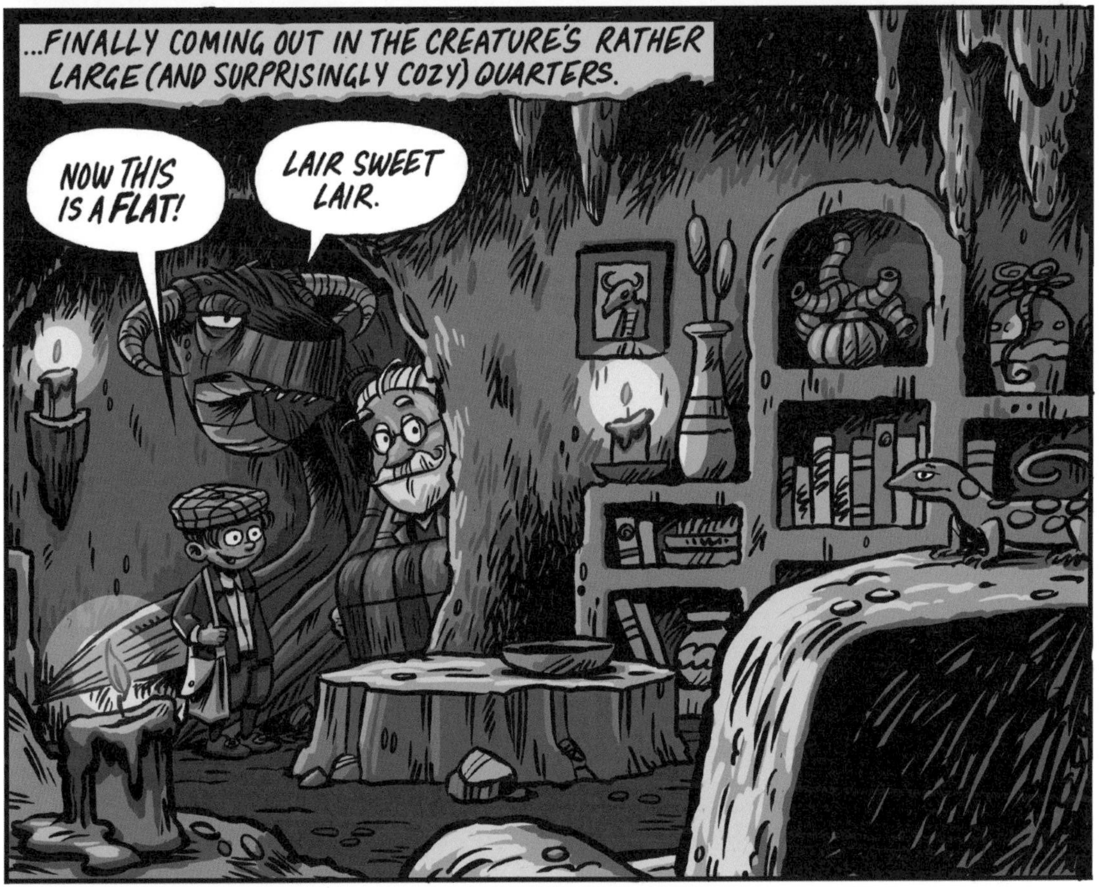
...FINALLY COMING OUT IN THE CREATURE'S RATHER LARGE (AND SURPRISINGLY COZY) QUARTERS.
NOW THIS IS A FLAT!
LAIR SWEET LAIR.

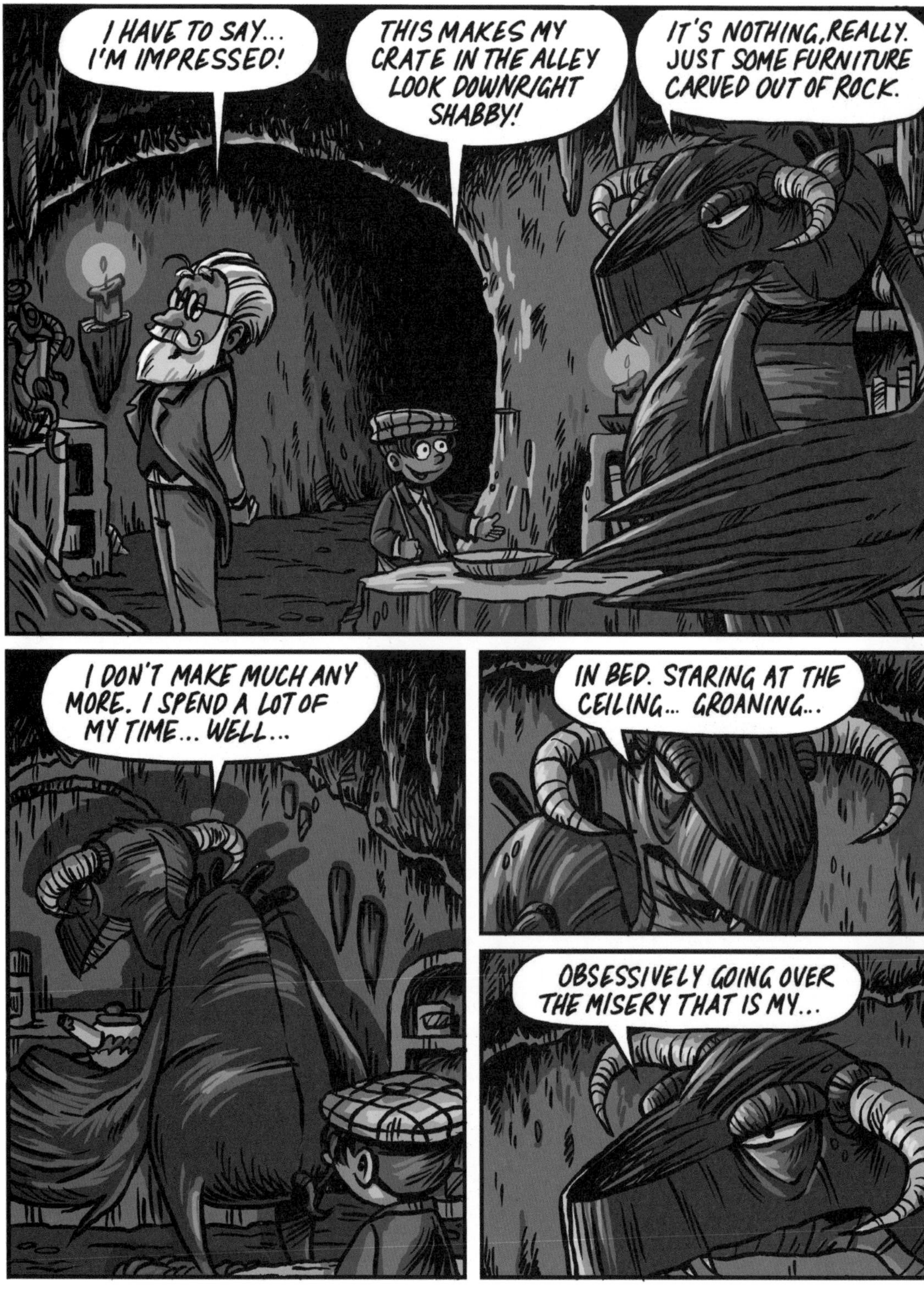
I HAVE TO SAY... I'M IMPRESSED!
THIS MAKES MY CRATE IN THE ALLEY LOOK DOWNRIGHT SHABBY!
IT'S NOTHING, REALLY. JUST SOME FURNITURE CARVED OUT OF ROCK.
I DON'T MAKE MUCH ANY MORE. I SPEND A LOT OF MY TIME... WELL...
IN BED. STARING AT THE CEILING... GROANING...
OBSESSIVELY GOING OVER THE MISERY THAT IS MY...

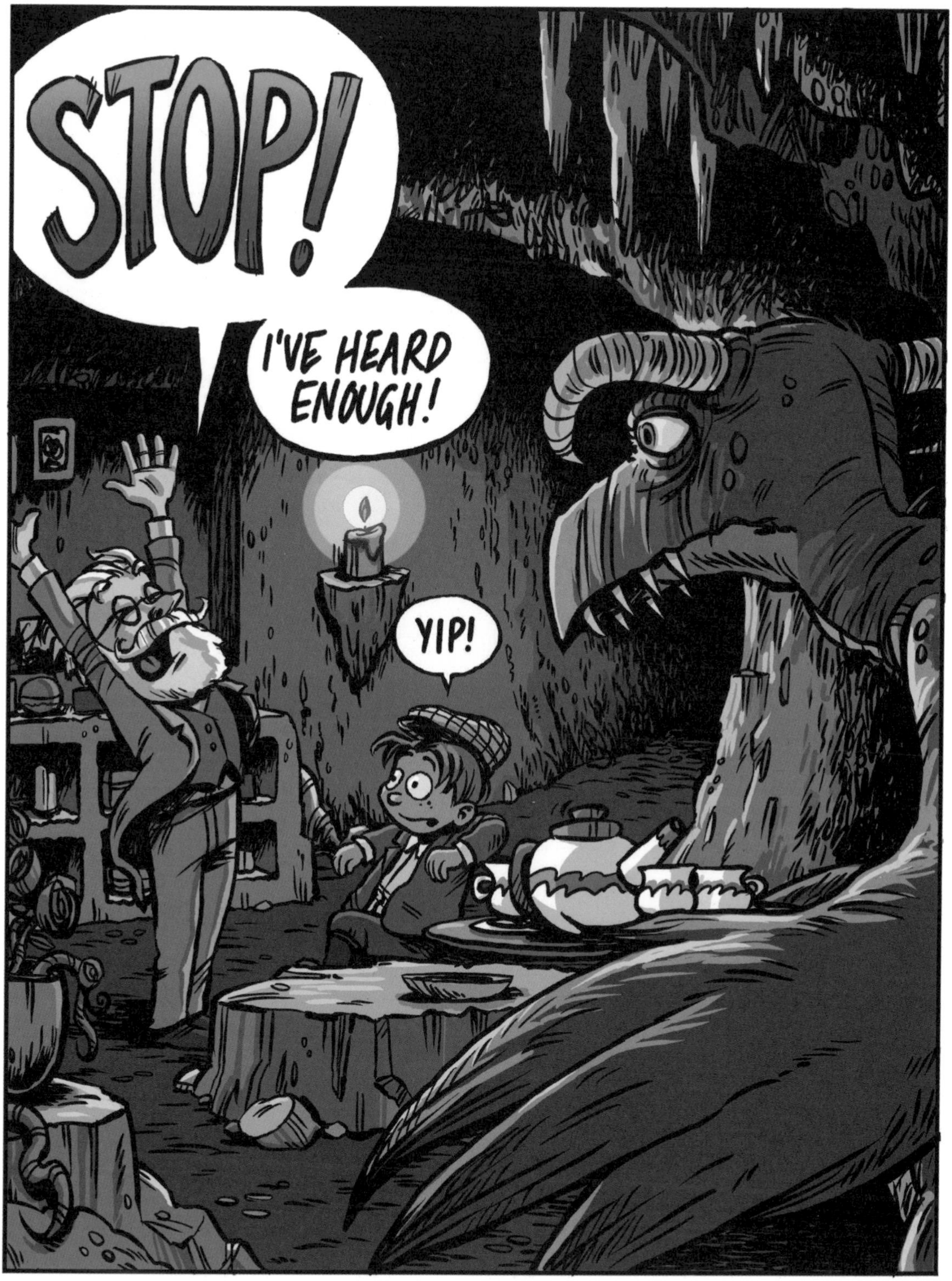
STOP!
I'VE HEARD ENOUGH!
YIP!

36

NO, NO! IT WORKS! MOST OF MY PATIENTS HAVE BEEN THRILLED WITH THE RESULTS.

YEAH. I'M SURE THEM WHAT SURVIVED WAS BLEEDIN' ECSTATIC.

I FEEL LIGHT-HEADED.

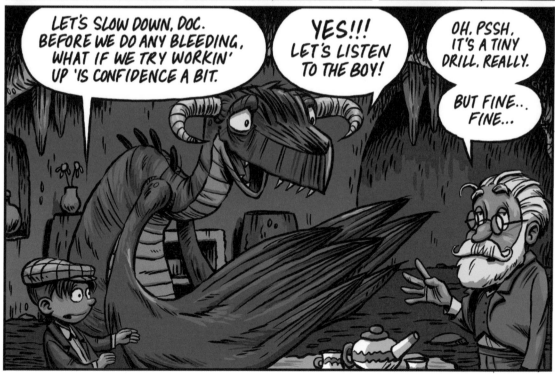

LET'S SLOW DOWN, DOC. BEFORE WE DO ANY BLEEDING, WHAT IF WE TRY WORKIN' UP 'IS CONFIDENCE A BIT.

YES!!! LET'S LISTEN TO THE BOY!

OH, PSSH, IT'S A TINY DRILL, REALLY.

BUT FINE... FINE...

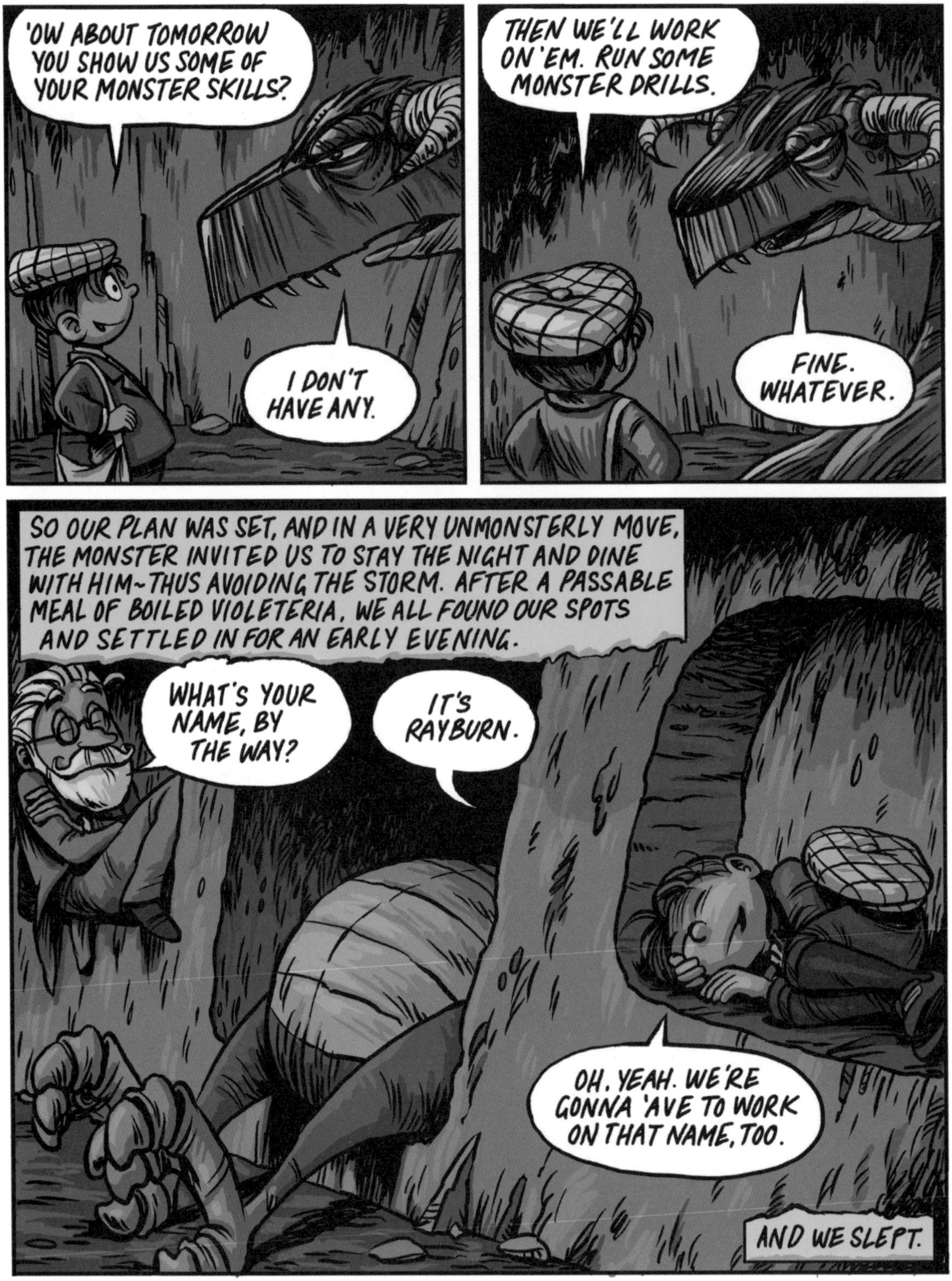
'OW ABOUT TOMORROW YOU SHOW US SOME OF YOUR MONSTER SKILLS?
I DON'T HAVE ANY.
THEN WE'LL WORK ON 'EM. RUN SOME MONSTER DRILLS.
FINE. WHATEVER.
SO OUR PLAN WAS SET, AND IN A VERY UNMONSTERLY MOVE, THE MONSTER INVITED US TO STAY THE NIGHT AND DINE WITH HIM~THUS AVOIDING THE STORM. AFTER A PASSABLE MEAL OF BOILED VIOLETERIA, WE ALL FOUND OUR SPOTS AND SETTLED IN FOR AN EARLY EVENING.
WHAT'S YOUR NAME, BY THE WAY?
IT'S RAYBURN.
OH. YEAH. WE'RE GONNA 'AVE TO WORK ON THAT NAME, TOO.
AND WE SLEPT.

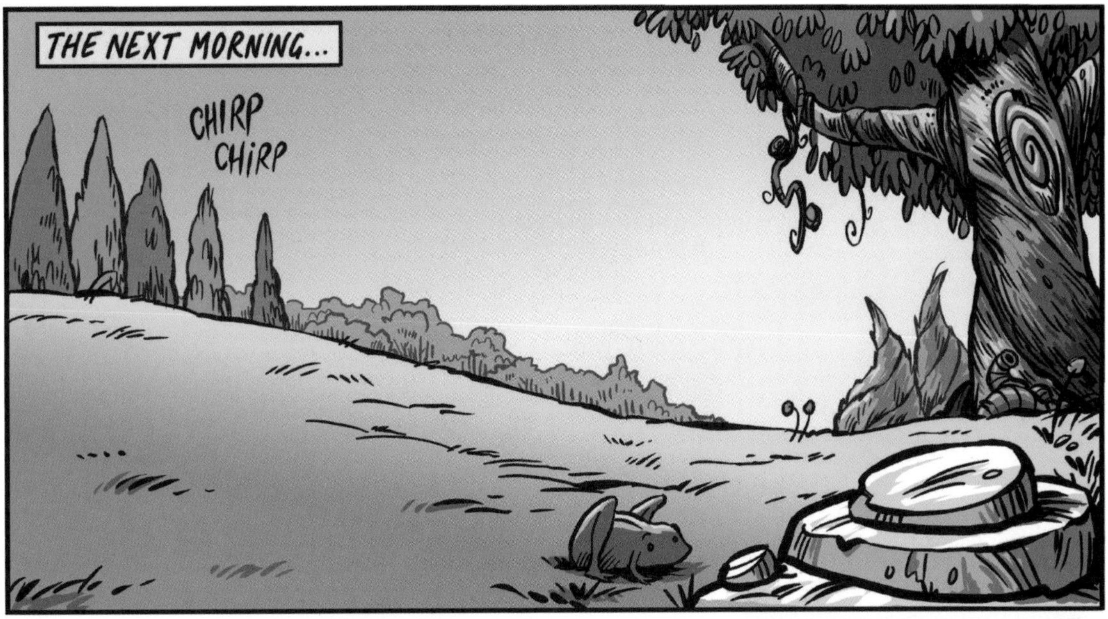
THE NEXT MORNING...
CHIRP CHIRP

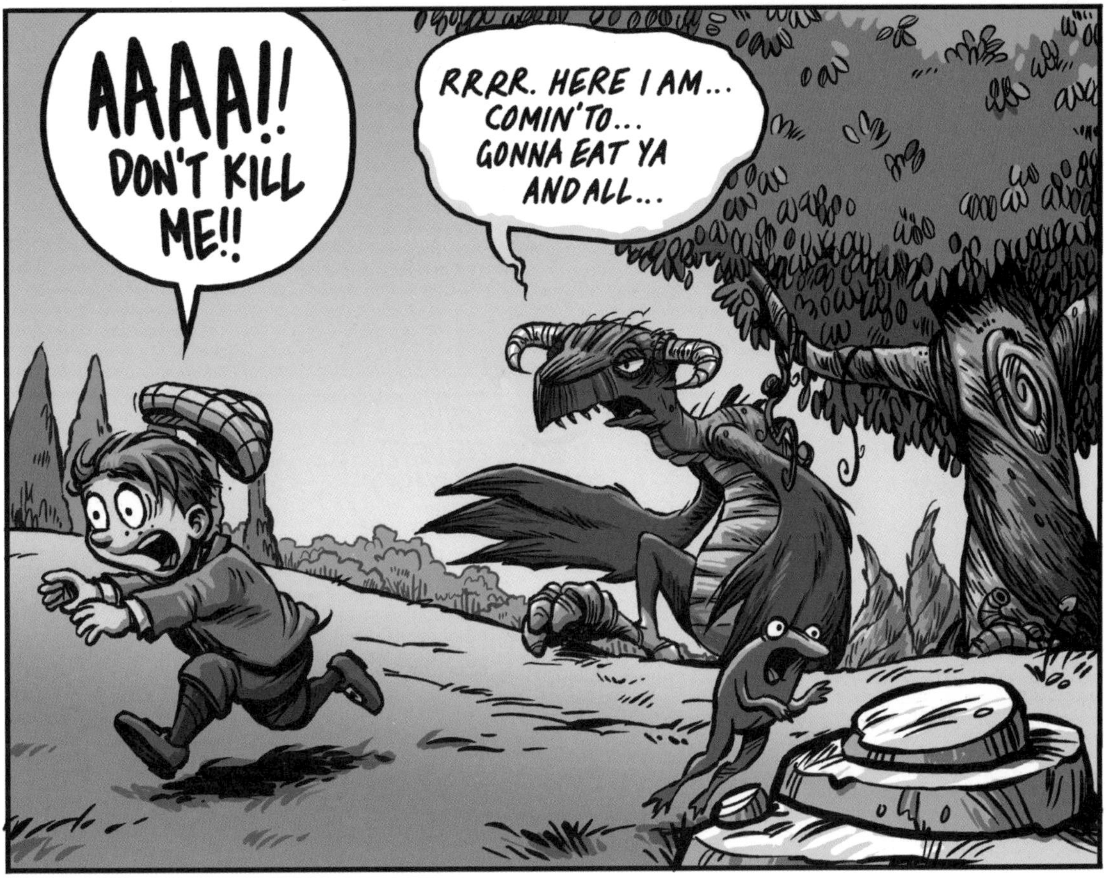
AAAA!! DON'T KILL ME!!
RRRR. HERE I AM... COMIN' TO... GONNA EAT YA AND ALL...

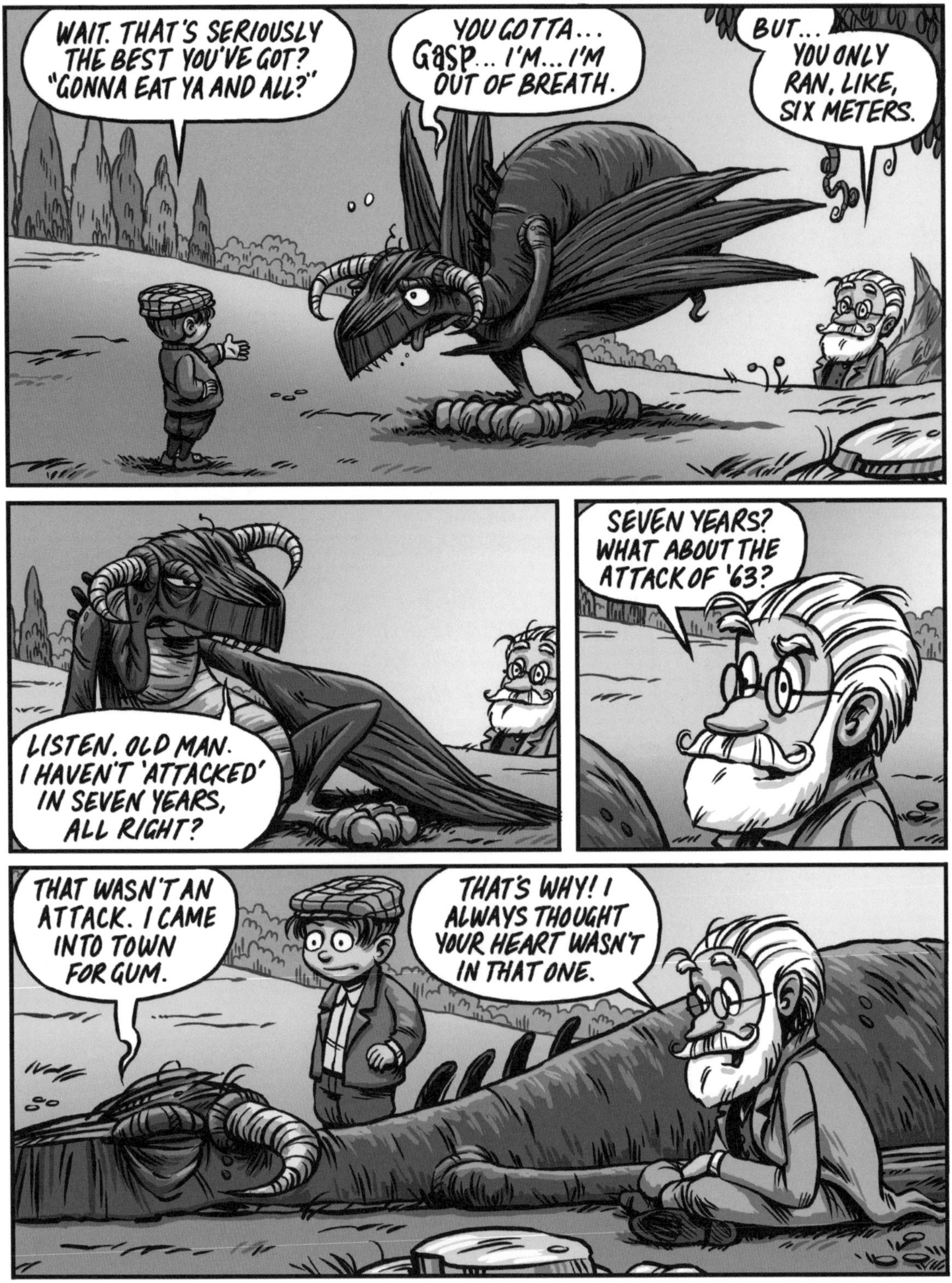
WAIT. THAT'S SERIOUSLY THE BEST YOU'VE GOT? "GONNA EAT YA AND ALL?"
YOU GOTTA... GASP... I'M... I'M OUT OF BREATH.
BUT... YOU ONLY RAN, LIKE, SIX METERS.
LISTEN, OLD MAN. I HAVEN'T 'ATTACKED' IN SEVEN YEARS, ALL RIGHT?
SEVEN YEARS? WHAT ABOUT THE ATTACK OF '63?
THAT WASN'T AN ATTACK. I CAME INTO TOWN FOR GUM.
THAT'S WHY! I ALWAYS THOUGHT YOUR HEART WASN'T IN THAT ONE.

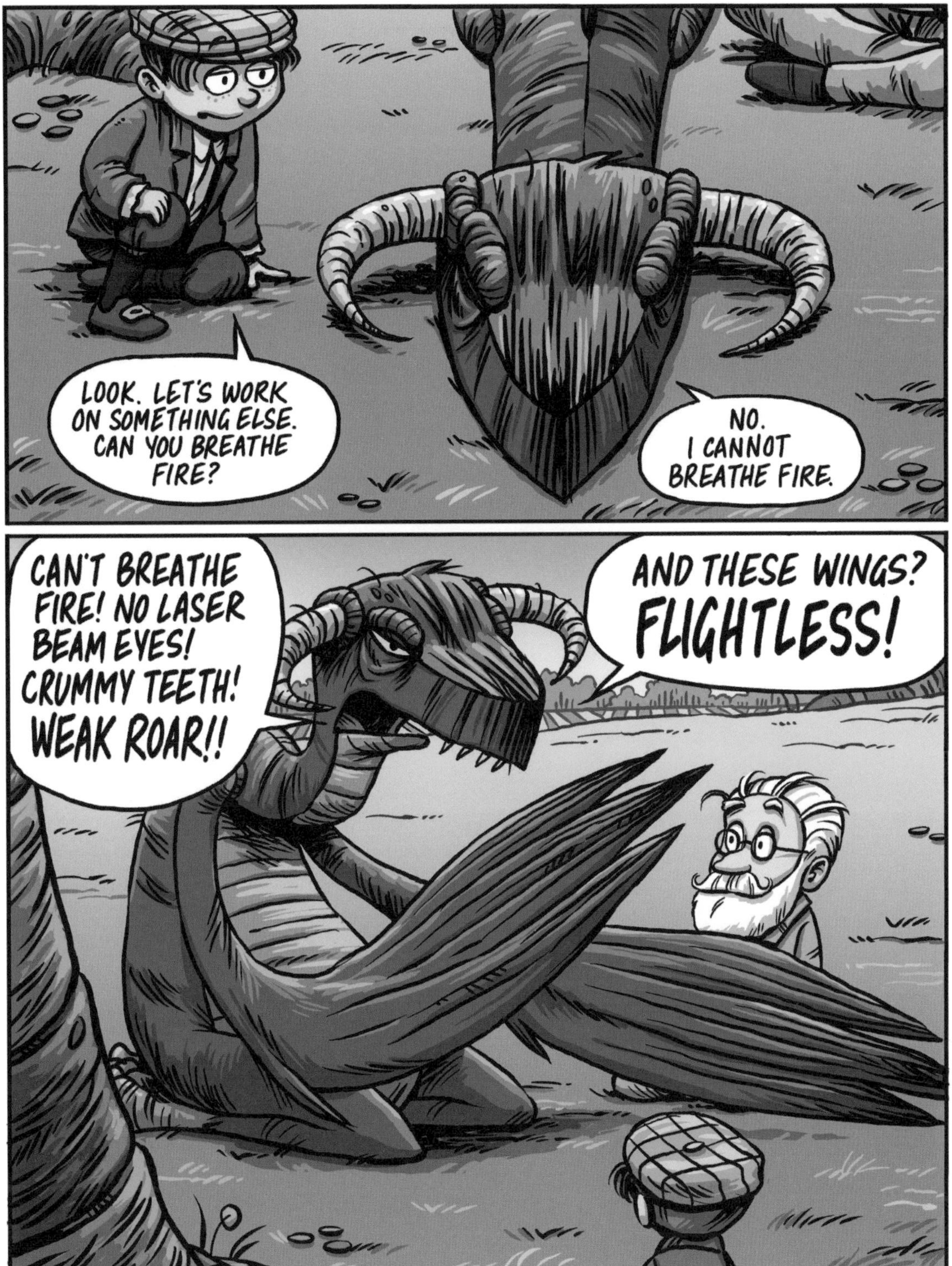
LOOK. LET'S WORK ON SOMETHING ELSE. CAN YOU BREATHE FIRE?
NO. I CANNOT BREATHE FIRE.
CAN'T BREATHE FIRE! NO LASER BEAM EYES! CRUMMY TEETH! WEAK ROAR!!
AND THESE WINGS? FLIGHTLESS!

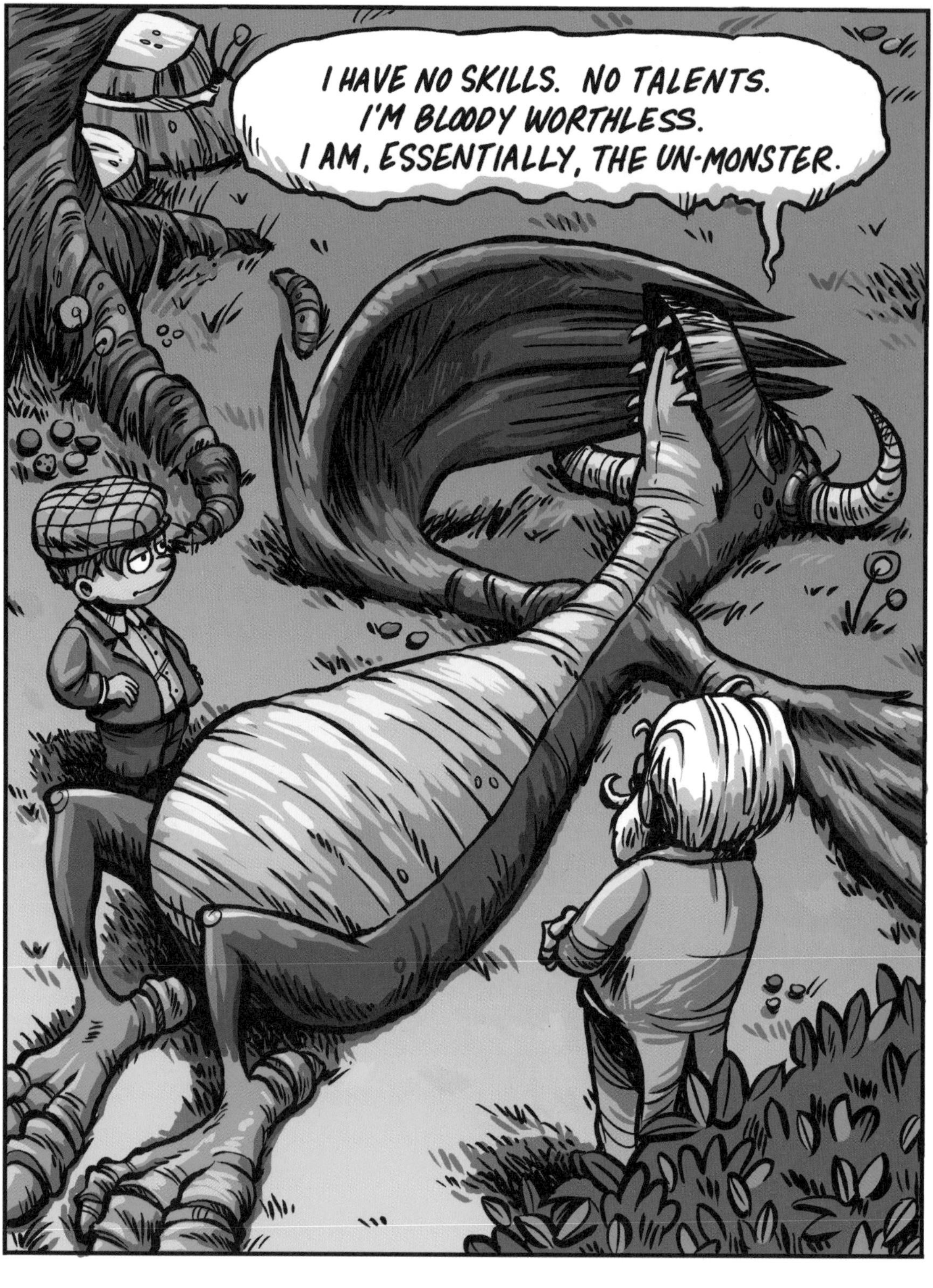
I HAVE NO SKILLS. NO TALENTS. I'M BLOODY WORTHLESS. I AM, ESSENTIALLY, THE UN-MONSTER.

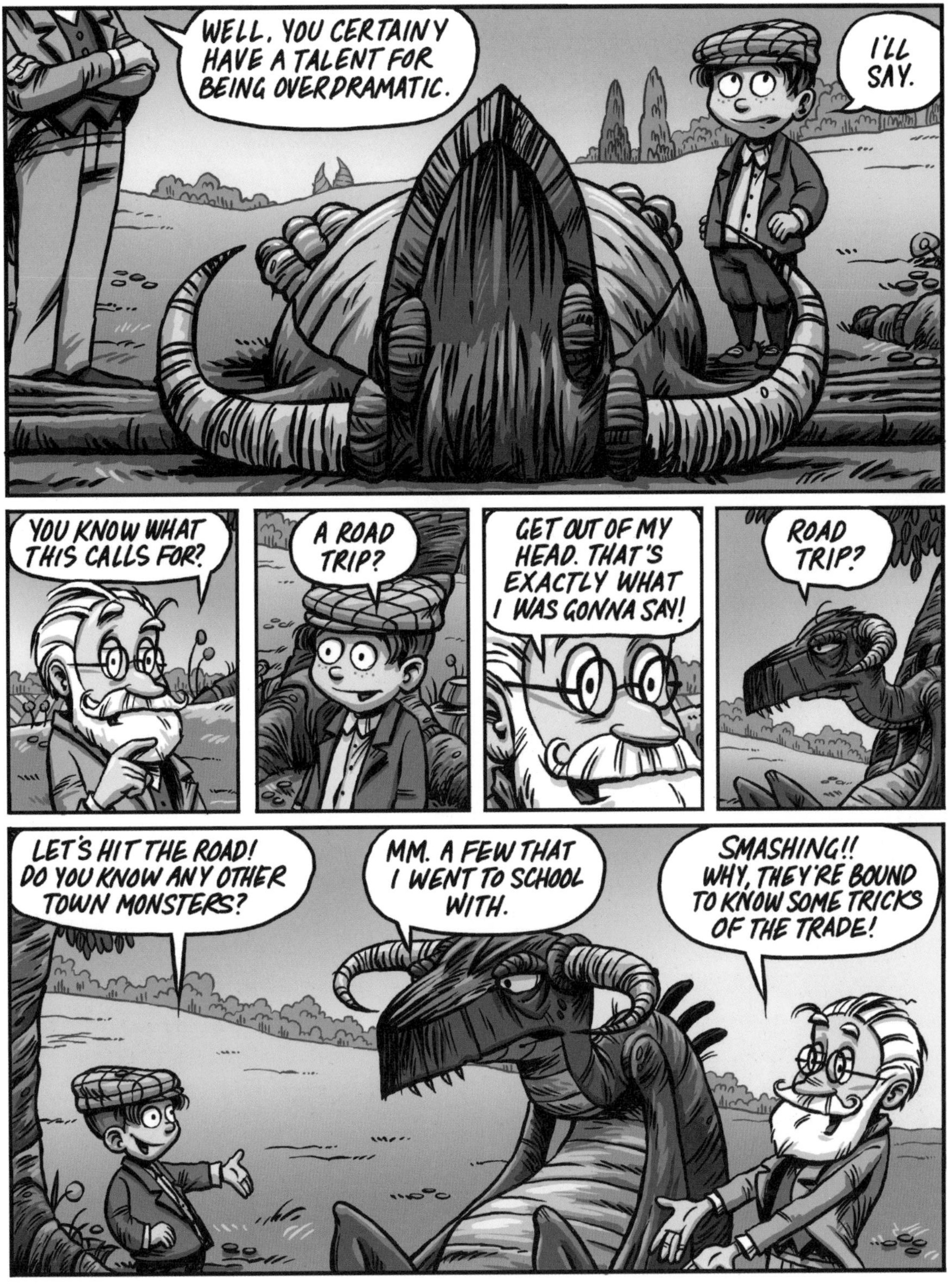
WELL, YOU CERTAINY HAVE A TALENT FOR BEING OVERDRAMATIC.
I'LL SAY.
YOU KNOW WHAT THIS CALLS FOR?
A ROAD TRIP?
GET OUT OF MY HEAD. THAT'S EXACTLY WHAT I WAS GONNA SAY!
ROAD TRIP?
LET'S HIT THE ROAD! DO YOU KNOW ANY OTHER TOWN MONSTERS?
MM. A FEW THAT I WENT TO SCHOOL WITH.
SMASHING!! WHY, THEY'RE BOUND TO KNOW SOME TRICKS OF THE TRADE!

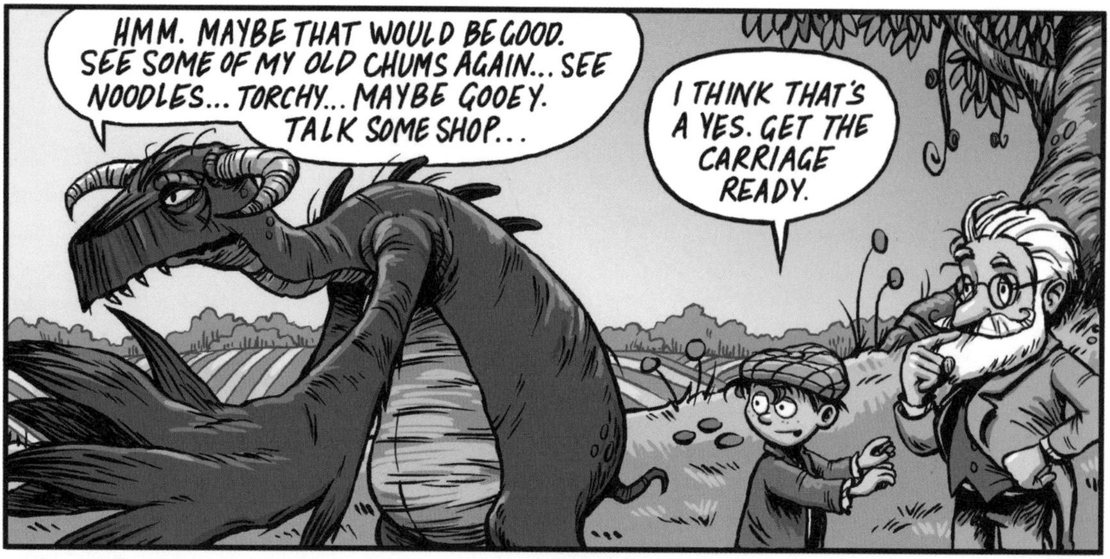
HMM. MAYBE THAT WOULD BE GOOD. SEE SOME OF MY OLD CHUMS AGAIN... SEE NOODLES... TORCHY... MAYBE GOOEY. TALK SOME SHOP...
I THINK THAT'S A YES. GET THE CARRIAGE READY.

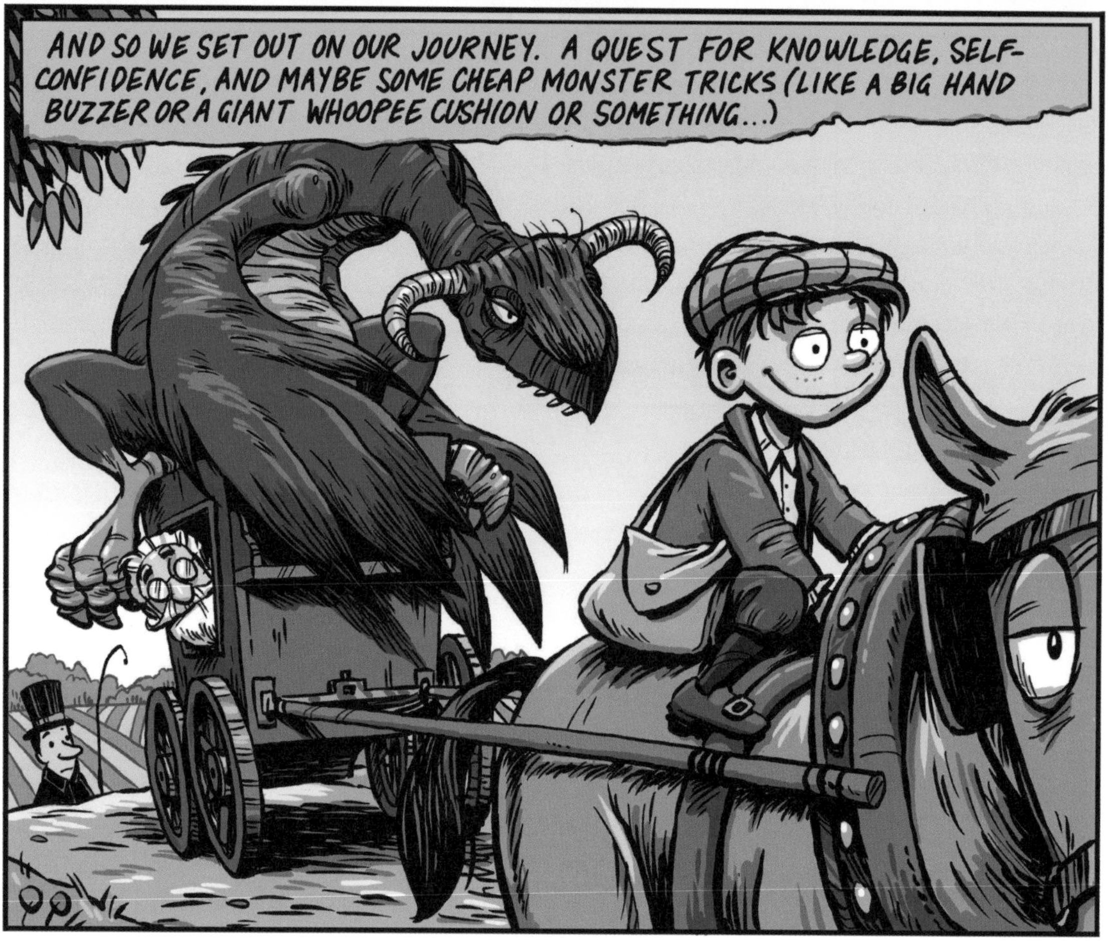
AND SO WE SET OUT ON OUR JOURNEY. A QUEST FOR KNOWLEDGE, SELF-CONFIDENCE, AND MAYBE SOME CHEAP MONSTER TRICKS (LIKE A BIG HAND BUZZER OR A GIANT WHOOPEE CUSHION OR SOMETHING...)

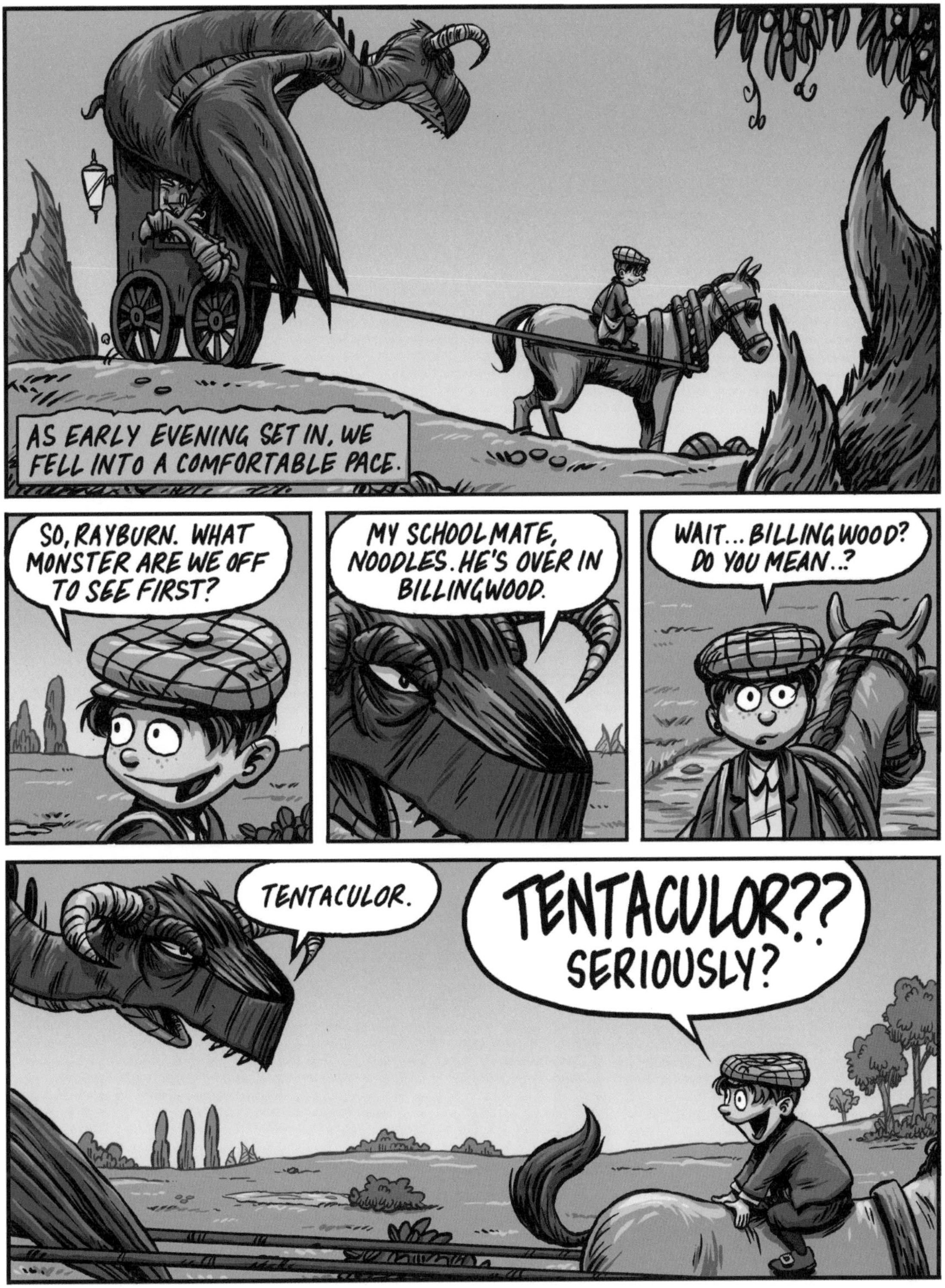
AS EARLY EVENING SET IN, WE FELL INTO A COMFORTABLE PACE.
SO, RAYBURN. WHAT MONSTER ARE WE OFF TO SEE FIRST?
MY SCHOOLMATE, NOODLES. HE'S OVER IN BILLINGWOOD.
WAIT... BILLINGWOOD? DO YOU MEAN..?
TENTACULOR.
TENTACULOR?? SERIOUSLY?

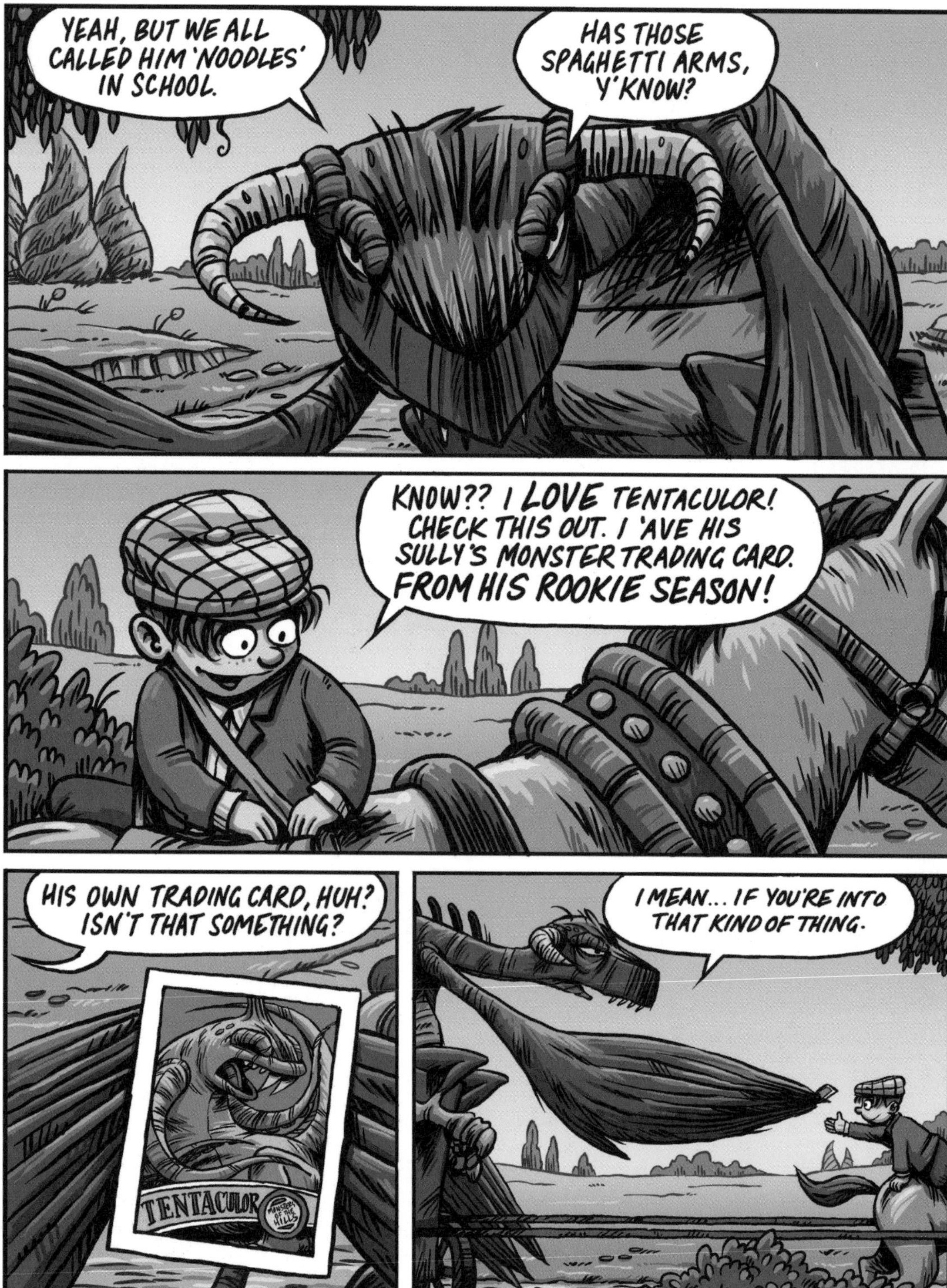
YEAH, BUT WE ALL CALLED HIM 'NOODLES' IN SCHOOL.
HAS THOSE SPAGHETTI ARMS, Y'KNOW?
KNOW?? I LOVE TENTACULOR! CHECK THIS OUT. I 'AVE HIS SULLY'S MONSTER TRADING CARD. FROM HIS ROOKIE SEASON!
HIS OWN TRADING CARD, HUH? ISN'T THAT SOMETHING?
TENTACULOR
MONSTERS OF THE HILLS
I MEAN... IF YOU'RE INTO THAT KIND OF THING.

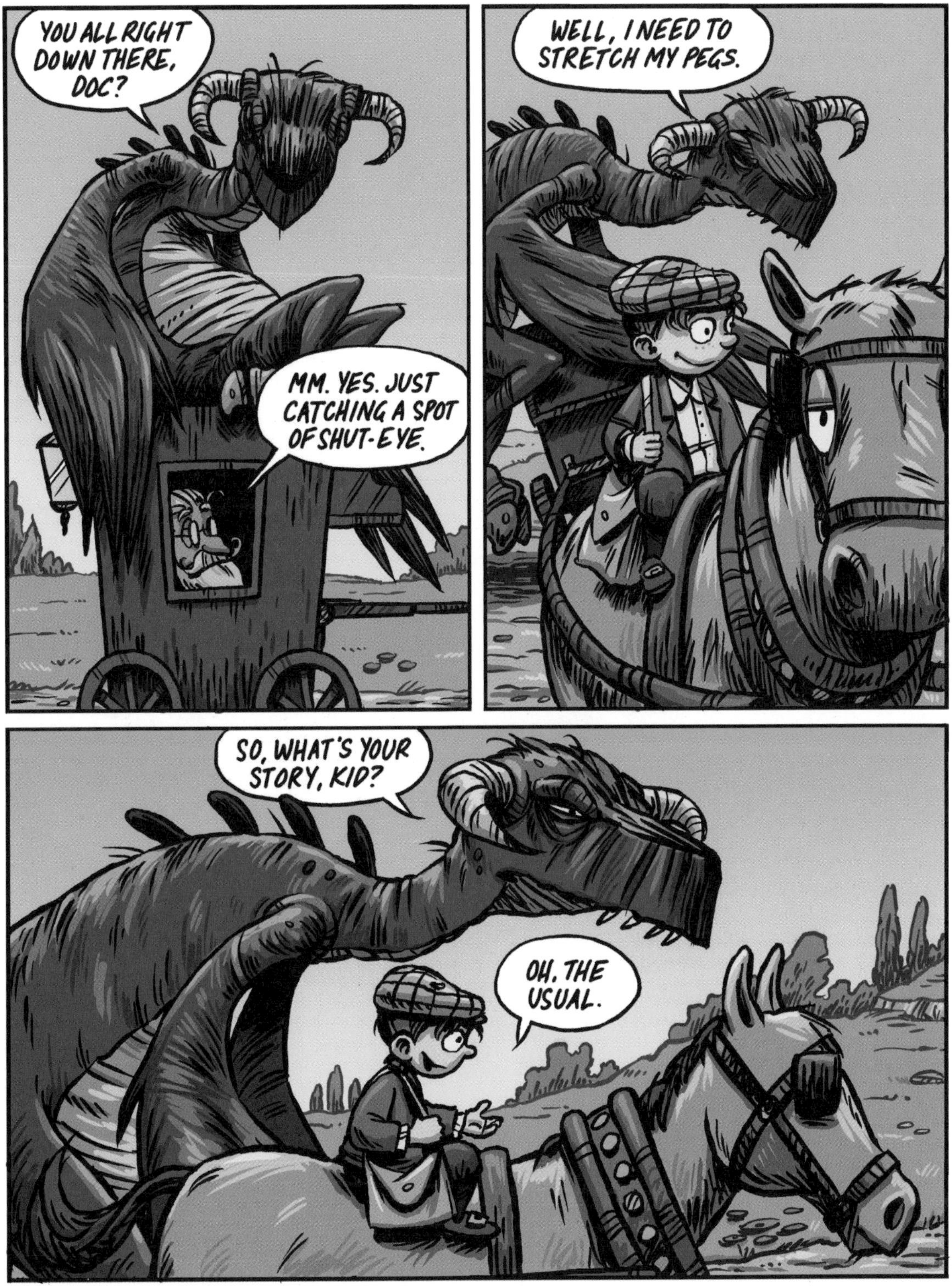
YOU ALL RIGHT DOWN THERE, DOC?
MM. YES. JUST CATCHING A SPOT OF SHUT-EYE.
WELL, I NEED TO STRETCH MY PEGS.
SO, WHAT'S YOUR STORY, KID?
OH, THE USUAL.

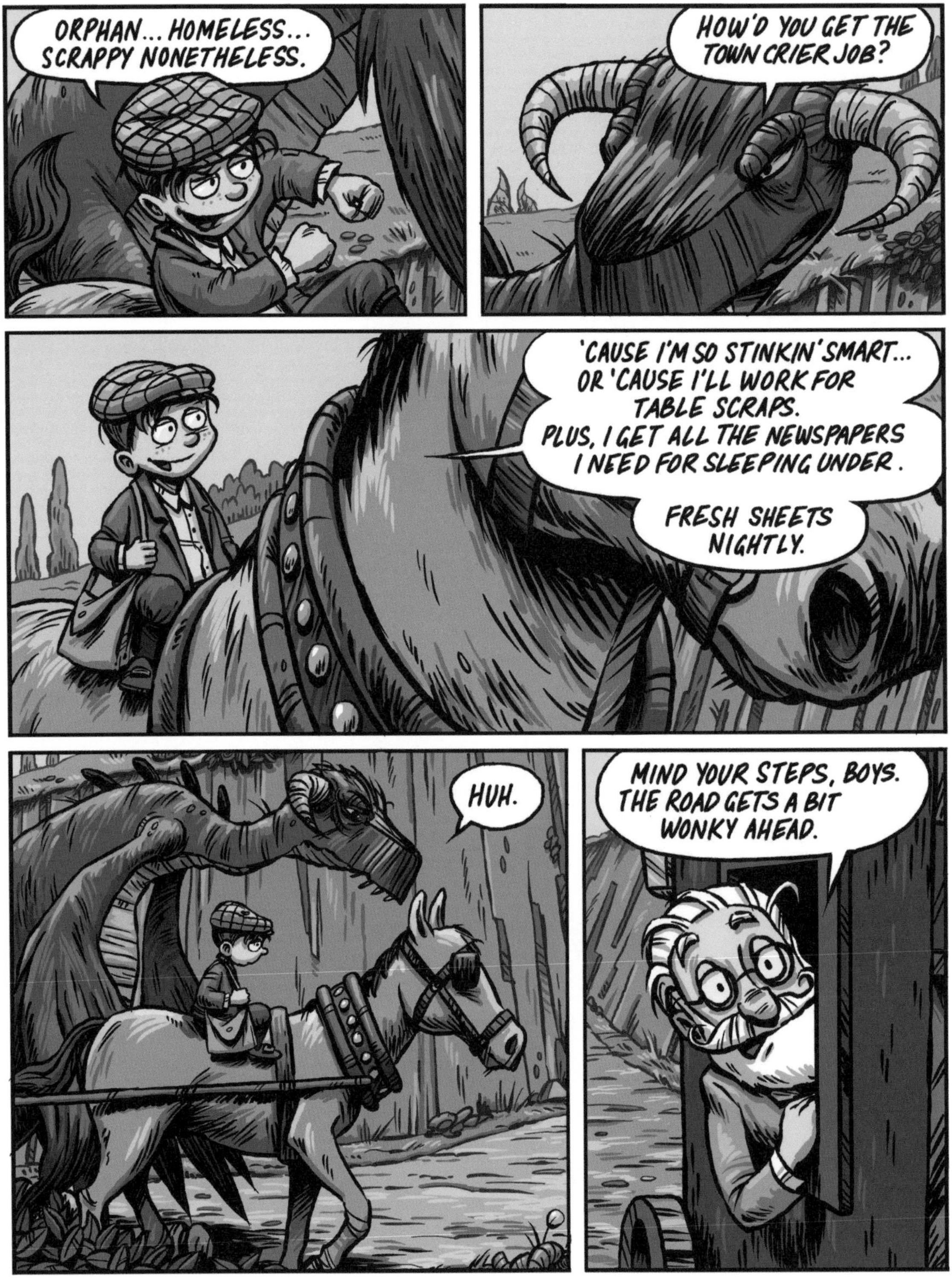
ORPHAN... HOMELESS... SCRAPPY NONETHELESS.
HOW'D YOU GET THE TOWN CRIER JOB?
'CAUSE I'M SO STINKIN' SMART... OR 'CAUSE I'LL WORK FOR TABLE SCRAPS. PLUS, I GET ALL THE NEWSPAPERS I NEED FOR SLEEPING UNDER.
FRESH SHEETS NIGHTLY.
HUH.
MIND YOUR STEPS, BOYS. THE ROAD GETS A BIT WONKY AHEAD.

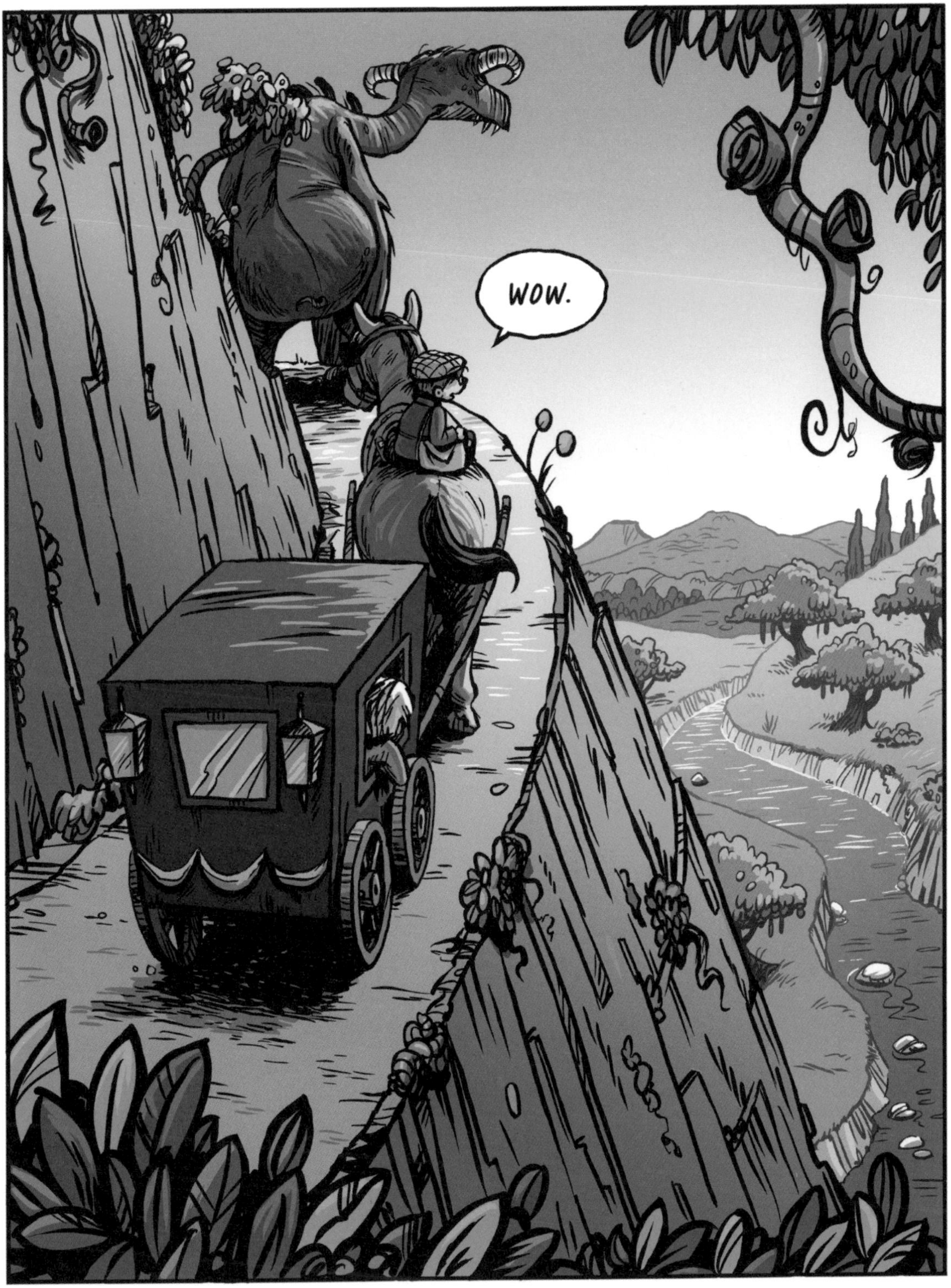
WOW.

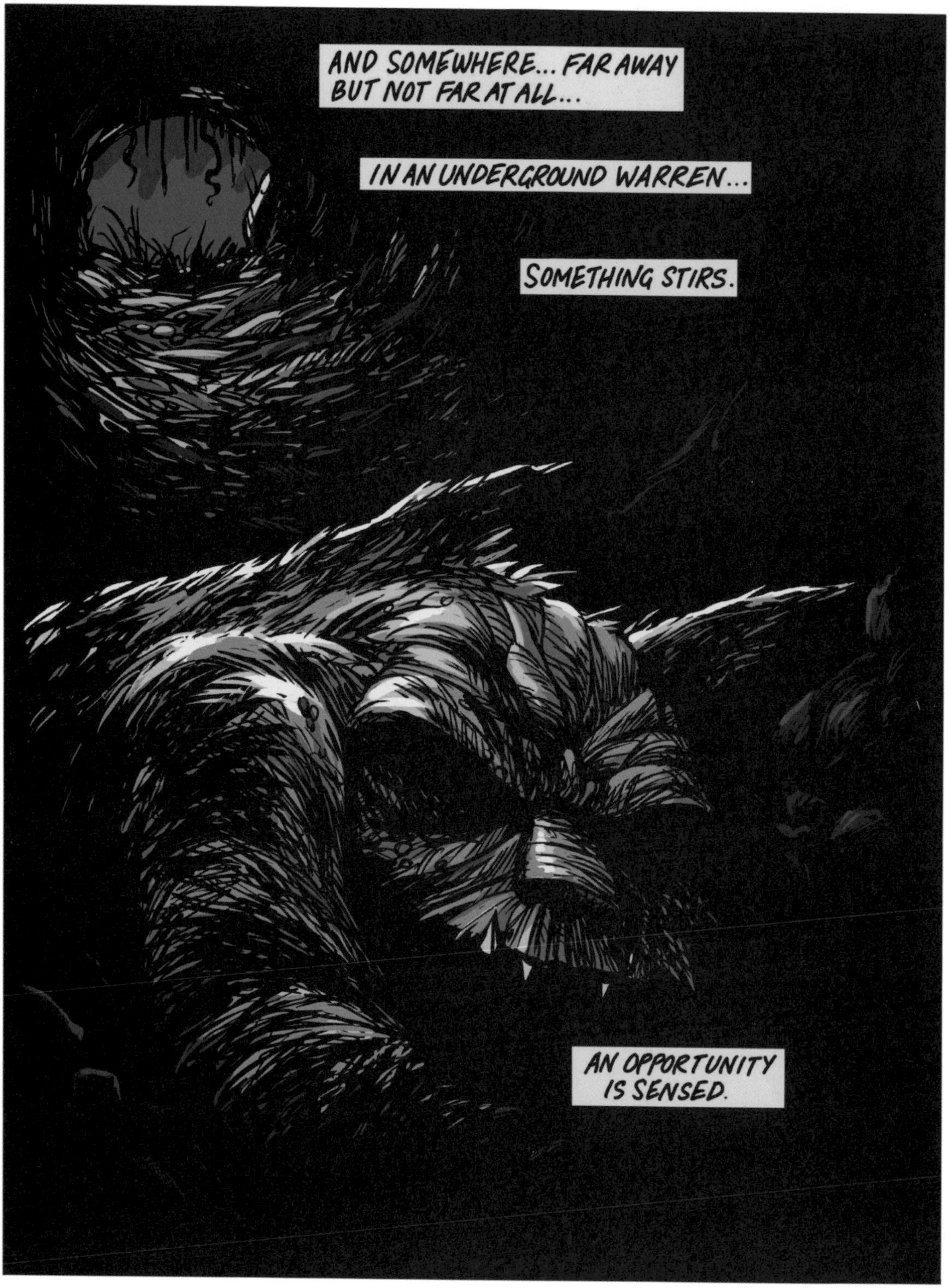
AND SOMEWHERE... FAR AWAY BUT NOT FAR AT ALL...
IN AN UNDERGROUND WARREN...
SOMETHING STIRS.
AN OPPORTUNITY IS SENSED.

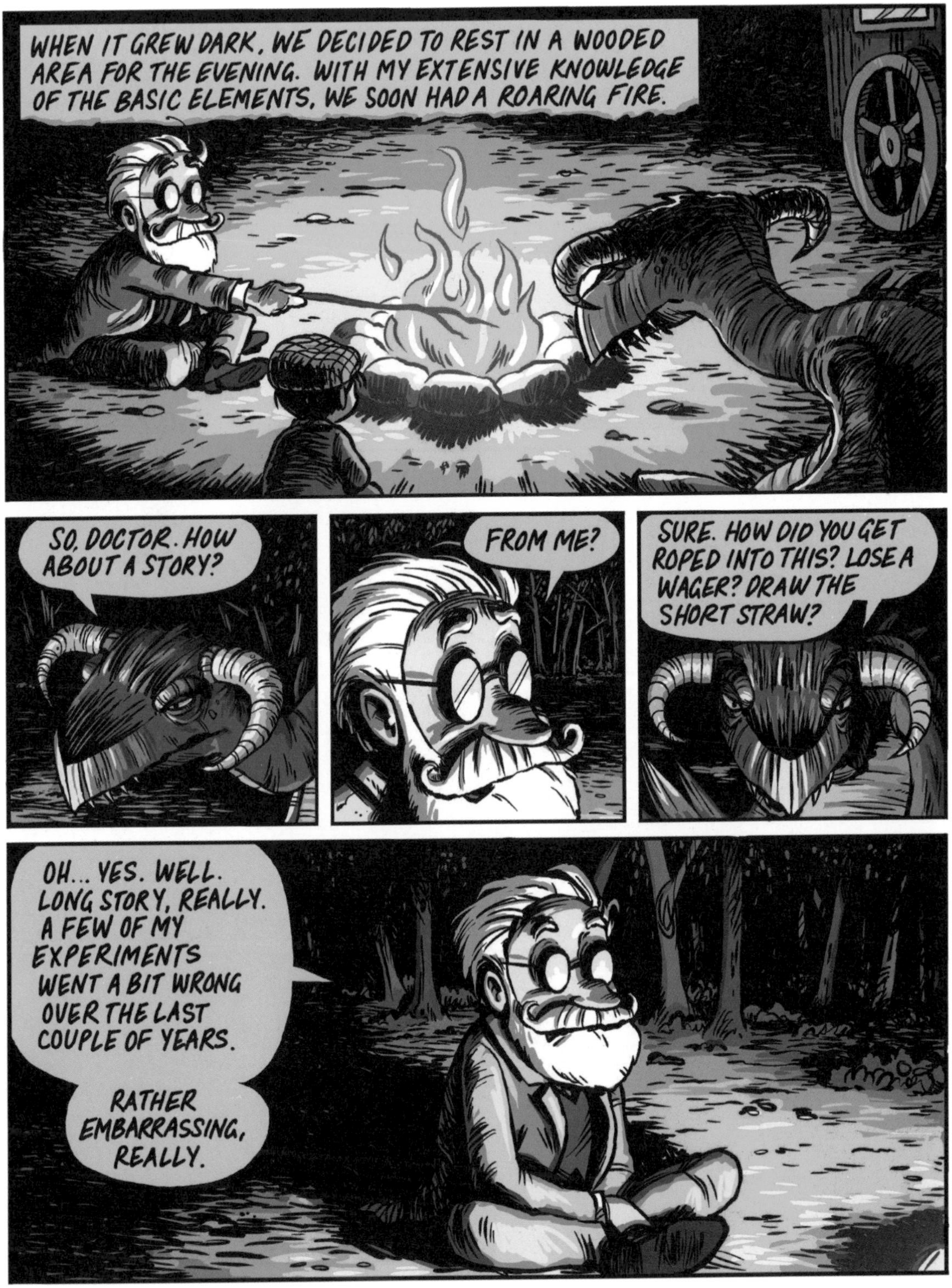

WHEN IT GREW DARK, WE DECIDED TO REST IN A WOODED AREA FOR THE EVENING. WITH MY EXTENSIVE KNOWLEDGE OF THE BASIC ELEMENTS, WE SOON HAD A ROARING FIRE.
SO, DOCTOR. HOW ABOUT A STORY?
FROM ME?
SURE. HOW DID YOU GET ROPED INTO THIS? LOSE A WAGER? DRAW THE SHORT STRAW?
OH... YES. WELL. LONG STORY, REALLY. A FEW OF MY EXPERIMENTS WENT A BIT WRONG OVER THE LAST COUPLE OF YEARS.
RATHER EMBARRASSING, REALLY.

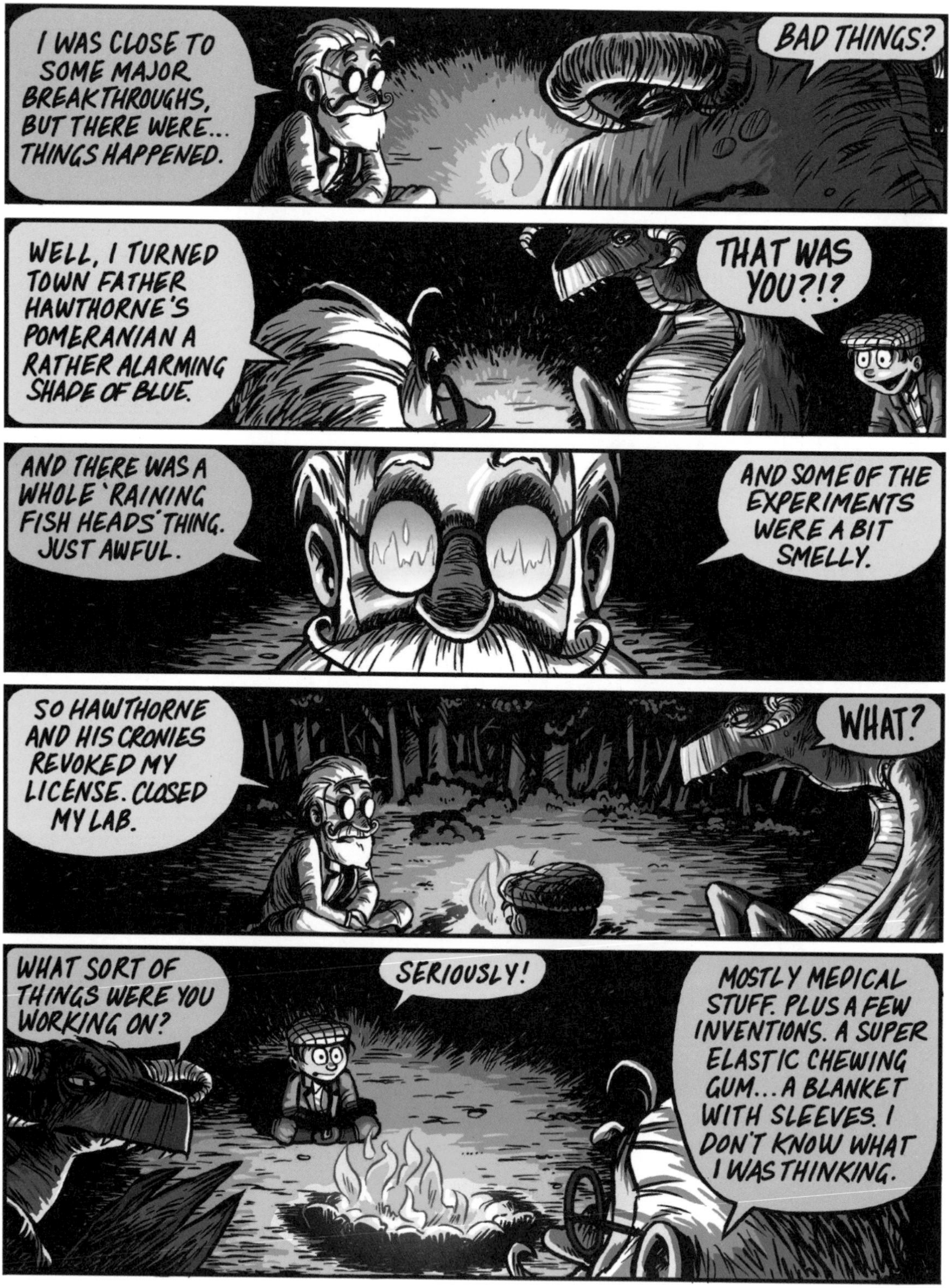
I WAS CLOSE TO SOME MAJOR BREAKTHROUGHS, BUT THERE WERE... THINGS HAPPENED.
BAD THINGS?
WELL, I TURNED TOWN FATHER HAWTHORNE'S POMERANIAN A RATHER ALARMING SHADE OF BLUE.
THAT WAS YOU?!?
AND THERE WAS A WHOLE 'RAINING FISH HEADS' THING. JUST AWFUL.
AND SOME OF THE EXPERIMENTS WERE A BIT SMELLY.
SO HAWTHORNE AND HIS CRONIES REVOKED MY LICENSE. CLOSED MY LAB.
WHAT?
WHAT SORT OF THINGS WERE YOU WORKING ON?
SERIOUSLY!
MOSTLY MEDICAL STUFF. PLUS A FEW INVENTIONS. A SUPER ELASTIC CHEWING GUM... A BLANKET WITH SLEEVES. I DON'T KNOW WHAT I WAS THINKING.

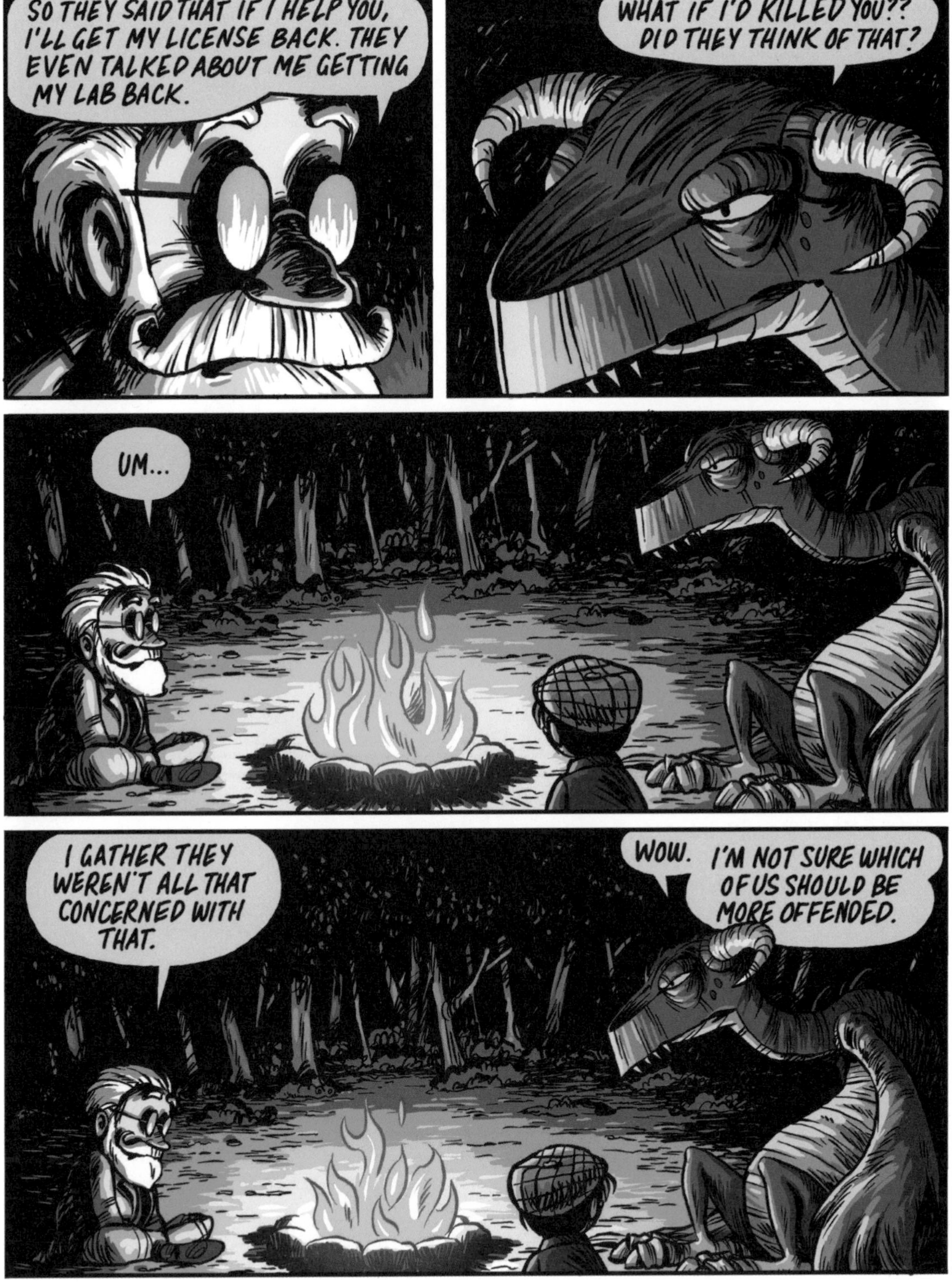
SO THEY SAID THAT IF I HELP YOU, I'LL GET MY LICENSE BACK. THEY EVEN TALKED ABOUT ME GETTING MY LAB BACK.
WHAT IF I'D KILLED YOU?? DID THEY THINK OF THAT?
UM...
I GATHER THEY WEREN'T ALL THAT CONCERNED WITH THAT.
WOW.
I'M NOT SURE WHICH OF US SHOULD BE MORE OFFENDED.

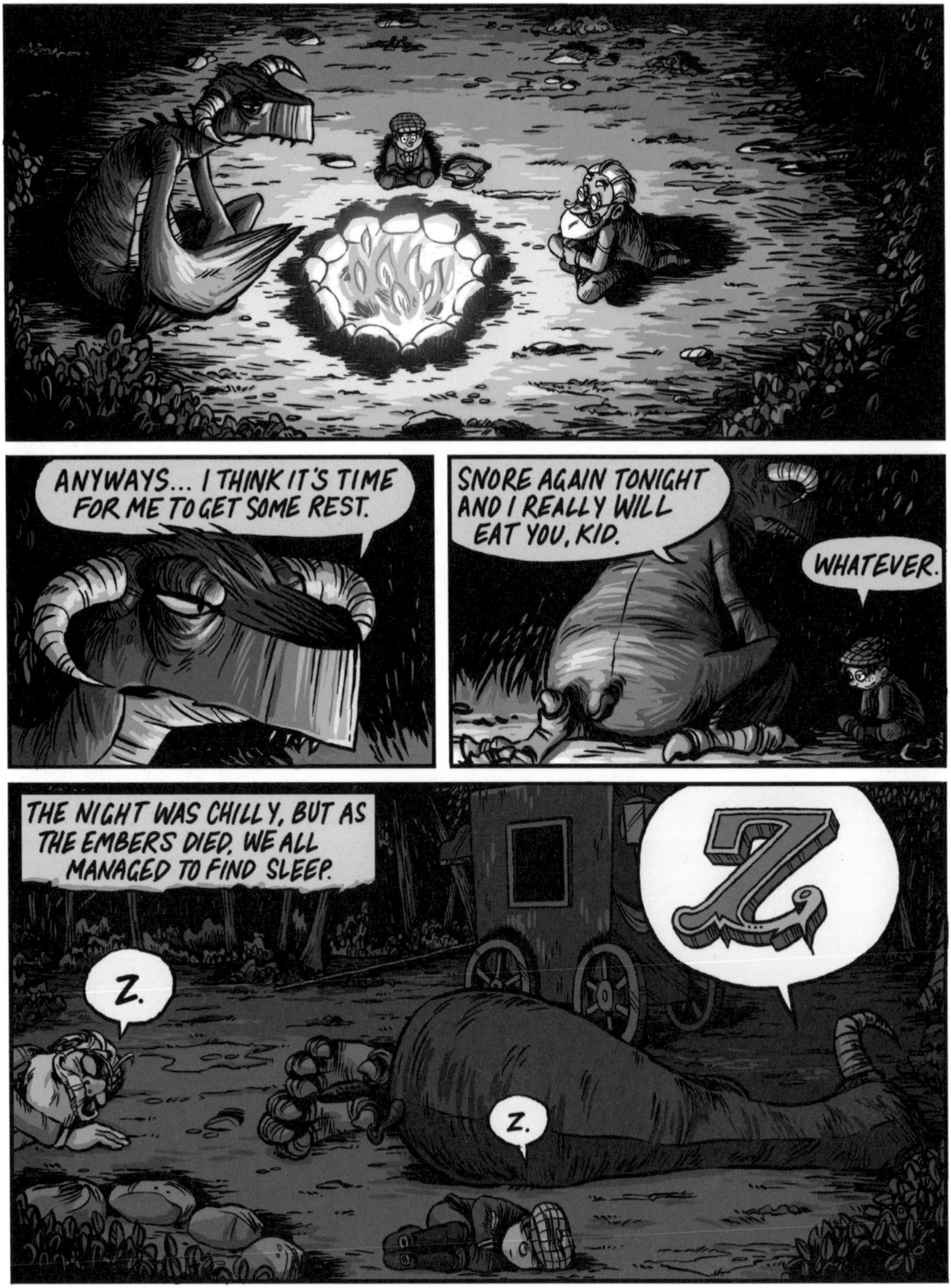
ANYWAYS... I THINK IT'S TIME FOR ME TO GET SOME REST.
SNORE AGAIN TONIGHT AND I REALLY WILL EAT YOU, KID.
WHATEVER.
THE NIGHT WAS CHILLY, BUT AS THE EMBERS DIED, WE ALL MANAGED TO FIND SLEEP.
Z
Z.
Z.

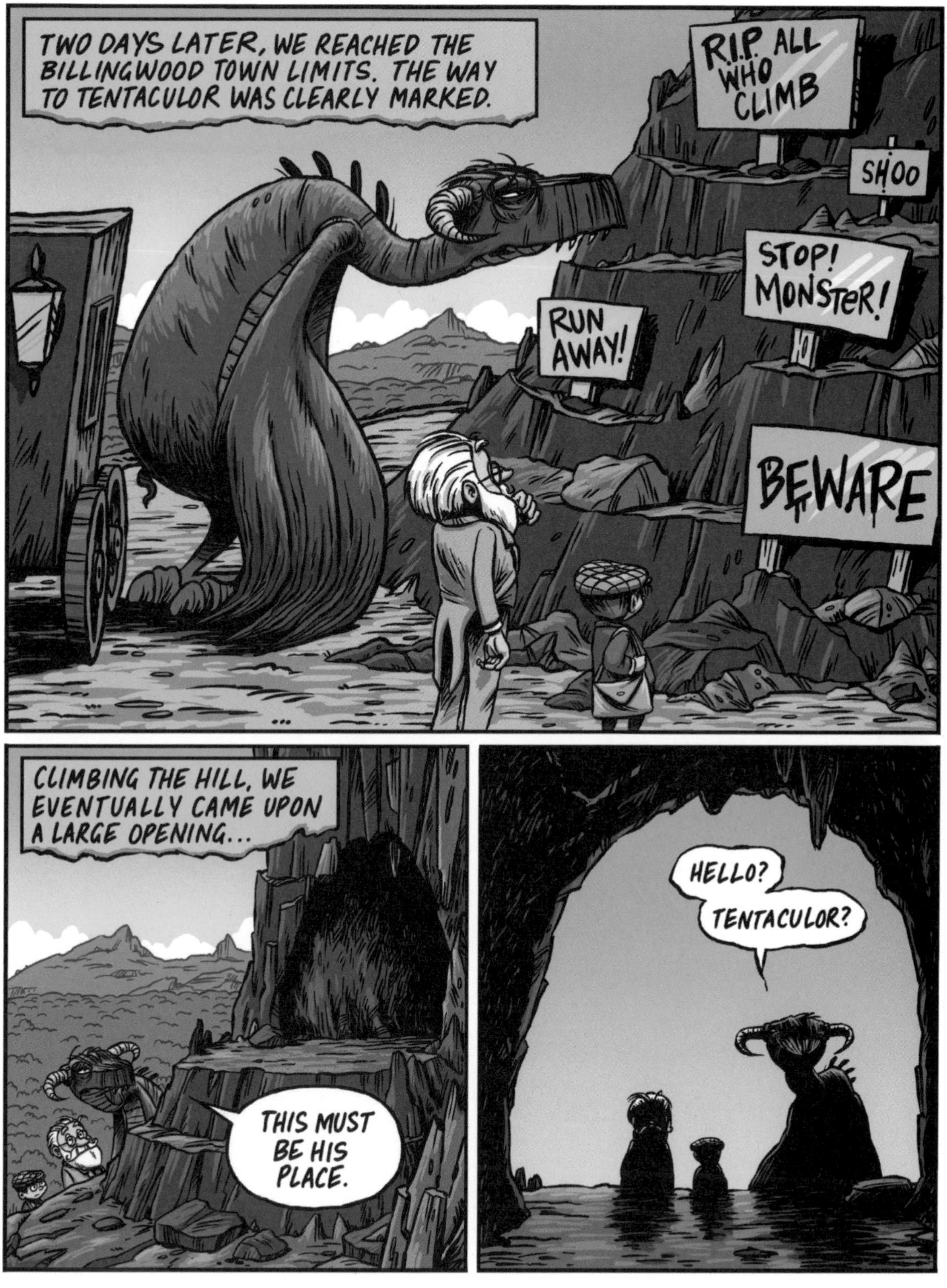
TWO DAYS LATER, WE REACHED THE BILLINGWOOD TOWN LIMITS. THE WAY TO TENTACULOR WAS CLEARLY MARKED.
R.I.P. ALL WHO CLIMB
SHOO
STOP! MONSTER!
RUN AWAY!
BEWARE
CLIMBING THE HILL, WE EVENTUALLY CAME UPON A LARGE OPENING...
THIS MUST BE HIS PLACE.
HELLO?
TENTACULOR?

RROAR

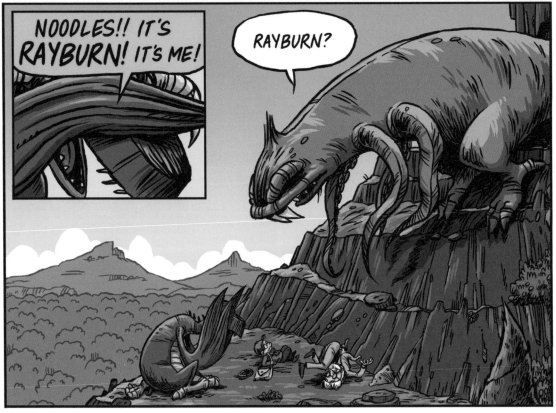

NOODLES!! IT'S RAYBURN! IT'S ME!

RAYBURN?

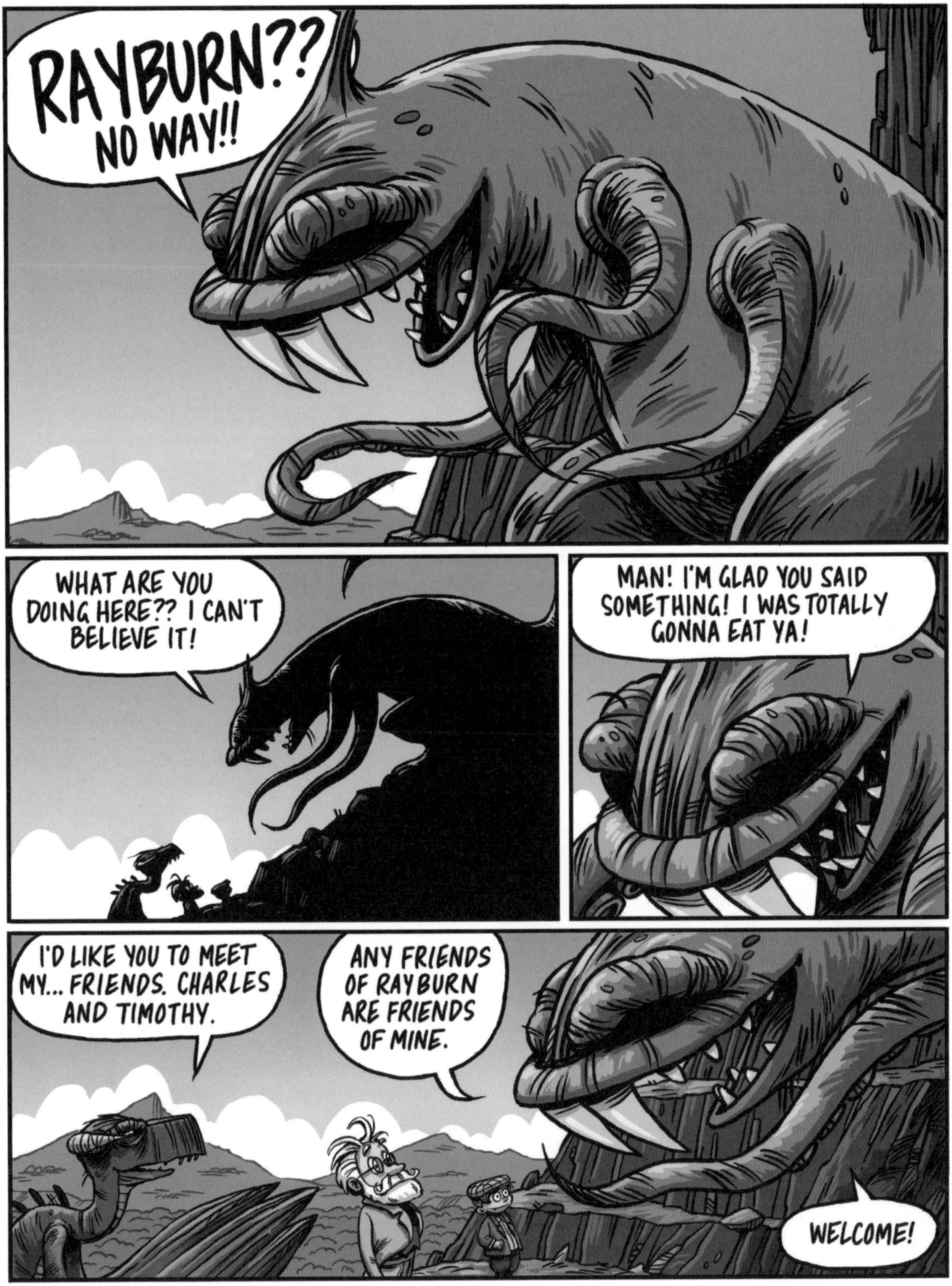
RAYBURN?? NO WAY!!
WHAT ARE YOU DOING HERE?? I CAN'T BELIEVE IT!
MAN! I'M GLAD YOU SAID SOMETHING! I WAS TOTALLY GONNA EAT YA!
I'D LIKE YOU TO MEET MY... FRIENDS. CHARLES AND TIMOTHY.
ANY FRIENDS OF RAYBURN ARE FRIENDS OF MINE.
WELCOME!

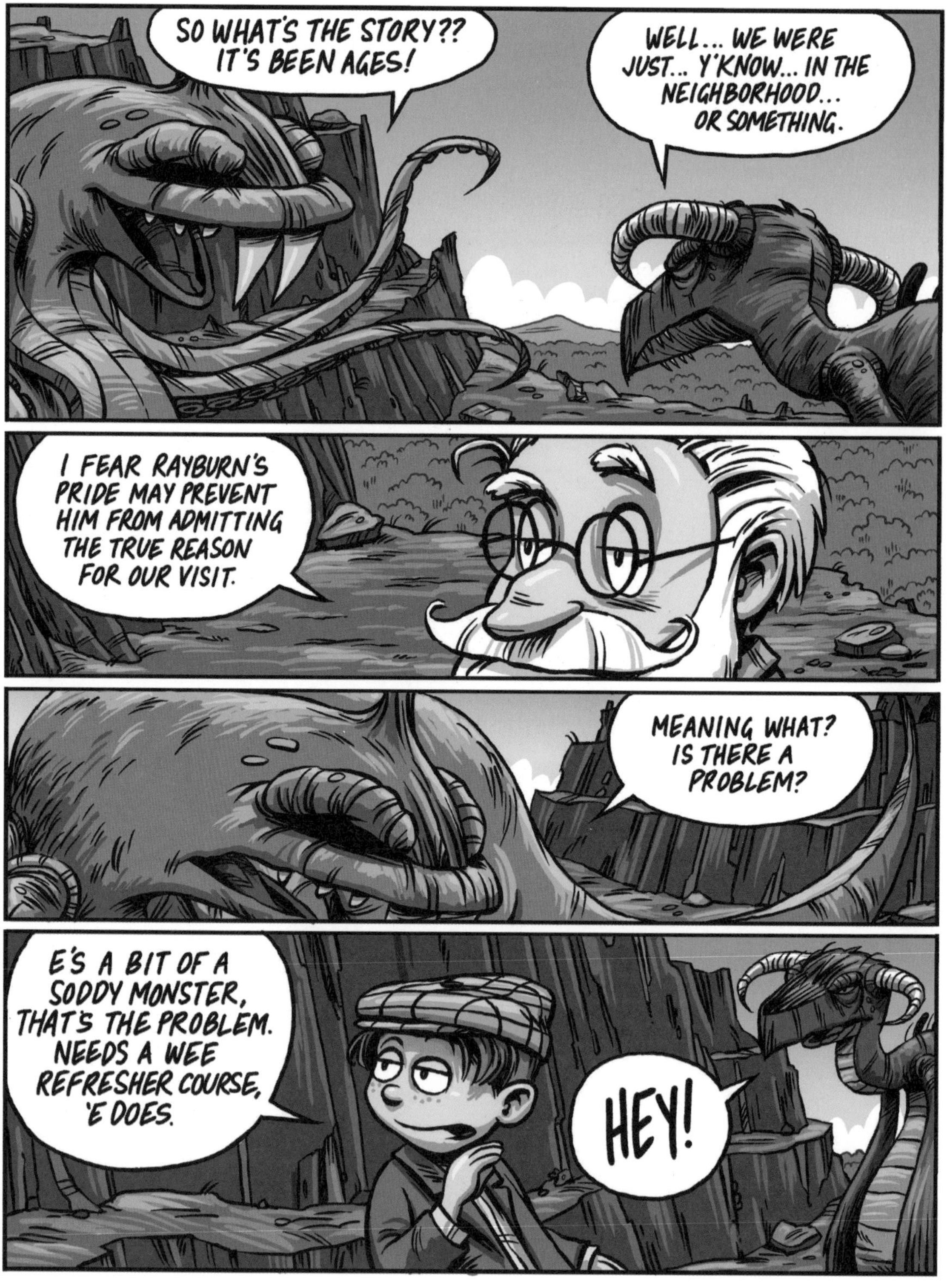
SO WHAT'S THE STORY?? IT'S BEEN AGES!
WELL... WE WERE JUST... Y'KNOW... IN THE NEIGHBORHOOD... OR SOMETHING.
I FEAR RAYBURN'S PRIDE MAY PREVENT HIM FROM ADMITTING THE TRUE REASON FOR OUR VISIT.
MEANING WHAT? IS THERE A PROBLEM?
E'S A BIT OF A SODDY MONSTER, THAT'S THE PROBLEM. NEEDS A WEE REFRESHER COURSE, 'E DOES.
HEY!

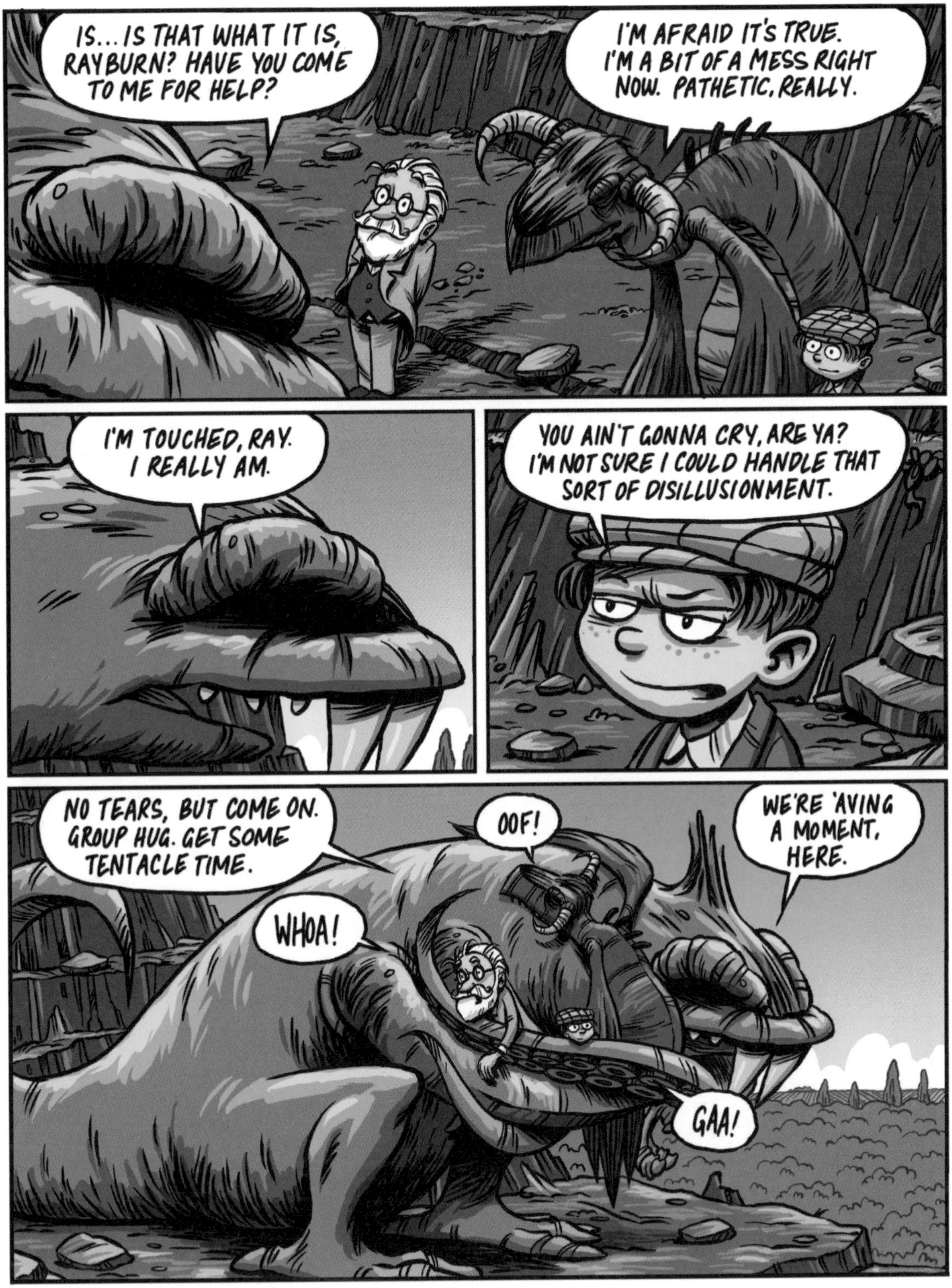
IS... IS THAT WHAT IT IS, RAYBURN? HAVE YOU COME TO ME FOR HELP?
I'M AFRAID IT'S TRUE. I'M A BIT OF A MESS RIGHT NOW. PATHETIC, REALLY.
I'M TOUCHED, RAY. I REALLY AM.
YOU AIN'T GONNA CRY, ARE YA? I'M NOT SURE I COULD HANDLE THAT SORT OF DISILLUSIONMENT.
NO TEARS, BUT COME ON. GROUP HUG. GET SOME TENTACLE TIME.
OOF!
WE'RE 'AVING A MOMENT, HERE.
WHOA!
GAA!

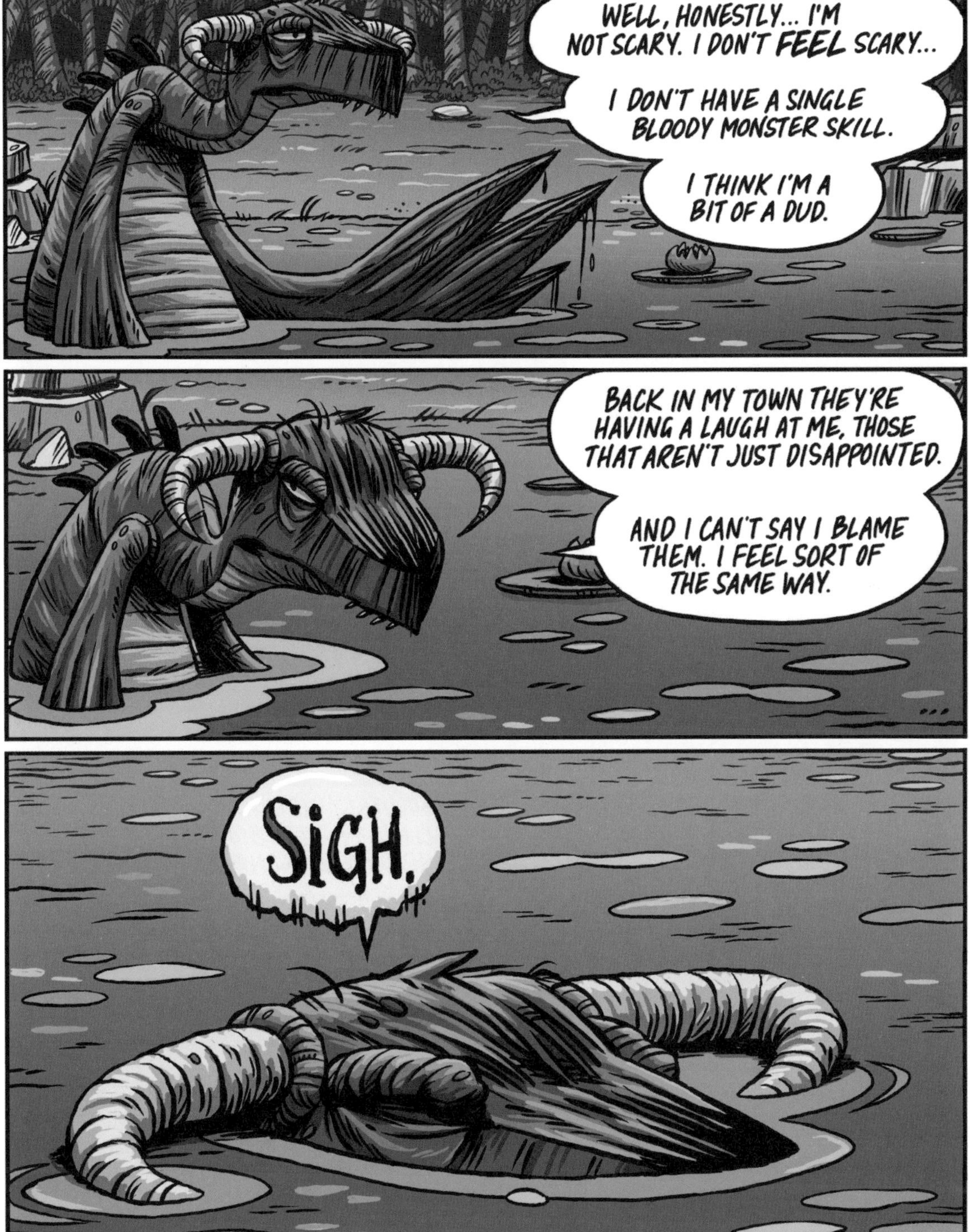
WELL, HONESTLY... I'M NOT SCARY. I DON'T FEEL SCARY...
I DON'T HAVE A SINGLE BLOODY MONSTER SKILL.
I THINK I'M A BIT OF A DUD.
BACK IN MY TOWN THEY'RE HAVING A LAUGH AT ME, THOSE THAT AREN'T JUST DISAPPOINTED.
AND I CAN'T SAY I BLAME THEM. I FEEL SORT OF THE SAME WAY.
SIGH.

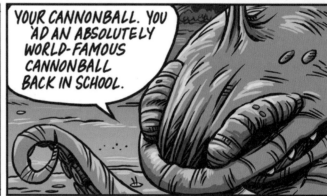

62

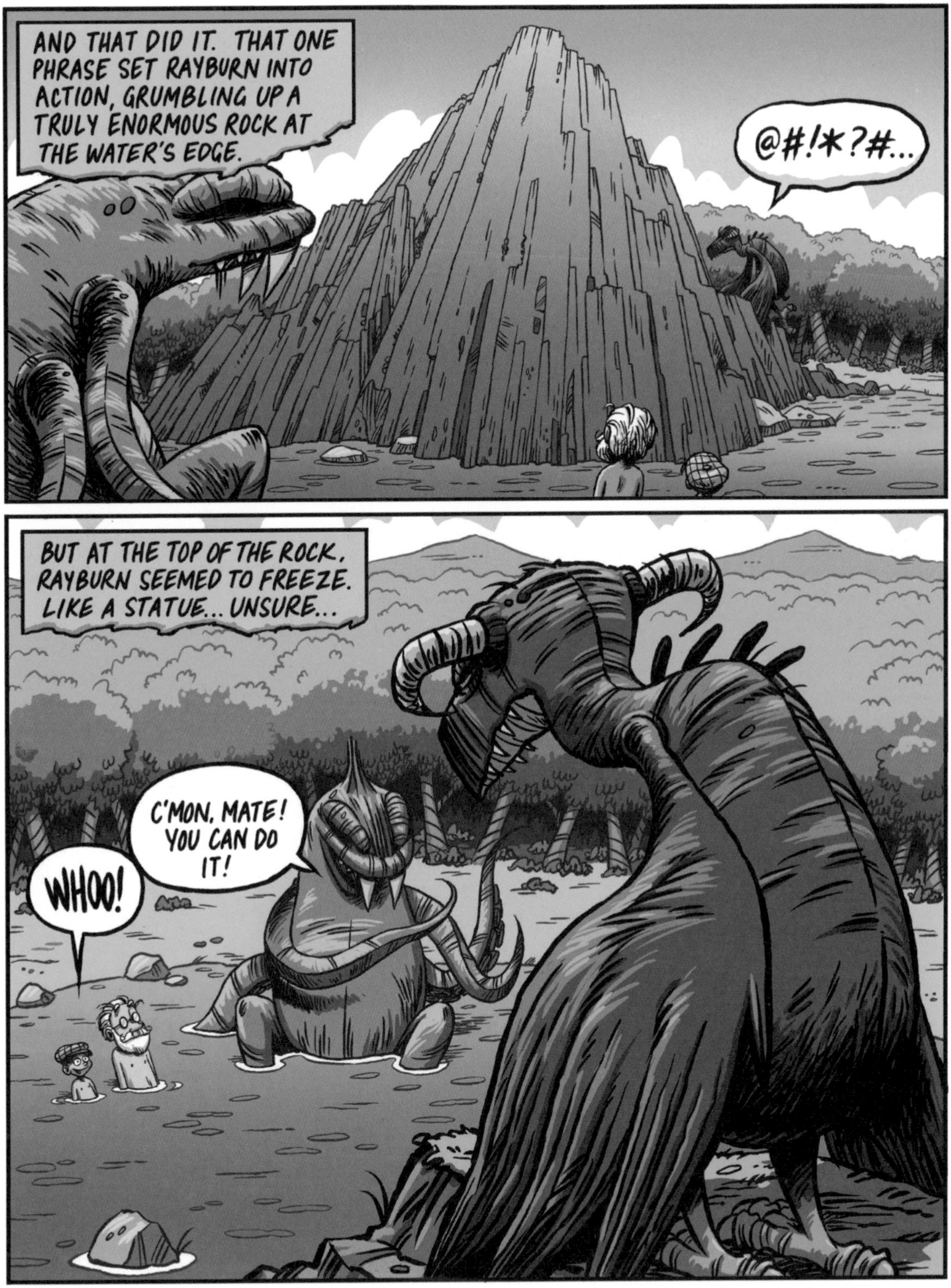
AND THAT DID IT. THAT ONE PHRASE SET RAYBURN INTO ACTION, GRUMBLING UP A TRULY ENORMOUS ROCK AT THE WATER'S EDGE.
@#!*?#...
BUT AT THE TOP OF THE ROCK, RAYBURN SEEMED TO FREEZE. LIKE A STATUE... UNSURE...
C'MON, MATE! YOU CAN DO IT!
WHOO!

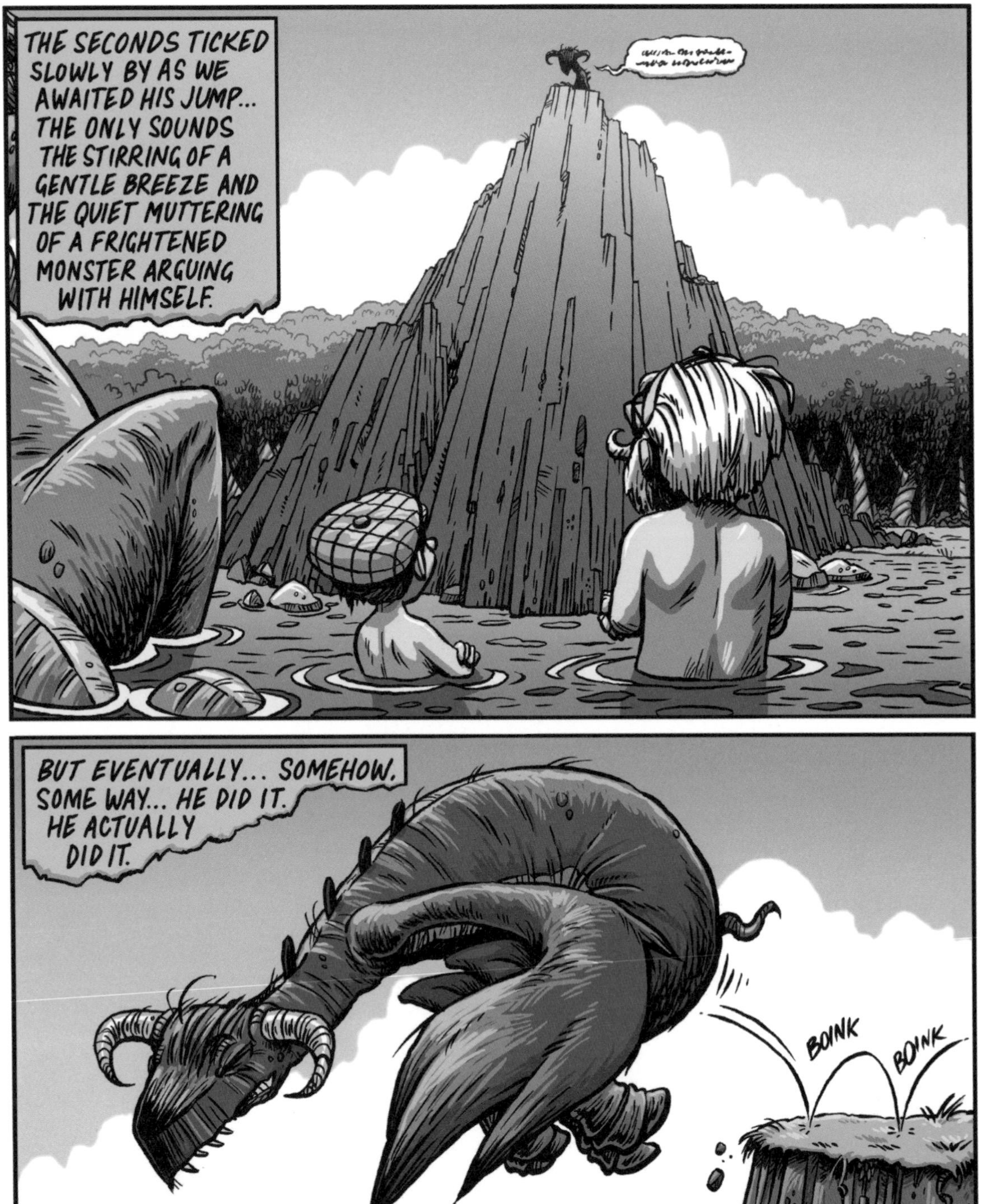
THE SECONDS TICKED SLOWLY BY AS WE AWAITED HIS JUMP... THE ONLY SOUNDS THE STIRRING OF A GENTLE BREEZE AND THE QUIET MUTTERING OF A FRIGHTENED MONSTER ARGUING WITH HIMSELF.
BUT EVENTUALLY... SOMEHOW. SOME WAY... HE DID IT. HE ACTUALLY DID IT.
BOINK
BOINK

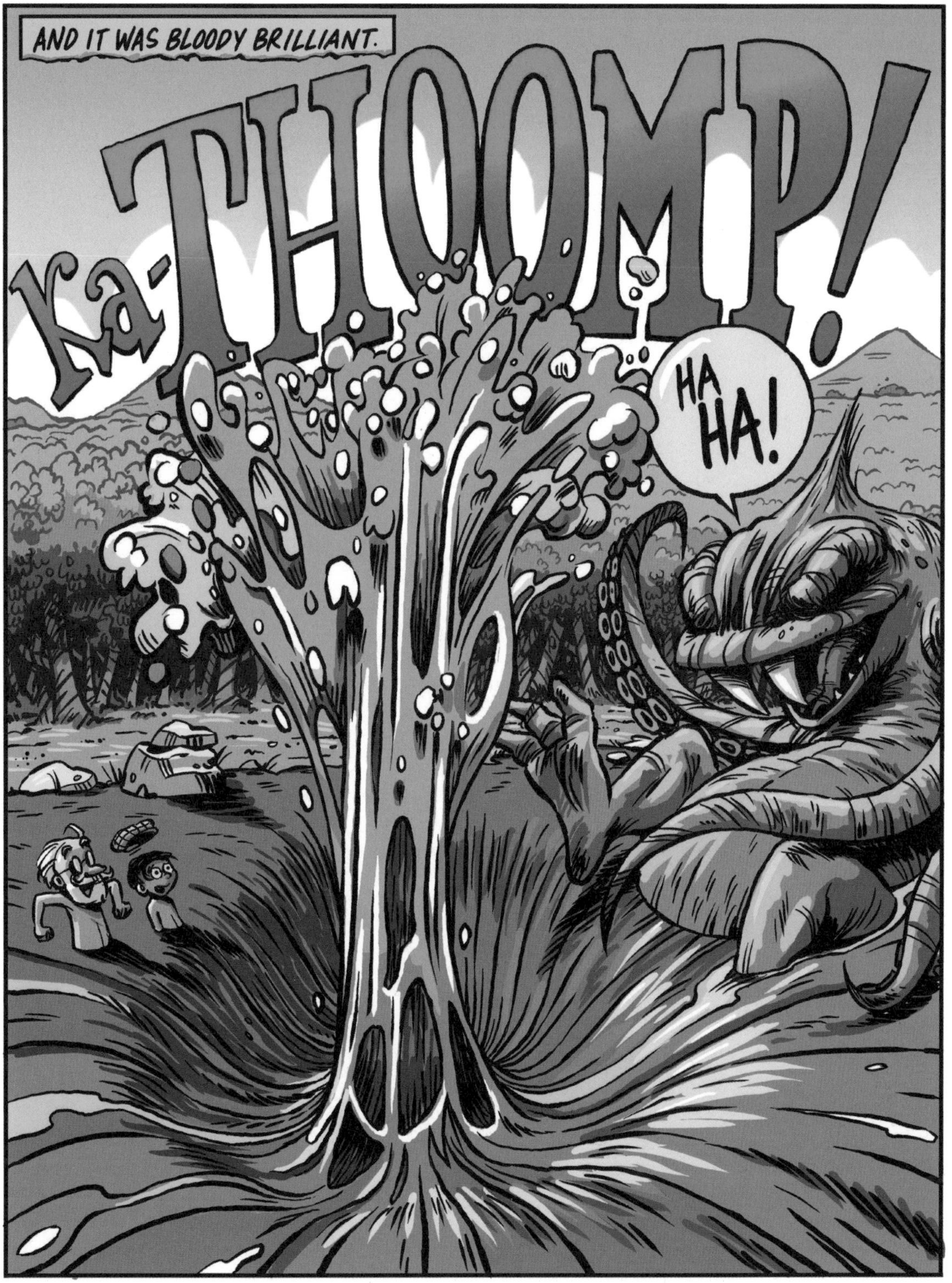
AND IT WAS BLOODY BRILLIANT.
KA-THOOMP!
HA HA!

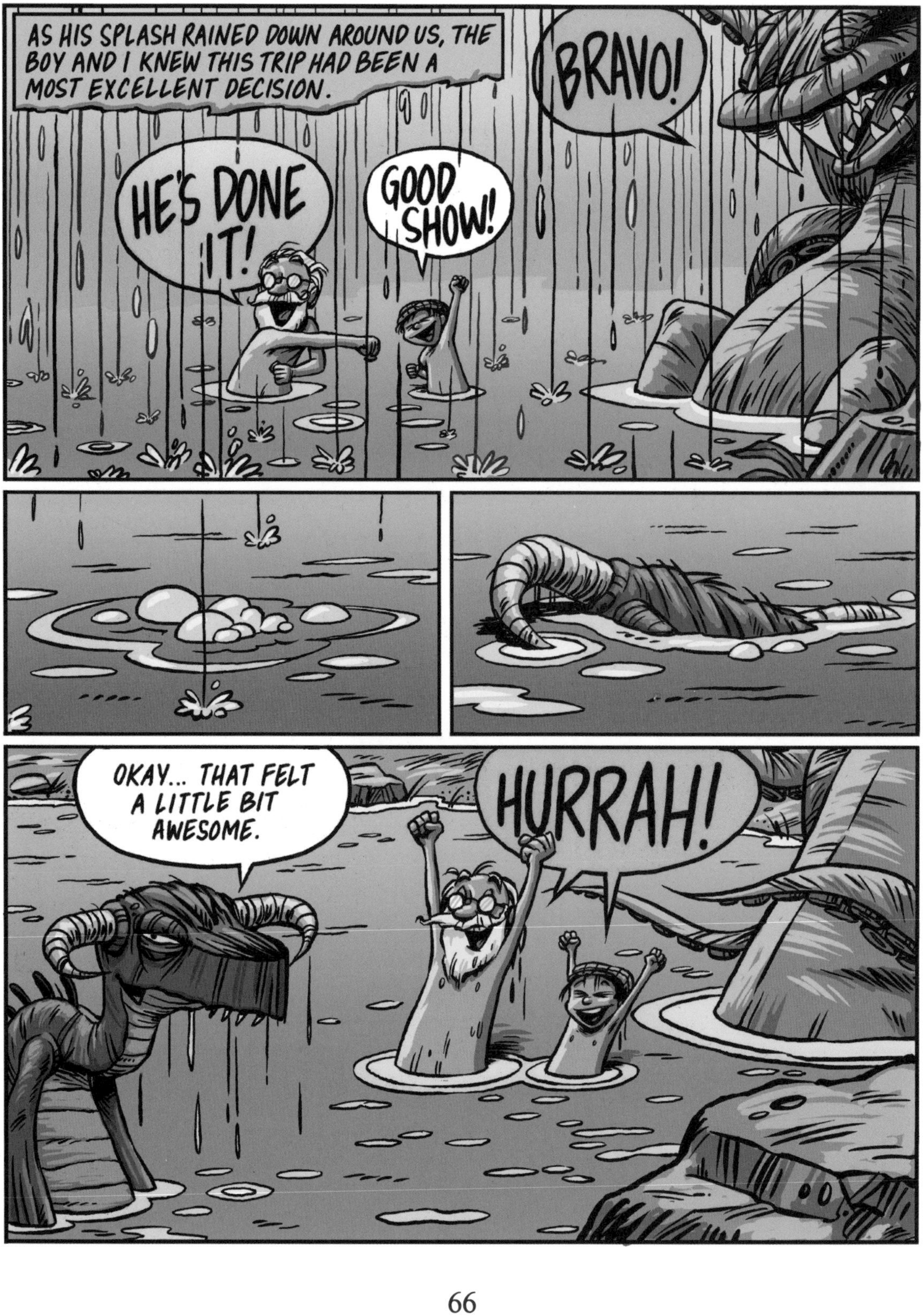
AS HIS SPLASH RAINED DOWN AROUND US, THE BOY AND I KNEW THIS TRIP HAD BEEN A MOST EXCELLENT DECISION.
BRAVO!
HE'S DONE IT!
GOOD SHOW!
OKAY... THAT FELT A LITTLE BIT AWESOME.
HURRAH!

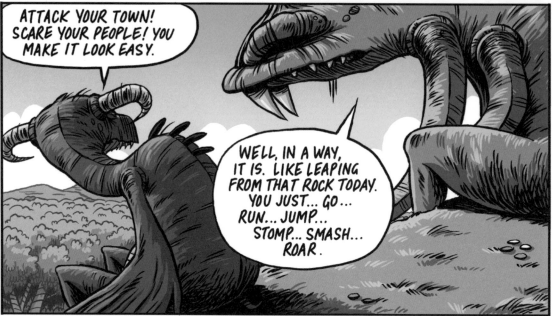

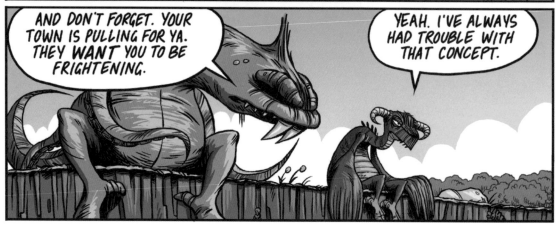

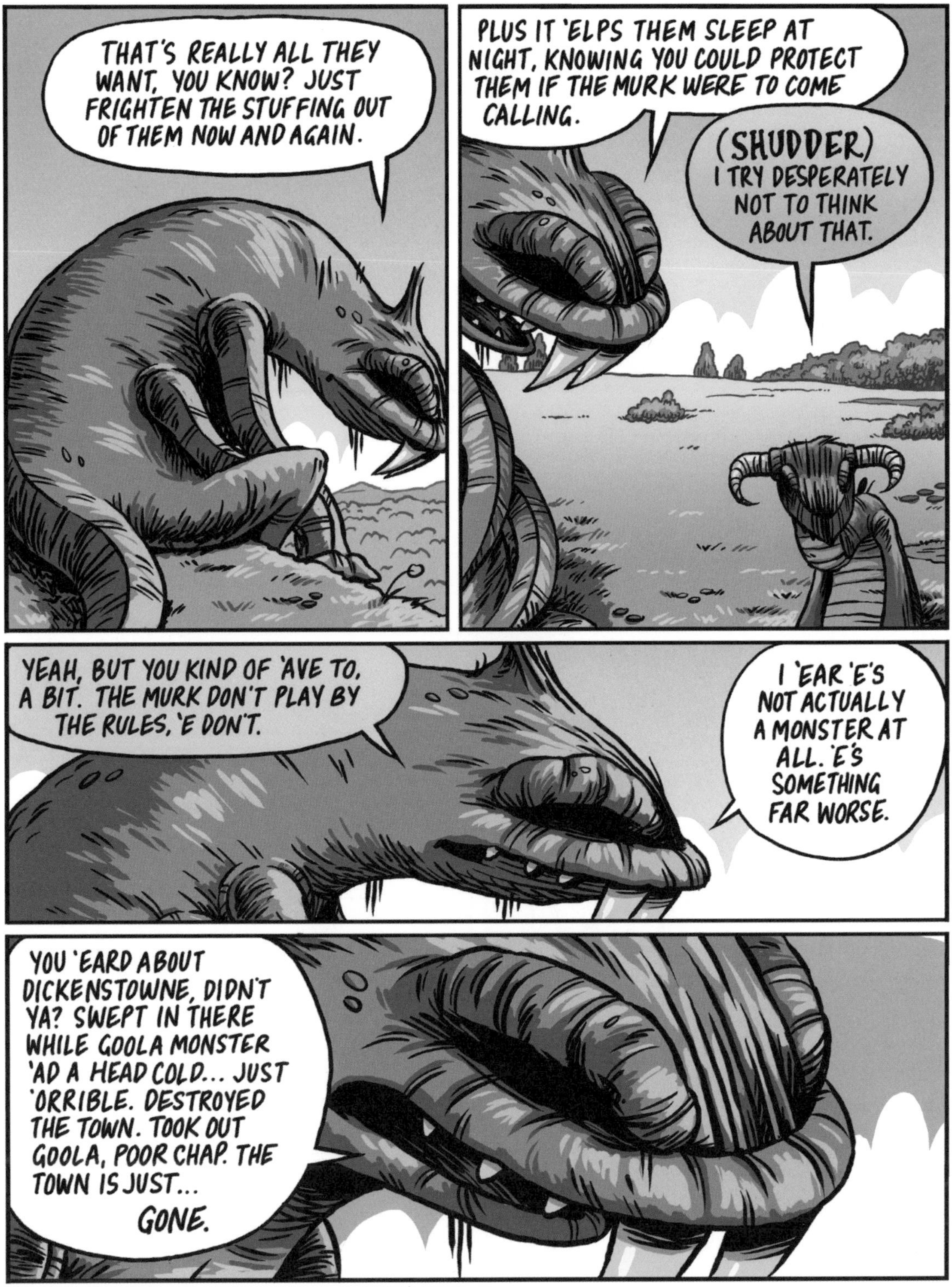
THAT'S REALLY ALL THEY WANT, YOU KNOW? JUST FRIGHTEN THE STUFFING OUT OF THEM NOW AND AGAIN.
PLUS IT 'ELPS THEM SLEEP AT NIGHT, KNOWING YOU COULD PROTECT THEM IF THE MURK WERE TO COME CALLING.
(SHUDDER) I TRY DESPERATELY NOT TO THINK ABOUT THAT.
YEAH, BUT YOU KIND OF 'AVE TO, A BIT. THE MURK DON'T PLAY BY THE RULES, 'E DON'T.
I 'EAR 'E'S NOT ACTUALLY A MONSTER AT ALL. 'E'S SOMETHING FAR WORSE.
YOU 'EARD ABOUT DICKENSTOWNE, DIDN'T YA? SWEPT IN THERE WHILE GOOLA MONSTER 'AD A HEAD COLD... JUST 'ORRIBLE. DESTROYED THE TOWN. TOOK OUT GOOLA, POOR CHAP. THE TOWN IS JUST... GONE.

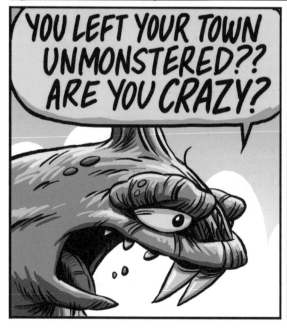

70

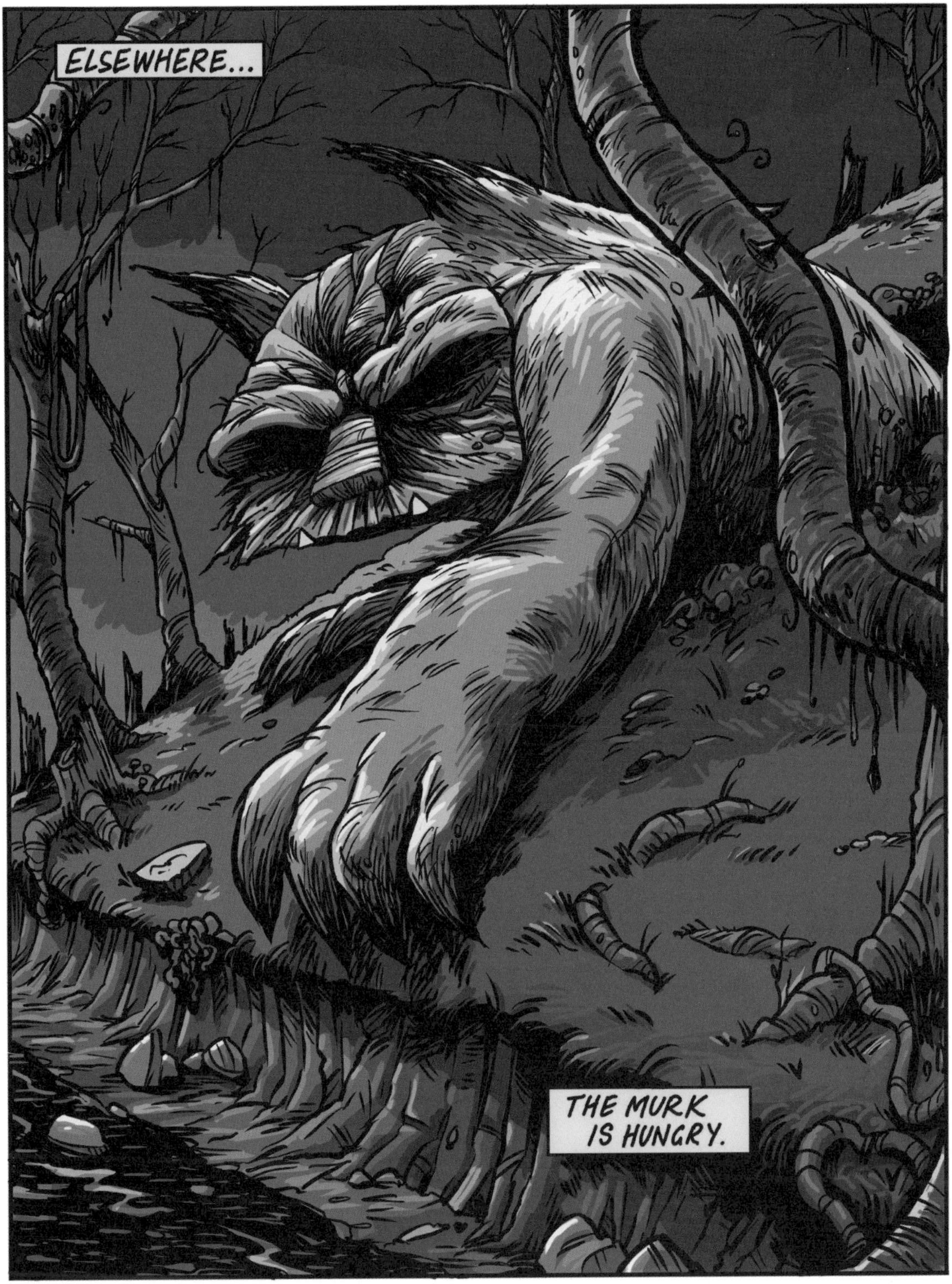
ELSEWHERE...
THE MURK IS HUNGRY.

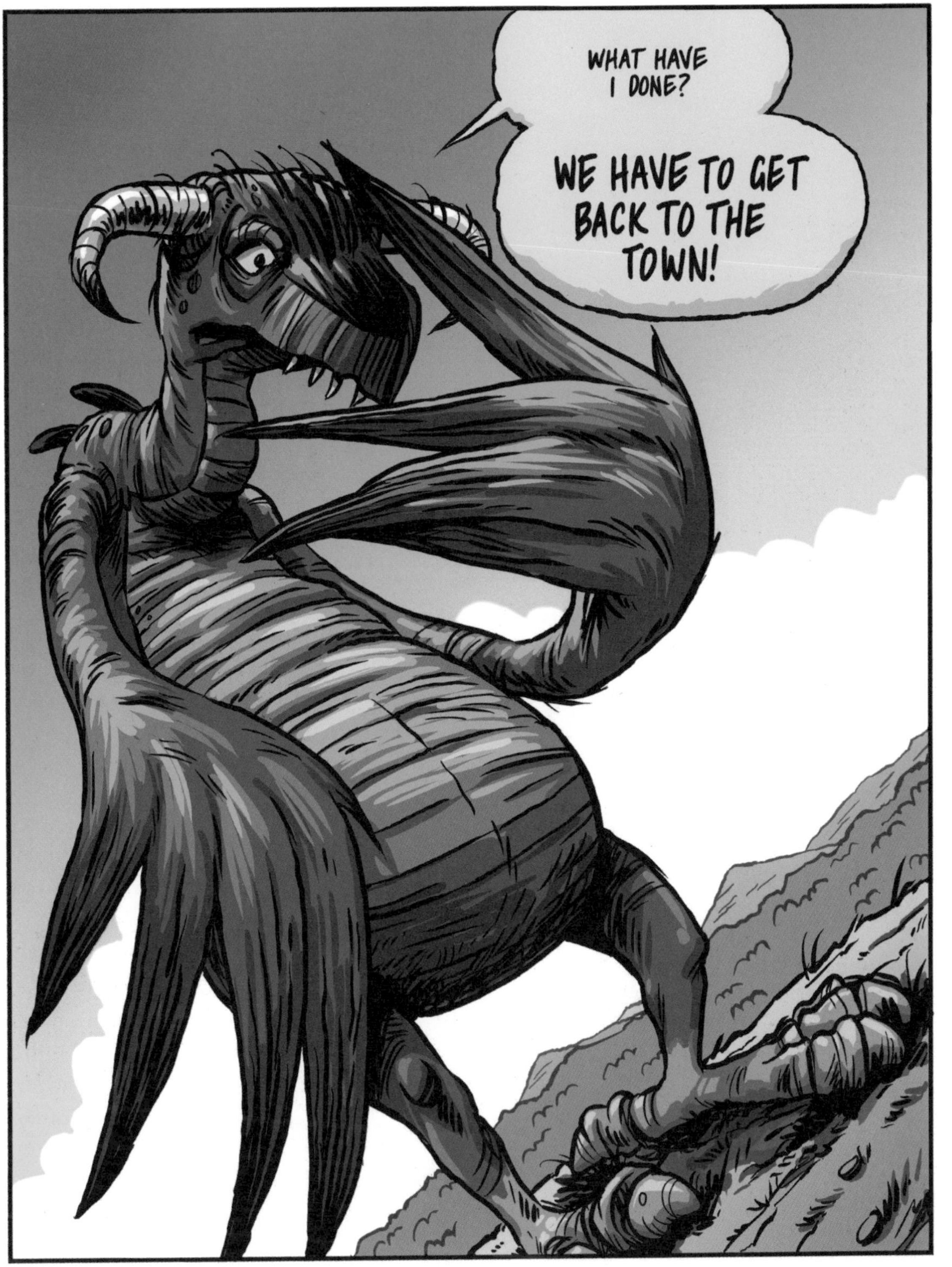
WHAT HAVE I DONE?
WE HAVE TO GET BACK TO THE TOWN!

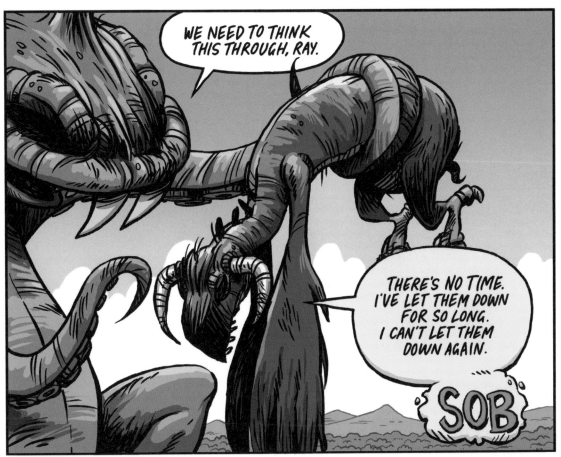

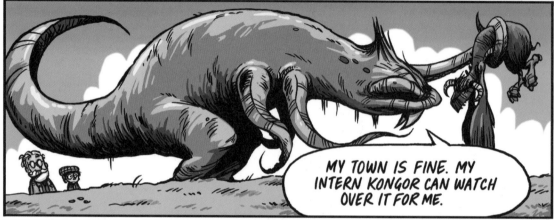

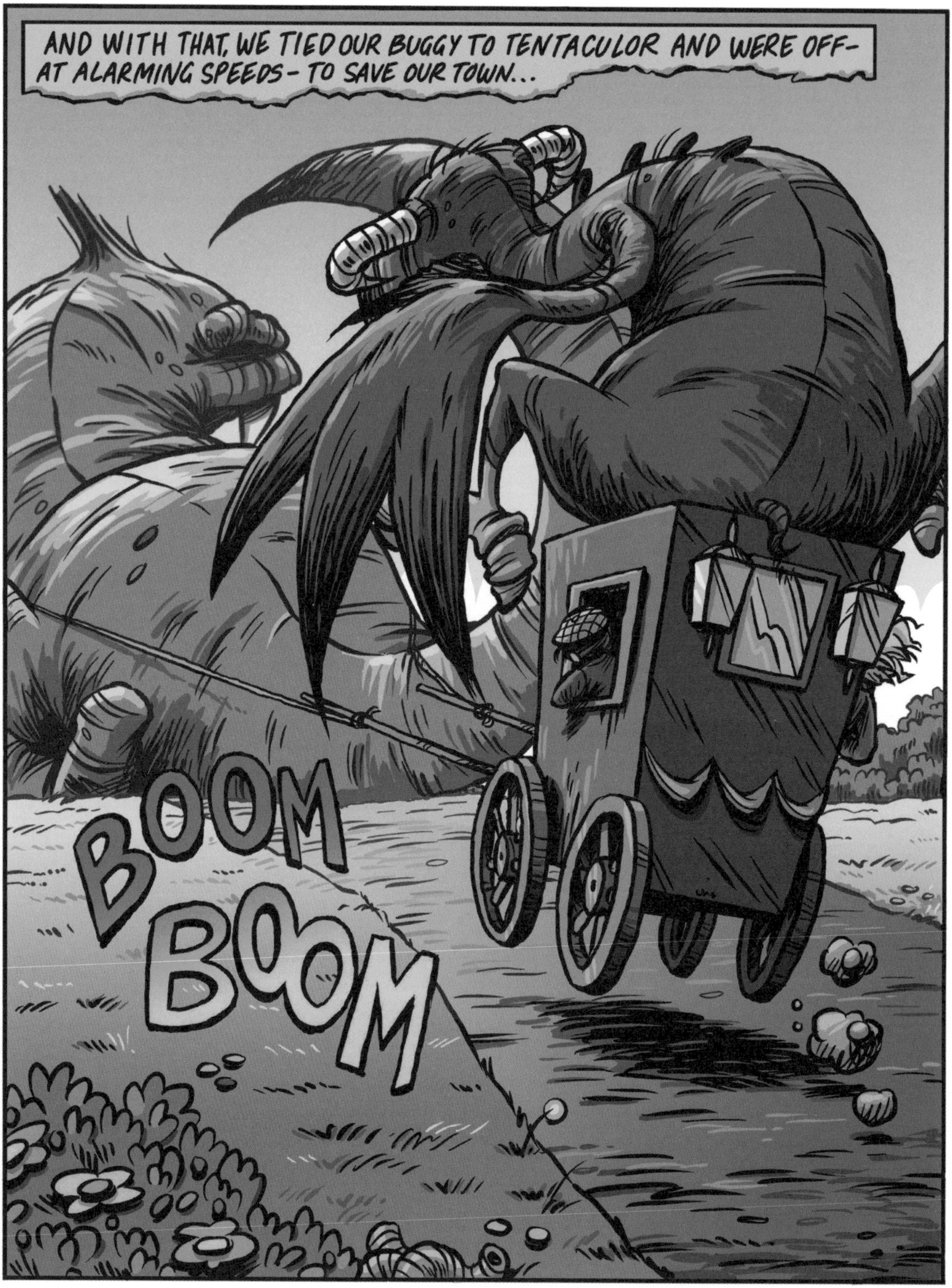
AND WITH THAT, WE TIED OUR BUGGY TO TENTACULOR AND WERE OFF- AT ALARMING SPEEDS- TO SAVE OUR TOWN...
BOOM
BOOM

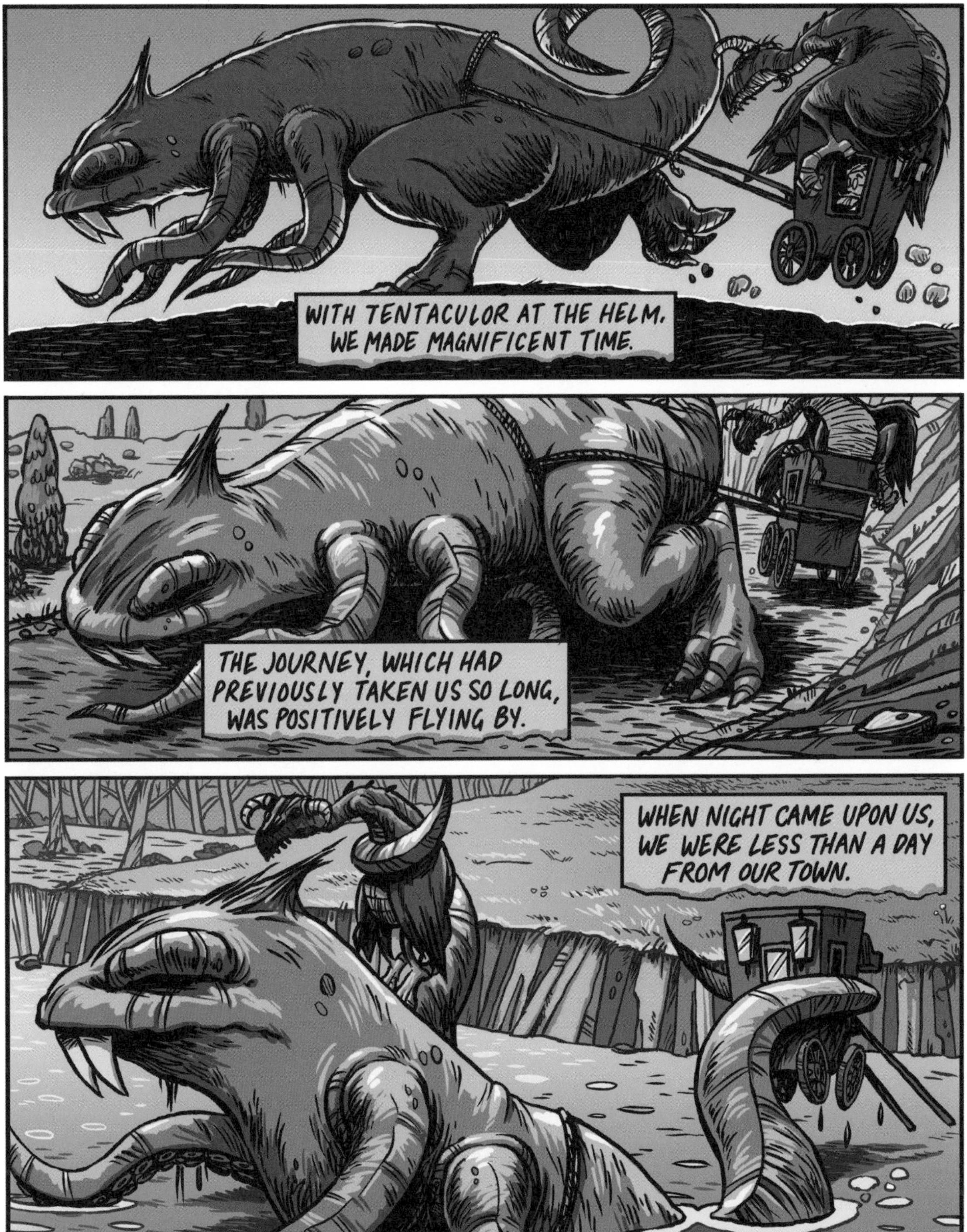
WITH TENTACULOR AT THE HELM, WE MADE MAGNIFICENT TIME.
THE JOURNEY, WHICH HAD PREVIOUSLY TAKEN US SO LONG, WAS POSITIVELY FLYING BY.
WHEN NIGHT CAME UPON US, WE WERE LESS THAN A DAY FROM OUR TOWN.

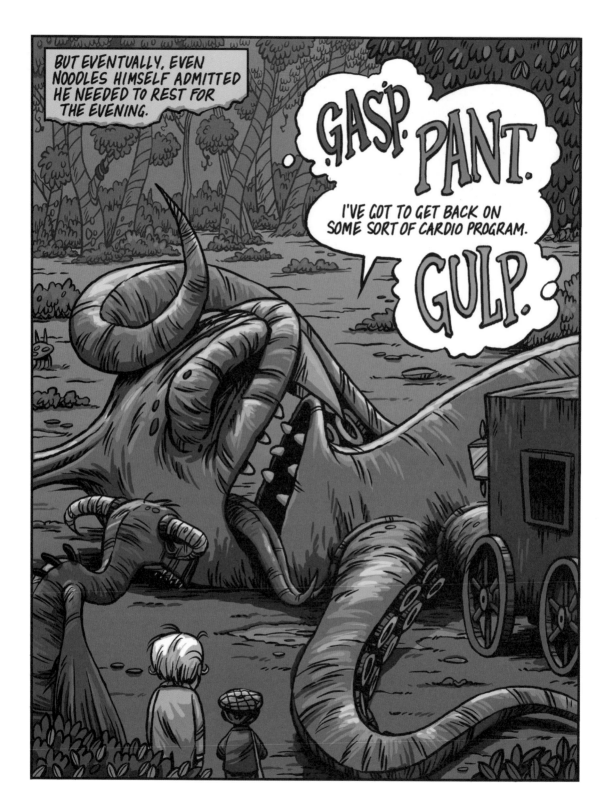

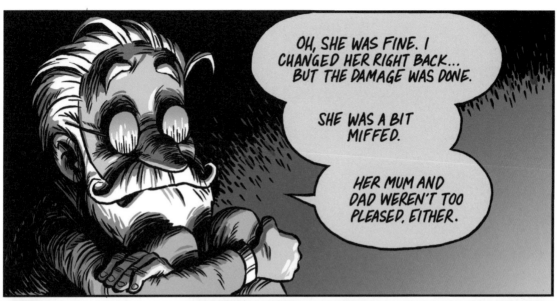

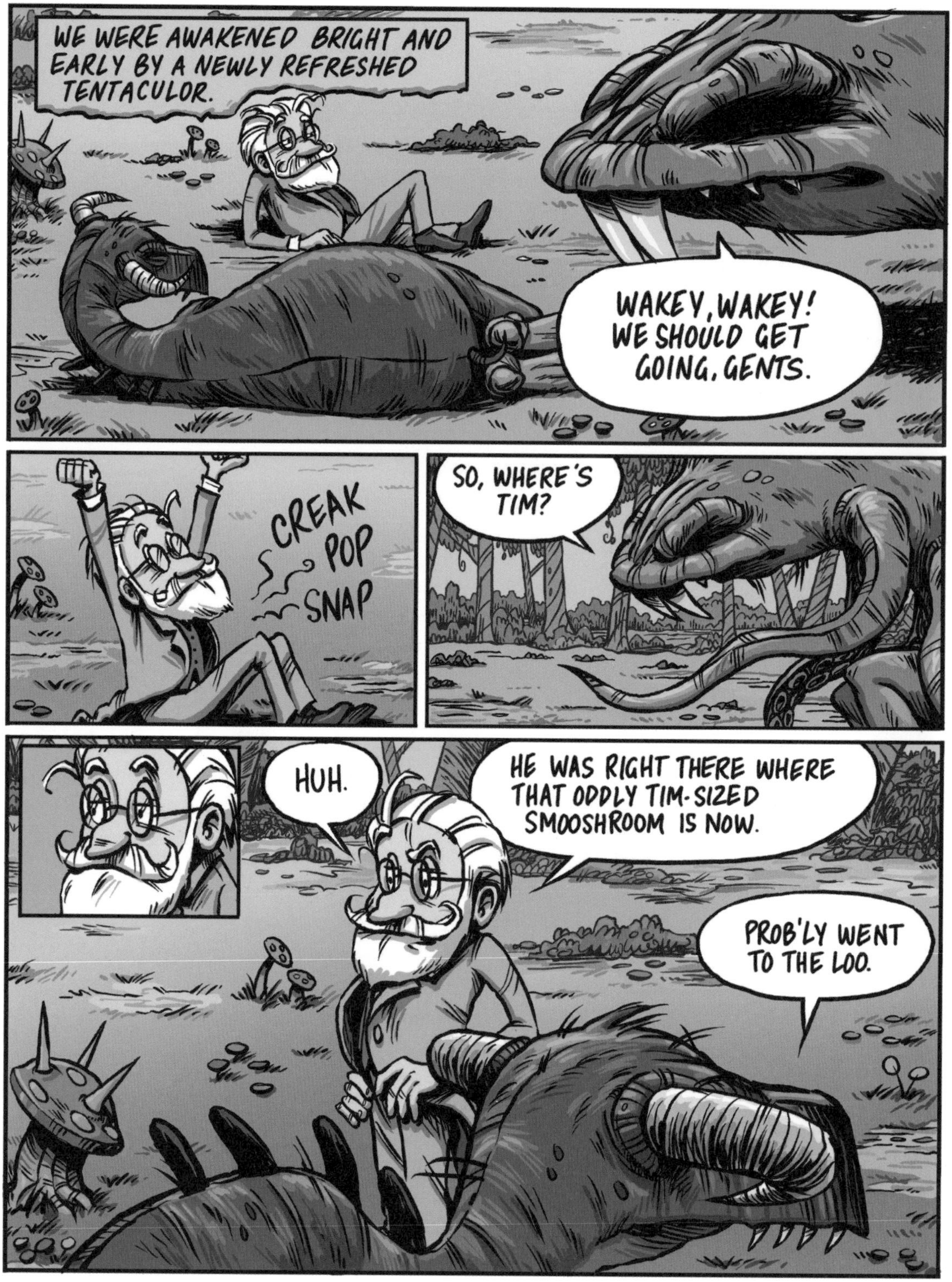
WE WERE AWAKENED BRIGHT AND EARLY BY A NEWLY REFRESHED TENTACULOR.
WAKEY, WAKEY! WE SHOULD GET GOING, GENTS.
CREAK
POP
SNAP
SO, WHERE'S TIM?
HUH.
HE WAS RIGHT THERE WHERE THAT ODDLY TIM-SIZED SMOOSHROOM IS NOW.
PROB'LY WENT TO THE LOO.

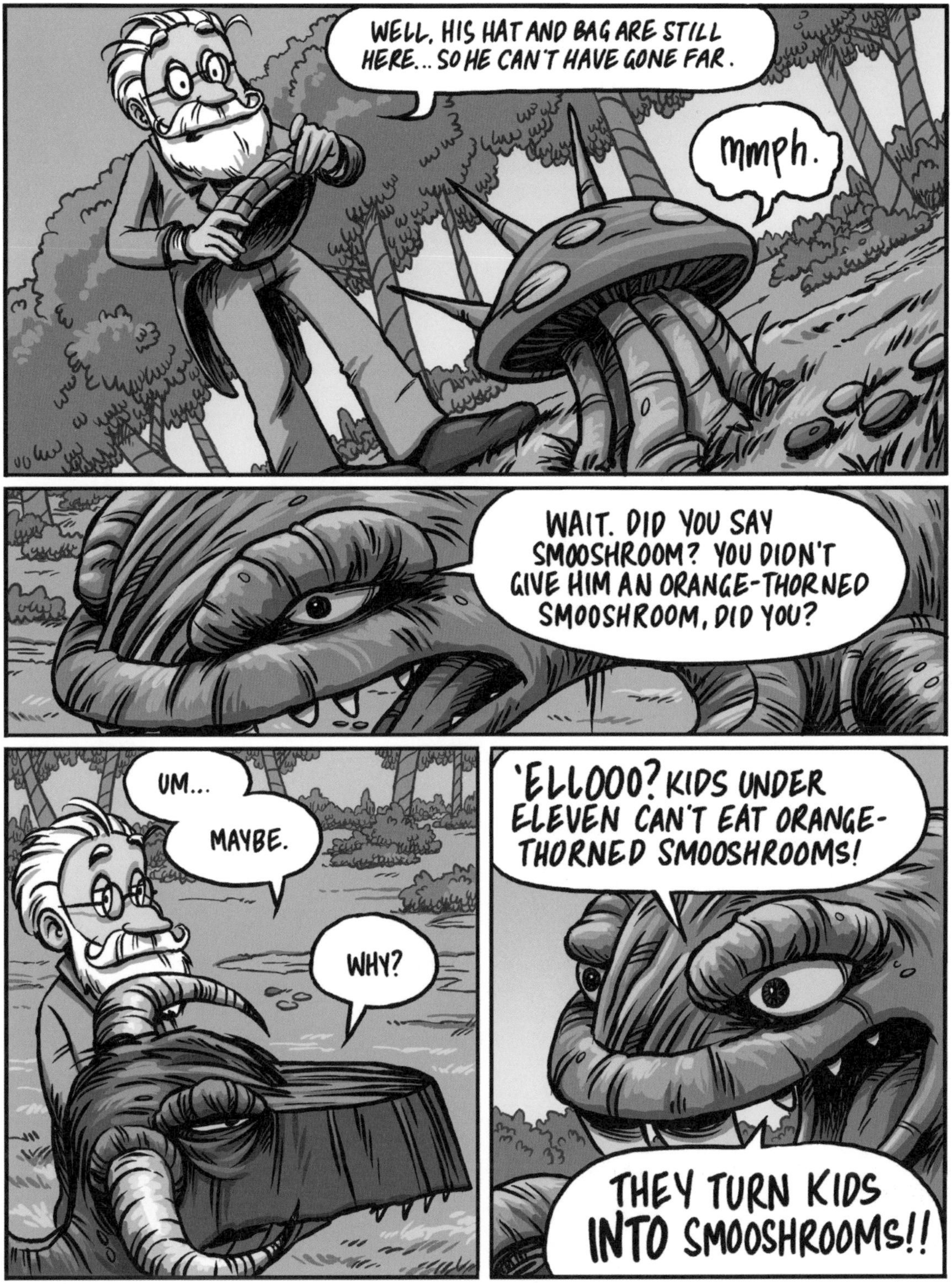
WELL, HIS HAT AND BAG ARE STILL HERE... SO HE CAN'T HAVE GONE FAR.
mmph.
WAIT. DID YOU SAY SMOOSHROOM? YOU DIDN'T GIVE HIM AN ORANGE-THORNED SMOOSHROOM, DID YOU?
UM...
MAYBE.
WHY?
'ELLOOO? KIDS UNDER ELEVEN CAN'T EAT ORANGE-THORNED SMOOSHROOMS!
THEY TURN KIDS INTO SMOOSHROOMS!!

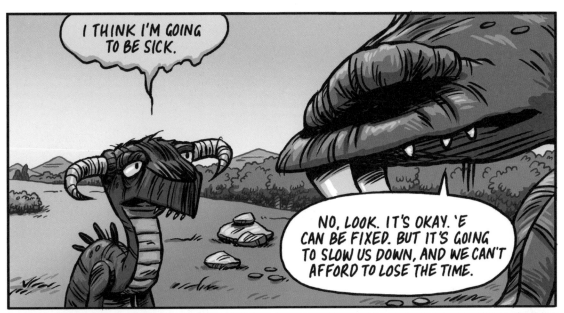

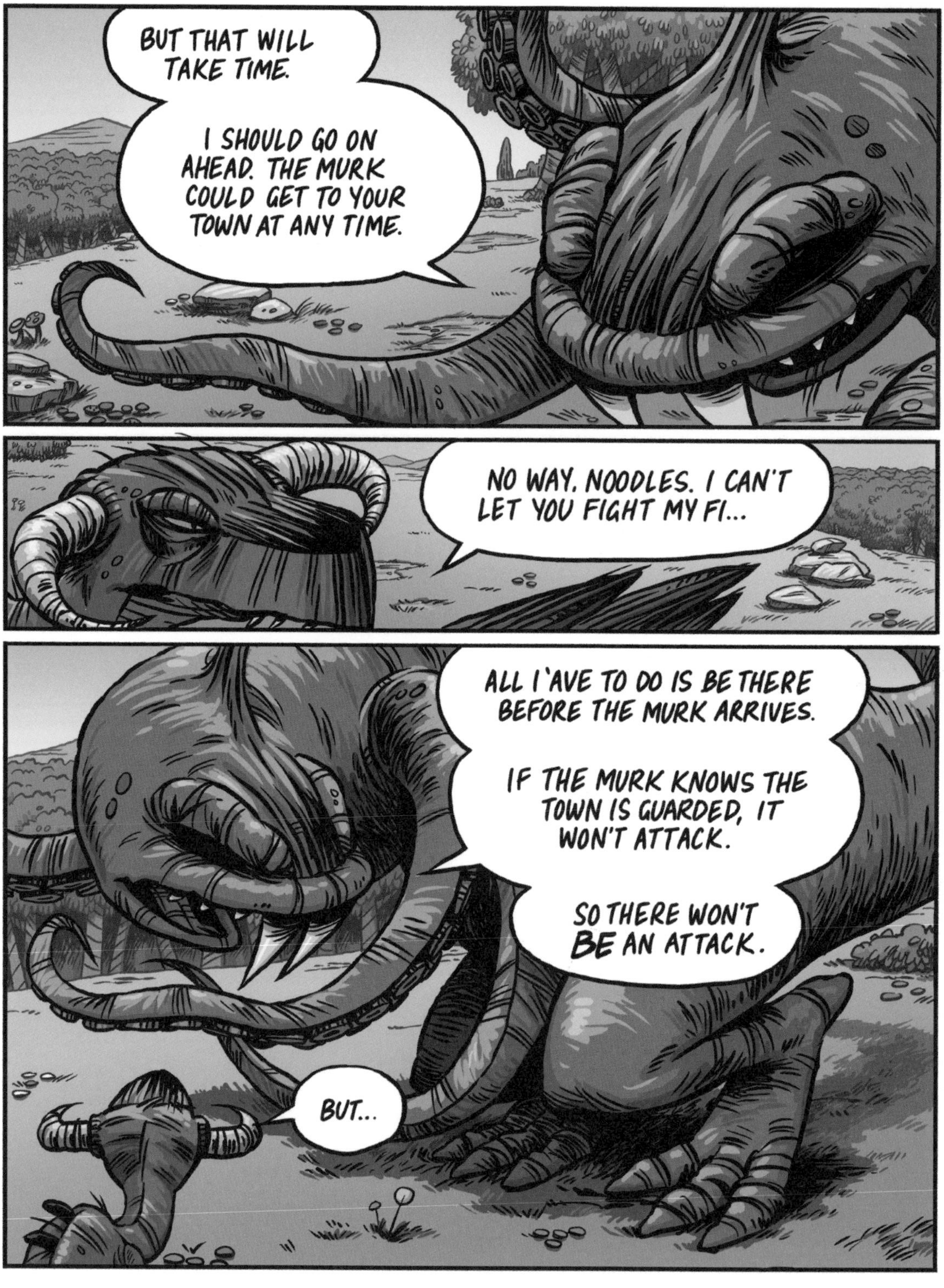
BUT THAT WILL TAKE TIME.
I SHOULD GO ON AHEAD. THE MURK COULD GET TO YOUR TOWN AT ANY TIME.
NO WAY, NOODLES. I CAN'T LET YOU FIGHT MY FI...
ALL I'AVE TO DO IS BE THERE BEFORE THE MURK ARRIVES.
IF THE MURK KNOWS THE TOWN IS GUARDED, IT WON'T ATTACK.
SO THERE WON'T **BE** AN ATTACK.
BUT...

93

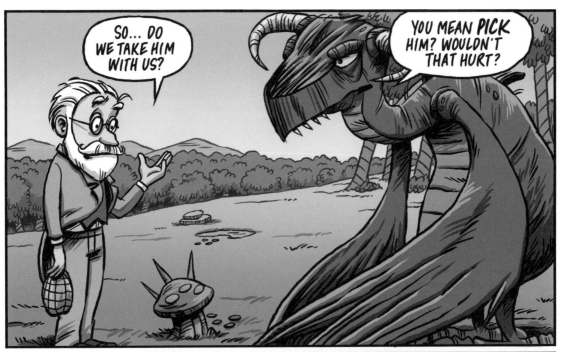

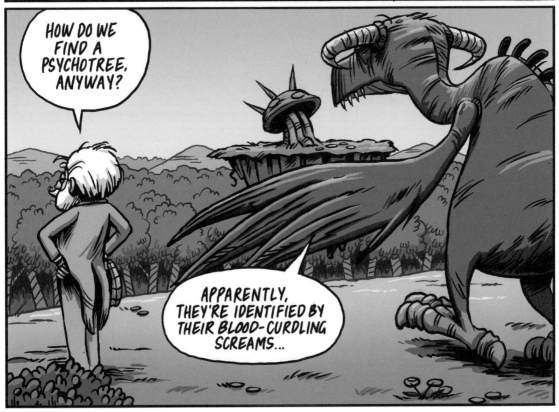

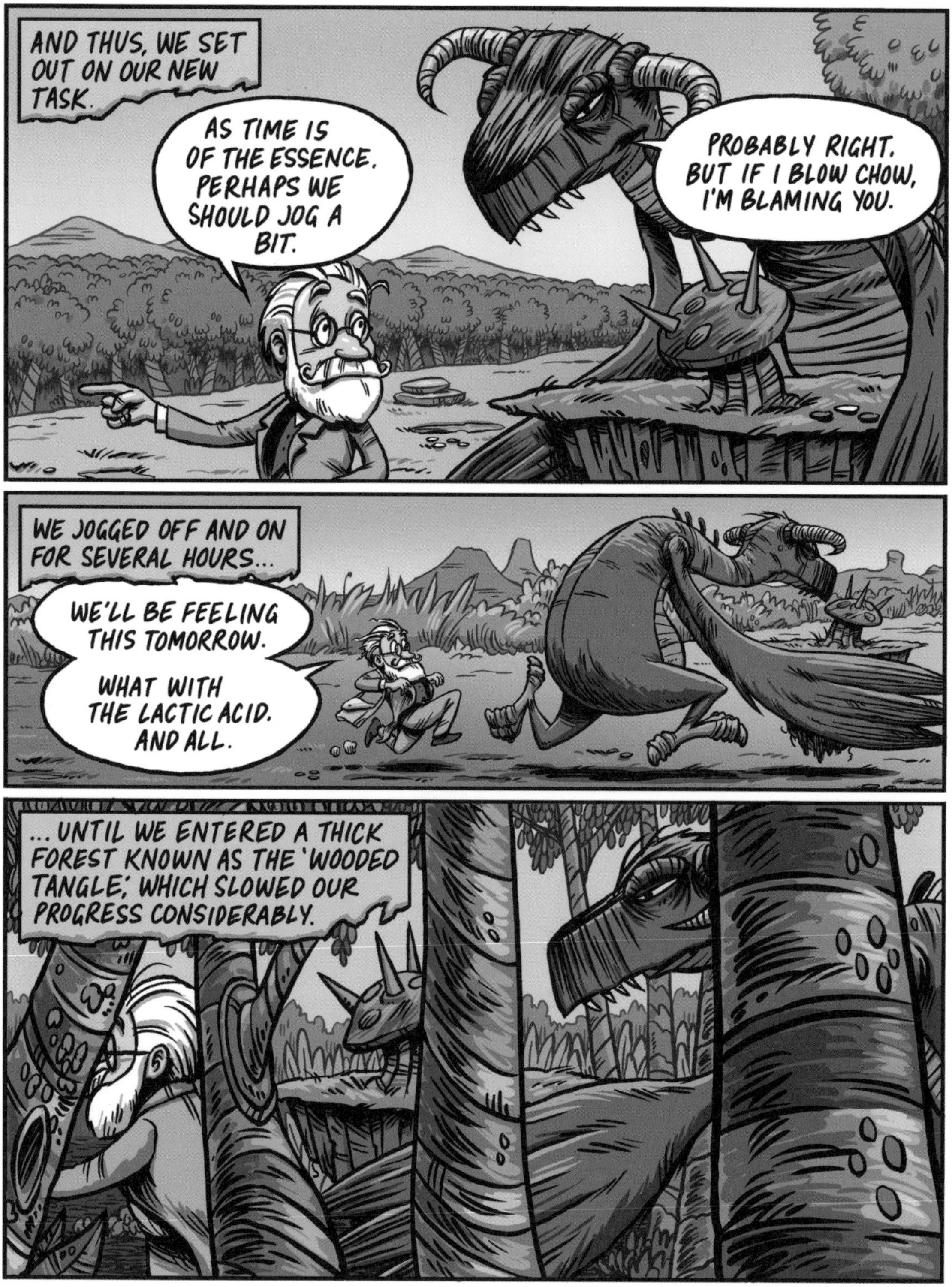
AND THUS, WE SET OUT ON OUR NEW TASK.
AS TIME IS OF THE ESSENCE. PERHAPS WE SHOULD JOG A BIT.
PROBABLY RIGHT. BUT IF I BLOW CHOW, I'M BLAMING YOU.
WE JOGGED OFF AND ON FOR SEVERAL HOURS...
WE'LL BE FEELING THIS TOMORROW.
WHAT WITH THE LACTIC ACID. AND ALL.
... UNTIL WE ENTERED A THICK FOREST KNOWN AS THE 'WOODED TANGLE,' WHICH SLOWED OUR PROGRESS CONSIDERABLY.

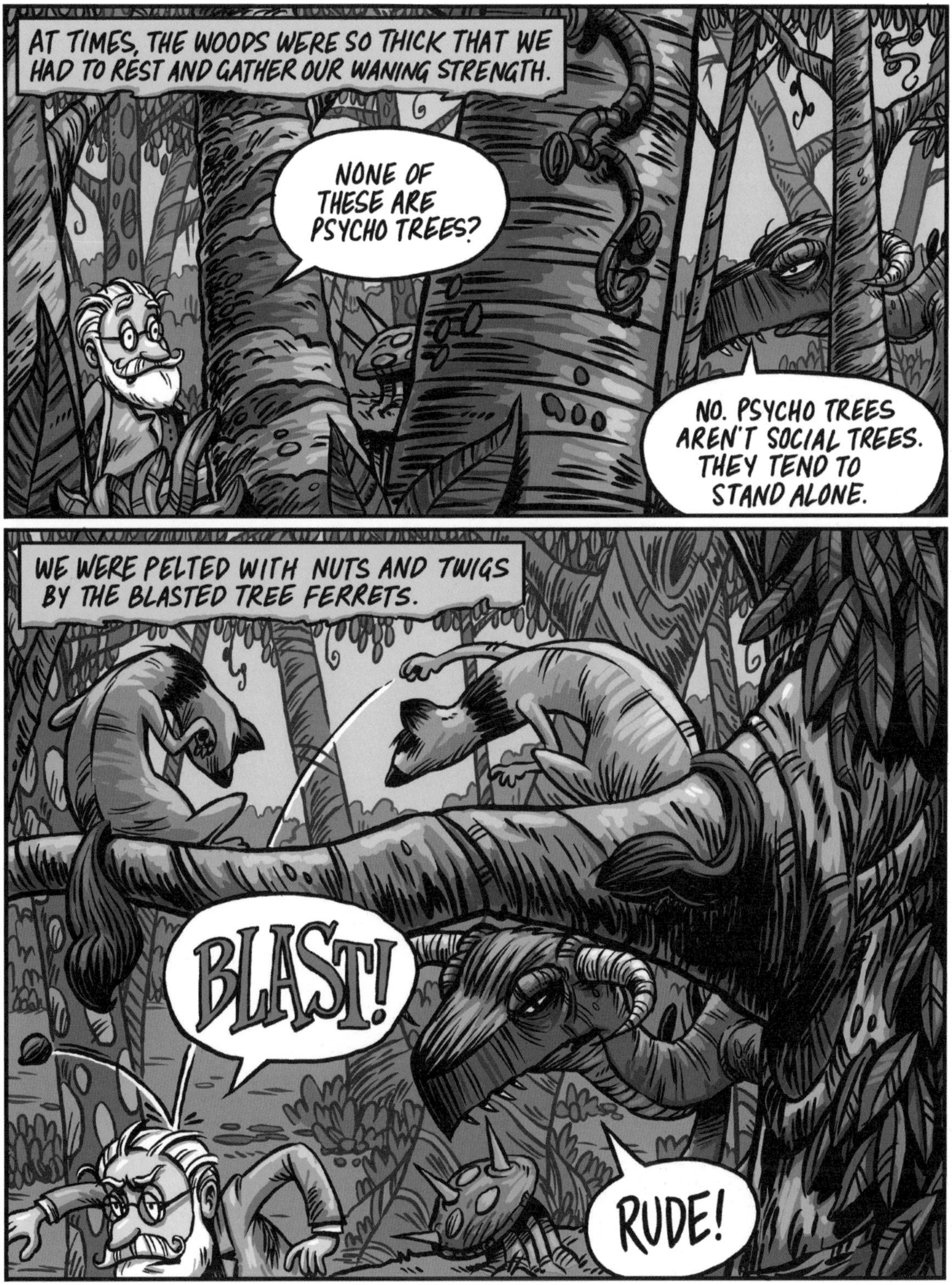
AT TIMES, THE WOODS WERE SO THICK THAT WE HAD TO REST AND GATHER OUR WANING STRENGTH.
NONE OF THESE ARE PSYCHO TREES?
NO. PSYCHO TREES AREN'T SOCIAL TREES. THEY TEND TO STAND ALONE.
WE WERE PELTED WITH NUTS AND TWIGS BY THE BLASTED TREE FERRETS.
BLAST!
RUDE!

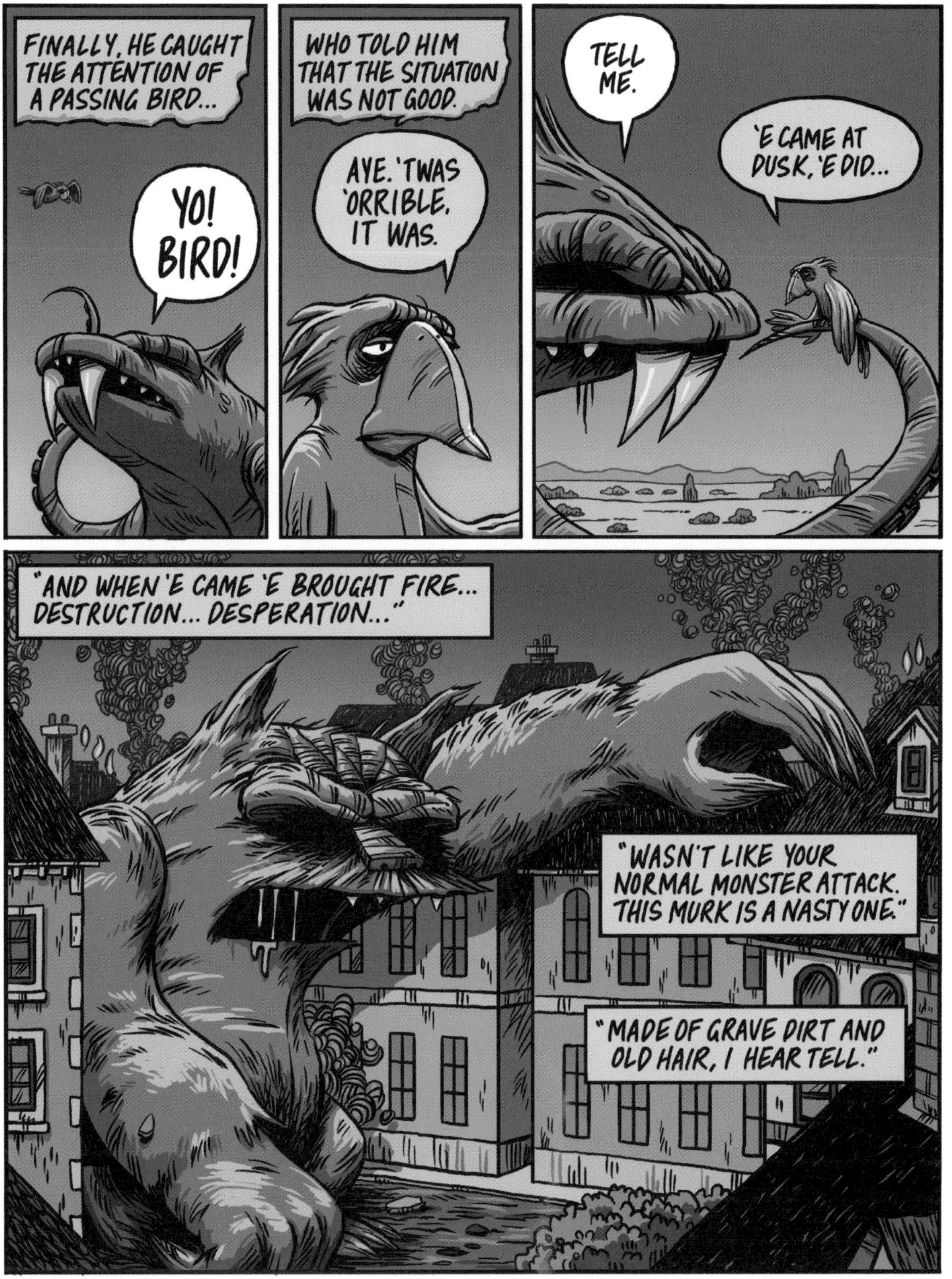

FINALLY, HE CAUGHT THE ATTENTION OF A PASSING BIRD...
YO! BIRD!
WHO TOLD HIM THAT THE SITUATION WAS NOT GOOD.
AYE. 'TWAS 'ORRIBLE, IT WAS.
TELL ME.
'E CAME AT DUSK, 'E DID...
"AND WHEN 'E CAME 'E BROUGHT FIRE... DESTRUCTION... DESPERATION..."
"WASN'T LIKE YOUR NORMAL MONSTER ATTACK. THIS MURK IS A NASTY ONE."
"MADE OF GRAVE DIRT AND OLD HAIR, I HEAR TELL."

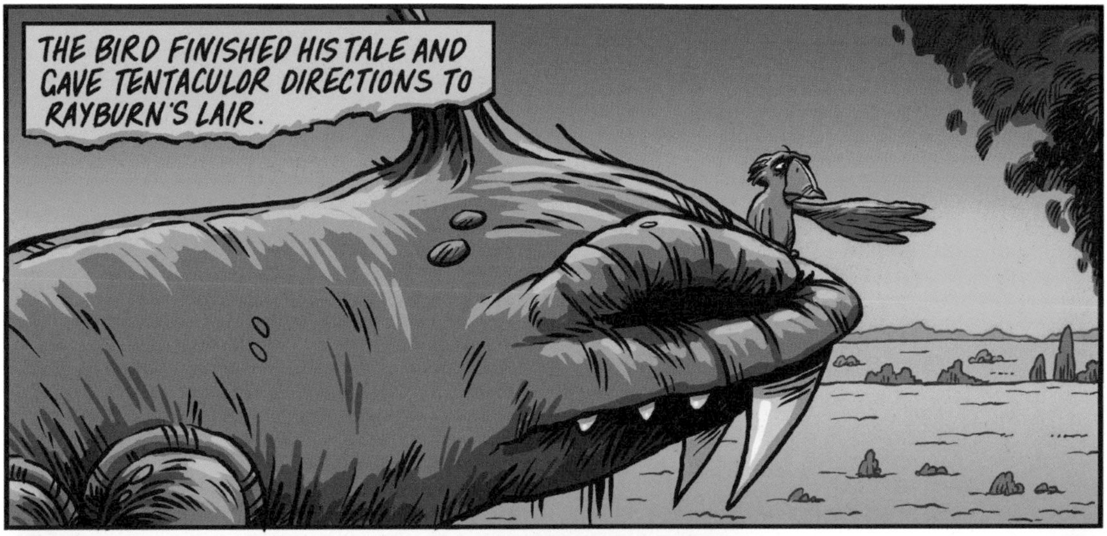
THE BIRD FINISHED HIS TALE AND GAVE TENTACULOR DIRECTIONS TO RAYBURN'S LAIR.

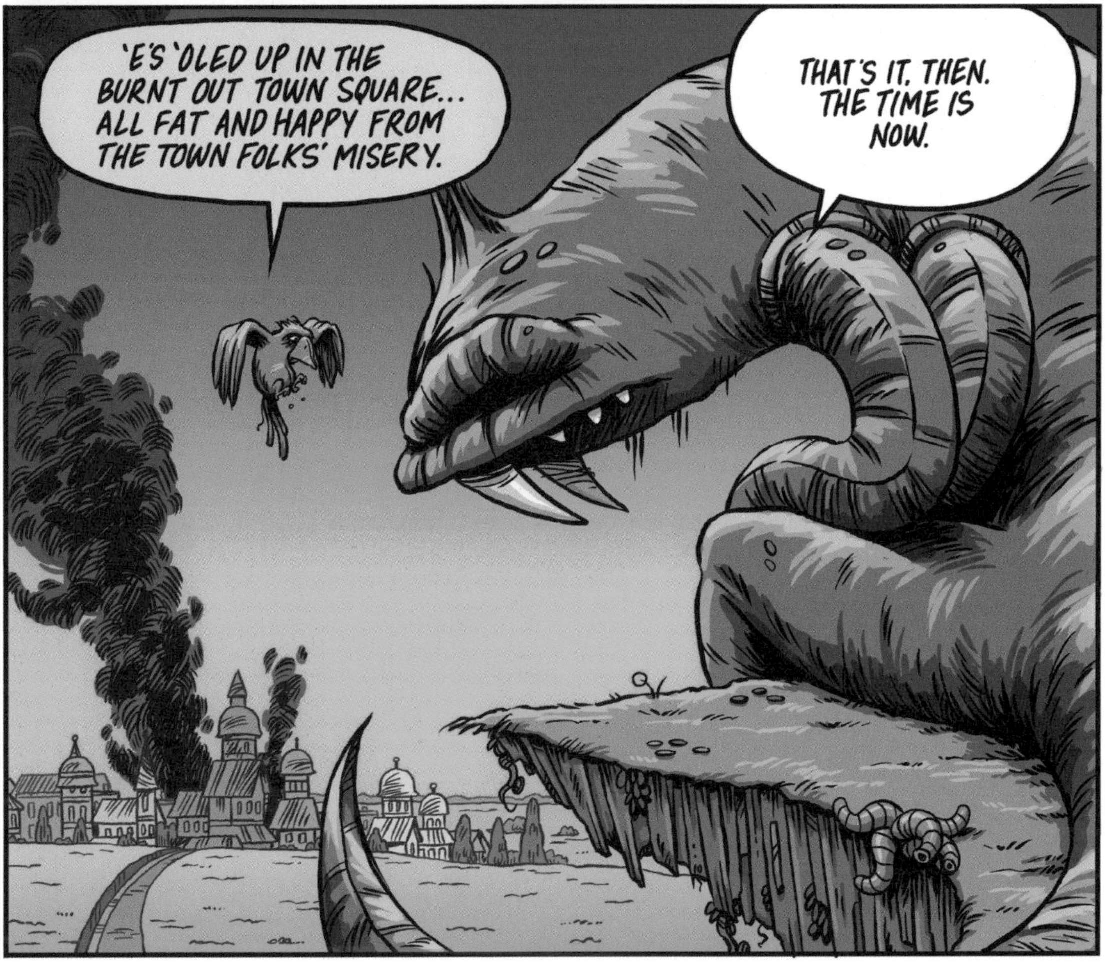
'E'S 'OLED UP IN THE BURNT OUT TOWN SQUARE... ALL FAT AND HAPPY FROM THE TOWN FOLKS' MISERY.
THAT'S IT, THEN. THE TIME IS NOW.

AND WITH THAT, TENTACULOR REARED UP AND LET OUT THE LOUDEST BATTLE CRY OF HIS LIFE.

A ROAR THAT SHOOK STOKER-ON-AVON TO ITS CORE...

...BEFORE RACING DOWN THE HILL TO FACE THE BEAST KNOWN ONLY AS 'THE MURK.'

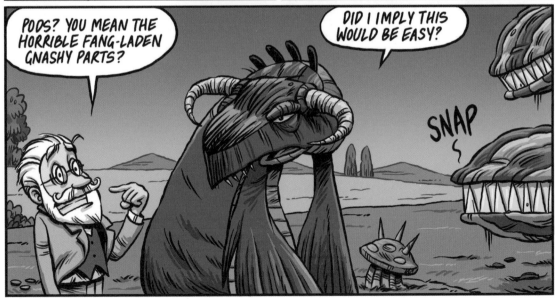

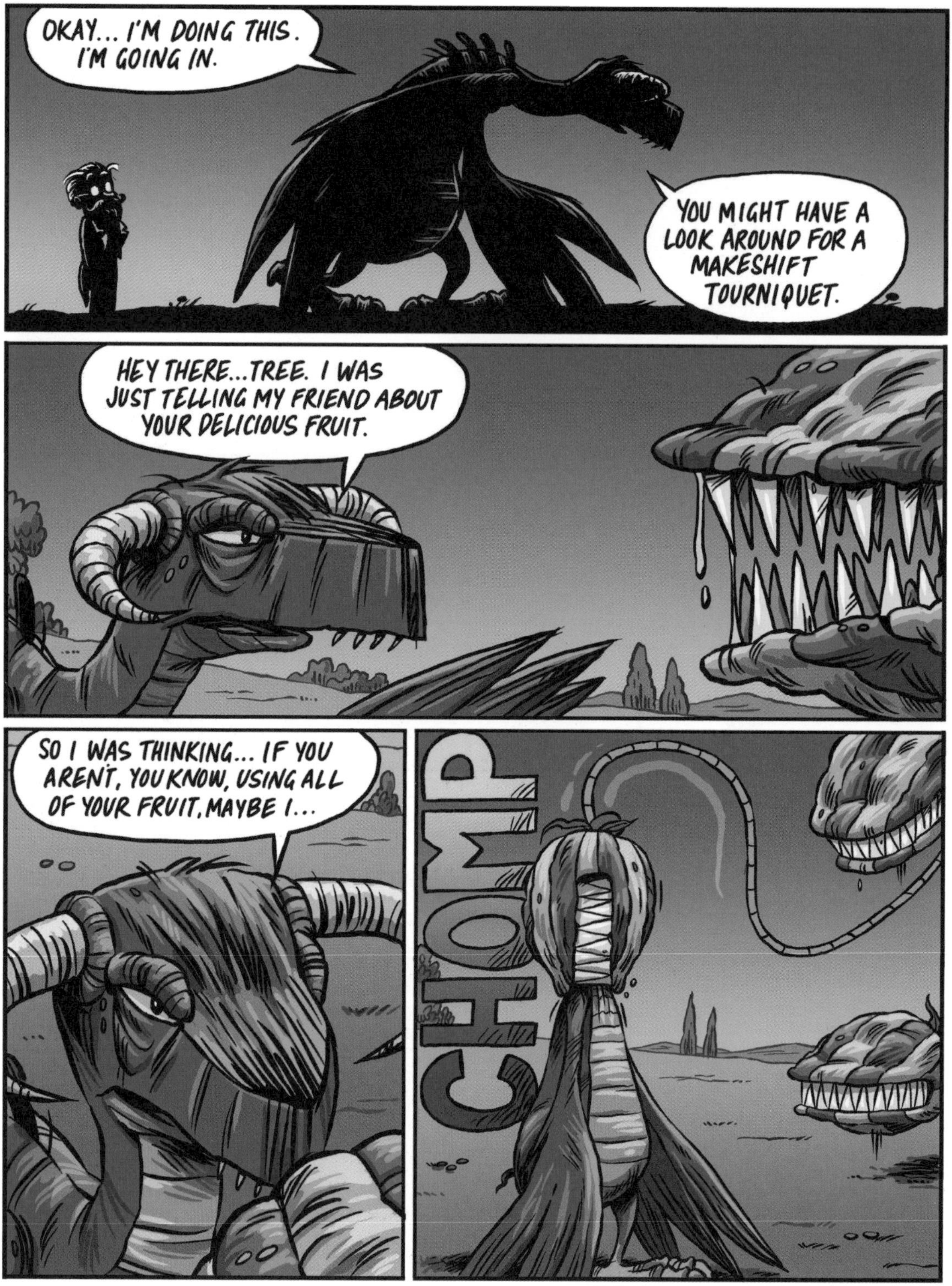
OKAY... I'M DOING THIS. I'M GOING IN.
YOU MIGHT HAVE A LOOK AROUND FOR A MAKESHIFT TOURNIQUET.
HEY THERE...TREE. I WAS JUST TELLING MY FRIEND ABOUT YOUR DELICIOUS FRUIT.
SO I WAS THINKING... IF YOU AREN'T, YOU KNOW, USING ALL OF YOUR FRUIT, MAYBE I...
CHOMP

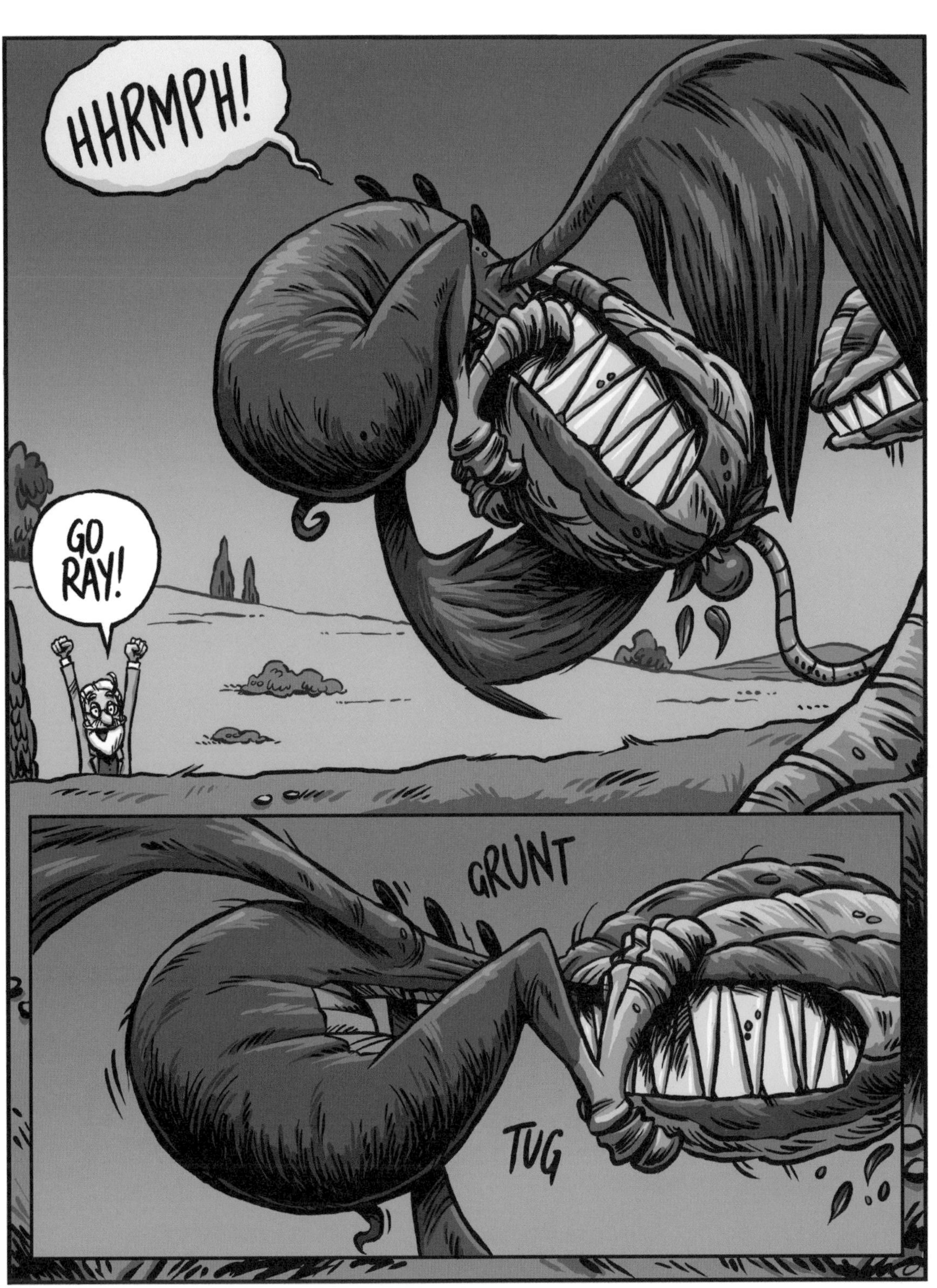
HHRMPH!
GO RAY!
GRUNT
TUG

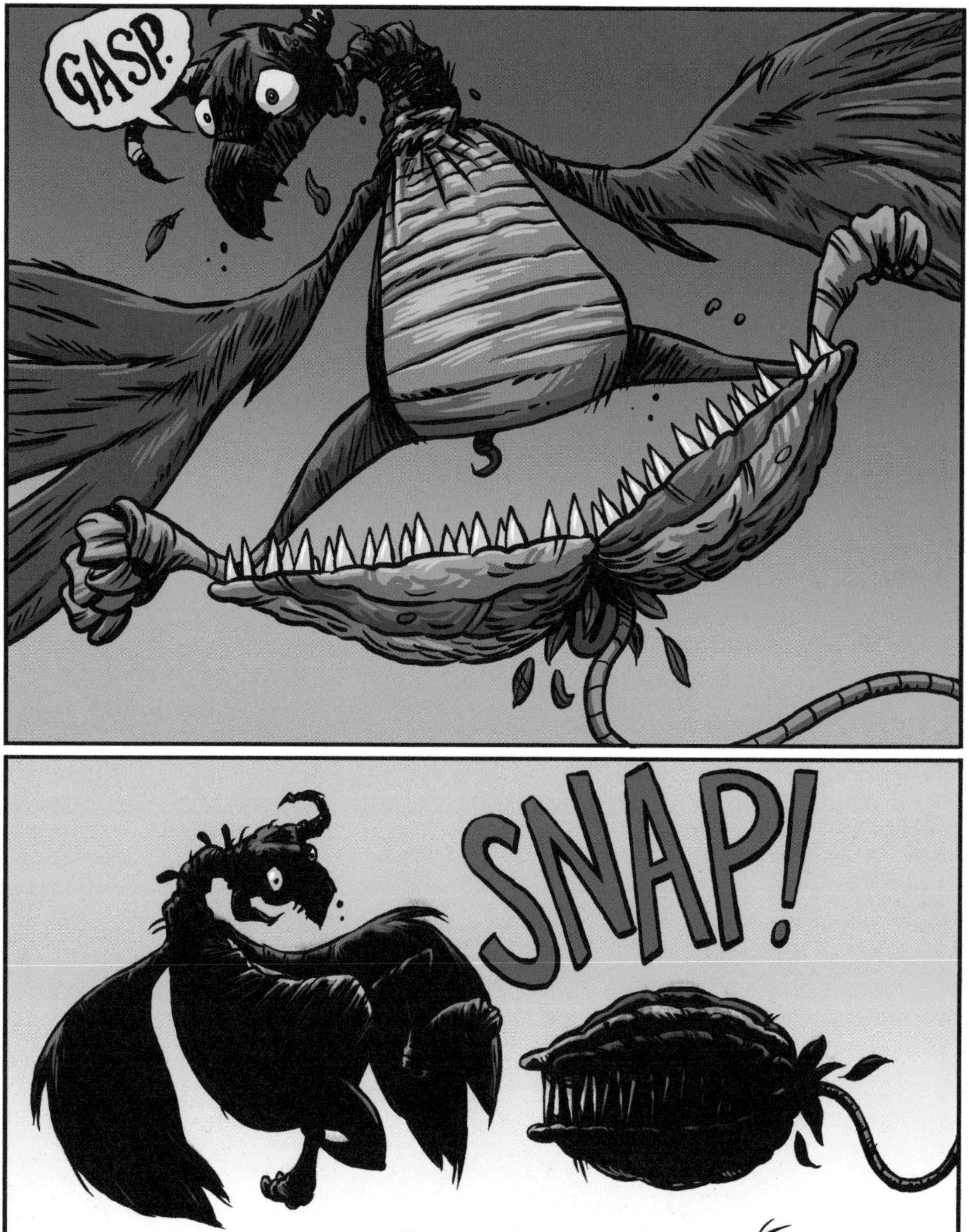
GASP.
SNAP!

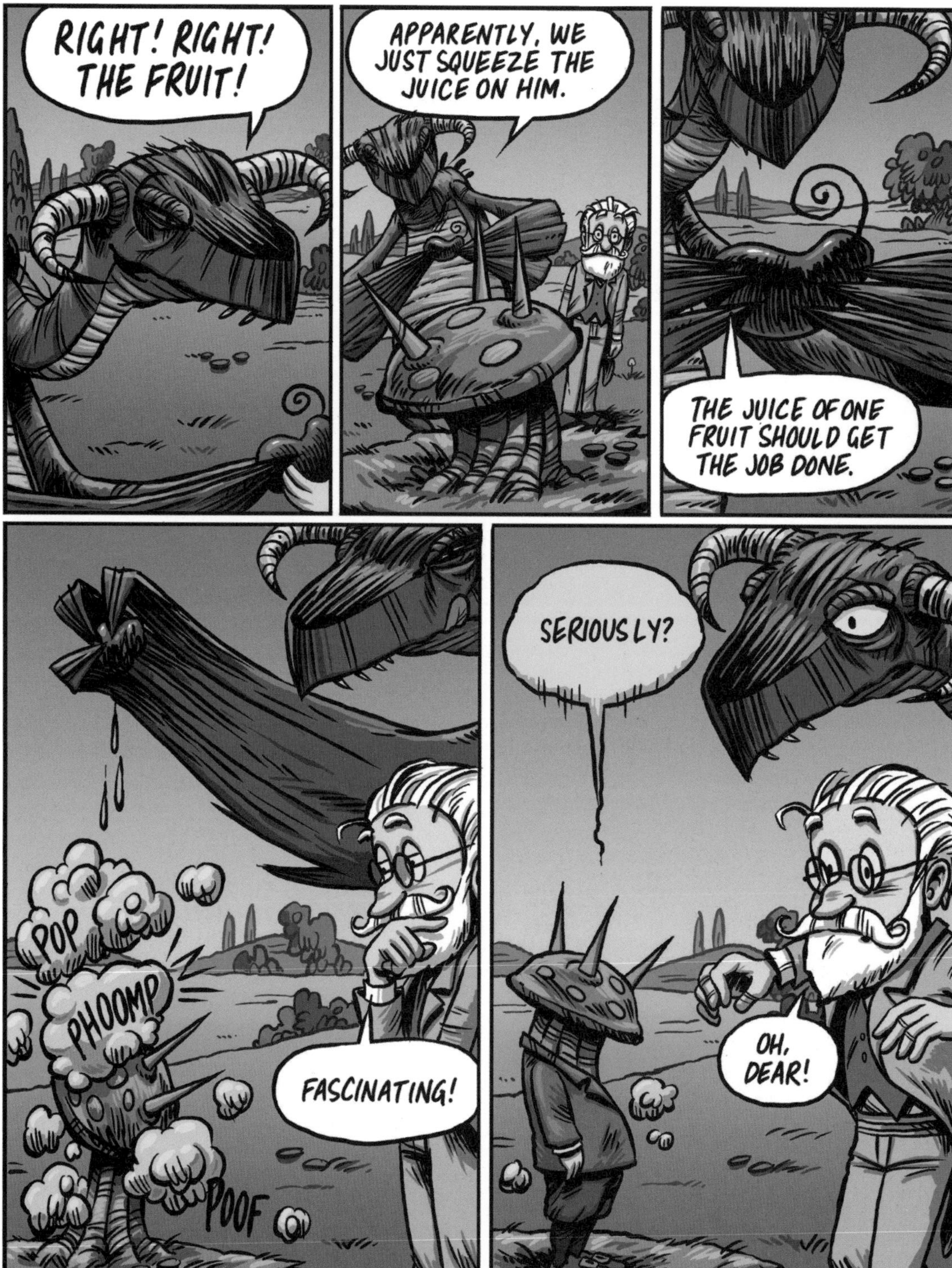
RIGHT! RIGHT! THE FRUIT!
APPARENTLY, WE JUST SQUEEZE THE JUICE ON HIM.
THE JUICE OF ONE FRUIT SHOULD GET THE JOB DONE.
POP
PHOOMP
POOF
FASCINATING!
SERIOUSLY?
OH, DEAR!

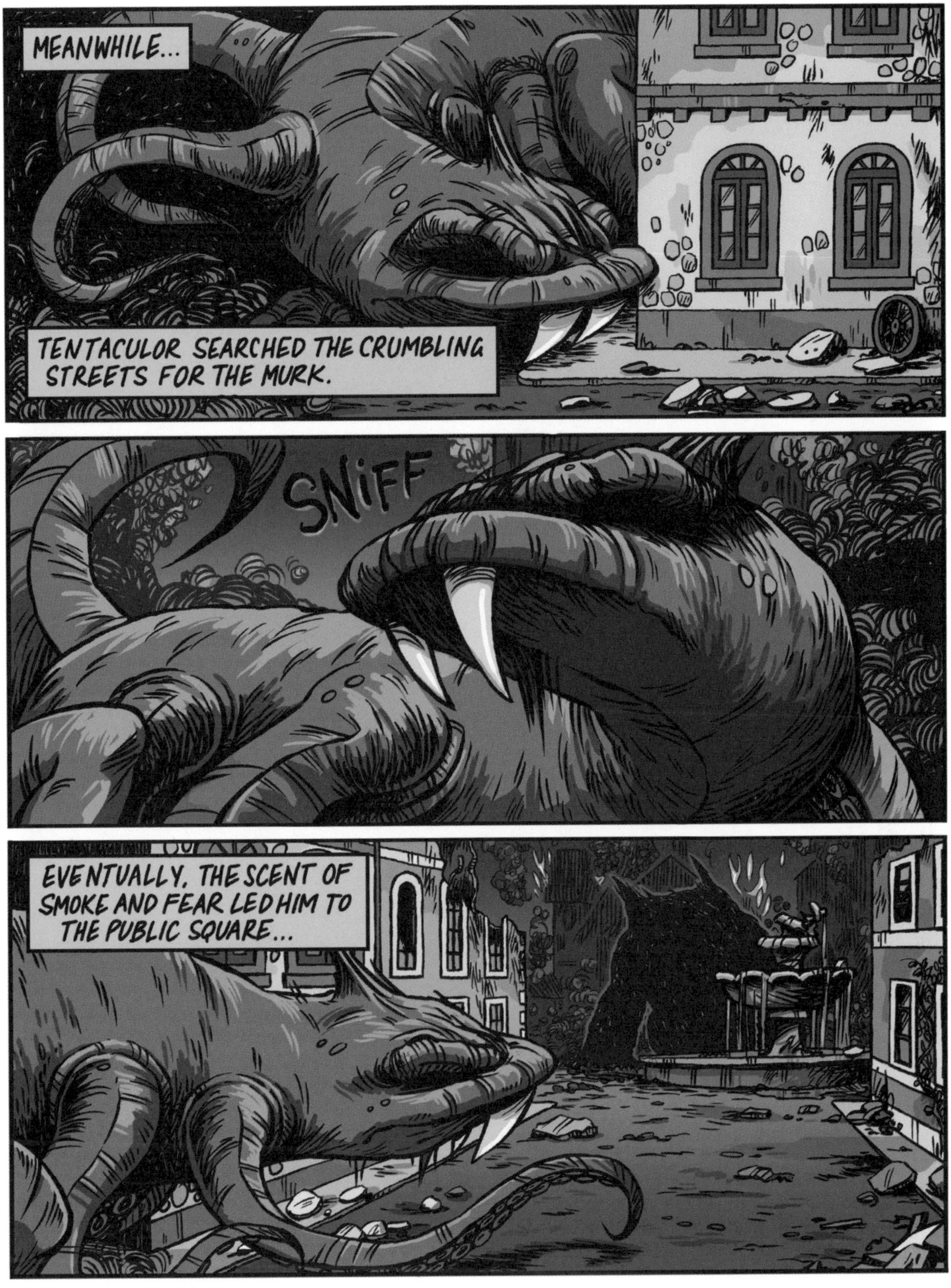
MEANWHILE...
TENTACULOR SEARCHED THE CRUMBLING STREETS FOR THE MURK.
SNIFF
EVENTUALLY, THE SCENT OF SMOKE AND FEAR LED HIM TO THE PUBLIC SQUARE...

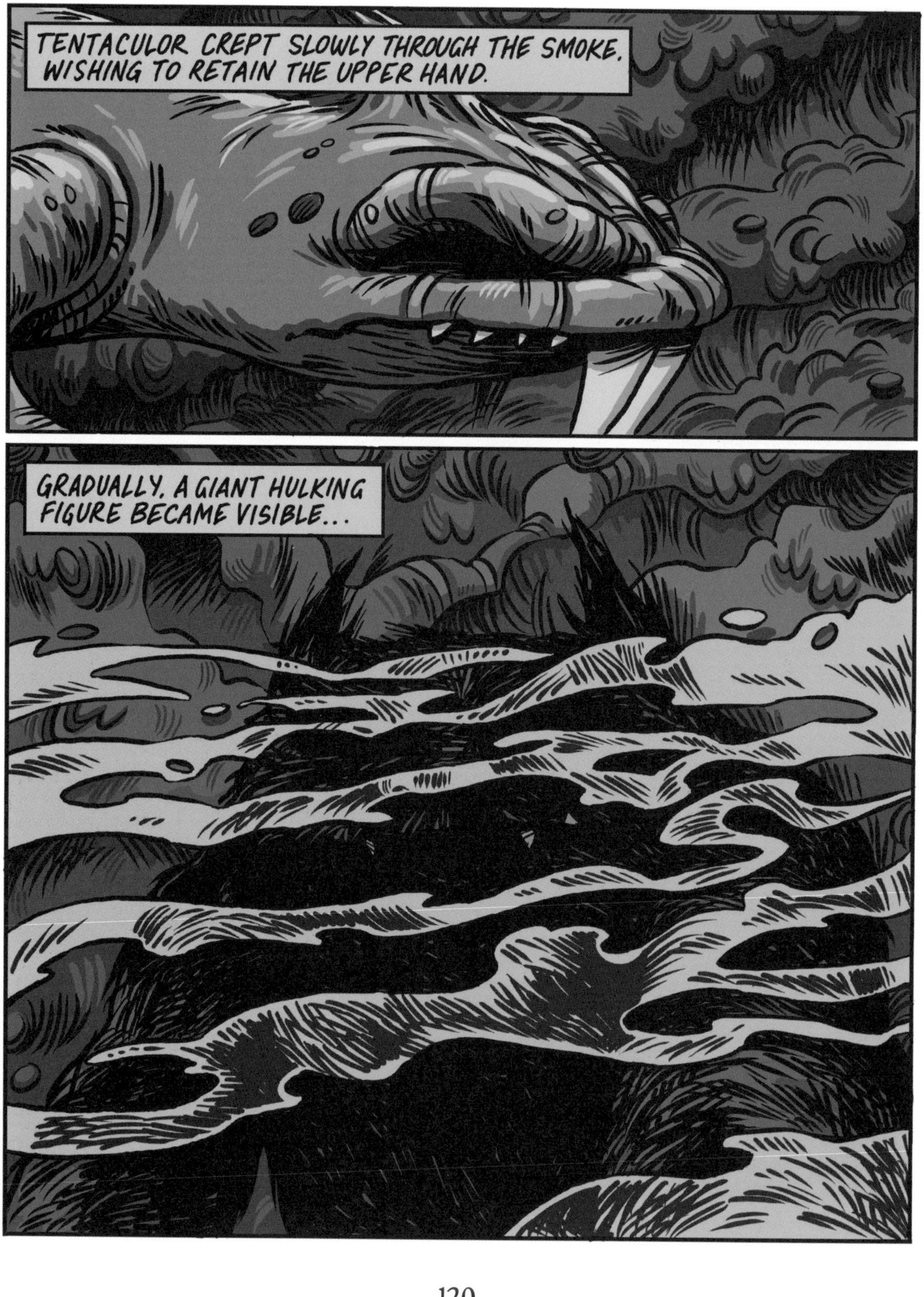
TENTACULOR CREPT SLOWLY THROUGH THE SMOKE, WISHING TO RETAIN THE UPPER HAND.
GRADUALLY, A GIANT HULKING FIGURE BECAME VISIBLE...

123

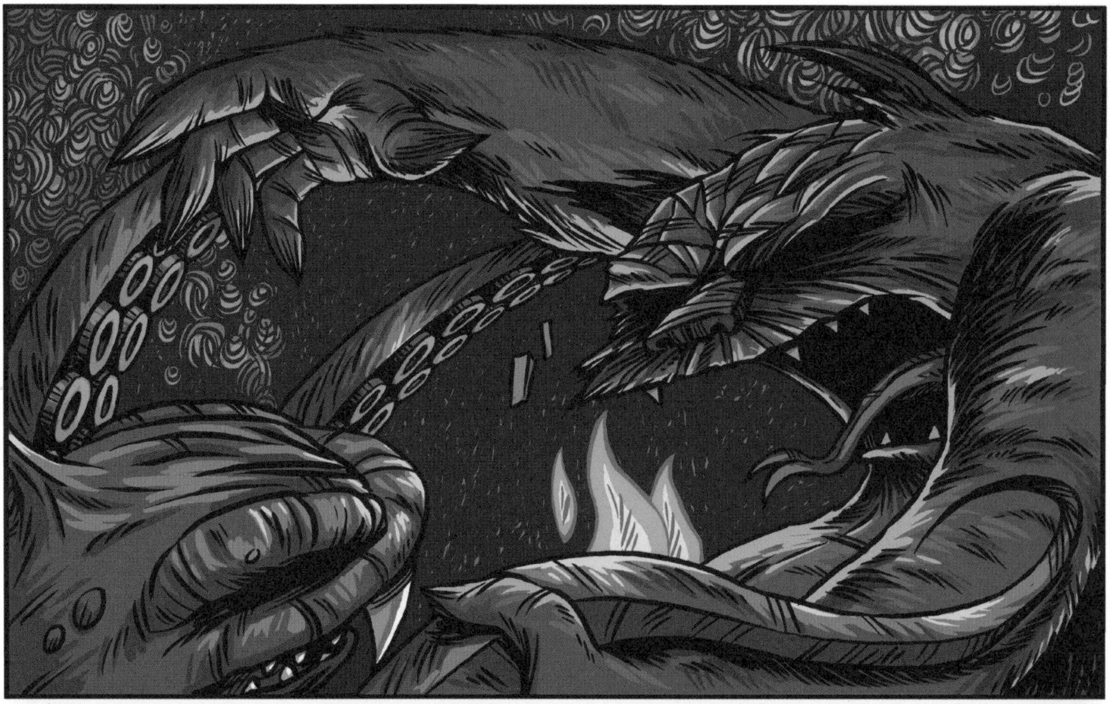

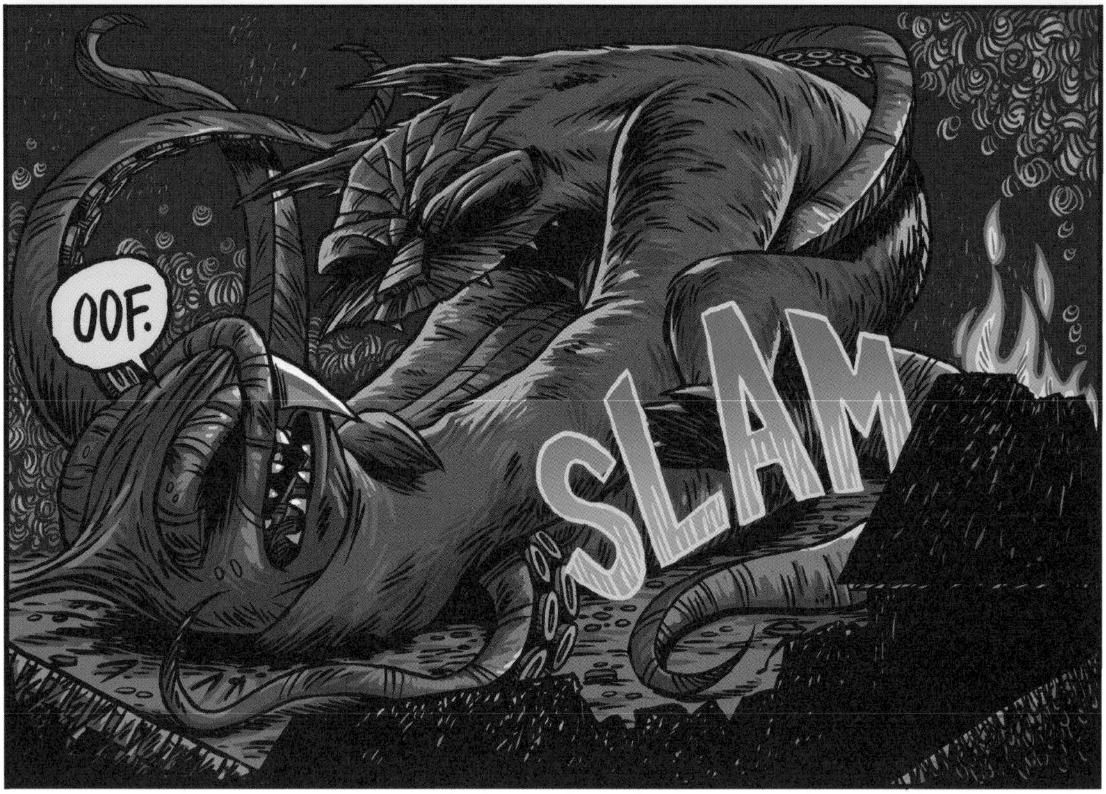
OOF.
SLAM

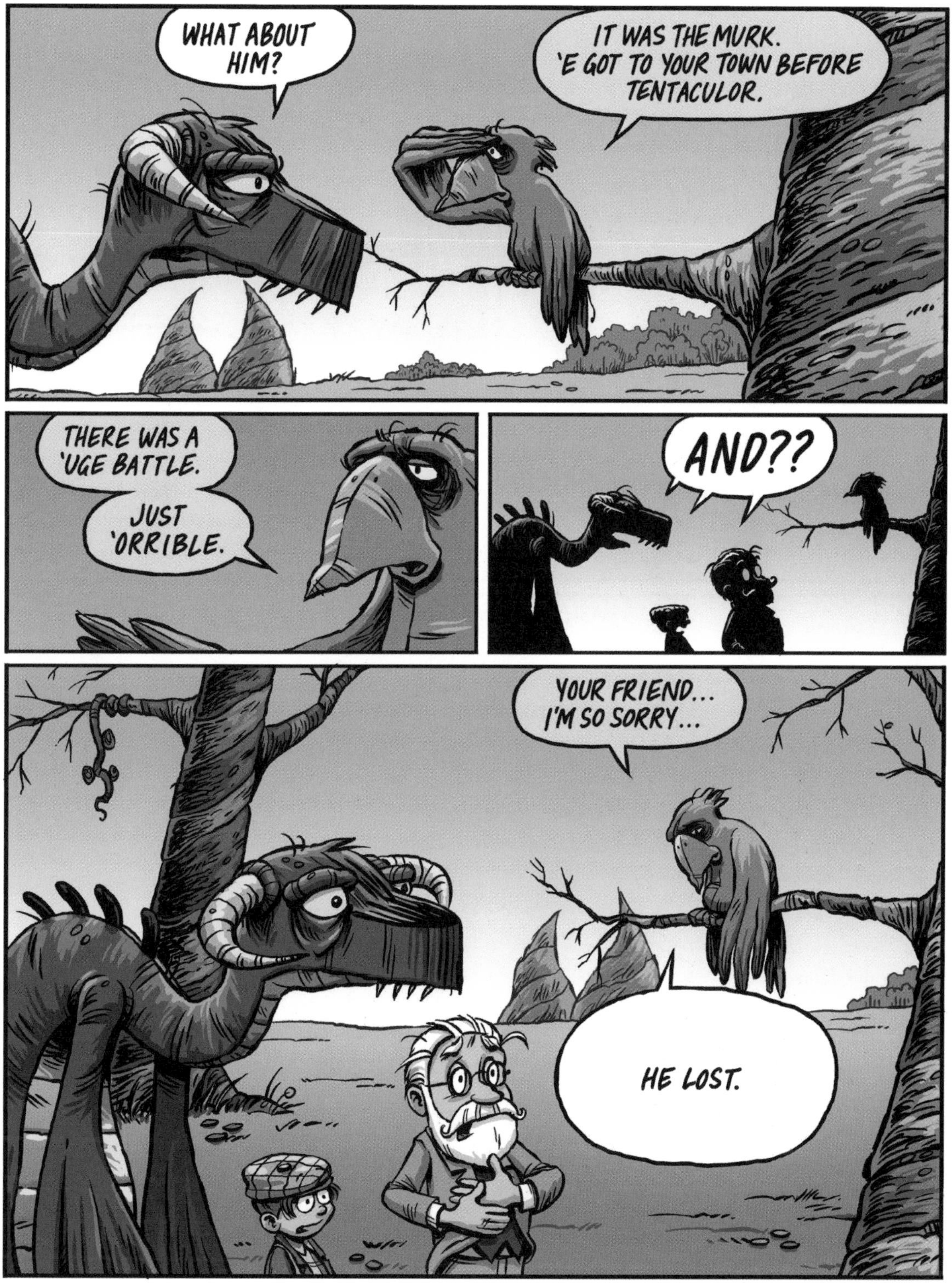
WHAT ABOUT HIM?
IT WAS THE MURK. 'E GOT TO YOUR TOWN BEFORE TENTACULOR.
THERE WAS A 'UGE BATTLE.
JUST 'ORRIBLE.
AND??
YOUR FRIEND... I'M SO SORRY...
HE LOST.

137

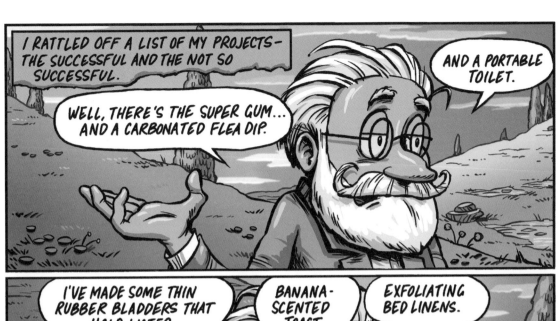

I RATTLED OFF A LIST OF MY PROJECTS—THE SUCCESSFUL AND THE NOT SO SUCCESSFUL.

WELL, THERE'S THE SUPER GUM... AND A CARBONATED FLEA DIP.

AND A PORTABLE TOILET.

I'VE MADE SOME THIN RUBBER BLADDERS THAT HOLD WATER...

BANANA-SCENTED TOAST...

EXFOLIATING BED LINENS.

THERE'S A PROPELLED HOT AIR FLYING THINGY.

PERMANENT CHALK.

AN EDIBLE MEGAPHONE.

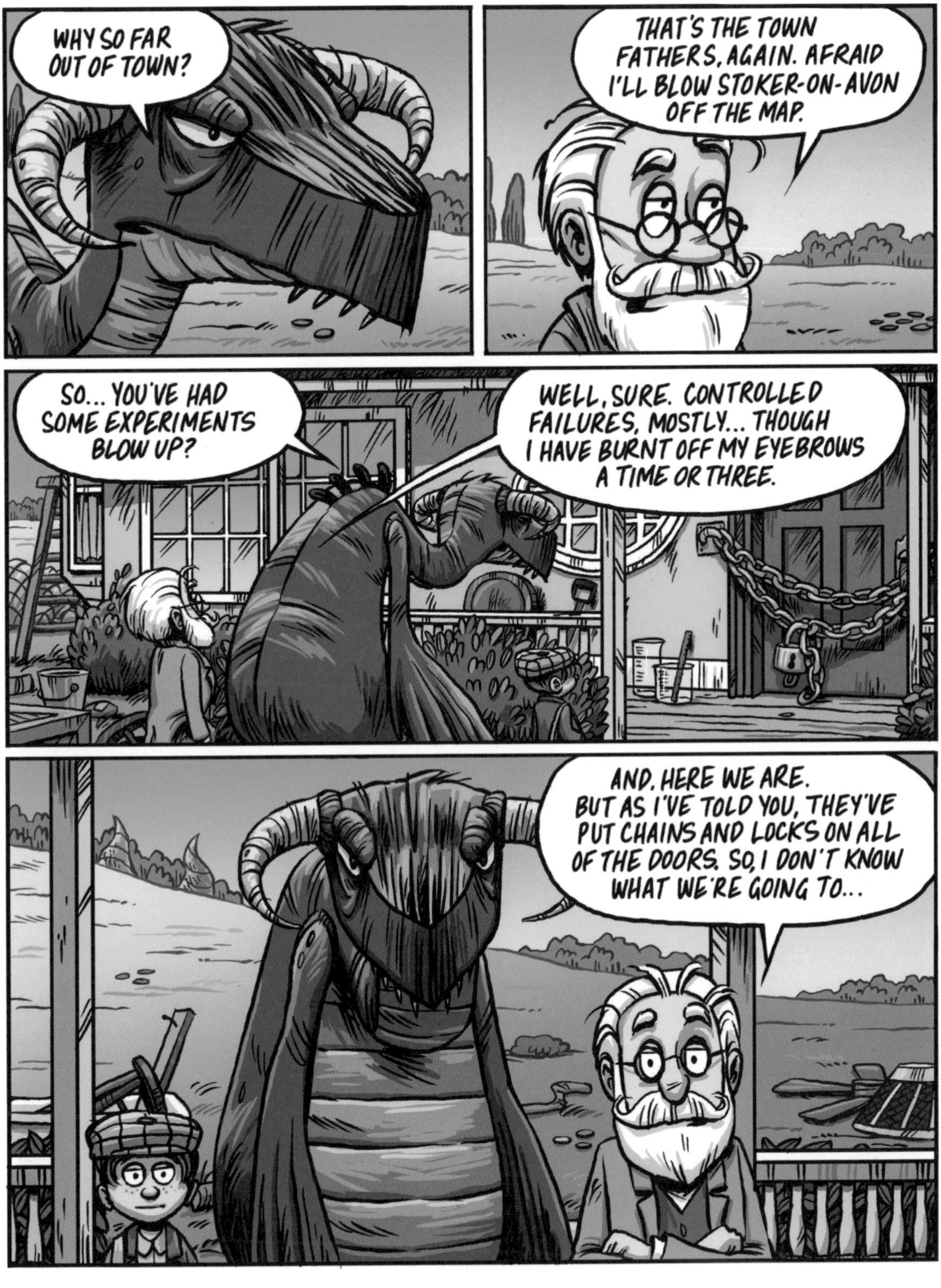
WHY SO FAR OUT OF TOWN?
THAT'S THE TOWN FATHERS, AGAIN. AFRAID I'LL BLOW STOKER-ON-AVON OFF THE MAP.
SO... YOU'VE HAD SOME EXPERIMENTS BLOW UP?
WELL, SURE. CONTROLLED FAILURES, MOSTLY... THOUGH I HAVE BURNT OFF MY EYEBROWS A TIME OR THREE.
AND, HERE WE ARE. BUT AS I'VE TOLD YOU, THEY'VE PUT CHAINS AND LOCKS ON ALL OF THE DOORS. SO, I DON'T KNOW WHAT WE'RE GOING TO...

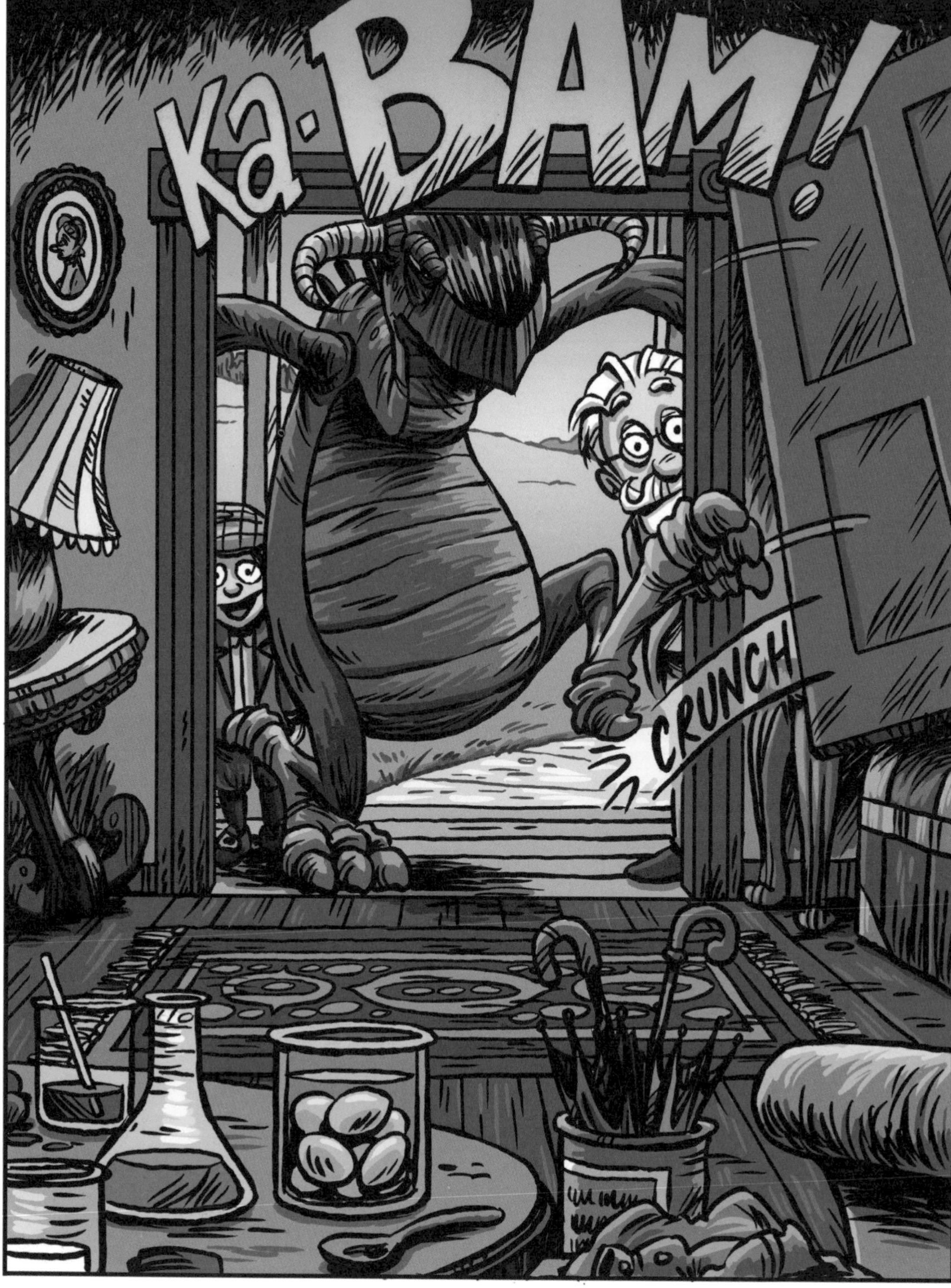
KA-BAM!
CRUNCH

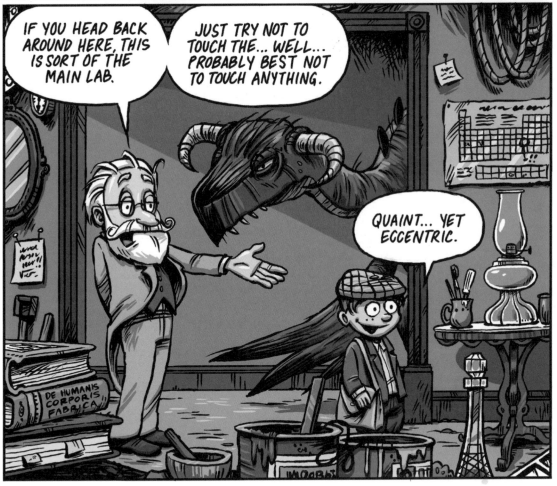

145

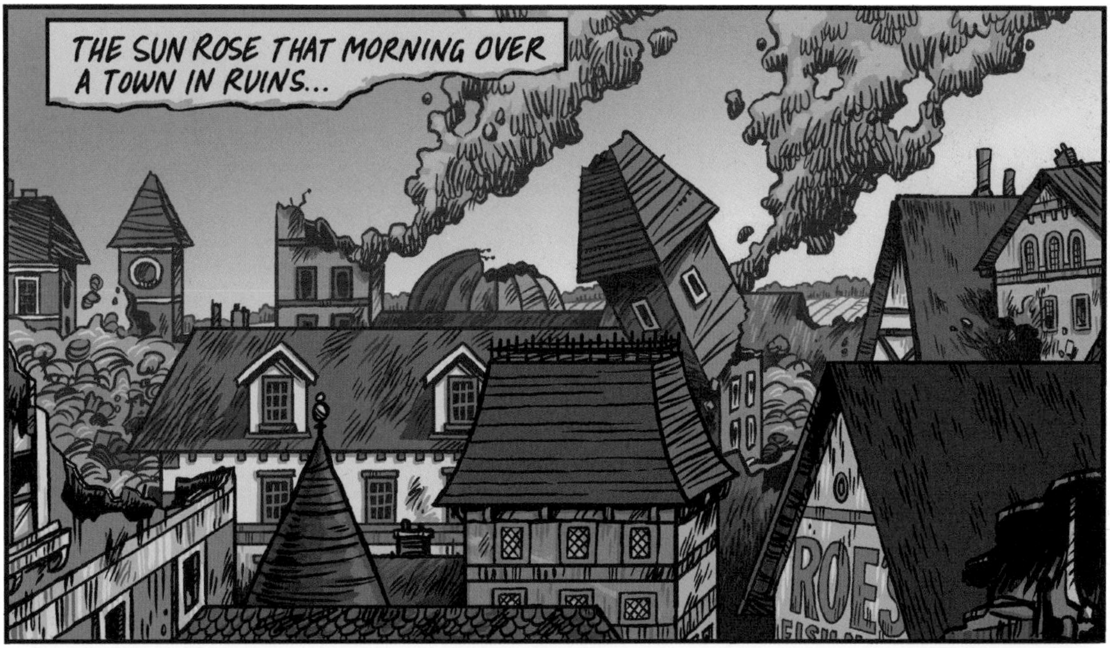
THE SUN ROSE THAT MORNING OVER A TOWN IN RUINS...
ROES

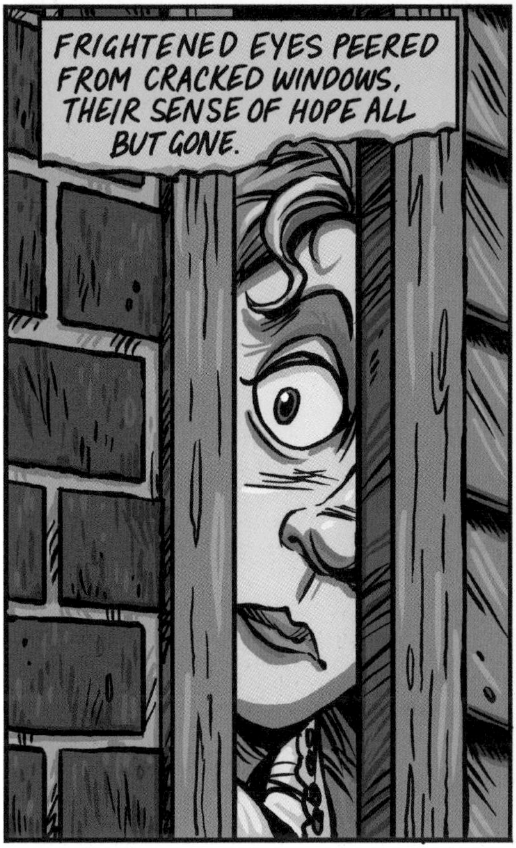
FRIGHTENED EYES PEERED FROM CRACKED WINDOWS, THEIR SENSE OF HOPE ALL BUT GONE.

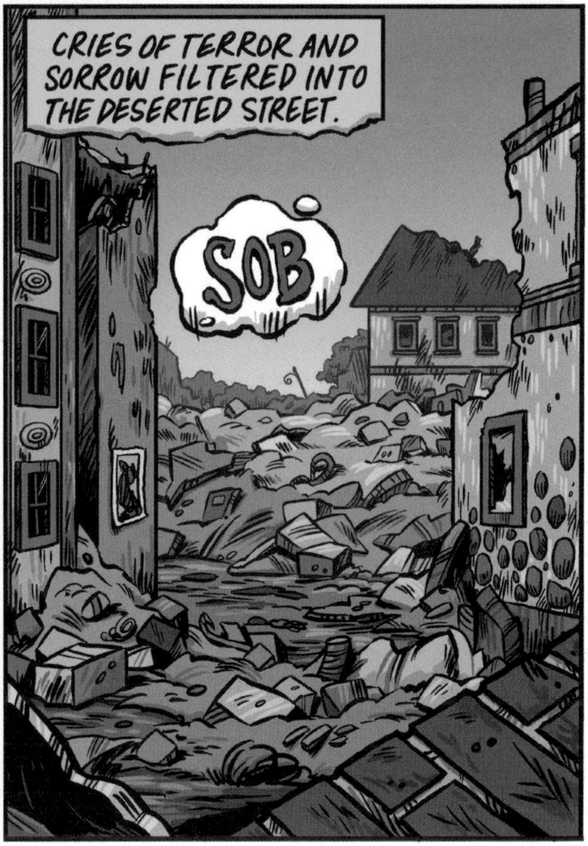
CRIES OF TERROR AND SORROW FILTERED INTO THE DESERTED STREET.
SOB

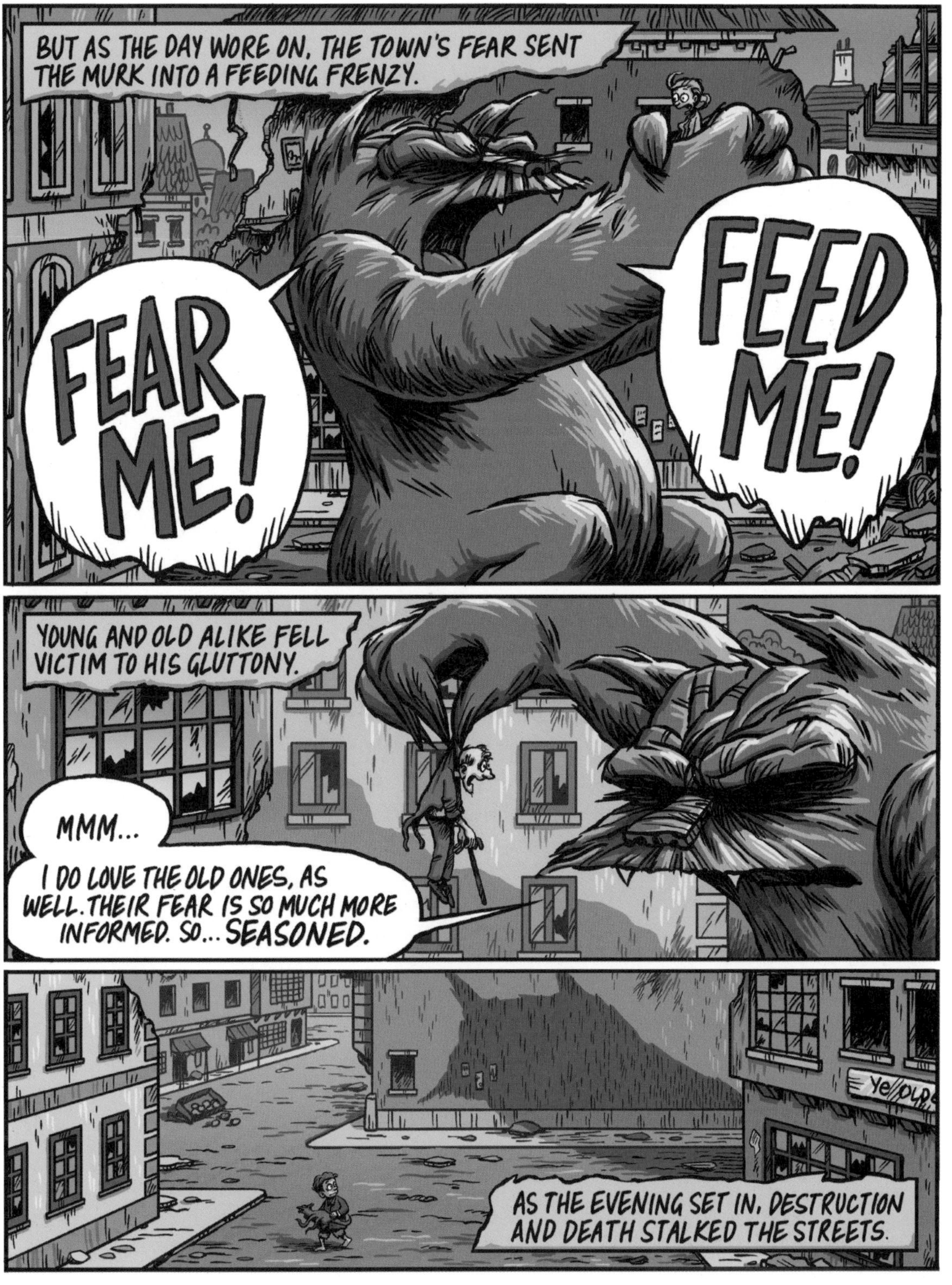
BUT AS THE DAY WORE ON, THE TOWN'S FEAR SENT THE MURK INTO A FEEDING FRENZY.
FEAR ME!
FEED ME!
YOUNG AND OLD ALIKE FELL VICTIM TO HIS GLUTTONY.
MMM...
I DO LOVE THE OLD ONES, AS WELL. THEIR FEAR IS SO MUCH MORE INFORMED. SO... SEASONED.
AS THE EVENING SET IN, DESTRUCTION AND DEATH STALKED THE STREETS.

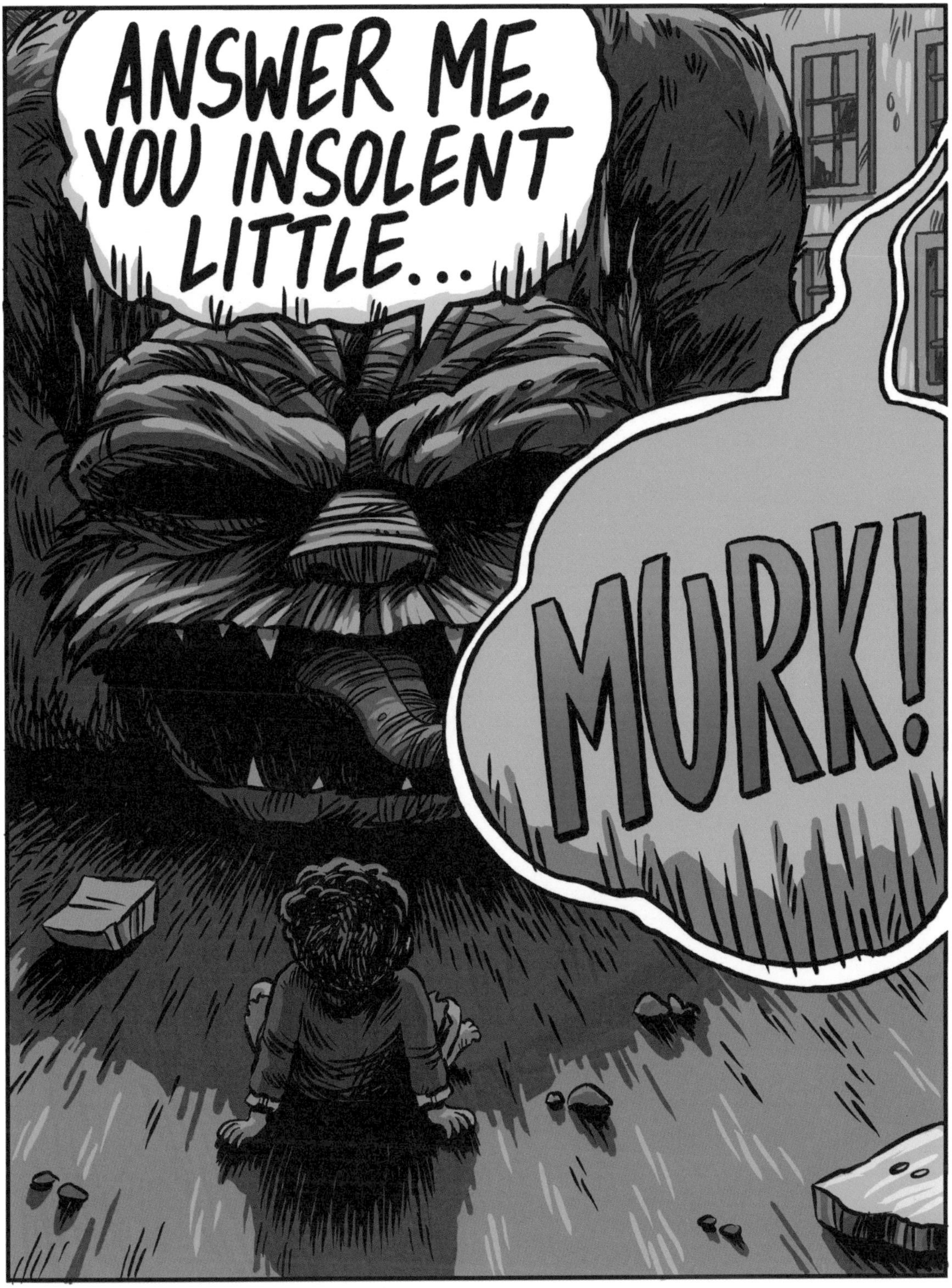
ANSWER ME, YOU INSOLENT LITTLE...
MURK!

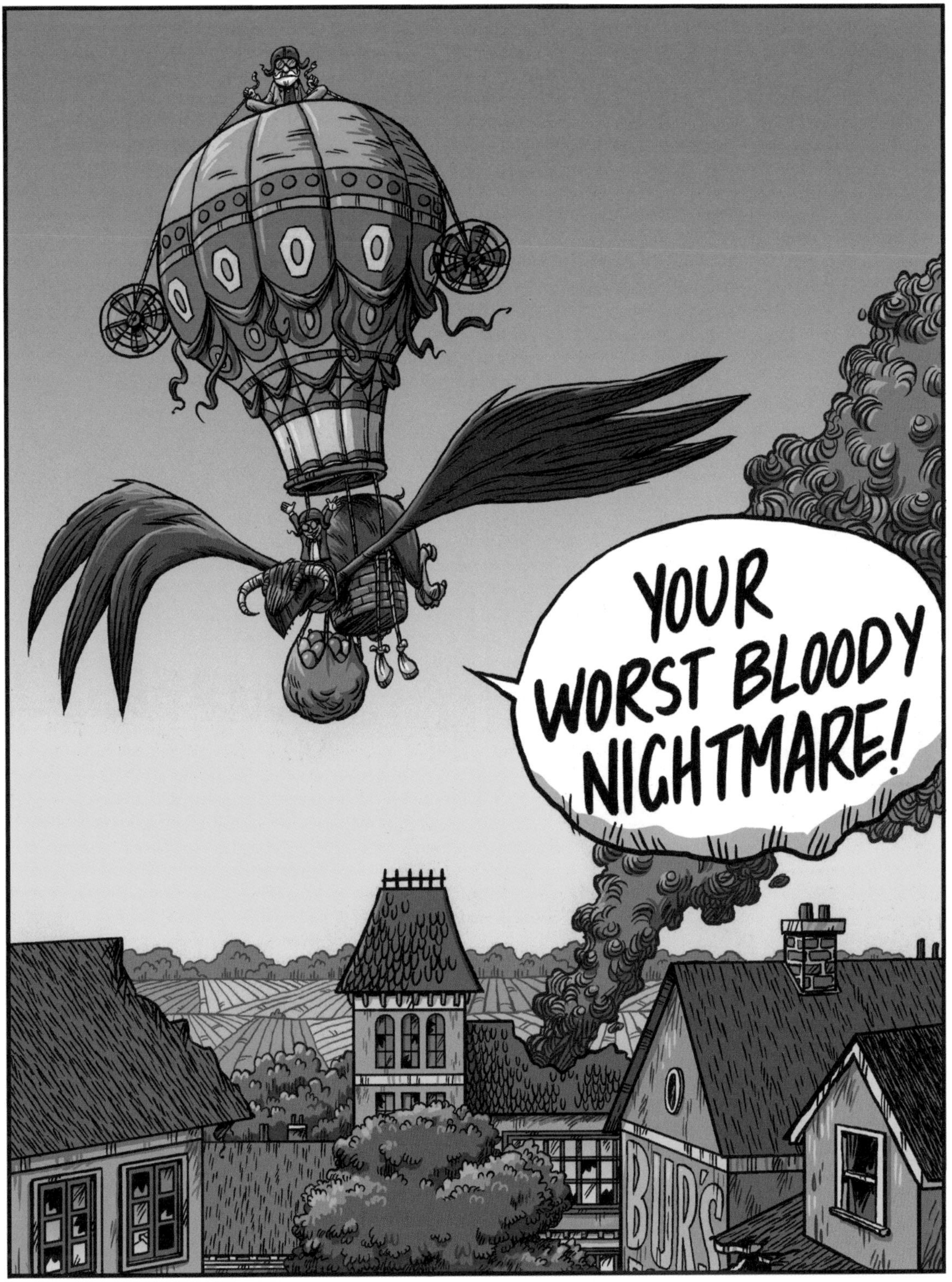
YOUR WORST BLOODY NIGHTMARE!
BUR'S

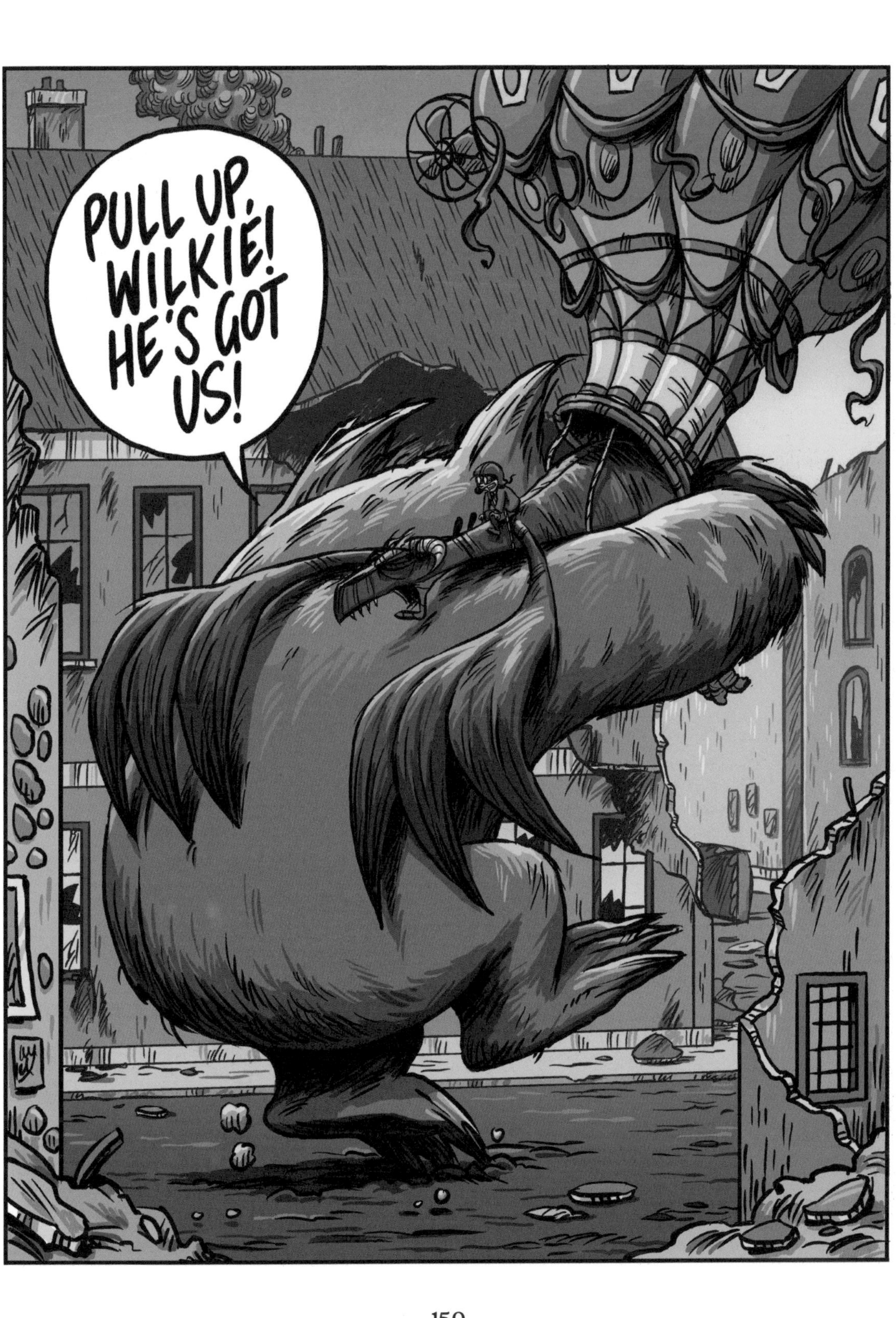
PULL UP, WILKIE! HE'S GOT US!

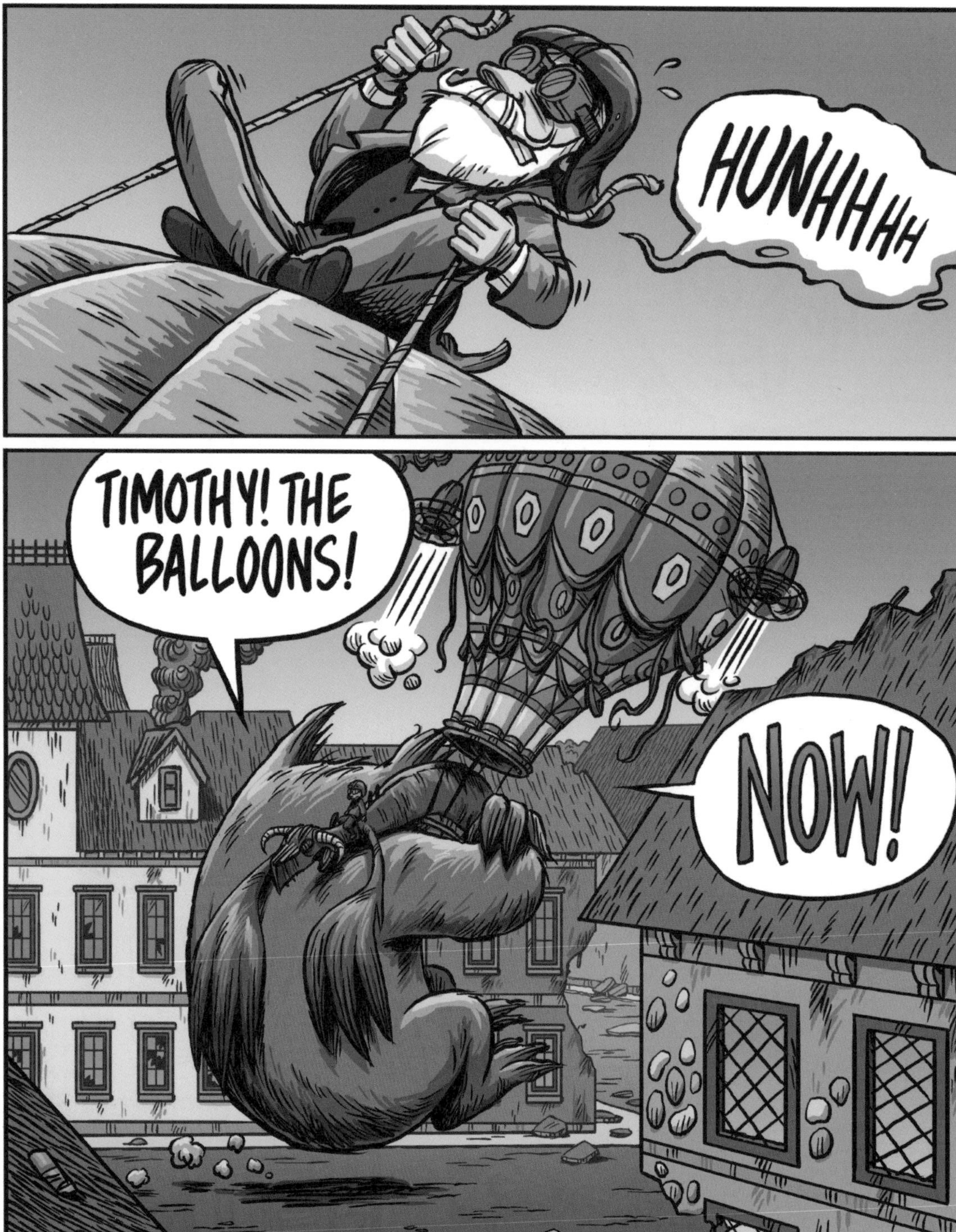
HUNHHHHH
TIMOTHY! THE BALLOONS!
NOW!

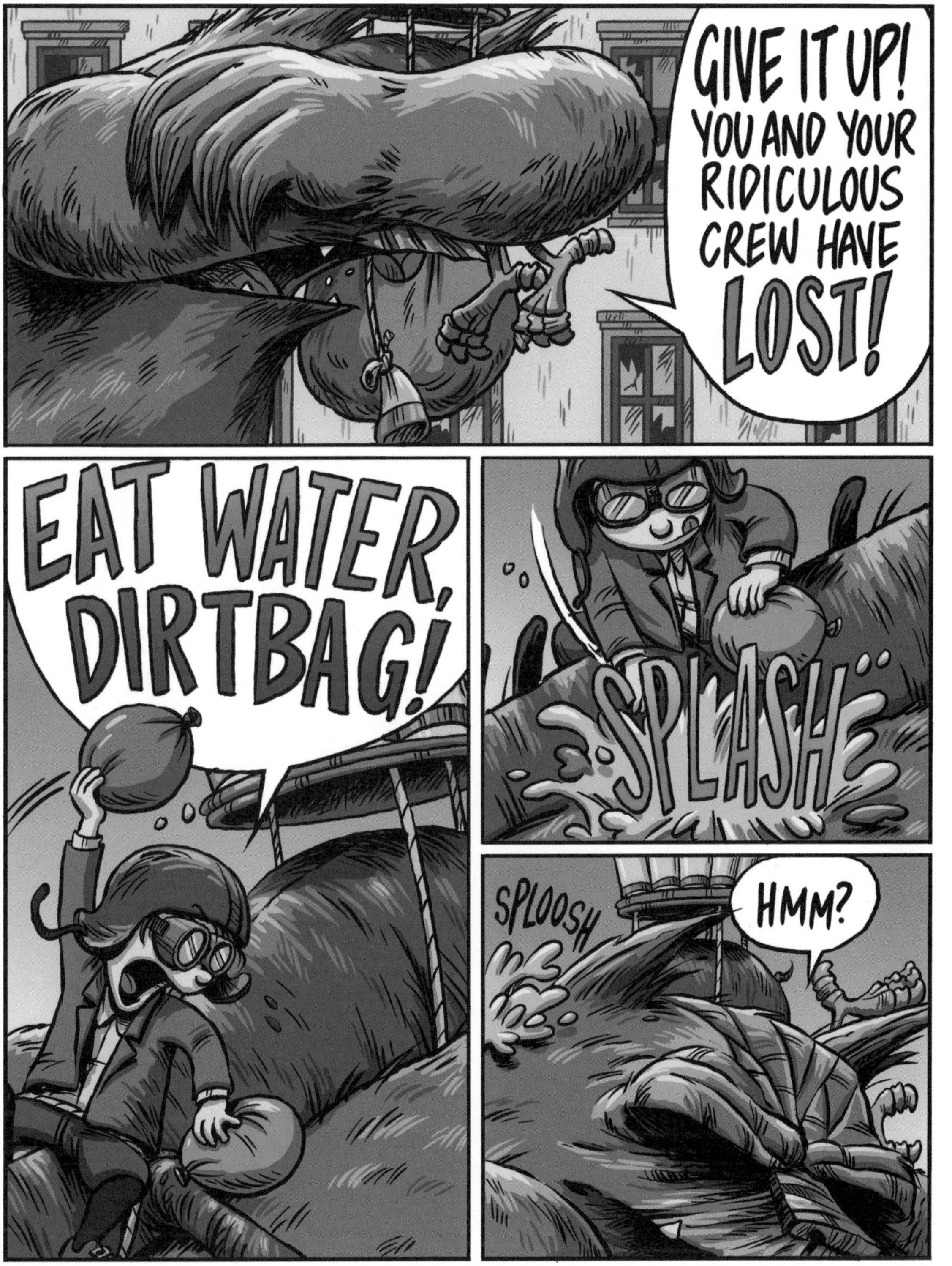
GIVE IT UP! YOU AND YOUR RIDICULOUS CREW HAVE LOST!
EAT WATER, DIRTBAG!
SPLASH
SPLOOSH
HMM?

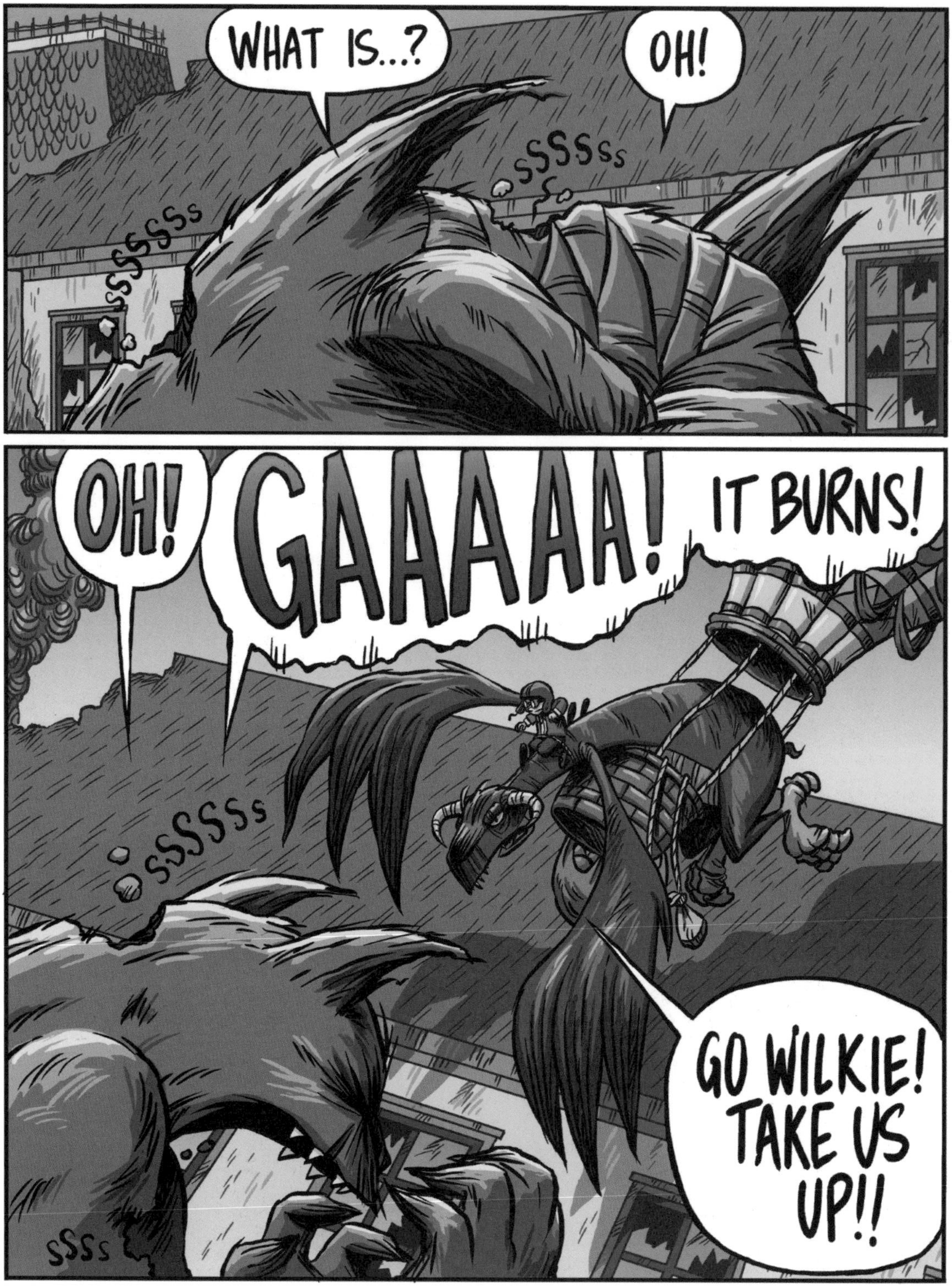
WHAT IS...?
OH!
SSSSSs
SSSSSSs
OH!
GAAAAA!
IT BURNS!
SSSSSSs
GO WILKIE! TAKE US UP!!
SSSs

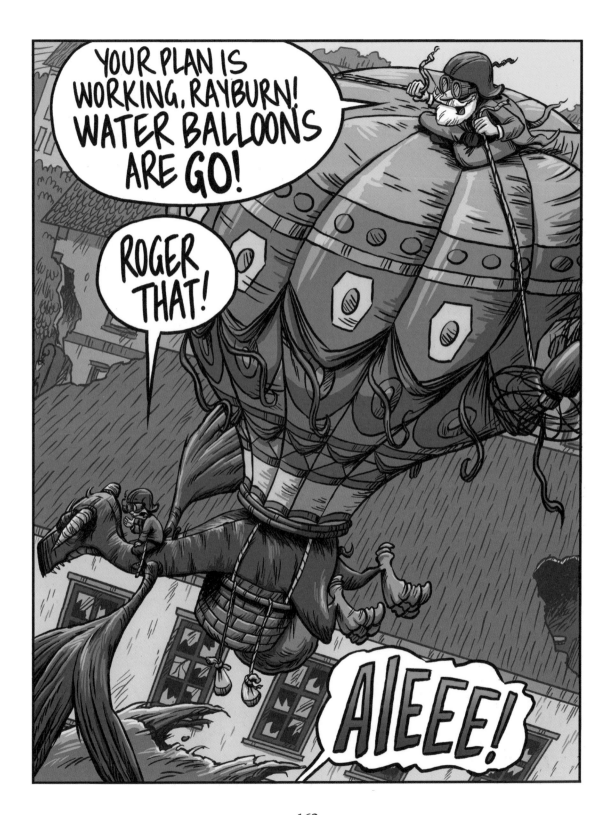

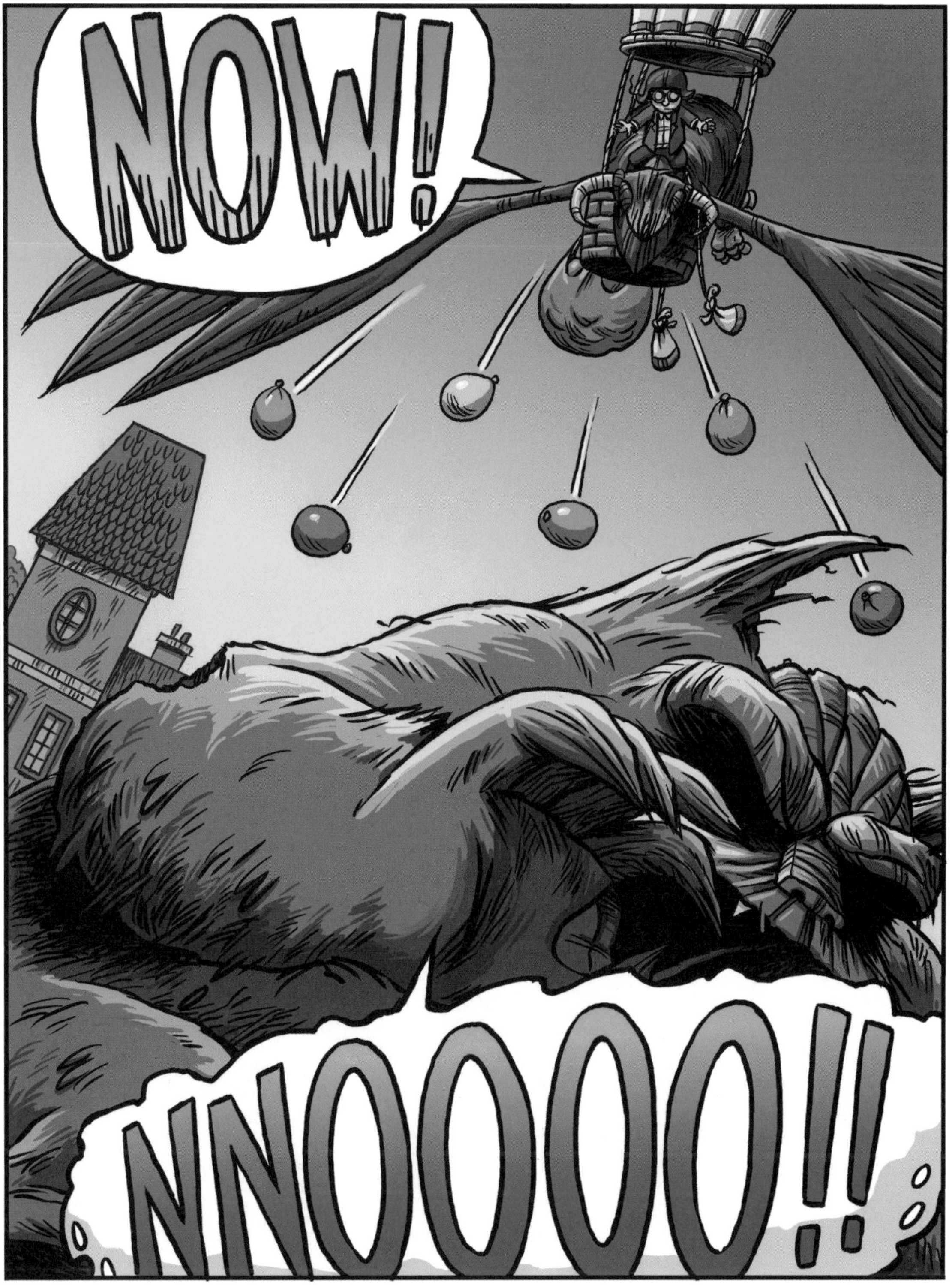
NOW!
NNOOOO!!

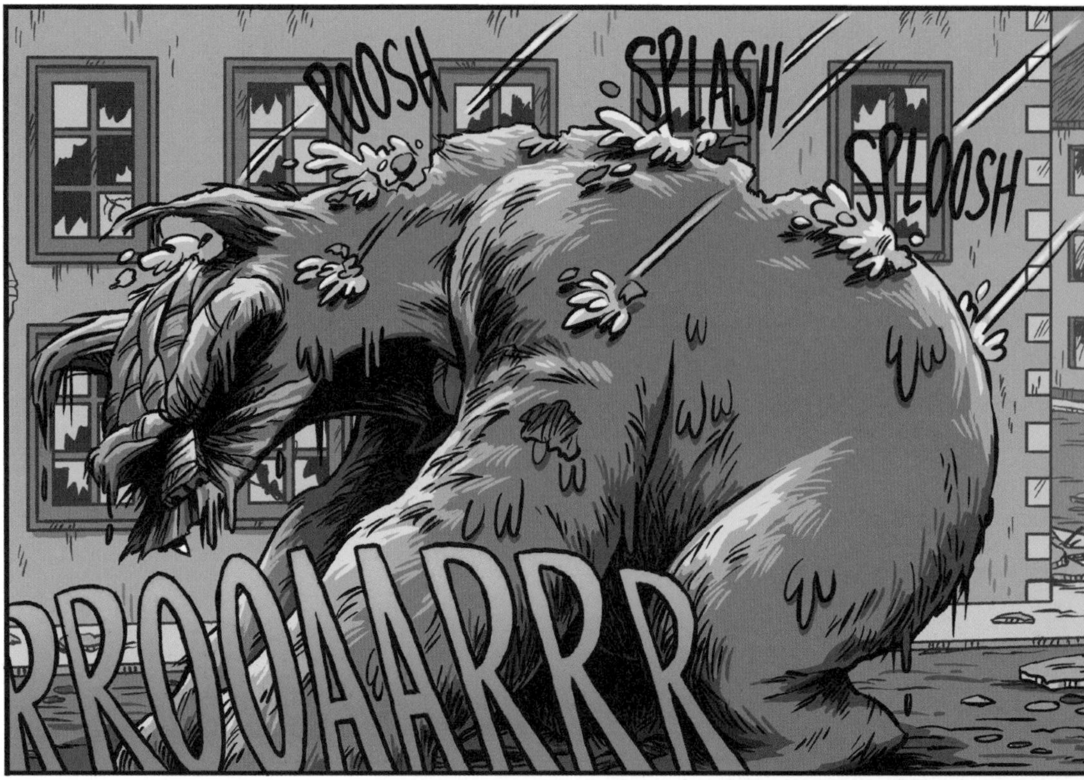
POOSH
SPLASH
SPLOOSH
RROOAARRRR

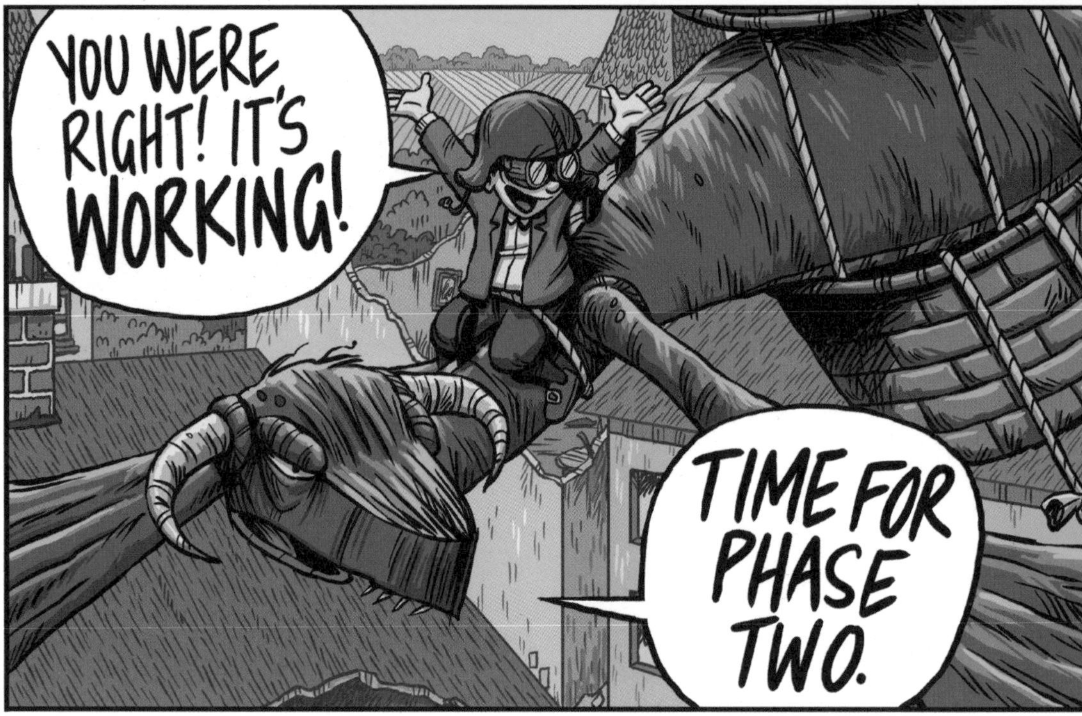
YOU WERE RIGHT! IT'S WORKING!
TIME FOR PHASE TWO.

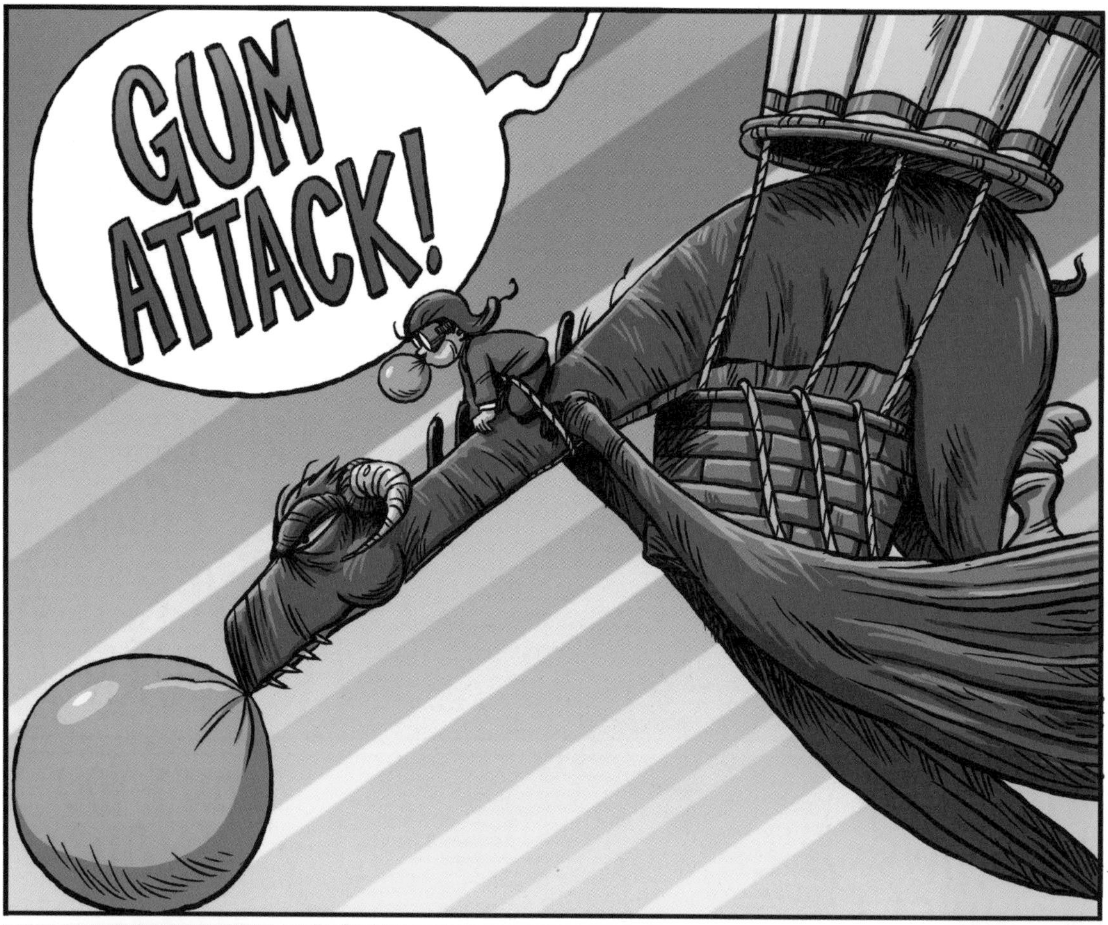
GUM ATTACK!

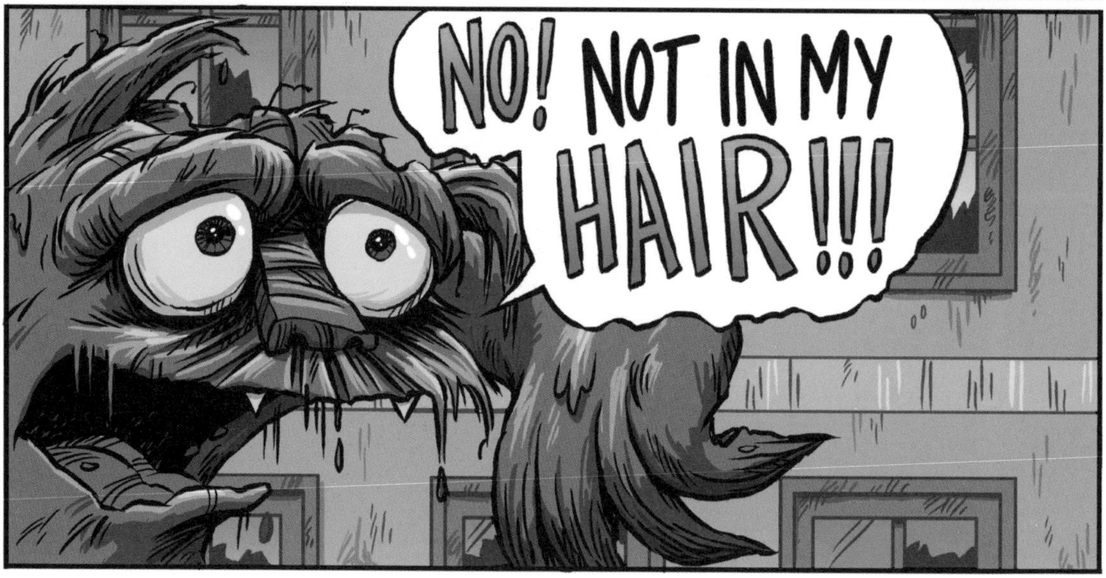
NO! NOT IN MY HAIR!!!

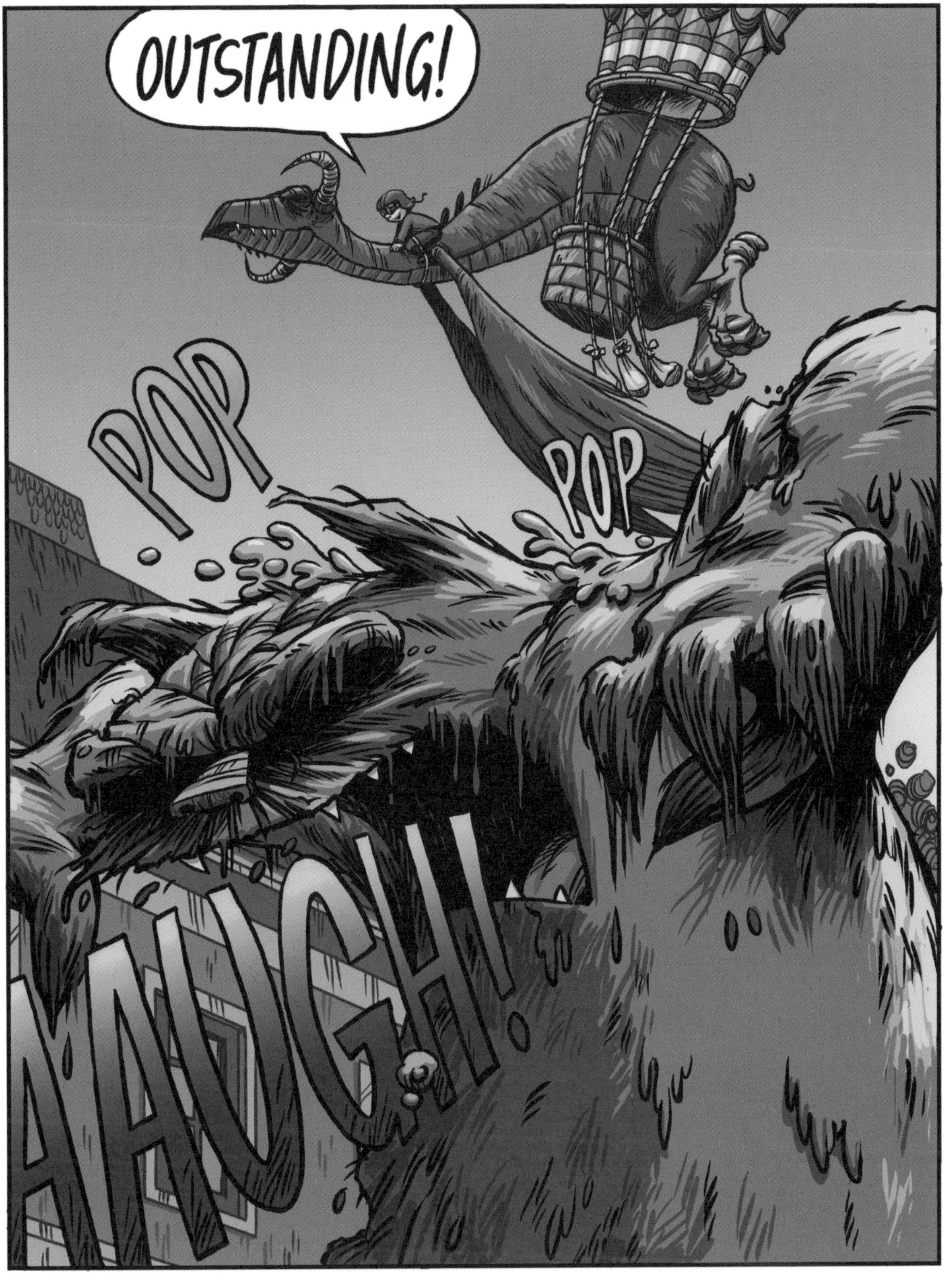
OUTSTANDING!
POP
POP
AAAUGH!!

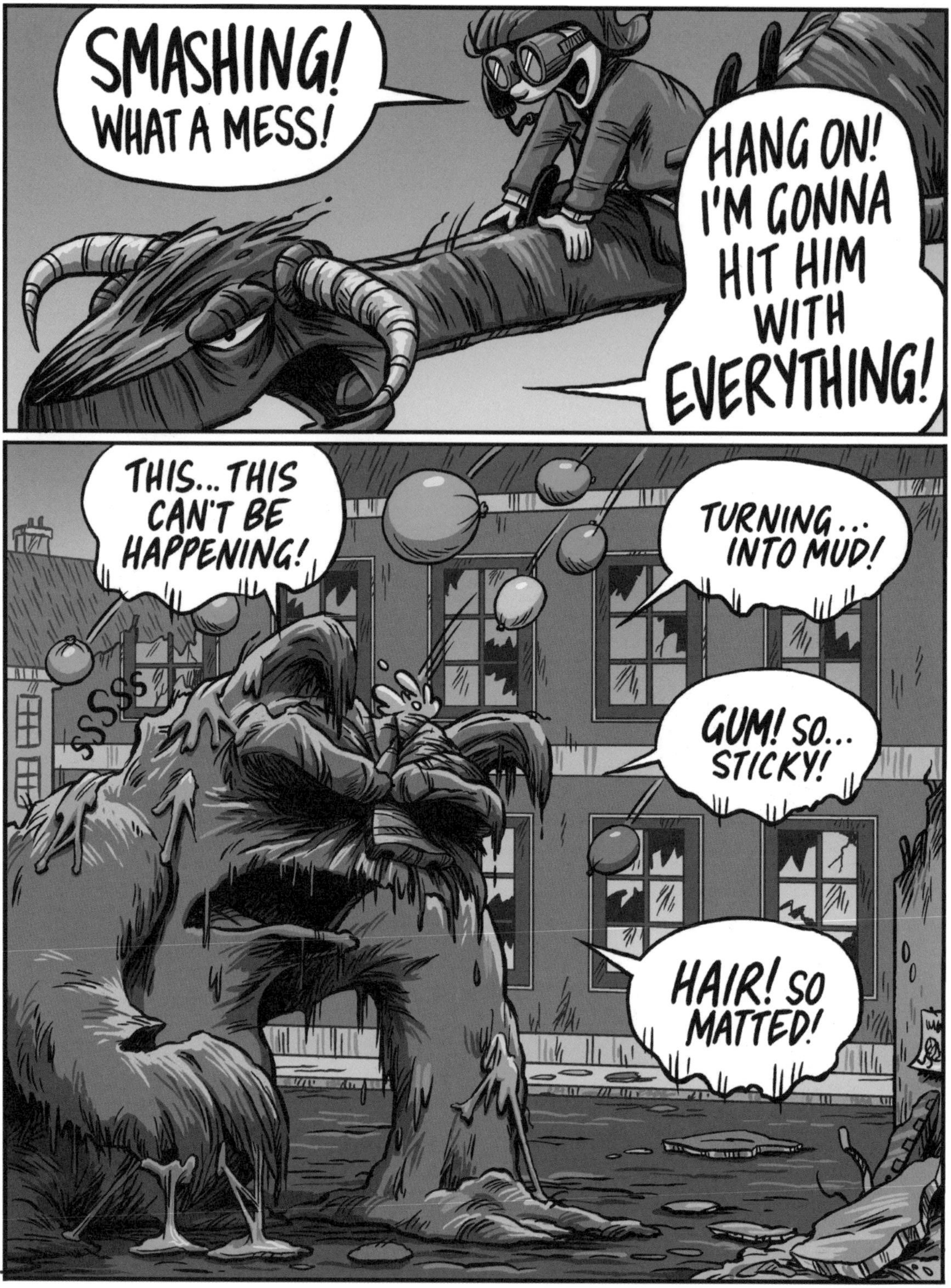
SMASHING! WHAT A MESS!
HANG ON! I'M GONNA HIT HIM WITH EVERYTHING!
THIS... THIS CAN'T BE HAPPENING!
SSSSS
TURNING... INTO MUD!
GUM! SO... STICKY!
HAIR! SO MATTED!

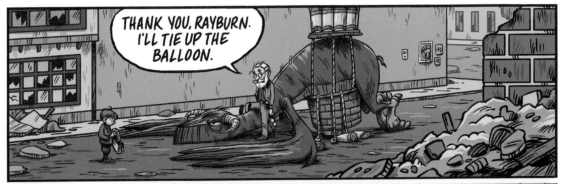

173

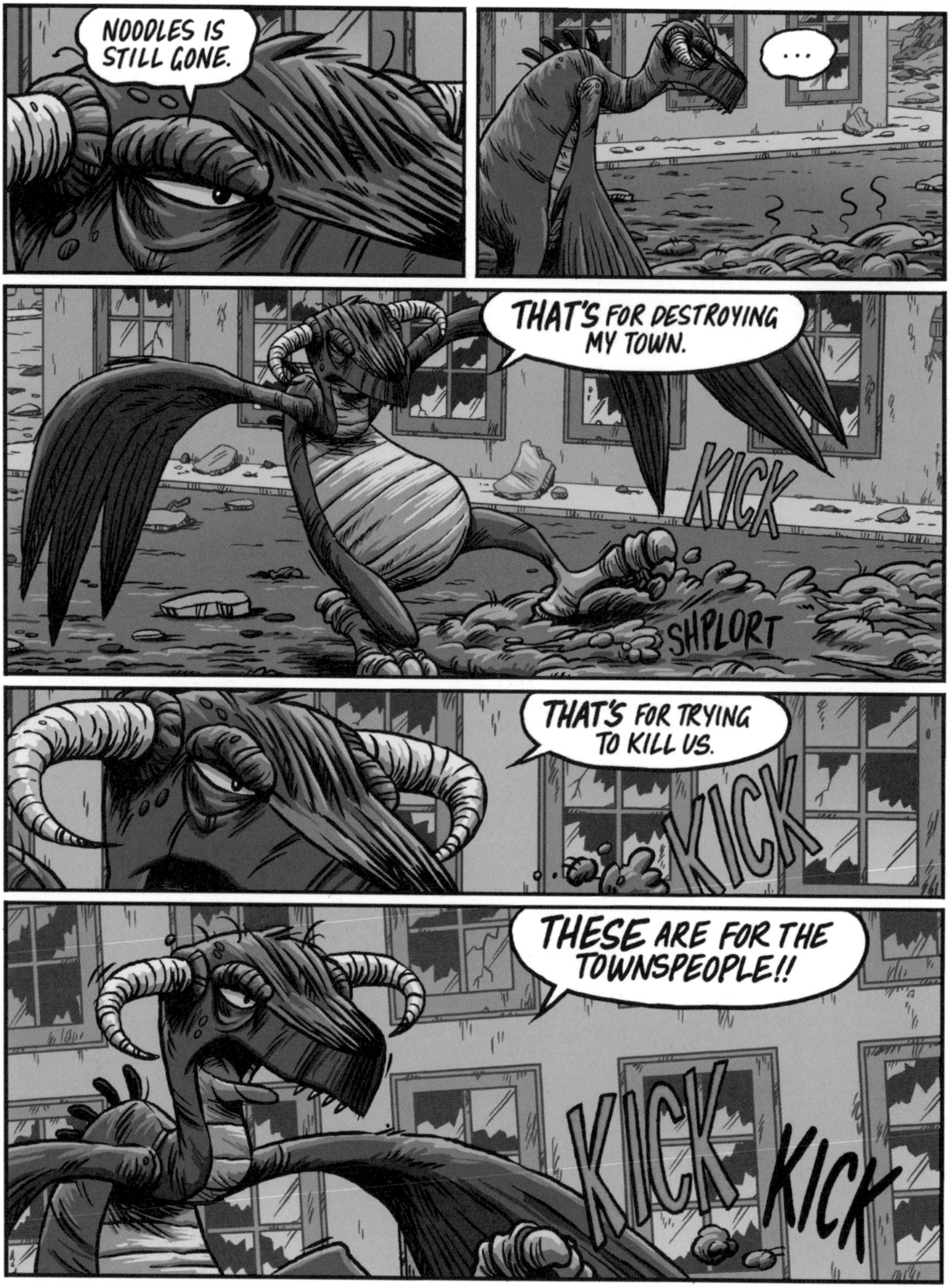
NOODLES IS STILL GONE.
...
THAT'S FOR DESTROYING MY TOWN.
KICK
SHPLORT
THAT'S FOR TRYING TO KILL US.
KICK
THESE ARE FOR THE TOWNSPEOPLE!!
KICK
KICK

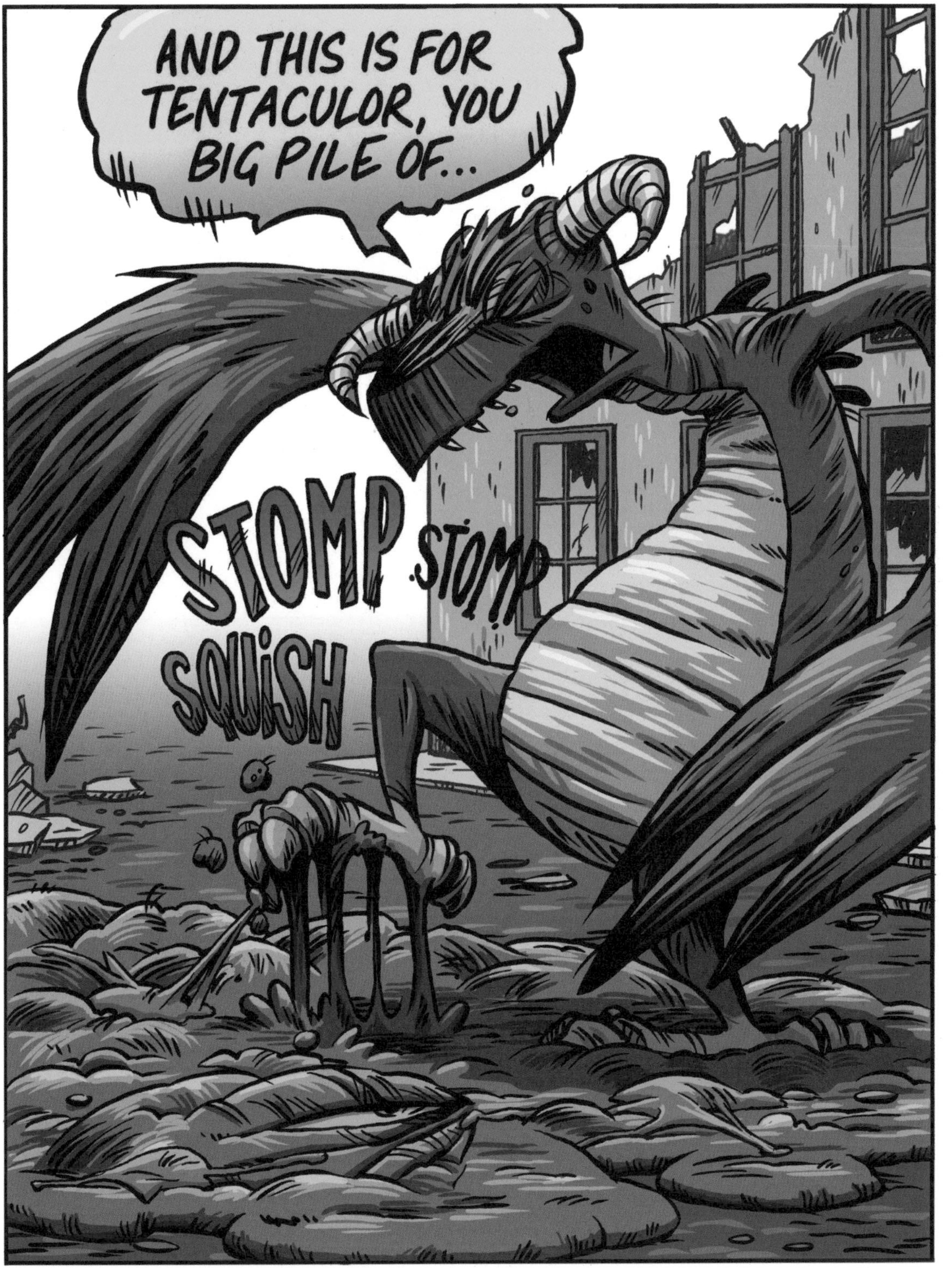
AND THIS IS FOR TENTACULOR, YOU BIG PILE OF...
STOMP
STOMP
SQUISH

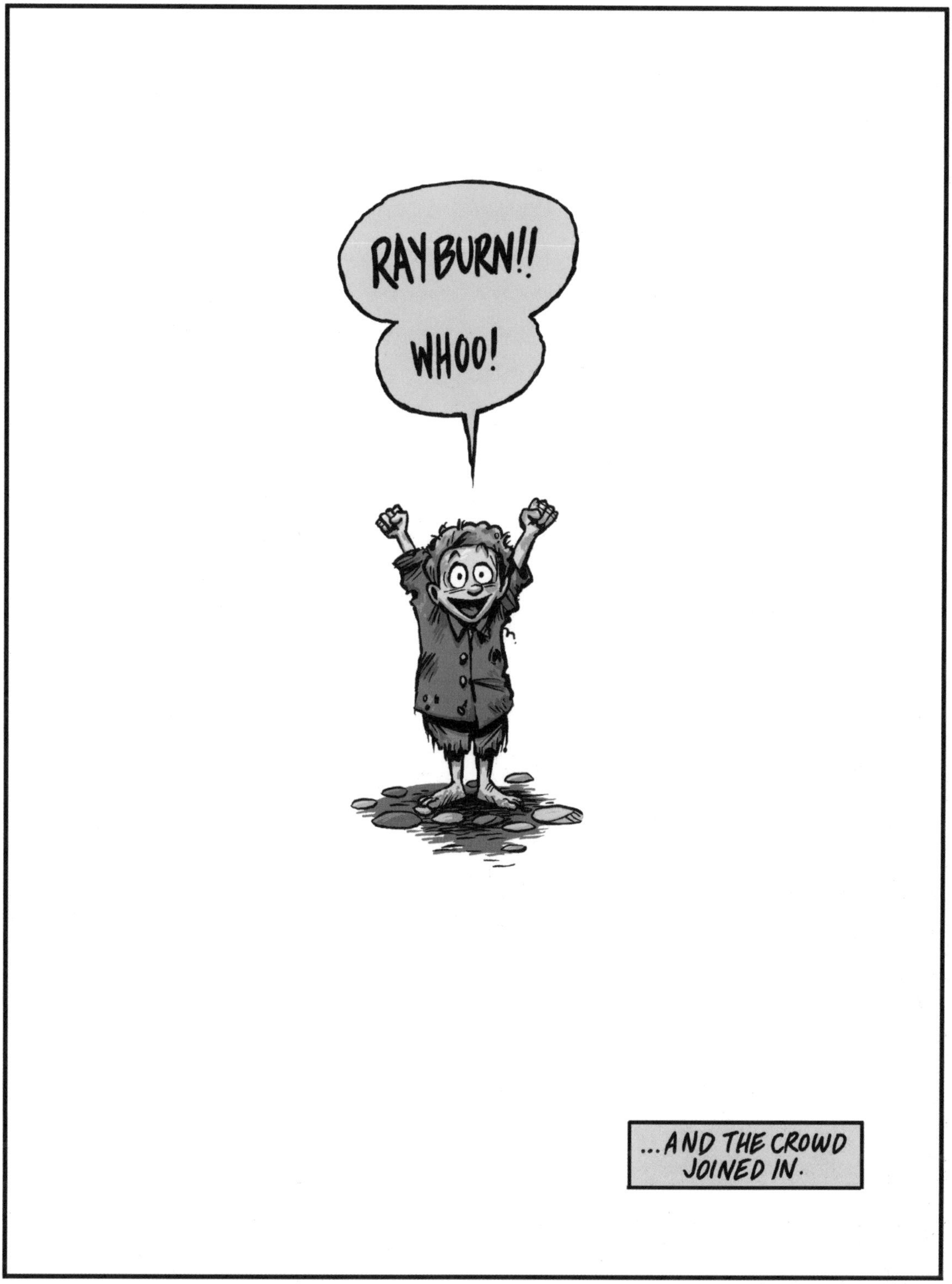
RAYBURN!!
WHOO!
...AND THE CROWD JOINED IN.

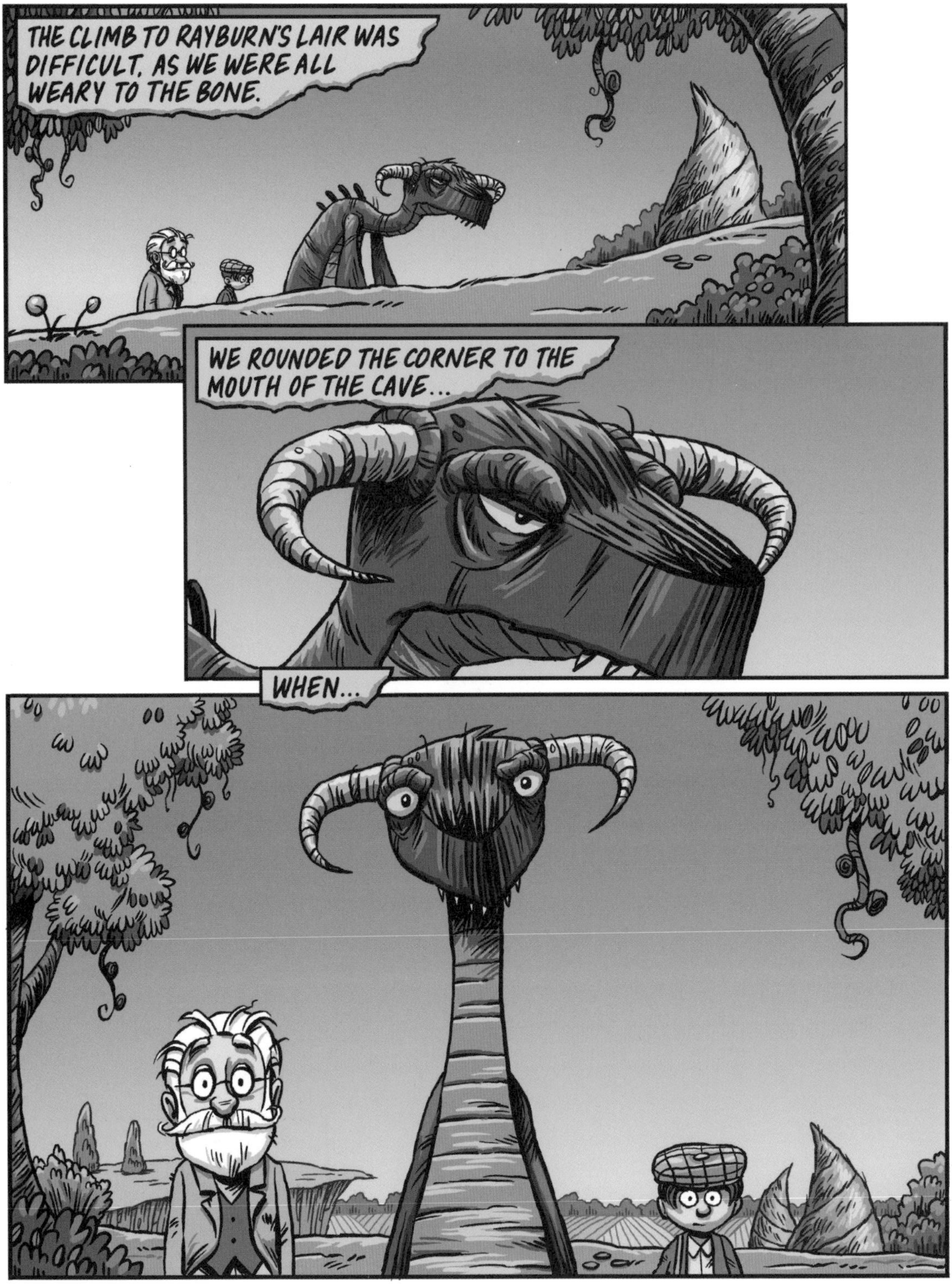
THE CLIMB TO RAYBURN'S LAIR WAS DIFFICULT, AS WE WERE ALL WEARY TO THE BONE.
WE ROUNDED THE CORNER TO THE MOUTH OF THE CAVE...
WHEN...

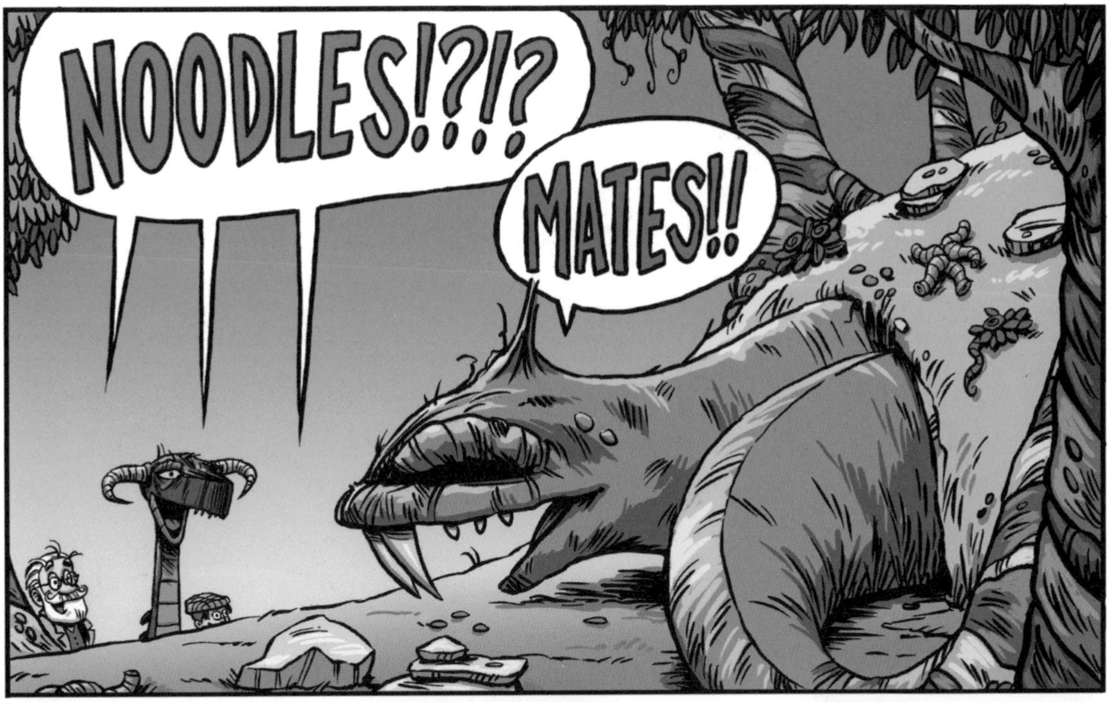
NOODLES!?!?
MATES!!

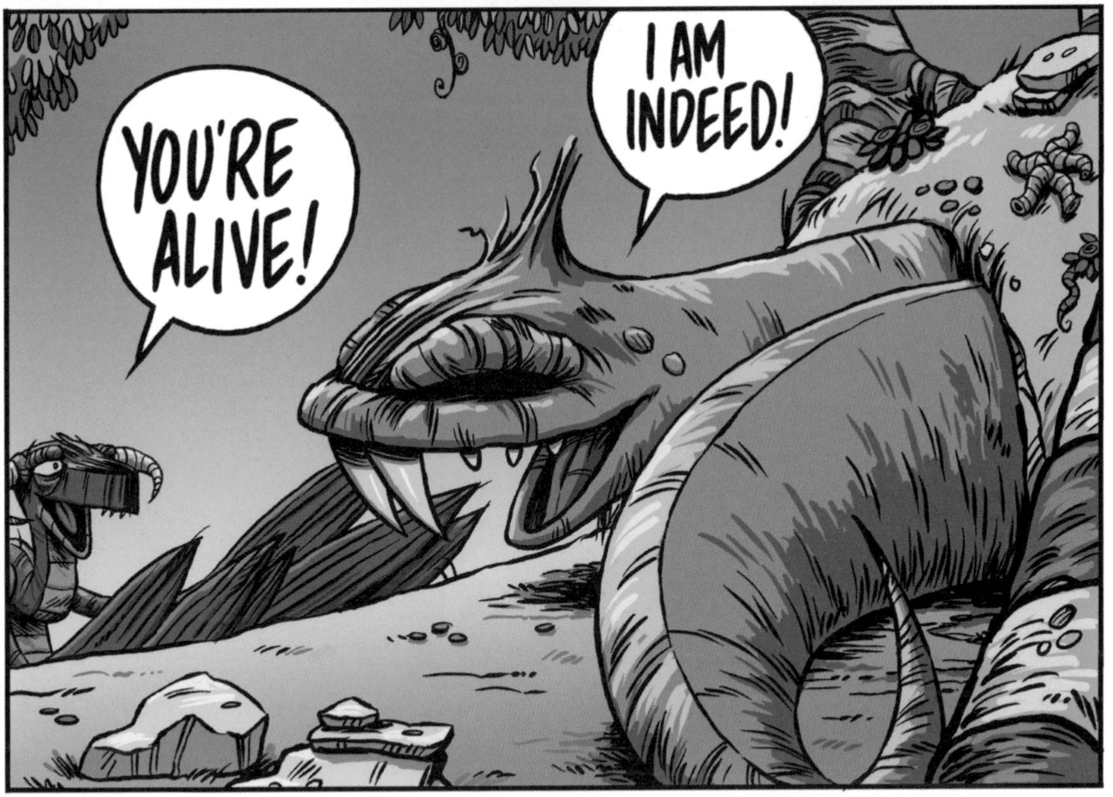
YOU'RE ALIVE!
I AM INDEED!

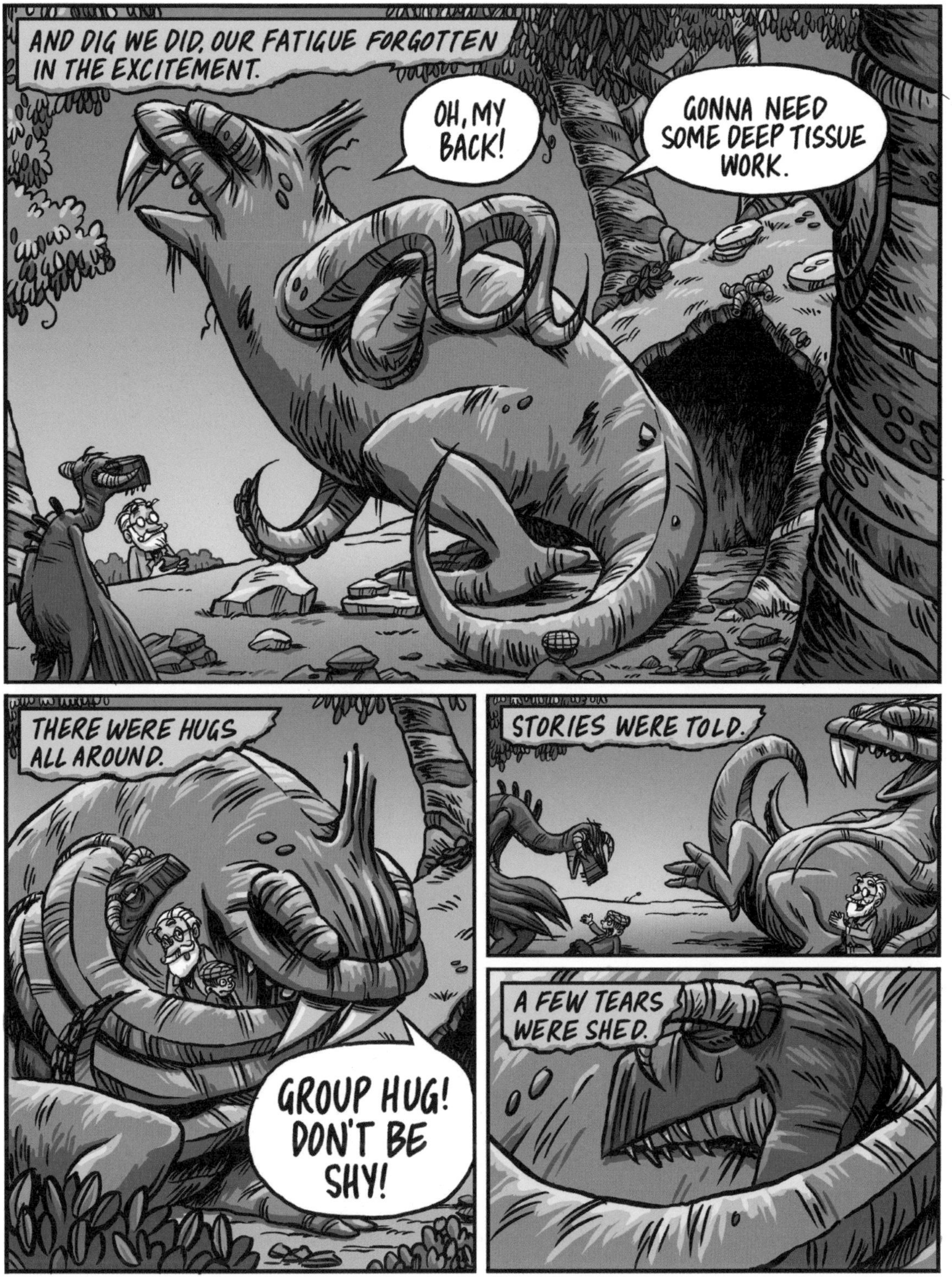
AND DIG WE DID, OUR FATIGUE FORGOTTEN IN THE EXCITEMENT.
OH, MY BACK!
GONNA NEED SOME DEEP TISSUE WORK.
THERE WERE HUGS ALL AROUND.
GROUP HUG! DON'T BE SHY!
STORIES WERE TOLD.
A FEW TEARS WERE SHED.

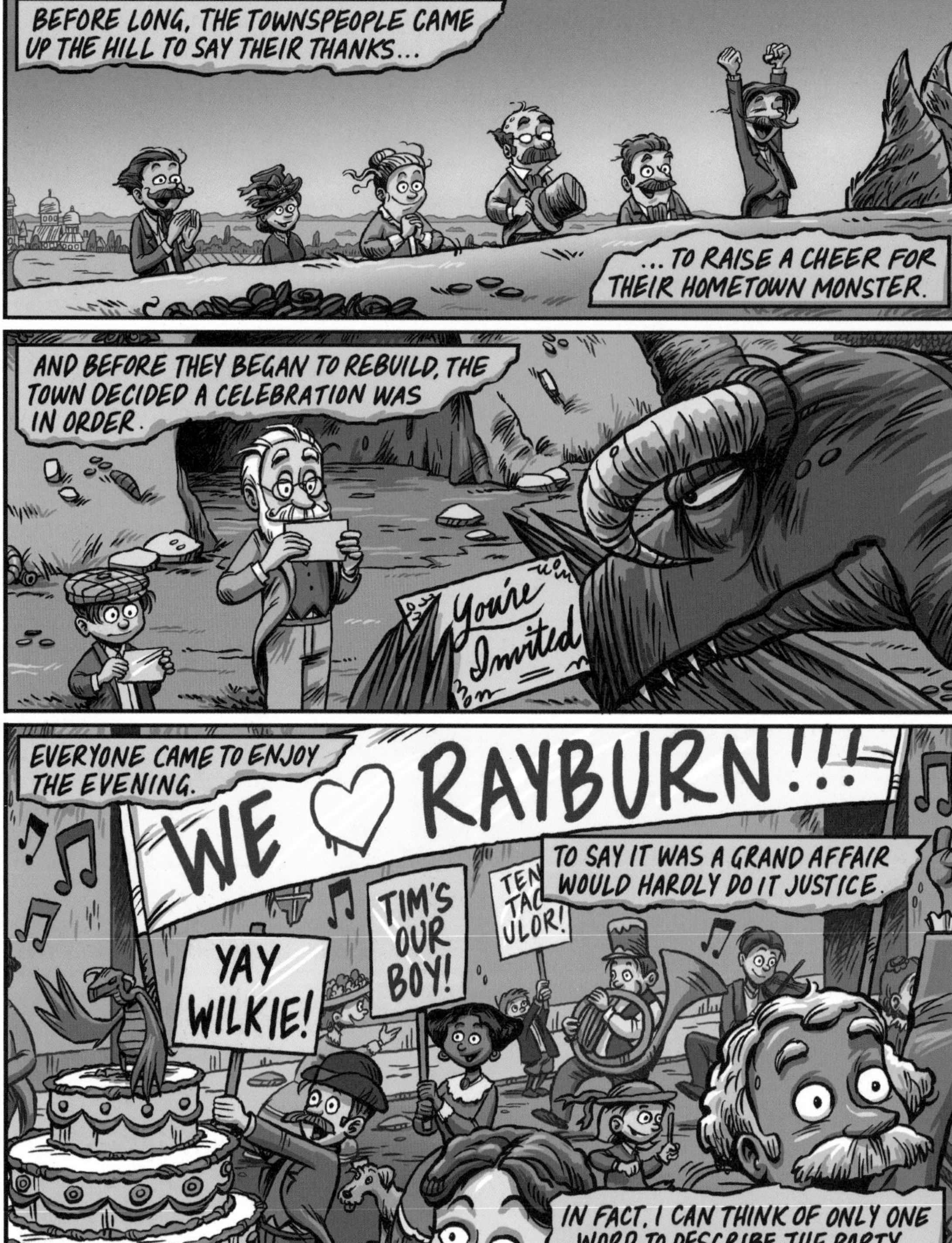
BEFORE LONG, THE TOWNSPEOPLE CAME UP THE HILL TO SAY THEIR THANKS...
...TO RAISE A CHEER FOR THEIR HOMETOWN MONSTER.
AND BEFORE THEY BEGAN TO REBUILD, THE TOWN DECIDED A CELEBRATION WAS IN ORDER.
You're Invited
EVERYONE CAME TO ENJOY THE EVENING.
WE ♡ RAYBURN!!!
TO SAY IT WAS A GRAND AFFAIR WOULD HARDLY DO IT JUSTICE.
YAY WILKIE!
TIM'S OUR BOY!
IN FACT, I CAN THINK OF ONLY ONE WORD TO DESCRIBE THE PARTY...

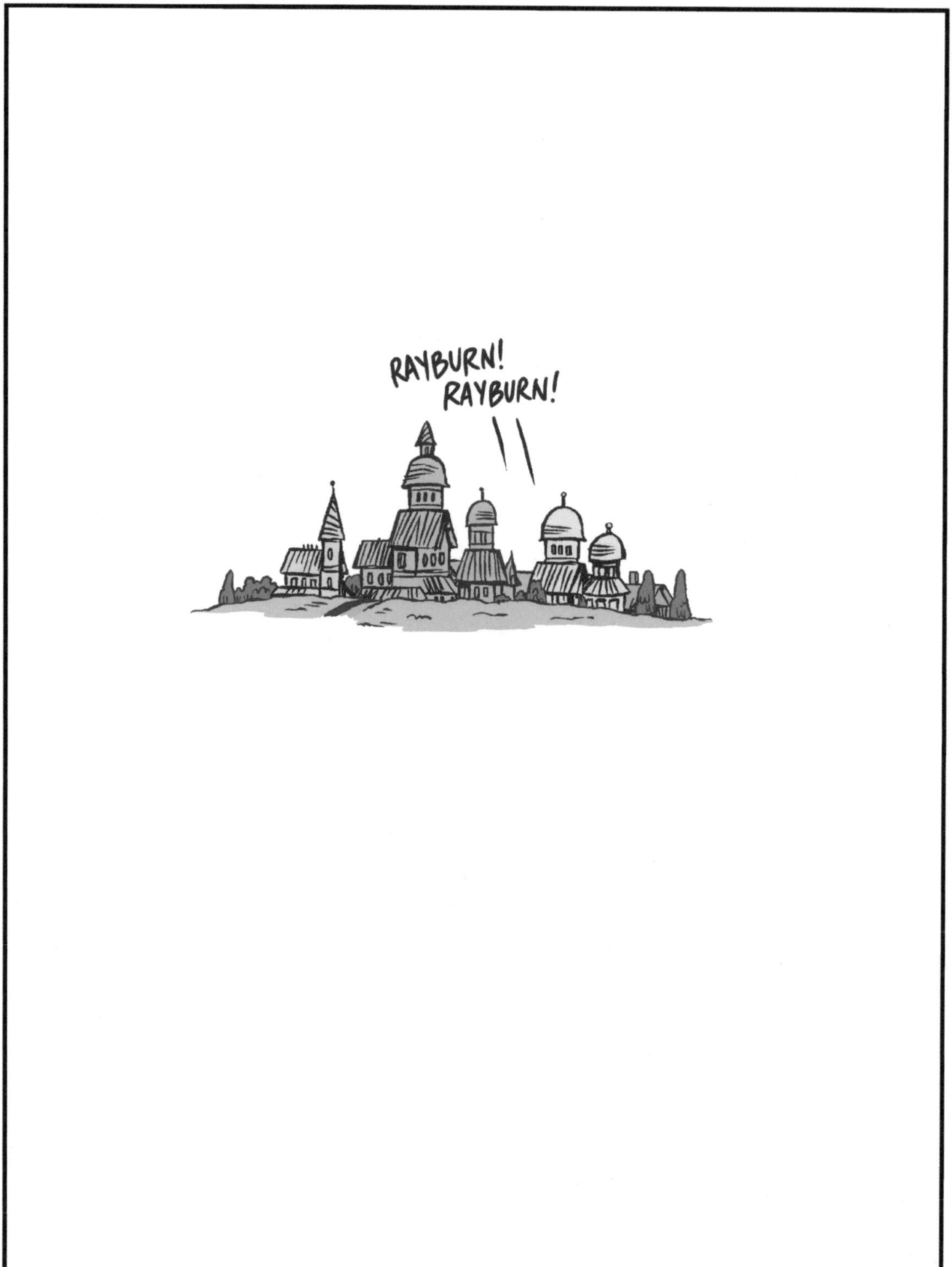
RAYBURN!
RAYBURN!

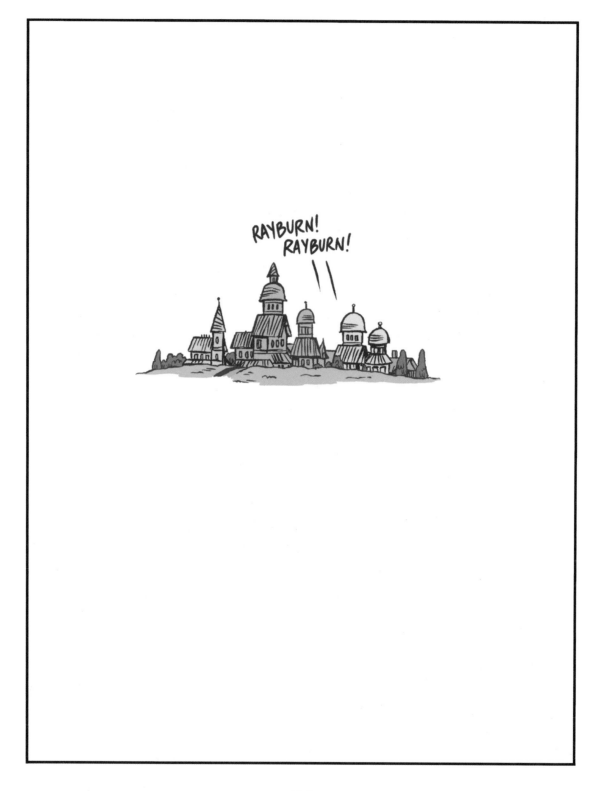

ONE YEAR LATER...

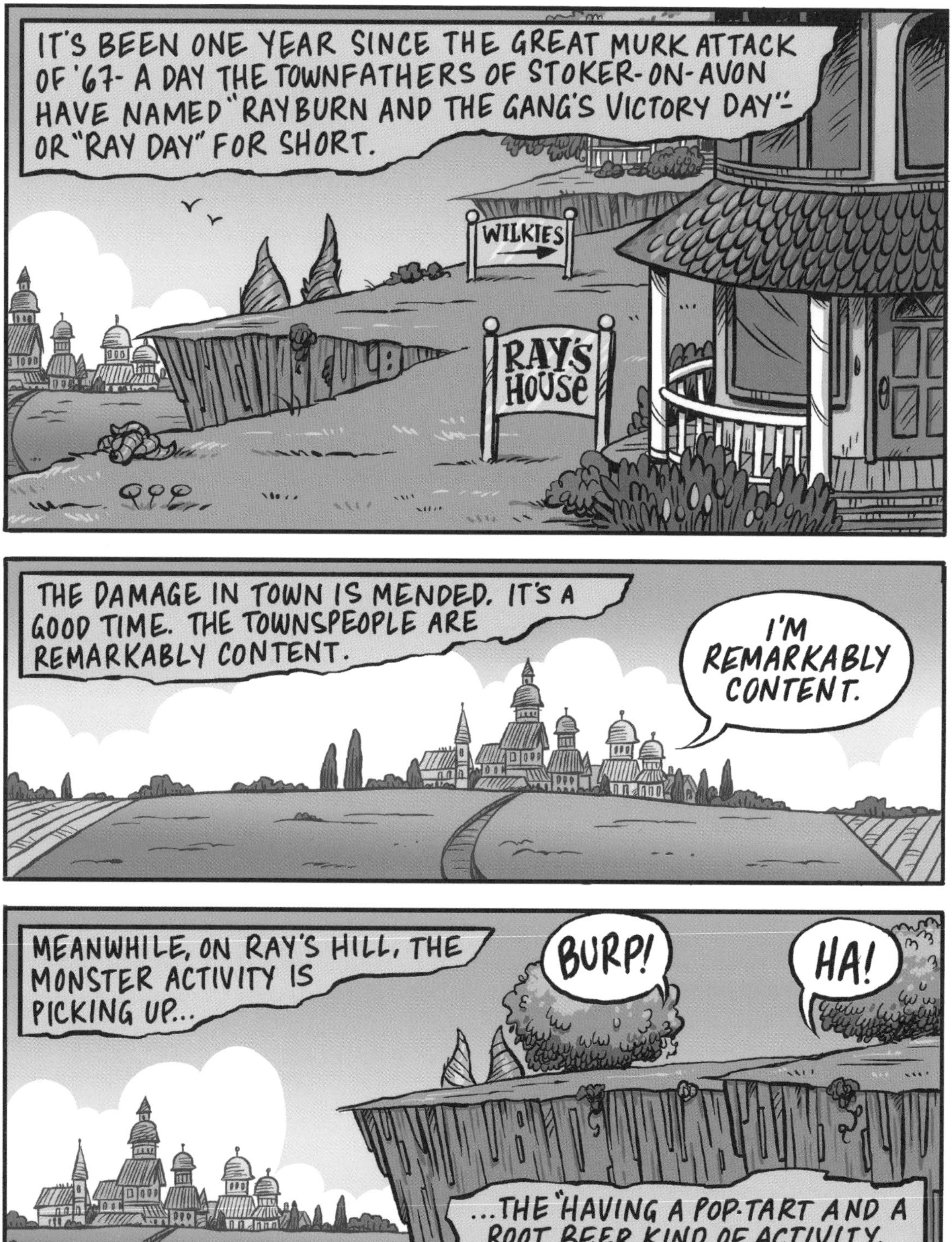
IT'S BEEN ONE YEAR SINCE THE GREAT MURK ATTACK OF '67- A DAY THE TOWNFATHERS OF STOKER-ON-AVON HAVE NAMED "RAYBURN AND THE GANG'S VICTORY DAY"- OR "RAY DAY" FOR SHORT.
WILKIES
RAY'S HOUSE
THE DAMAGE IN TOWN IS MENDED. IT'S A GOOD TIME. THE TOWNSPEOPLE ARE REMARKABLY CONTENT.
I'M REMARKABLY CONTENT.
MEANWHILE, ON RAY'S HILL, THE MONSTER ACTIVITY IS PICKING UP...
BURP!
HA!
...THE "HAVING A POP-TART AND A ROOT BEER KIND OF ACTIVITY.

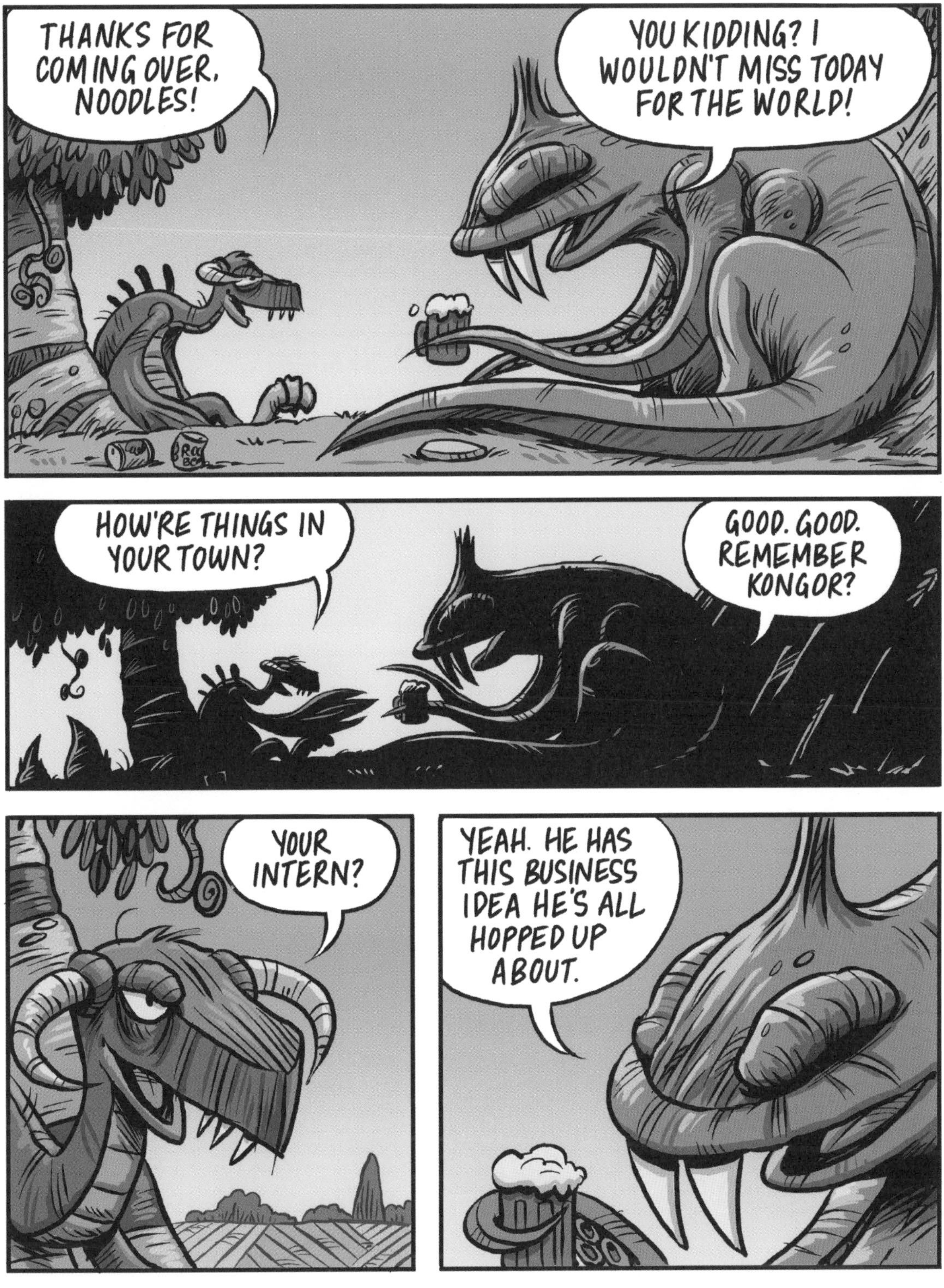
THANKS FOR COMING OVER, NOODLES!
YOU KIDDING? I WOULDN'T MISS TODAY FOR THE WORLD!
HOW'RE THINGS IN YOUR TOWN?
GOOD. GOOD. REMEMBER KONGOR?
YOUR INTERN?
YEAH. HE HAS THIS BUSINESS IDEA HE'S ALL HOPPED UP ABOUT.

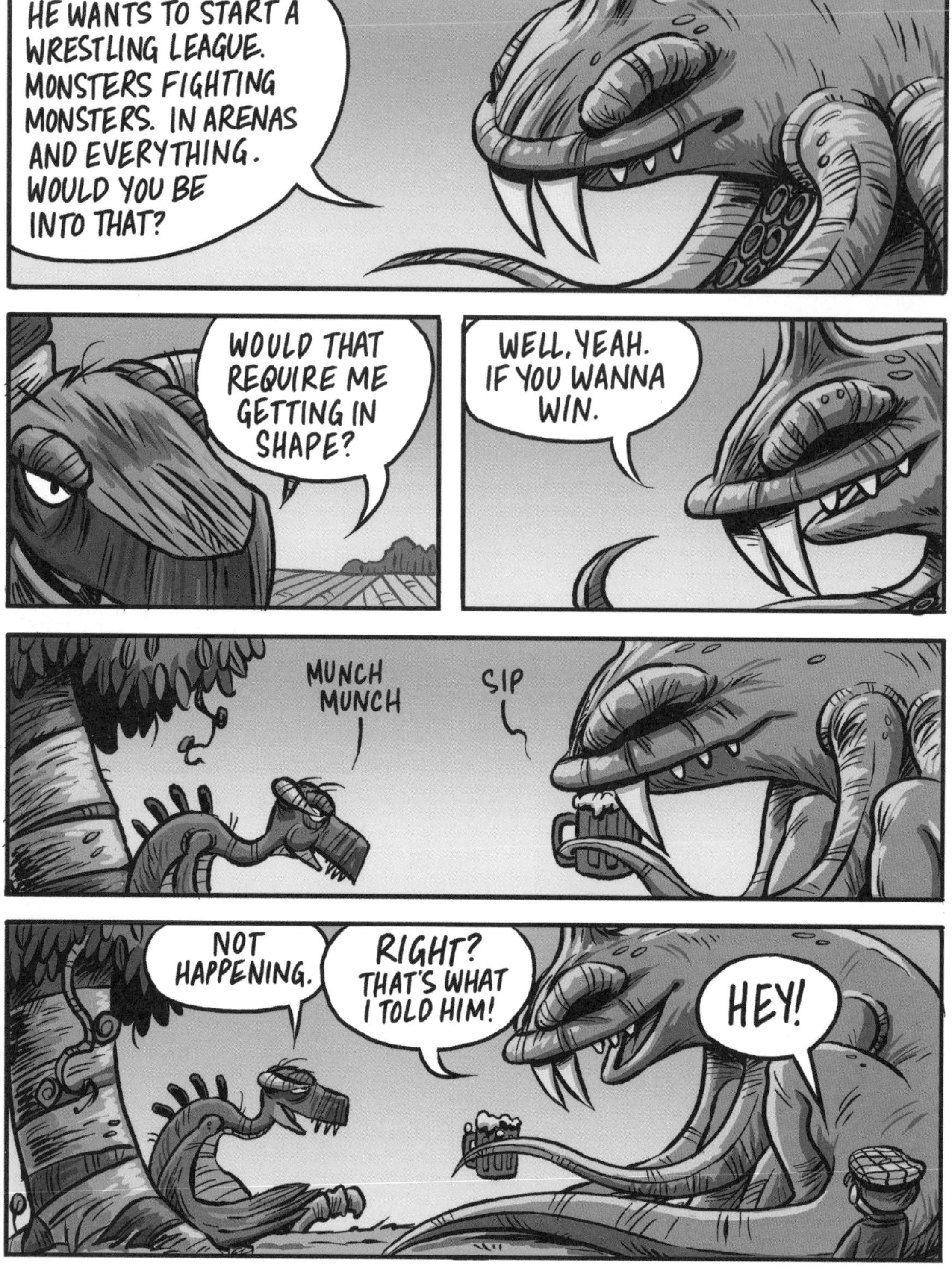
HE WANTS TO START A WRESTLING LEAGUE. MONSTERS FIGHTING MONSTERS. IN ARENAS AND EVERYTHING. WOULD YOU BE INTO THAT?
WOULD THAT REQUIRE ME GETTING IN SHAPE?
WELL, YEAH. IF YOU WANNA WIN.
MUNCH MUNCH
SIP
NOT HAPPENING.
RIGHT? THAT'S WHAT I TOLD HIM!
HEY!

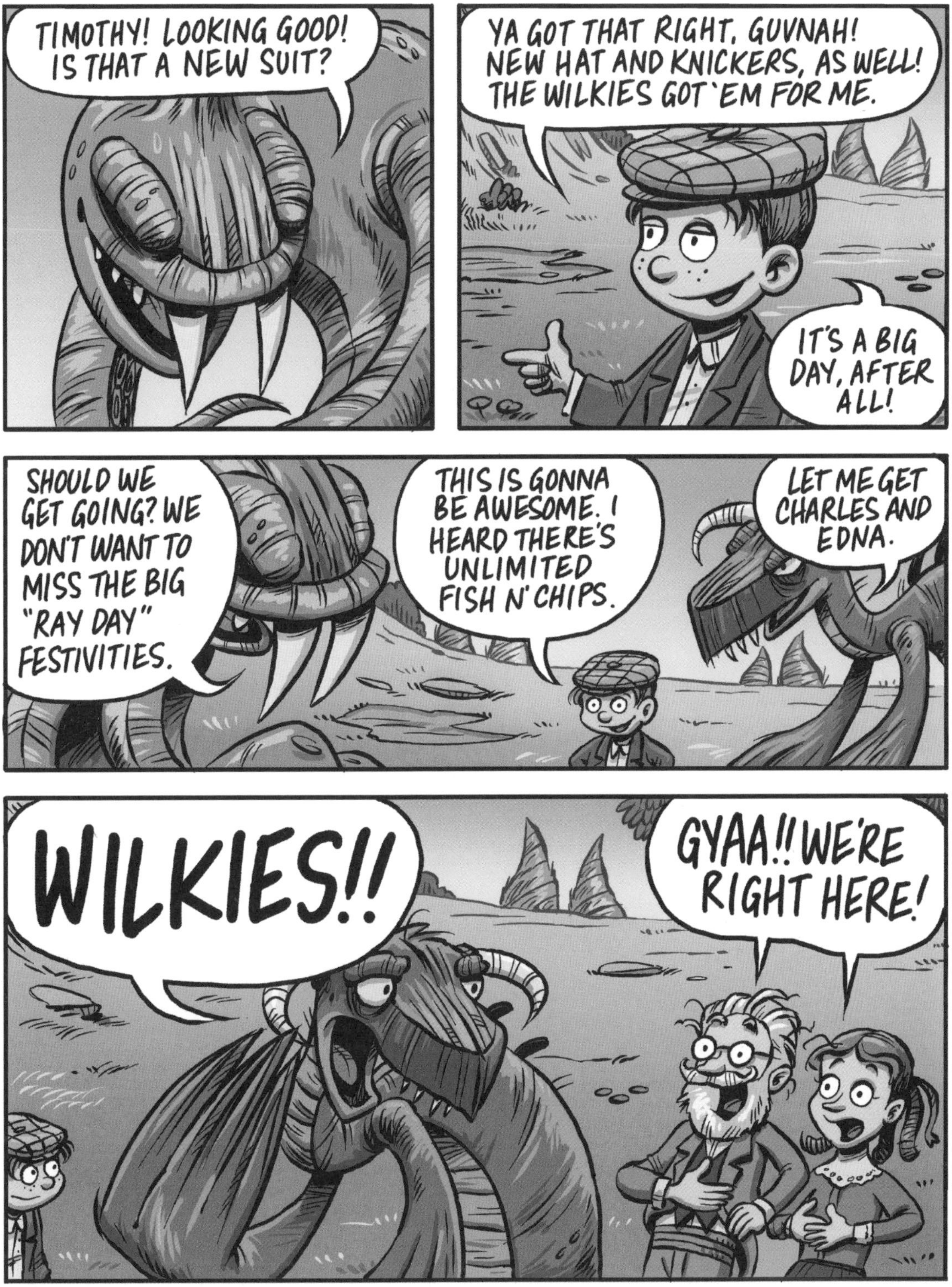
TIMOTHY! LOOKING GOOD! IS THAT A NEW SUIT?
YA GOT THAT RIGHT, GUVNAH! NEW HAT AND KNICKERS, AS WELL! THE WILKIES GOT `EM FOR ME.
IT'S A BIG DAY, AFTER ALL!
SHOULD WE GET GOING? WE DON'T WANT TO MISS THE BIG "RAY DAY" FESTIVITIES.
THIS IS GONNA BE AWESOME. I HEARD THERE'S UNLIMITED FISH N' CHIPS.
LET ME GET CHARLES AND EDNA.
WILKIES!!
GYAA!! WE'RE RIGHT HERE!

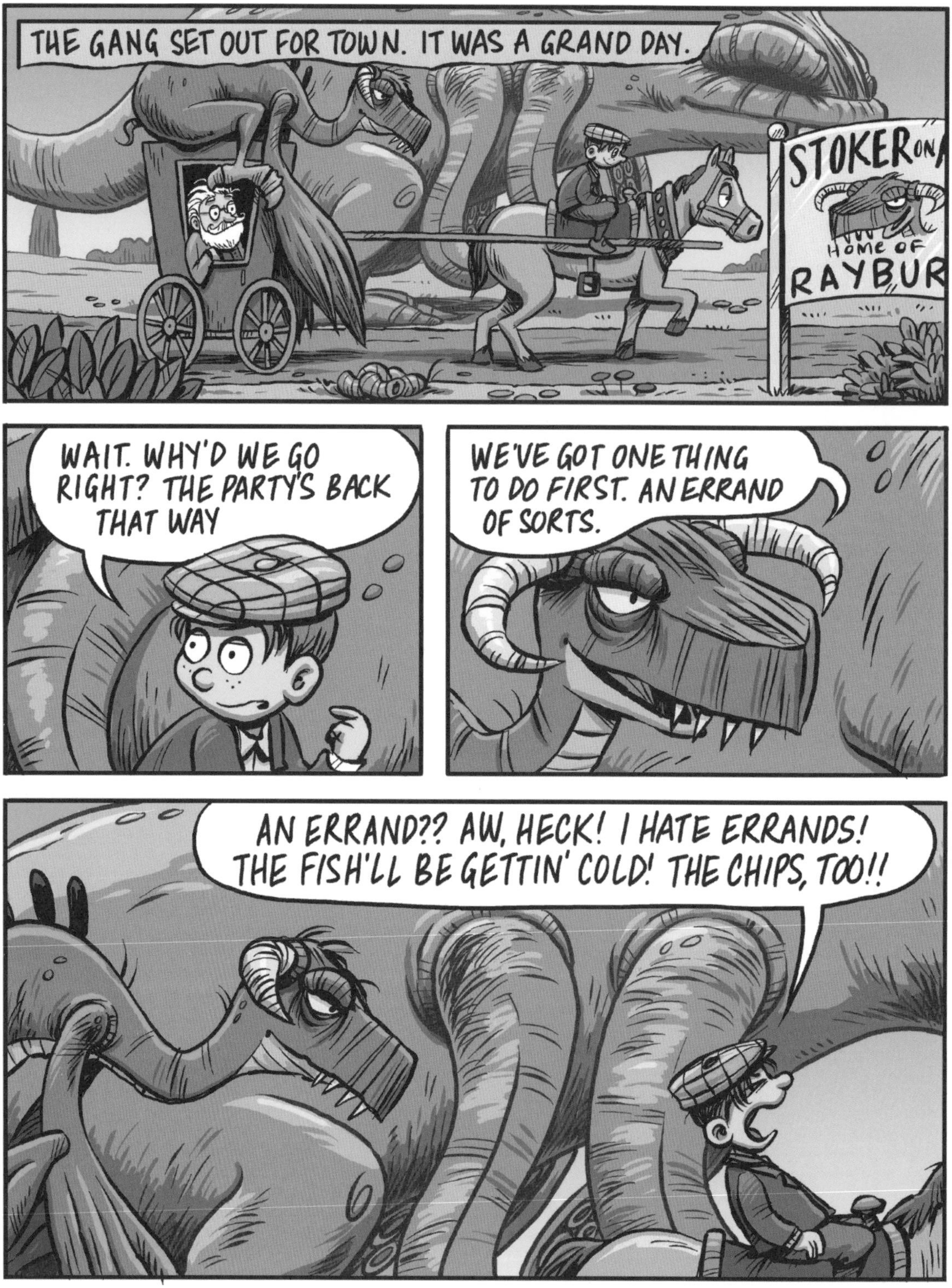
THE GANG SET OUT FOR TOWN. IT WAS A GRAND DAY.
STOKER ON
HOME OF
RAYBUR
WAIT. WHY'D WE GO RIGHT? THE PARTY'S BACK THAT WAY
WE'VE GOT ONE THING TO DO FIRST. AN ERRAND OF SORTS.
AN ERRAND?? AW, HECK! I HATE ERRANDS! THE FISH'LL BE GETTIN' COLD! THE CHIPS, TOO!!

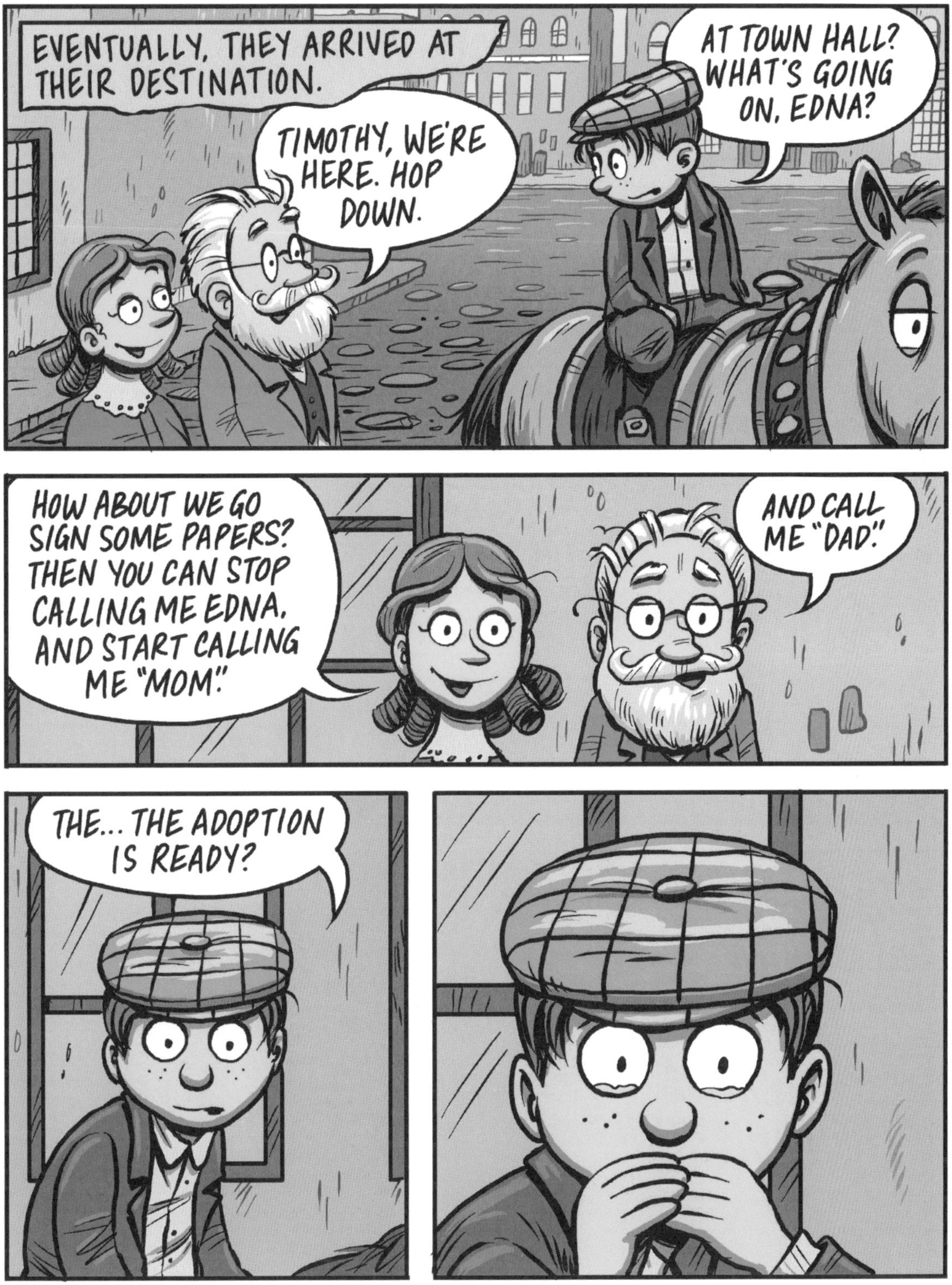
EVENTUALLY, THEY ARRIVED AT THEIR DESTINATION.
TIMOTHY, WE'RE HERE. HOP DOWN.
AT TOWN HALL? WHAT'S GOING ON, EDNA?
HOW ABOUT WE GO SIGN SOME PAPERS? THEN YOU CAN STOP CALLING ME EDNA, AND START CALLING ME "MOM."
AND CALL ME "DAD."
THE... THE ADOPTION IS READY?

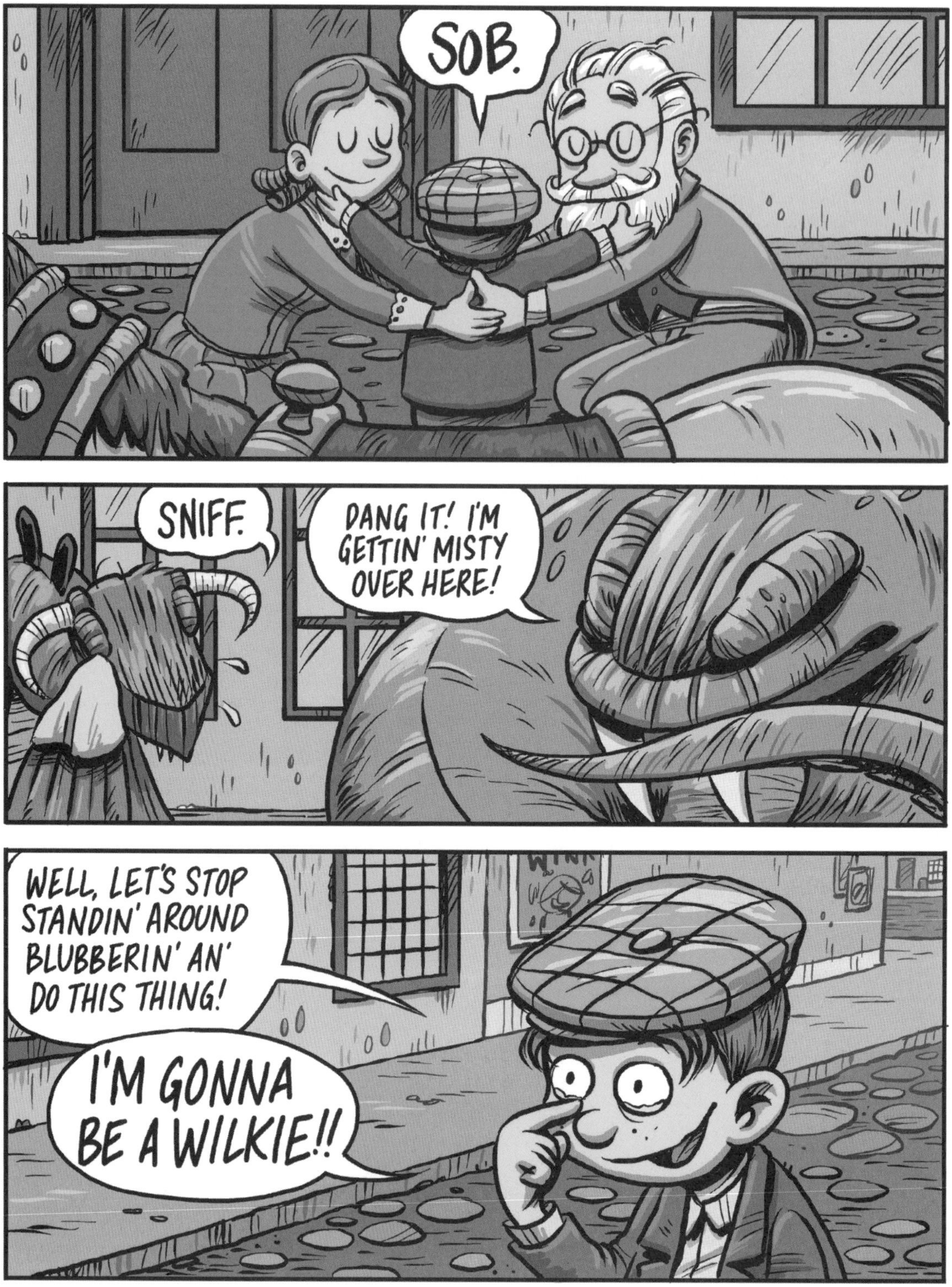
SOB.
SNIFF.
DANG IT! I'M GETTIN' MISTY OVER HERE!
WELL, LET'S STOP STANDIN' AROUND BLUBBERIN' AN' DO THIS THING!
I'M GONNA BE A WILKIE!!

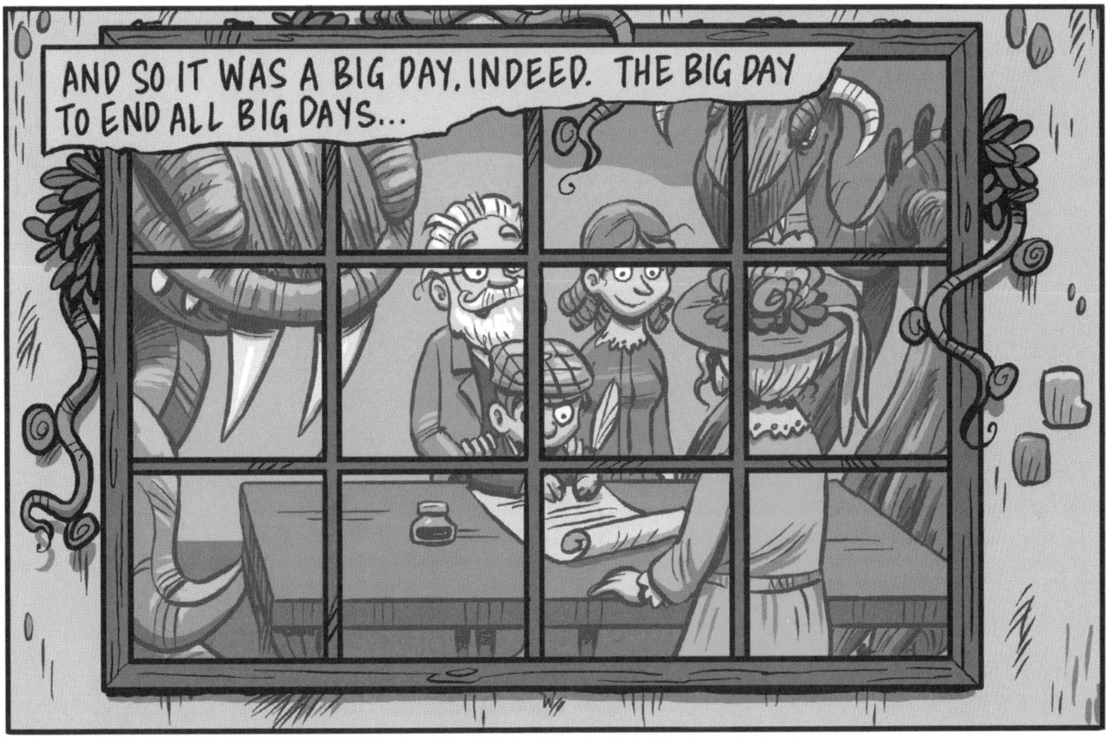
AND SO IT WAS A BIG DAY, INDEED. THE BIG DAY TO END ALL BIG DAYS...

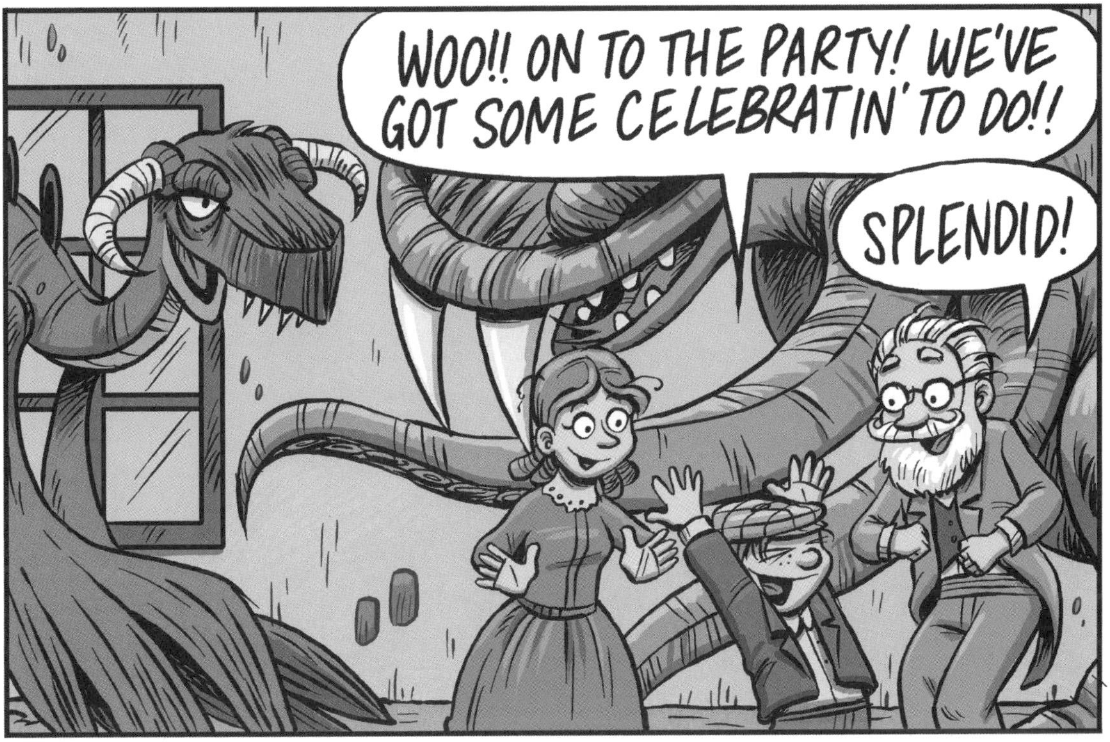
WOO!! ON TO THE PARTY! WE'VE GOT SOME CELEBRATIN' TO DO!!
SPLENDID!

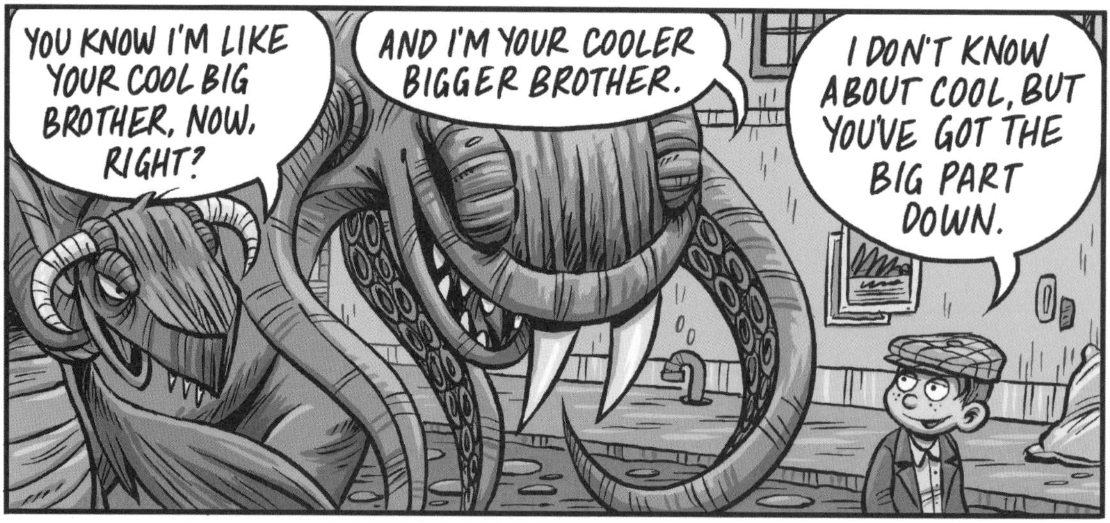
YOU KNOW I'M LIKE YOUR COOL BIG BROTHER, NOW, RIGHT?
AND I'M YOUR COOLER BIGGER BROTHER.
I DON'T KNOW ABOUT COOL, BUT YOU'VE GOT THE BIG PART DOWN.

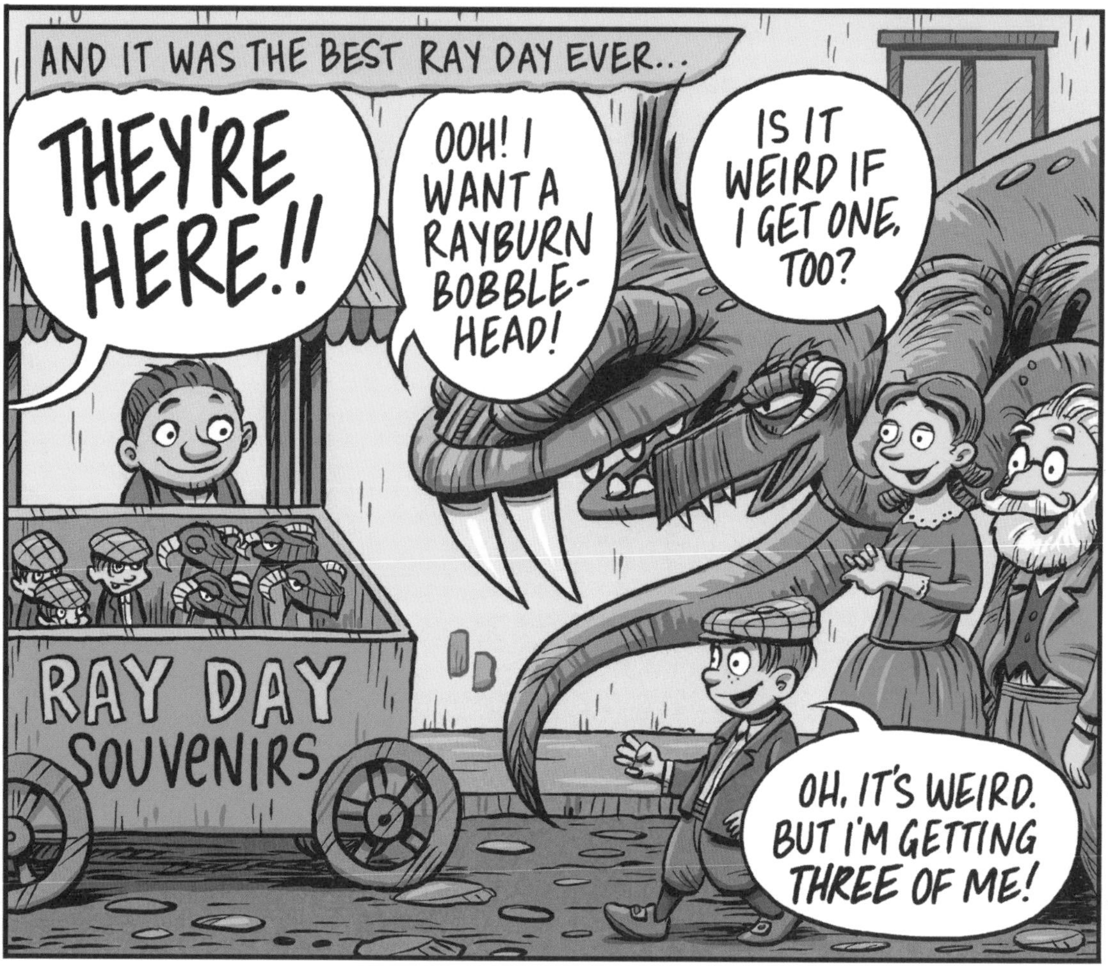
AND IT WAS THE BEST RAY DAY EVER...
THEY'RE HERE!!
OOH! I WANT A RAYBURN BOBBLE-HEAD!
IS IT WEIRD IF I GET ONE, TOO?
RAY DAY SOUVENIRS
OH, IT'S WEIRD. BUT I'M GETTING THREE OF ME!

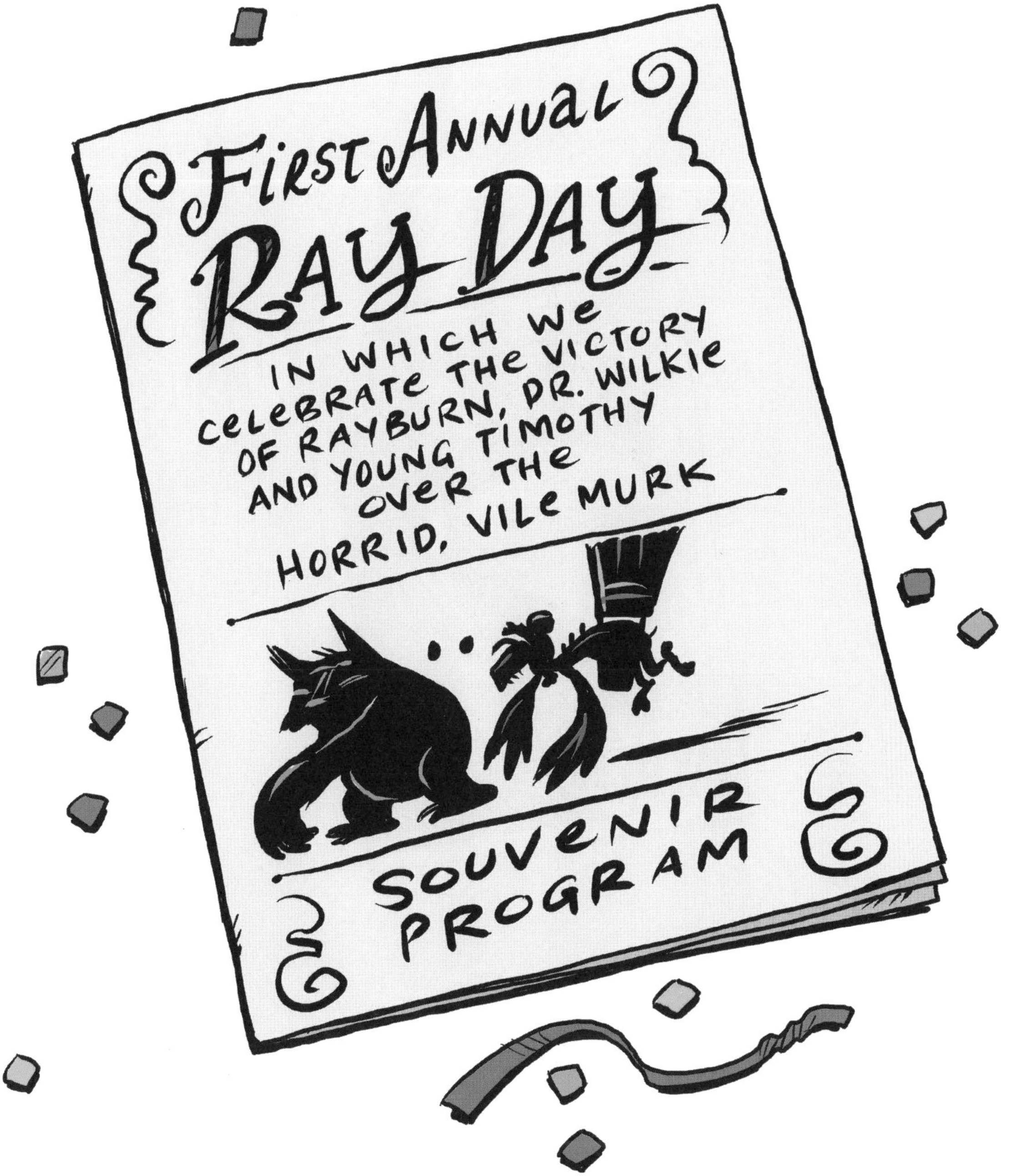
First Annual
Ray Day
IN WHICH WE
CELEBRATE THE VICTORY
OF RAYBURN, DR. WILKIE
AND YOUNG TIMOTHY
OVER THE
HORRID, VILE MURK
SOUVENIR
PROGRAM

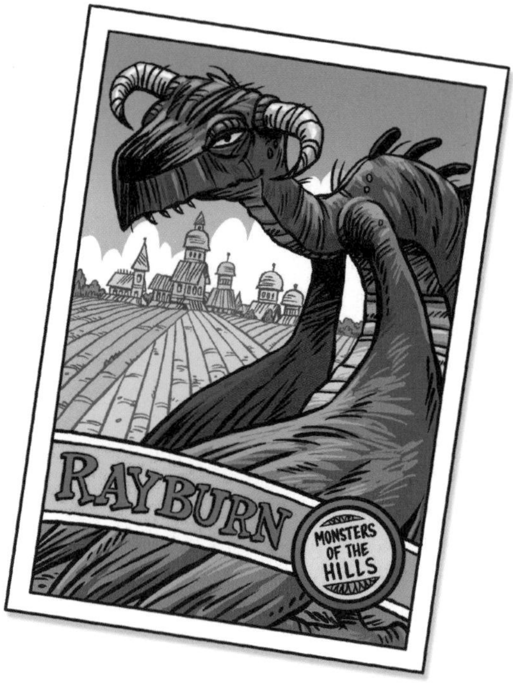
RAYBURN
MONSTERS OF THE HILLS

Acknowlegements

I would like to offer my sincere thanks to the following people for their help, support, and kindness: my incredibly patient family; my amazing and infinitely supportive wife, Amber; Chris Staros, Brett Warnock, Chris Ross, Leigh Walton, and everyone at Top Shelf; Jason Dravis; Josh Block; Jon Weed; Mark Pett; Team Dank; John Glynn and everyone at Universal; my amazing friends in Austin, Indianapolis, New York, and elsewhere; Bob Kingsley; and all of my personal Dr. Wilkies.

And finally, a special monstrous thank you to Wayne Beamer.

Rob Harrell wrote and drew the *Life of Zarf* series of books, as well as the novel *Wink*, published by Dial Books for Young Readers. He wrote and drew the daily comic strip *Big Top* from 2002 - 2007 and currently creates the strip *Adam@Home*.

He lives in Zionsville, Indiana with his wife, Amber, and their two dogs, Cooper and Kasey.

Visit him online at www.robharrell.com.